"I found it!"

"Good," Wade whispered to himself, growing more uncomfortable every moment with the heat, the stench, and the muted hum which now seemed to surround him.

He waited, wondering what story Gillie would cook up to explain their taking the skiff . . .

"Wade?"

Something in the tone of Gillie's voice sent a tiny chill trickling down his spine.

"Wade?"

Not a cry, not a loud call. "Wade?" Then rapidly: "Wade? Wade?" Then louder and louder.

He could see Gillie.

And smell the stench.

It burned the lining of his nostrils.

He could feel the air from the beat of wings.

And hear a smothered cry—nothing like Gillie's voice.

A blackness rose and spread, a black curtain closing, then slowly opening.

No scream.

Wade's skin turned cool and clammy.

Then his senses began to shut down.

TERROR LIVES!

THE SHADOW MAN   (1946, $3.95)
by Stephen Gresham
The Shadow Man could hide anywhere—under the bed, in the closet, behind the mirror . . . even in the sophisticated circuitry of little Joey's computer. And the Shadow Man could make Joey do things that no little boy should ever do!

SIGHT UNSEEN   (2038, $3.95)
by Andrew Neiderman
David was always right. Always. But now that he was growing up, his gift was turning into a power. The power to know things—terrible things—that he didn't want to know. Like who would live . . . and who would die!

MIDNIGHT BOY   (2065, $3.95)
by Stephen Gresham
Something horrible is stalking the town's children. For one of its most trusted citizens possesses the twisted need and cunning of a psychopathic killer. Now Town Creek's only hope lies in the horrific, blood-soaked visions of the MIDNIGHT BOY!

TEACHER'S PET   (1927, $3.95)
by Andrew Neiderman
All the children loved their teacher Mr. Lucy. It was astonishing to see how they all seemed to begin to resemble Mr. Lucy. And act like Mr. Lucy. And kill like Mr. Lucy!

Available wherever paperbacks are sold, or order direct from the Publisher. Send cover price plus 50¢ per copy for mailing and handling to Zebra Books, Dept. 2891, 475 Park Avenue South, New York, N.Y. 10016. Residents of New York, New Jersey and Pennsylvania must include sales tax. DO NOT SEND CASH.

BLOOD WINGS
Stephen Gresham

ZEBRA BOOKS
KENSINGTON PUBLISHING CORP.

ZEBRA BOOKS

are published by

Kensington Publishing Corp.
475 Park Avenue South
New York, NY 10016

First printing: February, 1990

Printed in the United States of America

A writer learns that there are places of darkness and places of light—for me, a place called Tyler's in Auburn, Alabama is one of light. And so it is that I dedicate this book to the place which greets me at dawn and allows me to sit and write and watch the world awaken, and to the people who frequent that establishment—familiar folk such as Rain Dance, Sam, the D.A., Ben and Lucy, Jim, Fred, Connie, and Tressie—and the strangers, too, whose names I'll never know, but whose faces I'll never forget.

A special thanks, also, to Amy Knight, who taught me how to tend to a sick boa constrictor.

—Stephen Gresham
June 6, 1989

Chapter One

1

"I can take care of myself."

"And I'm sayin' you can't. I'm sayin' you're a friggin' wimp."

"I *can* take care of myself. Been doin' it for a long, long time. And I ain't a friggin' wimp neither."

Both boys paused as a helicopter dipped low, thrumming, then climbed and banked sharply out over the slough and the mangrove swamp beyond it.

"Betcha never stole nuthin'. Betcha don't know how."

"I do so. I've stole stuff. Lotsa stuff. Back in Missouri."

"Okay, prove it. Go ahead and do it now. Walk right into Holly's and steal somethin'."

As he considered the challenge, Wade lifted his blue-green Miami Dolphin's cap, a perfect match for Gillie's, and squinted into the south Florida sun, trying to catch a final glimpse of the copter.

"Gillie, I can steal any ole thing you can steal. But I gotta case the place first. It'd be stupid not to."

Gillie started to laugh. His pink, sweaty cheeks rounded into shiny balls; his head jerked; his cap tumbled off. He rubbed furiously at his blond crewcut and stomped his feet until his blond-white rat's tail bobbed on the back of his neck like a hangman's noose dangling in the wind.

"Case the place! Oh, man, that's funny! That's so-o-o damn funny!"

His black eyes darting, fearing someone would hear the derisive laughter, Wade pushed his companion hard in the chest, and together they twisted around the concrete block wall at the rear of Holly's Grocery and Bait Shop. Continuing to laugh, Gillie buckled over, occasionally glancing up to check Wade's expression, exploding into fresh laughter at the other boy's seriousness.

Wade dug his fingernails into his palms, squeezing and unsqueezing, but his anger would not relent. He rocked forward on the balls of his feet and cleared his throat.

"Come on and I'll show you. I'll show you 'bout stealin' stuff. Florida people don't know nuthin' 'bout stealin'. St. Louis people, they know. I grew up there, and so I can tell you—they know."

Gillie's eyes bulged. His mouth stretched wide open in disbelief. "Florida people don't—! Frig it, sport, you're seriously wrong. I mean *seriously* wrong. Listen, I growed up in Miami before my folks sent me here to Orchid Springs. I'm tellin' you, people in Miami *invented* stealin'. Killin', too. Ask anybody, sport."

A car rattled along the dusty white, shell-based road winding into the mobile home park behind Holly's, stirring fine particles which the breeze snatched and tossed into the boys' faces.

Wade blinked hard. "Don't call me that, Gillie. Don' call me 'sport.' I really hate that. What's it mean anyway?"

Gillie shrugged and slapped the bill of Wade's cap.

"I hate *that*, too. You tryin' to piss me off, Gillie?"

His companion laughed. "No, sport." He feigned fear

8

as Wade clenched a threatening fist.

"I mean it, Gillie."

"Hey, wait, man. Nuthin' wrong with the word 'sport.' It's Aussie."

"So what's Aussie?"

"Australian. You know, like Miss Freda over at the wildlife refuge. She uses words like that. It's a friendly word."

Wade let his glance drift doubtfully across the slough and the roadway bridge into the Maxwell Schreck Wildlife Refuge, Orchid Springs' chief tourist attraction. He had never met Miss Freda. Wasn't eager to do so, either.

"You sure it doesn't mean something like 'asshole'?"

Gillie grinned and swiped at his sweaty face. "You got kangaroos under your tophat, mate?"

Wade glared. "More Australian stuff?"

"Yeah. It means, 'Are you crazy'?"

"Why don't they just say, 'Are you crazy?' Lot easier."

Gillie shrugged. "Beats the shit outta me. Let's get movin'. We got us some stealin' to do. You with me?"

He bounced on ahead in a loping, sneaky gait like that of a fox or a coyote, and Wade watched him, watched him carefully because of one simple fact: Wade Martin worshipped Gillie Roth. Worshipped the air that he breathed and the dust that he spit upon. Gillie was the coolest, street-smartest, bad-ass eleven-year-old Wade had ever known. Or could imagine. But that didn't mean, as Wade often reminded himself, he should let Gillie walk all over him. You had to draw the line sometimes. And yet—well, he would have paid money unhesitatingly to be in Gillie's company. The rat-tailed scavenger could take care of himself. He was, in Wade's eyes, totally awesome.

"I'm with you," he whispered, twenty feet behind.

At the glass double doors to Holly's, Gillie wheeled around. "So whatcha gonna steal?"

Wade took a deep breath and peered into the aisles of bread, aspirin, and cookies, the racks of sunglasses and visors and lotion, and the tangle of dip nets and rods.

"Haven't decided. Maybe some candy or . . . triple geez, no."

"Watcha see?"

"My *mom*'s in there talkin' to Holly. I think she's gonna ask for a job waitin' tables at the bar next door." Disappointed, he faced Gillie. "I gotta wait till she leaves. I'm not goin' in there while my mom's there."

Gillie shook his head. "You're a big-time stealer all right. Man, I can't believe this—the kid's scared of his mom."

"Am not. But a smart stealer, he don't take unnecessary chances," Wade exclaimed, hoping his words echoed enough cockiness and street wisdom to sound convincing.

Gillie seemed to be studying him, and it made him uncomfortable.

"You know what your problem is, Wade ole friend? You're a coward. Got no guts. I shoulda seen it before. You're 'fraid to go into forbidden territory."

The words "coward" and "no guts" reactivated Wade's palm pressing; but the words "forbidden territory," the mystique of them, the surprising ease with which they slipped from Gillie's tongue, startled him.

And he found himself listening.

"Yeah, that's what it is," Gillie continued. "You say you got the guts to take care of yourself, and maybe you do when things is safe; but what about when they're not? What about when you got to do things and go into places where you could get your ass burned? You got to have the guts to cross the line. These here doors is your line, man.

10

You gonna cross it?"

Shamed, fuming within, Wade stared at the white silt standing in tiny mounds where the doors came together; then he raised his eyes and caught the profile of his mother's face, the black ringlets of her hair.

"I can take care of myself. I ain't a coward."

Gillie made a deprecatory sound with his lips; two drops of spittle landed on Wade's flushed cheek.

"See this nickel?" Gillie taunted, holding it up against the glare of the noonday sun. "I'm gonna walk in there and buy me one Blue Volcano Jaw Teaser, but I'm comin' out with a stash—I'm talkin' at least two candy bars and a bag of M & M's."

"Big deal," said Wade, his heart racing as he followed Gillie's swagger into the air-conditioned store.

Can he really deliver on this one? It would be too awesome. Too friggin' awesome.

The door alert, a string of flat, metallic shells, rang discordantly.

Holly Webster, proprietress, looked up from her conversation with Anita Martin and smiled, and when she commenced talking again, Wade could see her fat jowls quiver. He avoided his mother's glance. In fact, he stayed mostly out of sight, over near the ice cream freezer, as Gillie went to work.

Cool. Gillie was so-o-o cool. He strolled by the candy rack, passing it while keeping his hand tucked in the stomach pouch of his windbreaker. He turned and sought eye contact with Wade. Gaining it, he slowed his steps on a return pass at the candy rack, his head cocked to one side as if listening to every word Holly and Mrs. Martin exchanged.

Cool. Careful. Awesome.

Wade held his breath and tiptoed from aisle to aisle. He momentarily lost sight of his friend, but could hear him clink his nickel on the counter and purchase the Teaser.

11

The indistinct give and take between the purchaser and Holly was muffled. Then a pleasant, fat lady chuckle was followed by another few words. And then Gillie was on his way to the glass doors.

Forbidden territory.

The words rumbled through Wade's thoughts like thunder rolling over the nearby Everglades. Gillie had ventured into Holly's, claiming he could load up. Stealing. Forbidden territory. So cool. Had he pulled it off?

"Couldn't have," Wade whispered to himself.

He would have bet money Gillie failed.

2

Surprised beyond words, Wade wrapped his fingers around the Snicker's bar as if doubting it were real. He and Gillie hunkered down behind Holly's to examine the loot: Besides the Snicker's, there was an Almond Joy, a bag of Peanut M & M's, a half dozen caramel squares, and, of course, the Blue Volcano Jaw Teaser.

Wade touched each item; a string of saliva escaped from one corner of his mouth.

Gillie laughed. Then he said, "Hey, your eyes are big as pool balls. Whatsa matter, didn't you think I could pull it off?"

Wade shook his head very slowly, the kind of head shake every boy understands to have been generated by envy or astonishment.

"You did pretty good, Gillie."

"Pretty good? Friggin' right, I did."

"Not bad."

Gillie leaned closer and whispered, "Now it's your turn. You ain't freezin' up on me, are you?"

"Huh? Me? Freezin' up? No way. No way."

Gillie seemed to study him again; Wade pushed himself to his feet to elude the unnerving scrutiny.

"Here," said Gillie, "you can have half my Almond Joy. After you steal somethin', I'll show you a cool thing we can do with the caramels."

"What's the cool thing?"

Wolfing down the candy, Gillie gargled, "Huh-uh. Later."

They dipped into the M & M's, crunching, and on such a warm day in late May they discovered that the candy-coated goodies do indeed melt in your hand—and get smeared on your shirt and shorts and chin—even your sneakers.

"You know what, Gillie? This stuff makes me thirsty. You thirsty?"

"Yeah. Bad thirsty."

Hands on hips, head cocked at a mischievous angle, Gillie surveyed a wisp of cloud far to the north. Wade, whose estimation of his friend had just climbed a dozen rungs, thought Gillie looked too cool to be true. Off the scale cool.

"Here's the plan," Gillie exclaimed suddenly. "While I'm buyin' a can of Cherry Coke, you cruise the candy rack and fill your pockets—little shit like bubble gum and jaw breakers, they're the easiest. Bags of M & M's and Skittles make too much noise if you're just startin' out stealin'." He paused. "Listen, I'll be a distraction, you know, so you can make a clean lift. It'll be a piece of cake."

Wade wanted to protest, wanted to maintain that he needed no such assistance. *I can take care of myself.* But he kept his mouth shut. Obviously Gillie was in a class by himself when it came to lifting goodies.

And so, backs of his knees the consistency of Jell-o, Wade trailed into Holly's behind Gillie. The scenario unfolded in an orderly fashion. Gillie worked his special

13

magic at the soft drink cooler and ambled toward the checkout counter, where Holly and Wade's mom pursued their seemingly idle chatter.

"Piece of cake," Wade whispered, attempting to pump up his courage.

He threaded his way past the bags of potato chips and cheese curls, one ear glued to Gillie's progress; and then it presented itself, heart-plunging and larger than life—the candy rack. It was a profusion of colors and anticipations of tastes.

Gillie, Cherry Coke in hand, had reached the counter.

Better hurry up and take something, Wade told himself.

He scanned the rack, scrambling his brain to recall Gillie's advice. And suddenly panic—he couldn't decide. Colors and items and sizes blurred. He could hear Holly's chuckle, but he could also imagine her meat-hook of an arm swinging down upon him: *Put that back!* And what about his mom? She would pitch a major fit. She would send him on the longest guilt trip of his young life.

He grabbed at a Blue Volcano and tried to jam it into the pocket of his shorts.

But he dropped it. It bounced twice and rolled, luckily just as the cash register drawer rattled open.

Why am I doing this? I've never really stolen anything except once at school I took a couple of baseball cards out of a kid's locker. I've been in fights and been sent to the principal's office, but I've never, ever stolen stuff from a real store.

He conjured up Gillie's cocky grin.

Coward. No guts.

He dived to the floor after the Blue Volcano; it was wedged beneath the rack.

Gillie was starting to leave.

Grab something! Anything!

Wade got to his feet and without looking snatched at one of the display boxes and, heart beating like a jambox, poked the item in his pocket. Then he hustled out of the store.

Once outside, he ran. He didn't stop until he reached the halfway point of the small bridge that joined Orchid Springs with the Schreck Wildlife Refuge. Beneath his feet, the wooden planks continued to echo the hammering of his footfalls.

Huffing and puffing, Gillie jogged up, and they rested their elbows on the railing, eyes drawn to the coffee-colored water of the slough as it flowed sluggishly below them, moving inexorably toward its destination: the Everglades.

"Let me see what you got," Gillie prodded.

Wade hesitated; it was a stomach-turning realization: He had no idea exactly what he had thrust into his pocket before desperately escaping Holly's.

"Sure. I made a super-clean lift. You didn't need to be a distraction for me." He brought his hand free of his pocket and slowly uncurled his fingers.

Gillie frowned. "A pack of wintergreen gum? All the neat junk in there and you stole a pack of wintergreen gum? You friggin' serious?"

The tips of Wade's ears burned; his throat filled with sawdust as he stared down at the gum.

He swallowed, and the resultant gulp was audible.

Time to stonewall it, he reasoned. "Hey, I like wintergreen gum. It's my favorite kind. It's what I wanted to steal."

Charade under way, he tore into the pack, unwrapped a piece, and popped it into his mouth. He immediately hated the taste, the semi-sweet coolness with a bite all its own.

"Want a piece?"

Gillie grimaced. "Not on a bet."

He opened his can of Cherry Coke and slipped a second can to Wade, who almost sent the partially chewed gum on a journey into his bowels.

"You got two!"

"Couldn't leave out my buddy, could I?"

Impressed, Wade took a long draw on the sickeningly sweet drink, a draw imitative of Gillie's, and then he noticed that his friend's gaze was glued to a skiff tied up thirty yards beyond them—a skiff that belonged to Mr. C.M. Bradshaw, real estate developer and self-appointed mayor of Orchid Springs.

Eyes never abandoning the skiff, Gillie said, "It's gonna be a good summer. Monday's the last day of school, and you and me are gonna be cocks of the rock."

"That Australian? 'Cocks of the rock'?"

"Naw—it's somethin' my Granny Roth says."

When Gillie wasn't looking, Wade sneaked the wintergreen out of his mouth and gave it a hard flick behind his back. He took another swig at his Cherry Coke, all the while admiring the final inches of Gillie's rat's tail and wondering how much his mom would scream if he dyed his own coal-black hair blond. Some pretty serious screaming, he guessed, but he didn't care; it would mean he was more like Gillie.

Bradshaw's skiff continued to occupy his hero's attention. Wade finished his Coke and belched loudly, earning him an appreciative smile from Gillie, who volleyed an even louder belch, and they pursued the impromptu competition until Wade's stomach hurt and Gillie gained an unceremonious victory.

Then Wade said, "Anything every scare you, Gillie? I mean, really, really scare you? Scare you shitless?"

"Shitless?" He thought a split-second. "No."

Wade grinned. Yeah, it was going to be a great summer. In the company of a cool dude like Gillie, how could it be anything else?

"Hey, wanna have some fun?" Gillie exclaimed.

Nodding, Wade finished his soda.

Eyes twinkling mischievously, Gillie held up two caramel squares.

"Feeding time."

3

The kangaroo, an elderly female named Ruthie, worked her velvety lips like fingers, but no matter how hard she tried, the sticky caramel squares eluded her control. At one point, she rolled onto her back, pawing at her mouth, chewing as furiously as her ancient jaws would allow.

Gillie and Wade cackled.

But as they watched the shackled animal, Wade shot a wary glance now and again at the Key-West-type, white-frame house at the rear of the refuge.

"What if Miss Freda sees us?" he offered in a sober moment between laughs.

Gillie waved him off. "She never comes outta her house. Not for nuthin'. She's got a housekeeper, a real live aborigine from Australia who does everything for her. Houston Parker and old Hash are supposed to tend the animals and keep up the grounds—but you don't see *them* around, do you?"

After Ruthie had managed to worry the caramel squares into a more consumable texture, the boys grew weary of her performance and moved to the koala cage and the pen holding the large ostrichlike rhea. From there they migrated to the gator area and hovered at the chain-link fence, hoping to see one of the muddy gray-green monsters snap into action.

None did.

"Let's go tease at Houston's albino," Gillie suggested.

The pure white gator, a five-footer, had a shallow concrete pool of its own. Gillie waited for a couple of tourists to move on before searching in the nearby vegetation for a wire-looped bamboo pole used for dangling snacks near the mouth of the rare reptile.

"Houston's chopper be headin' in soon," Wade warned.

"I ain't 'fraid of Houston," said Gillie, tapping the gator on its snout until, irritated, it lunged, snapping, whipping its tail to show that it meant business. "Houston thinks he's hot stuff, you know. Thinks he looks like Don Johnson; thinks all the women are warm for his bod. Your mom likes him—I can tell that."

A flame torched in Wade's chest.

"She does *not!* She thinks he's a jerk—least *I* think he's a jerk."

Winning several more angry snaps from the gator, Gillie tossed the pole aside and said, "I bet Houston's humpin' your mom."

Wade froze; the fury started at the soles of his feet and spiraled up through his stomach and chest, and when it reached his mouth he growled low and mean. Then he charged.

It wasn't much of a fight. More of a shoving match in which Gillie easily held off the smaller boy, giggling madly as he did so.

"Is not! Is not! Is not!" Wade yelled.

A tourist or two in the distance might have taken notice; but the basking gators did not, and when the dust had settled, Gillie apologized. Sort of.

"Look, I'd've never said anything 'bout your mom and Houston if I'd known how it'd freak you. Wow, you got seriously freaked."

Embarrassed, Wade caught his breath.

"Didn't mean to jump you," he mumbled. "Don't talk 'bout Houston and my mom no more, okay?"

"Gotcha."

Wade looked around. He had forgotten about something, lost as he had been in the aura of Gillie's company—even if Gillie could ignite his anger any second.

"You seen Timmy?"

"Nope."

"Geez, I'm supposed to keep an eye on him. Mom says I got to."

"Glad I don't got a little brother," said Gillie. "They can be real pissers."

"Come on. I gotta see if I can find him."

Back over the bridge they rumbled. Late spring traffic going into the refuge was very light as usual. The world of Orchid Springs seemed to belong exclusively to the two boys.

"There he is," Wade exclaimed. "Down by the slough."

"Yeah, and look who's with him."

Both boys snickered.

The scene they came upon consisted of a nine-year-old, black-haired boy and a heavyset girl, eleven, lightly spotted with freckles which matched her strawberry-blond hair. The boy was Timmy Martin; the girl was Sara Beth Bradshaw, the mayor's daughter. They were farting around near the skiff, perhaps toying with the daring idea of taking a ride in it, but much too timid to ever attempt it.

As Wade and Gillie approached them, Gillie became animated.

"It's happy, happy hippo, happy, happy hippo," he chortled, dancing down the gentle bank toward the slough, working his arms so that they resembled a huge mouth opening and closing.

"Happy, happy hippo," Wade chimed in, and almost immediately, Timmy echoed the taunt aimed at the overweight girl.

Sara Beth retaliated with a throaty shriek and more.

She lifted one of the long wooden poles out of the skiff and jabbed it at Gillie's feet as if she were a medieval jouster wielding a lance.

"Get out of here!" she screamed. "Stop it, Timmy! Whose side are you on?"

She turned on her little turncoat friend, but he was swayed by the company of the older boys. The taunting continued for several minutes, much sound and fury—no injuries beyond Sara Beth's humiliation.

Wade grasped Timmy's arm eventually and pulled him up the bank. "Mom don't want you so close to the slough."

"Aw, why not? I can swim."

"Don't be so stupid, Timmy. There's alligators in there. They'd bite your face off if they got a chance."

Timmy thoughtfully touched at his nose and cheeks as if entertaining images of such a horrific event.

"You and Sara Beth go on up and play around the trailers," Wade added.

"We can play wherever we want to. My father owns most of Orchid Springs," said the flush-faced girl.

"Hippo, hippo, hippo," Gillie chanted, charging at her, sending her scrambling up the bank, scalded by his aggression.

"Go on, get," Wade said.

Timmy and Sara Beth lingered. Then she said, "You better leave my father's boat alone."

"It's hippo season, Sara Beth, you better get your fat ass outta here," Gillie called out. And he and Wade laughed riotously.

But not for long.

In Gillie's teeming brain, an idea was forming.

"Wade, ole friend, you ever been to Pelican Pond?"

The two boys flopped down in the cool grass bordering the slough. Wade glanced over his shoulder, making certain that Timmy was minding him.

20

"No. Where is it?"

Gillie gestured vaguely toward the mangrove swamp. "Some miles out there."

"What's so special about it?"

Rolling over so that he could look directly into Wade's eyes, Gillie whispered, "It's forbidden territory."

"You're full of shit, Gillie."

But the words had, once again, tapped a nerve. Wade felt tingly all over.

"And you're a friggin' coward."

They shoved at one another playfully before Wade asked, "So how do we get there?"

"How do you think, snothead—we fly!"

Gillie jumped to his feet and flailed his arms and circled Wade like a huge winged thing, soaring, gliding, and finally swooping down to attack.

"I'm serious," Wade protested, fighting off the predatory Gillie-creature.

Speaking very slowly, as if explaining something to the mentally handicapped, Gillie said, "We borrow Mr. Bradshaw's skiff."

"What? Come on, Gillie, if we steal that skiff, Bradshaw'll have our butts in a sling."

"Did I say 'steal'? Read my lips—'bor-row.' We're going to borrow it just as soon as I get my spear. Stay here. I'll be back in a second."

Pelican Pond. Forbidden territory.

Wade sat nervously contemplating the situation: *Stealing candy's one thing—but stealing a boat!* The notion scared him, yet curiously thrilled him. Could he back out of it? Could he tell Gillie he needed to stay and watch after Timmy?

No guts.

Gillie's claim echoed through the empty rooms of his thoughts.

"I can take care of myself," he whispered. "I ain't no

21

baby, and I ain't no coward."

Conflict resolved.

Mostly.

The sight of Gillie returning cheered him, reaffirming his decision.

"Is that your spear?" Wade asked.

Halfway down the bank, Gillie stopped. "No, it's a friggin' toothpick! Course it's my spear. Here, jump in the skiff and hold on to this while I push us off."

He tossed the object at Wade, who muffed it before he got control of it and gingerly stepped into the skiff. The spear was a masterwork of boyhood ingenuity: An axe handle with a long, nasty-looking butcher knife lashed to one end with wire and twine and black electrician's tape.

"Geez oh God, Gillie—this thing's wicked."

"Might need it where we're goin'."

As the skiff eased away from the bank and Gillie leaped aboard, Wade felt a draught of cool air gust through his insides.

Borrow, not steal, he reminded himself.

Wade remained seated, but Gillie stood, maneuvering the pushpole, straining to coax the skiff out into the current.

From a vantage point somewhere out of sight, Sara Beth's voice screeched, "I'm going to tell my father!"

"Hippo, hippo, hippo!" Gillie called back, and as they caught the sluggish current, he and Wade laughed and whooped and felt a particular surge of energy that only boys can understand.

In a matter of minutes, they were drifting free of Orchid Springs. Holly's store and her bar, the mobile home park, the scattering of cheap condos and the area's only motel diminished rapidly. The slough meandered slightly to the right, rimming the edge of the Schreck Wildlife Refuge. Grassy banks transformed into the low tangle of mangrove trees, their roots threatening to claw

22

their way out to the skiff.

"Comin' up on Hash's cabin," Gillie announced.

Behind the small, derelict building stood a tall tower with an observation deck for bird-watchers. As they passed the cabin, Wade thought about the man called Hash, a man who reminded him of the actor Telly Savalas, except that Hash looked meaner, his eyes dark and hard like those of a shark.

"Didja know Hash has a talking parrot and a pet boa constrictor?" Wade asked.

"Sure. I've helped him feed Danbhalah—that's the snake's name. And Ibo, the parrot—man, he can swear like a sailor—neat bird."

Disappointed that Gillie knew more about Hash than he did, Wade sat back and surveyed the scenery and soaked up all the good feeling of being out on such an adventure. There might be hell to pay when his mom heard of it, but, well, it would be worth any punishment.

"I've been thinkin' 'bout somethin'," said Gillie, guiding the skiff expertly down the ever-narrowing slough. "How'd you like to go halves with me on my paper route? *Miami Herald.* It's a good deal. I've had the route 'bout a year now."

"You serious?" said Wade. "That'd be super."

"Thing I've been thinkin' is—you and me, we're a lot alike, you know."

Wade warmed to the suggestion. "Yeah, I guess maybe you're right."

"I mean, take dads, for example—neither of us got one. Mine left my mom when I was just a baby."

"Mine's not around neither," Wade confirmed. "One night my mom loaded up me and Timmy, and we headed out of St. Louis and came here because Holly—she's my mom's aunt—she told mom we could come here if Dad kept gettin' meaner."

"Your dad pretty mean?"

"Yeah. But—well, he told my mom if she left him, he'd find us and pay her back—you know, get revenge for taking me and Timmy away. My mom's 'fraid he'll show up one of these days and there'll be trouble. We been here two whole months, and so far he hasn't come."

"I don't need a dad," said Gillie. "A mom neither. Livin' with Granny Roth's okay. She don't rag me much. I don't mind nuthin' she tells me to do."

"Where's your mom?"

For a few seconds, Gillie fell silent, then he forced a half chuckle. "She's in Miami. She's a hooker. You know, a whore. A prostitute. Makes pretty good money sometimes."

Wade frowned, and his lip curled as if he had tasted something sour. "She's not really, is she?"

Gillie wheeled in sudden anger. "God damn it, I said she was."

"I'm sorry," said Wade timidly, though it didn't seem to him like quite the right thing to say.

Conversation waned. Gillie let the slow current take them; he used the pole only to keep the skiff centered. A trio of brown pelicans winged above them, and off to their left a couple of wood storks stirred up the mud searching for food.

"Hey, there's a gator nest up ahead," Gillie announced, and Wade felt relieved that the focus of attention had shifted from Gillie's mom.

To their left, the saw grass grew tall, creating an interesting contrast to the low-growing snarl of mangrove trees to their right.

"We gonna look at it?" asked Wade.

"Sure. You can't pass a gator nest and not poke around in it."

"What if the mama gator's 'round? Won't she be protectin' it?"

"That's why I brought my spear. You can cover me

while I snatch us both a baby gator."

Gillie maneuvered the skiff up to within a few feet of the nest, a surprisingly large mound of vegetation hugging the bank.

"You want *me* to cover *you?*"

"Don't be so friggin' dense—yeah, I'd like to stay in one piece."

When the skiff nosed against the mounded nest, Gillie scrambled out onto it. Wade, spear in hand, crouched low, scanning the slough for any suspicious movement.

"Gillie, could a mama gator bite this boat in two?"

His curiosity running full speed, Gillie gently pawed through the top layer of sticks, paying no attention to his friend's anxiety.

"Gillie? I'm serious . . . Gillie, I think somethin's under the boat. You better leave the nest alone."

Spear poised to thrust into the water, Wade stood and squinted into the brackish water.

"Gillie?"

"Will you stop buggin' me!"

"All right, but I'm tellin' you . . . somethin's under the boat."

"Mud and swamp peat. That's what's under the boat, Wade. You're friggin' imaginin' things."

Gillie continued to remove sticks from the top of the nest until he happened to glance into the saw grass nearby. "Shit! Look at that."

"Gator comin'?" Wade tensed, tightening his grip on the spear handle.

"Somebody beat us to it," said Gillie as he tossed something white into the skiff.

Wade tiptoed reflexively away from it.

"What *is* that?"

"Broken gator egg," said Gillie. "Raccoons have been here. Couple dozen broken eggs over in the grass."

Fears relenting, Wade said, "I wouldn't want to be that

coon if mama gator finds him."

Gillie stepped back into the skiff. "Me neither. But she won't. Coons—they're real good at stealin' and gettin' away with it. Kinda like you and me."

He winked and rubbed at the blond stubble beneath his cap. Wielding the pushpole, he swung the skiff out into mid-current. For another hundred yards, they rode upon the rhythm of the swamp, the mangroves thickening, snowy egrets and blue herons watching them disinterestedly from knobby limbs.

"Hey, Gillie, you think it's 'bout time we turned 'round?"

"And miss Pelican Pond? Hang on. It's only another mile or so."

"Oh, yeah, I forgot, you know, 'bout Pelican Pond."

4

As they ventured onward, deeper and deeper into the labyrinth, Wade felt the mangroves take on a sinister air, their prop roots bending in graceful arcs resembled giant webs harboring an unseen spider creature beneath them somewhere in the muck. The waxy green foliage of the trees concealed furtive movement, completing the atmosphere of potential terror.

"This is neat," Wade exclaimed, hiding his real feelings.

"Beats the hell outa bein' in school, don't it?"

Wade smiled. The next mile passed slowly, and his smile gradually faded as the afternoon sun began to slip westward in earnest. The breeze soon died away, and the swamp's humidity closed around them oppressively.

"Skins! Skins!" Gillie suddenly exclaimed.

Wade jolted out of his reverie, his eyes darting from side to side, expecting to see a gator or perhaps that spider

26

creature his fear had spawned. But then he saw that Gillie was peeling off his windbreaker and T-shirt, and so he followed suit, keeping his cap on, as did Gillie, to ward off the possibility of a badly sunburned face.

They floated on, a lazy, dreamlike experience; the slough narrowed, then doglegged right. And Gillie whooped, sending a foursome of egrets winging straight at the sun.

"We made it!"

Wade stood up; the scene he surveyed weakened the backs of his knees.

Forbidden territory.

"This is it, isn't it? Pelican Pond."

"Damn right," said Gillie, his sweaty face beaming with a pride that suggested ownership.

"I don't see any pelicans," said Wade.

Gillie laughed. "You're not for real, man. It's just a friggin' name. Maybe pelicans *used* to nest here—who knows. Just a friggin' name. Waddaya think of the place?"

Gillie brought the skiff virtually to a stop. Wade drank in his surroundings as if he were dying of thirst: The slough emptied into a circular pond twenty to twenty-five yards in diameter, its water gray-black and locked in an almost imperceptible counter-clockwise swirl. To its right crowded the mangroves; top center, the slough resumed meandering still again to the right. But to the left of the pond, a hummock rose, an island of firmament covered in saw grass and dwarfed pines.

"This is weird," Wade muttered. "Super weird. But, hey, what's that wooden thing?"

At the far end of the hummock, railroad ties had been shaped into a boxlike platform and sunken into the grass.

"It belongs to Hash. There's a sinkhole over there, and he's got this pump that dredges up mud. He comes out here to look for fossils."

"Fossils?"

"You know, like old bones. He sells them to some rich guy in Miami—prehistoric shit like leg bones of saber-tooth lions. Haven't you ever seen some of Hash's bones out at his cabin?"

"Oh . . . yeah, sure. But why isn't he out doin' this more often?"

"'Cause he's a drunk. Whenever he looks for bones, he comes back and goes on a big drunk."

"Why?"

Gillie shrugged. "Who cares?"

They poled along the right edge of the bank. Wade was lost in thought over Hash's activities, but the sharp eyes of Gillie slammed him back to reality.

"It's mine!" he cried, grabbing his spear. "I saw it first!"

Out onto the mangrove roots he scampered, negotiating them as if they were a massive playground junglegym.

5

"Gillie? What do you see?"

Wade followed Gillie's acrobatics, saw the mangrove limbs bow and strafe, but could not detect the source of his animation. Not at first.

"Look at the size of that mother!" Gillie exclaimed, using the spear like a balance pole.

"Gillie?"

The rustle of wings in the near distance weakened the hold of the pond's humidity, and something more—the outer edge of a stench, the stink perhaps of the swamp itself, decaying, putrefying, feeding upon its own death—wafted through the air.

Gillie had stopped. "You see it?"

"No, what are you after?"

"Corn snake, dummy. Great big sucker. Six feet, I'd bet."

A slip of movement near the prop roots, and Wade caught sight of the orange-banded, gray-brown reptile.

"Down there, Gillie." Wade pointed.

"Keep the skiff close," Gillie called out as he gave chase.

Plunging the pushpole into the water, Wade smiled at his friend's energy.

"I'm comin'."

Gillie crashed forward, yelping with glee; soon he clambered around the turn and was out of sight, though Wade could hear his voice and the protest of the mangrove limbs.

The pond seemed alive with the vibration of wings. Everywhere wings; a thrumming, heavy and ominous. Wade looked up, expecting to see Houston Parker's copter, but his eye was greeted only by white wisps of clouds.

Wade wrinkled his nose. More of the swamp stench.

"Shit, I lost him!" Gillie's words filtered through the humidity. Having failed but not having been defeated, he climbed back into the skiff.

"Stinks 'round here, don't it?" said Wade.

"I missed that son-of-a-bitch by this far." He held up a thumb and forefinger, indicating a distance of two inches or so.

Wade was about to ask him why the corn snake held such importance when he noticed something. "Hey, where's your spear?"

"Friggin' straight—musta left it where I 'bout stuck that mister. Be right back."

"Well, hurry up, okay? We been gone long enough.

My mom's gonna jump my butt."

"Keep your pants on," Gillie exclaimed over his shoulder.

He rambled across the six-to seven-foot tops of the mangroves, then swung beyond view. Wade poled to the point at which the slough bled away from the pond, meandering right.

"I found it!"

"Good," Wade whispered to himself, growing more uncomfortable every moment with the heat, the stench, and the muted hum which now seemed to surround him.

He waited, wondering what story Gillie would cook up to explain their taking the skiff. Mr. Bradshaw would complain to Holly and Holly would probably inform his mom and—

"Wade?"

Something in the tone of Gillie's voice sent a tiny chill trickling down his spine.

"Wade?"

Not a cry, not a loud call.

Wade poled into the renewed current; the mangroves blocked his vision. "Gillie, where are you?"

Once again, Gillie said, "Wade?" Then repeated it rapidly: "Wade? Wade?" Then louder and louder: "Wade! Wa-a-a-de!"

The boy poled faster; the skiff caught the swing of the current, and suddenly he could see a wide expanse of mangroves.

He could see Gillie.

And smell the stench.

It burned the lining of his nostrils; mucous streamed down over his lips.

He could feel the air from the beat of wings.

And hear a smothered cry—nothing like Gillie's voice.

A blackness rose and spread, a black curtain closing, then slowly opening.

No scream.

Wade's skin turned cool and clammy.

His stomach gurgled once.

He held on to the pushpole as if letting go of it would plunge him into a bottomless abyss.

Then his senses began to shut down.

The world became a gigantic drive-in movie screen, white and blank.

Chapter Two

1

"I'm going to forget about men and become the perfect mother."

Anita Martin hesitated, waiting for her aunt's response to her declaration.

"Holly, did you hear what I said? No more men. I can't trust them. I have no judgment about them—look at the mess I made the first time around. Dean was a lousy choice—a lousy husband, a lousy father—a lousy everything. But I chose him."

Holly busied herself at the cash register, breaking open a new roll of quarters. Her broad back trembled as she tried to repress laughter, but she was not having much success.

"Holly, you're laughing. Don't make fun of me."

The older woman turned and cackled; it was a good-natured, free-swinging laugh, somehow endearing. Rolls of fat clinging to the undersides of her forearms quivered; her hazel eyes danced, and so did the large red freckles on her forehead and cheeks. Her red hair, shading to gray, picked up a ray of late-afternoon sun and shone like spun glass.

"Anita, honey," she replied, placing her doughlike hands on her niece's shoulders, "I'm on your side. But you got to be up front with me, girl. It's time for some realistic self-appraisal."

"You don't think I can be a good mother, do you?"

Holly chuckled softly, an infectious little laugh.

Anita had to smile. "So go ahead, set me straight."

Staring directly into her eyes, Holly said, "How old are you, hon?"

"Twenty-nine."

"What kind of cook are you?"

"A good cook . . . pretty good cook."

"Hon, I've tasted your broccoli casserole and your burned pork chops."

"All right . . . I have trouble timing things. Mama never taught me how to cook. If I can't microwave something, I'm in trouble."

"Can you keep a neat home? Keep it spic-and-span? Orderly?"

"Oh, Holly, you've seen our trailer."

"Yes, and when I did I thought to myself: It would be easier to walk through a minefield."

"Holly, that's not fair."

"No, you're right. I was being too kind." She hugged her niece, and they began to laugh before Anita pulled away.

"But I'm great with the boys. They have clean clothes most of the time, and now that we're in Orchid Springs, they have a safe place away from their father. Timmy and Wade get lots of love."

"Do you watch 'em closely?"

"Of course I do."

"Then you can tell me what Wade filched when he was in here a couple of hours ago."

Anita blinked. She shook her head, and her black hair glimmered.

34

"Filched? You mean like steal? Are you saying Wade *stole* something from this store?"

Holly smiled and nodded. "So did his friend, Gillie. Gillie Roth."

"Holly, no. Wade wouldn't—I mean, he's gotten into some trouble at school, but he wouldn't steal."

"It's okay. I'm sure Gillie put him up to it."

Indignant, Anita said, "I'll make certain he doesn't play with that boy ever again."

"Not a good idea. There are no other boys in the area Wade's age. Don't forget, Orchid Springs is ninety-five percent elderly. He would have a lonely summer if you ruled Gillie off-limits."

"But I can't have him stealing."

"I'll put them to work for the equivalent value of what they took. It's a system Gillie and I have developed."

"You mean *he* knows that *you* know he's stealing?"

"Yes. A game we play. Gillie's real mixed up. But under that cocky, street-smart mask, he's a good kid. The world's been mean to him, and so, every so often, he has to be mean back to it—like teasing the animals over at the refuge. He won't be such a bad friend for Wade."

Perplexed, Anita walked away. "What you're saying, Holly, is that I'm a failure as a mother, just like I failed at my job in Homestead and failed in my marriage. So what's left?"

She wasn't about to let Holly see the tears that were threatening.

"Ease up, girl. All I'm saying is that you shouldn't close the door on men so fast. You made one rotten choice. But eventually those two boys of yours will need a father figure around again."

"I don't know, Holly. I just don't know."

"Listen, hon. You're a very attractive young woman. Why, just the other day somebody told me you could double for Cher—and they're right. Remember *Moon-*

35

struck? Cher found someone. So will you."

"That was a movie. Not real life. And besides, *you* don't have a man, and you haven't had one for a long time, and you've run a store and built the bar next door . . . I can be as independent as you."

"I'm a tough ole gal, hon. When my Roy passed away, I went through a long, hard blue spell. I about gave in; fact is, I wouldn't want to see you go through all of those lonely years the way I did."

Anita leaned forward onto the counter. "I appreciate your concern; and, well, Orchid Springs is a beautiful, peaceful spot, and I like it and the boys seem to, too. But the average age of the men is about sixty-five. Even that dreadful Hash is old enough to be my father. The only younger man I've met is Houston Parker."

"And you can cross *him* off your list."

Amused at Holly's stern tone, Anita said, "Why? Is he taken?"

"No young woman who has a good head on her shoulders would be interested in him."

"He's great-looking. Has a smile that makes me feel like a little girl."

"You *are* a little girl."

"Hey . . . not fair."

"Maybe not. Point is, don't let yourself get anything started between you and Houston."

"Does he have a wife somewhere?"

"No. No wife."

"My God, he's not gay, is he?"

Holly shook her head and chuckled despite herself. "Oh, I'd say most likely not. He loves the ladies—every chance he gets."

"You think he's too young, is that it? What is he— twenty-four, five? It's the '80s, Holly, nobody except old prunes objects to a woman seeing a younger man."

36

"Age isn't the problem, hon."

"Then what is? Because I have a feeling that any day now Houston's going to ask me out, and since I see no good reason for saying no, I'll probably say yes."

Busying herself wiping the countertop, the older woman appeared to be sifting through thoughts and explanations as if weighing them on some inner scale. "I've known Houston for years. I remember when he was smaller than Wade, about Timmy's age, in fact, and he would come in and read the hot rod magazines, or look at the pictures, at least.

"But he was the nicest, politest little guy. Then, oh, I suppose it's been twelve, thirteen years ago, he lost his daddy. Some kind of accident out in the swamp. Well, it like to tore the boy's heart out. Jane Ellen, Houston's mother, she took the loss even harder than the boy did. A year or so later she moved away from Orchid Springs."

"What happened to Houston? He went along with her, didn't he?"

Holly sighed heavily. "Roy and I kept him, were his foster parents. Or we tried to be. During his teenage years, Houston turned wild, restless, in and out of trouble. He left the area for a few years, but something called him back."

"Probably a sense of obligation to you. With Roy gone, he knew you needed help."

"No. Houston thinks only of himself. It's a mystery to me what holds him here. Seems like he's given up on any kind of future. He'd rather charge through the sky in that helicopter or between here and Miami on that motorcycle. And now the drugs. If Miss Freda over at the refuge finds out he's taken tourists up in that copter when he's been high on something, he'll lose his job. And should."

"Sounds like he needs a good woman to give him direction."

37

"What he needs is a good distance—a good distance from Orchid Springs and whatever is clawing away at him."

"I feel sorry for him."

"Don't, hon. I know Houston Parker. I've tried to mother him and love him. His heart's too cold to accept any of it. If you get involved with him, he'll bring you down. Bring you down even lower than you've been."

2

The afternoon wore on. A few customers trickled in, most wanting fishing supplies, prodding Holly for insider information; a few bought a bag of groceries.

"This near to summer is it always so slow?" Anita asked. It was an idle question. She couldn't take her mind off Houston Parker. An inner resolve was collecting, and yet she respected Holly's advice. Would a clash with her be unavoidable?

"We would do better if we were ten miles closer to Miami," said Holly. "Too isolated being out here in the boondocks. Folks need more than gators and an old kangaroo to attract them out this far. I keep telling C.M., you know, Mr. Bradshaw, that we have to come up with a gimmick. Maybe a bass rodeo."

"A bass rodeo?"

"Uh-huh. A big fishing contest. That lazy ole slough out there has lots and lots of largemouth bass. Some real lunkers, too. See that one Roy caught?" She pointed to a huge bass mounted on the wall behind them.

Anita nodded vaguely. Then her brow wrinkled. "As it is, how do you pay your bills? You've had so little business this afternoon. I was hoping. . . ."

A tall, elderly gentleman, thin to the brink of emaciation, timid and surprisingly pale, entered the

38

store. Holly introduced him to Anita as the evening counterman. She called him by his nickname: Wimp.

"I know what you've been hoping," she replied to Anita as she cleared the register. "We'll talk. Let's go next door—I'll buy you a beer."

Anita smiled wearily. "Best offer I've had all day."

Holly's bar was dark and cool, a womblike shelter from the blazing sun and stifling humidity. It possessed a decidedly south Florida decor—lots of dark cedar, shells, tropical plants and fishing nets as well as an obligatory set of shark's teeth and a plastic replica of a leaping tarpon.

"I really like what you've done with the bar," said Anita. "It's cozy."

"I'd rather it be 'cashy,' if you know what I mean. Next week I'll start up a happy hour around five, and we'll stay open till midnight every day except Sunday."

Holly went behind the counter and expertly pulled a draught beer.

"There you are—on the house."

"Thanks."

Anita sipped at the beer's foamy head and brushed a few bubbles from her nose. "Aren't you having one?"

"Beer gives me gas," said Holly. "So does pizza."

"Mama used to love pizza. Did you remember that?"

"Carolyn loved all kinds of food. And that snip of a girl could eat like a fieldhand and not gain an ounce. Me—oh, land's. Food treats me like I'm a balloon that needs to be blown up."

Anita nursed her beer, lost momentarily in memory. "Mama had a nickname for you. You remember it?"

"No, but I used to call her scarecrow."

"Mama said that when you were growing up, she called you the big red hen."

Remembering, Holly instantly cackled. "How could I have forgotten that?"

Anita laughed, too. "And sometimes I would ask

39

mama: 'When are we going to see the big red hen?' I never called you by your name because I don't even think I knew it."

"I wish your mother hadn't suffered so long with that ole cancer."

Nodding soberly, Anita stared at the beer. Then she glanced at her watch. "I better get home and see what I can throw in the microwave for the boys' supper." She hesitated. "Holly, I . . . wanted to ask you. . . ."

Holly reached out and patted the woman's hand. "Wanted to ask me for a job, right?"

"You knew all along. I didn't have the nerve to ask you earlier. Losing that job in Homestead has made money a problem. Dean's supposed to pay child support, but somebody'll have to put a gun to his head before he will. Anyway, I've got to stand on my own two feet and take care of my family."

"You ever waited tables?"

Anita shook her head.

"Well, it ain't difficult. I could use you five nights a week, six till closing. Course, something will have to be done about the boys. Might find a babysitter around."

"Oh, Holly, I'll do it. I'll arrange it somehow. When do I start?"

"Next week sound okay?"

"It sounds wonderful."

She lurched across the bar to hug the woman, knocking over the glass of beer.

"Holly! Oh, damn, look at me!"

But her aunt only laughed. "That comes out of your tips."

"I won't be a klutz, Holly. I promise I won't."

"Good. Wouldn't want you to run afoul of the big red hen."

Anita didn't catch the pun, sending the heavyset woman into another round of body-trembling laughter.

40

The Florida sunset bronzed the western sky as Anita left the bar. She saw Timmy and Sara Beth down by the slough and called out for her son to come home. He turned the command into a challenge—a race.

"Watch me fly, mom!"

"You'll eat my dust, hot shot," she responded, and for ten yards she matched him stride for stride. Then, panting as if she had just finished a marathon, she slowed to a walk. "Your mother's getting too old for races."

And too old to chase down a man?

The thought jangled like a flashing neon sign. Self-doubts dominated her emotions. But she reminded herself that at least she had a job, thanks to Holly, and despite what Holly said about the boys needing a father, she clung to her resolve that a man wasn't absolutely essential.

Yet, a dark and hidden wish conjured Houston Parker's smile.

Bits and pieces of Holly's account of Houston's life filtered back, and again she found herself feeling sorry for him: *he's not another Dean. He's not.*

In the approaching twilight, she suddenly looked toward her trailer, number eight, and saw a man hunkered down as if something underneath it held his attention.

Her breath lodged in her throat.

My God, it's Dean!"

For several moments, fear seized her; she began to shake. An empty, queasy, about-to-pass-out feeling rushed over her.

Timmy! Had he raced into the trailer? Where was he?

"Oh, dear God, I can't let this . . . oh, dear God."

As she began running for the trailer, she chided herself for not having, long ago, purchased a gun, a small pistol of some type.

Should she call the police?

Or Holly?

She slowed. The man, dressed in dark coveralls, was strolling alongside the trailer, seeming to be examining it, sizing it up.

"Anita?"

The soft, dry, raspy voice caused her to stop and turn.

"Granny Roth? Oh, what is it? I'm sorry, I can't . . . I'm in a hurry. I'm afraid—"

"Have you seen Gillie?"

The old woman crept nearer, keeping her balance by placing one hand against her trailer.

Anita glanced over her shoulder to locate her former husband. He had slipped out of sight.

"No. No, I haven't. I can't talk now. Please."

She scrambled ahead, leaving the old woman locked in deliberate, spiderlike movements, her lips quivering.

Anita gritted her teeth.

I'll fight him. He's not taking my boys.

Exhaustion threatening every step, she reached the end of her trailer and listened. The man was knocking on the front door.

She slammed around the corner screaming, "Timmy! Timmy, don't open it! Do not open the door!"

The man stepped back at her approach.

"Leave us alone. I'll call the police. Don't think I won't."

She was half crying, half gasping, and the man was continuing to back away, hands up in front of his chest, palms out.

"Ma'am . . . hey, settle down. Settle down."

Her eyes widened, and she cupped a hand over her mouth: The hair, the physique—the man was a dead ringer for Dean. She stared at him. A patch on his coveralls read, "THE BUG FORCE."

"All I wanted, ma'am, is to see if you'd like to have our exterminating service come in once a month and . . . I can come back another time."

"I'm sorry. I thought you were . . . my husband."

"Yes, ma'am . . . I see," he whispered, ducking away.

He had not gotten out of hearing range before she felt an urge to surrender to a good cry. Instead, she laughed—at herself and at the lingering image of the exterminator's expression of utter confusion.

4

"Wade and Gillie stole a boat. They did. Me and Sara Beth saw 'em, and Sara Beth's gonna tell her daddy and Wade and Gillie gonna be in trouble. Will you make Wade stay in his room all summer?"

"Baby, do you want pepperoni or sausage?"

Not quite recovered from the episode with the exterminator, Anita held out the two small pizza containers. "Which one, Timmy? Come on, Mama has a headache."

"Hm-m-m . . . I'll take sausage . . . no. No, I want pepperoni. No—which one does Wade want?"

"Baby, Wade's not home yet. You choose. Wade's late, and he'll have to take whichever one you don't want."

Timmy applauded. "Oh, that's what he gets for stealing the boat."

"What boat?"

Anita shoved the pizzas in the microwave and punched the appropriate buttons. She sat down at the table, and over the hum of the appliance, she asked again, "Timmy, what boat?"

The boy was dipping a spoon into his grape Kool-Aid, slurping it as if it were soup.

"The one I been tellin' you about. Gillie and Wade. Sara Beth's daddy's boat. They took it out in the slough and wouldn't let us go too."

"He knows better than that. He'll have to be punished when he gets home. And don't you ever, *ever* go into the slough unless an adult is with you."

"Yeah, because the gators will bite your face off. Wade told me. They could bite *his* face off, too, maybe. You think they really could, mom?"

But she was resting her chin upon her hand, thinking. Thoughts kaleidoscoped: dark and knife-edged fears of Dean returning; the comically absurd darkness of her attack on the exterminator; lighter shades and more pleasant shapes—circles and mandalas—for thoughts of her new job at the bar; and a centerpiece, more intensely colored, shaped to complete the picture. That centerpiece image was of Houston Parker—dark and light, perfectly symmetrical, yet somehow formless.

Timmy continued to slurp his Kool-Aid.

Anita sighed.

Then the microwave beeped her back to reality.

Chapter Three

1

After he put the copter to bed, Houston Parker followed his quitting time ritual. With twilight deepening, he wandered over to the white alligator's pen and stared at it, and, as always, he couldn't avoid thinking about how long his father had searched the swamp region unsuccessfully to find one—a personal quest Houston never quite understood but reverenced nevertheless.

But he did not linger more than a few minutes; an urgency of a different type held him firmly. He could see it manifested in his trembling fingers, and on the final tourist run of the afternoon, he had experienced some disorientation as he landed.

His mouth was drier than dust, though he had put away three cold cans of Coke since noon. His cheeks felt flushed, and yet he shivered. He snuffled at his runny nose as he clawed into a front pocket of his jeans.

For an instant, hell opened up. He could imagine the fire raging in its throat and sharklike teeth rimming its lips. It was the picture he had seen in a Sunday school pamphlet once, and it had convinced him—at least when he was younger—that a person didn't *go* to hell but rather was *swallowed* by hell. Eaten alive.

Hell was also filled with winged things. Thousands and thousands of black, menacing winged things.

He fumbled at the pocket desperately.

Then he touched the rolled up dollars, and relief coursed through him. In the meager light, he counted the money—one hundred dollars. Better. He began to feel better. He relaxed a notch and tried to think pleasant thoughts.

Anita Martin, her shimmering black hair, the dark eyes and kissable mouth, came to mind. Those long, delicious legs and perfectly molded hips. Small, firm breasts high against her blouse. The image of her spread like fire through his thoughts. But finally she could not compete with another drive, another need which burned more eagerly than any sexual desire he could dream of.

Rap.

A simple, grayish powder, a combination of synthetic mescaline and an amphetamine—plus one secret ingredient. Rapture was the drug's official name, though some preferred Miami Ice as an alternative. On the street, they called it rap—but all that Houston Parker knew was that he needed it and that only one man in the area supplied it.

Life was an endless series of chasing-your-own-tail horrors without it.

He climbed onto his ancient Harley, kicked it, and listened to its growl. On good days, days when he wasn't strung out, the Harley's engine sounded like a metallic symphony. On bad days, it produced a shriek of demons.

2

"Can you fix Bella?" Dominick Hashler offered a chair across the small table from him.

"I told you before. It needs a new bleeder valve. That pump's on its last leg. Why don't you junk it and get you another one?"

The man called Hash puffed at a long, thin cigar and sipped straight rum from a plastic cup. Sunglasses were perched high on his gleaming bald head, and when he smiled, his large, pointed ears almost seemed to flap like wings. His black eyes evidenced predatory intent.

"Give up Bella? Hell, she's the most dependable female I've ever laid a hand on. Cranks up and does her thing any time I ask her to. No way I'm ditchin' Bella." He leaned back, and through the dim light in the foul-smelling cabin, he studied Houston.

"You fix her," Hash continued. "Hear me? Part of our little arrangement, remember. Mr. Bones is eager to add to his collection these days—I should have my ass at Pelican Pond dredging as many days as possible before summer rains come. So I need your help—and I'm *real sure* you need mine. Am I right?"

"Sorry sumbitch! Sorry sumbitch!"

"Hey, make that bird shut up," said Houston.

Hash laughed softly and gestured mockingly, helplessly. "I have no control over Ibo—he's a free spirit. He calls them as he sees them."

On a far wall, perched on a stick lodged in the opened jaws that once belonged to a monstrous shark, Ibo shifted restlessly.

"Come down here, trash mouth," said Hash, still not bothering to contain his laughter. "You've insulted our guest."

The air seemed to come alive with the sound of beating wings. Houston pitched back in his chair as the bird swung unnecessarily close to him before landing on top of an empty chair.

"Ibo, you mean little mother . . . don't you be dive bombing guests," reprimanded Hash.

47

The bird appeared to clear its throat, and in a voice perfectly imitative of Hash's, he said, "Mean little mother. Mean little mother."

"Pretty good impression, huh?"

Houston tried to repress a grin, but failed. "Yeah. Yeah, you've got you one damn weird bird."

"One damn weird bird. One damn weird bird," Ibo echoed, and this time the voice strikingly resembled Houston's.

"Jesus," Houston muttered. "You teach him to do that? It's kinda spooky."

Delighting in the young man's discomfort, Hash smiled and gave the bird an admiring glance. "Not really. Ibo's an African Gray parrot. They have an excellent facility to change voices and deliver lines of speech. He can even tell dirty jokes—tells them better than I can. Wanna hear one?"

"No. No, listen, I've got the money. I brought it. All of it."

It took several seconds for him to wrestle around in his pocket for the bills. He plopped them on the table, hands shaking.

"One hundred bucks. Count it if you don't trust me."

Hash frowned. "I hate to see a man grovel, Houston. Don't you, Ibo?"

He winked at the parrot, and in turn, the bird exclaimed in its own voice, "Count it if you don't trust me. Sorry sumbitch. Sorry sumbitch."

Throwing his head back, Hash laughed hard.

"I don't have all night," said Houston. "I've got things I need to do."

"Me and Ibo like to conduct business at a leisurely pace, don't we?"

"What's your hurry, asshole? What's your hurry?" squawked the parrot.

"My sentiments exactly. Some rum to calm your nerves?"

"No. No, nothing to drink. Nothing for me." Houston pointed at the wad of bills. "The money's there. It's all there."

Hash poured a splash of rum into another plastic cup and pushed it across the table. "That money appears to be ruining our evening together. Ibo, take care of this."

He tapped the table near the money; the bird cocked its head, then flapped forward, picked up the bills in its beak, and flew back to his shark's jaws.

"Hey, God damn it! Hey, what's he doing? Those are good bills, Hash."

"I'm sure they are. You see, Ibo's my accountant. Handles the paper work on our little deals."

Houston's eyes darted uneasily from the parrot to Hash and back to the parrot. "Will he do whatever you tell him to?"

Hash shook his head. "He can be a stubborn bastard. Most of the time he'll mind if I lean on him pretty hard. Just like people, I suppose."

Trying to relax, Houston asked, "Does he understand anything he says?"

"Naw. He picked up all the profanity from me. He repeats the damndest things."

"He wouldn't tear up those bills, would he? Wouldn't swallow them, I mean, would he?"

"Hell, yes. If I haven't fed him—which reminds me, another one of my children needs some dinner. You don't mind waiting awhile longer, do you? Drink your rum."

Digging a handkerchief from his back pocket, Houston mopped at the beads of sweat on his forehead and throat. "Hash . . . man, I can't."

Ibo shifted the bills from his beak to his strong claws.

49

"Sorry sumbitch. Sorry sumbitch."

"Enough over there!" Hash shouted. "Be quiet or I'll feed you to Danny Boy."

From a huge ceramic pot, the man lifted a large snake and draped it around his neck.

"How you feeling, big man?" he cooed to the snake.

He sat down and held the snake's head so that Houston could see it more clearly. "This is Danbhalah. But me and Ibo call him Danny Boy. He's a Peruvian boa constrictor—all ten feet of him."

"Danny Boy's in deep shit. Danny Boy's in deep shit."

"Hey, nobody pulled your string. What Ibo's referring to is Danny Boy's eating problems. His main diet is baby mice—pinkies—but the last couple of months he's stopped eating. Maybe he's anorexic; hell, I don't know. Been feeding him a little mixture that's supposed to make mice look like a sirloin steak to him again."

Houston nervously fidgeted with the cup in front of him; he watched his nemesis lovingly fondle the snake, and he knew that there was no way to rush him—he was totally at the man's mercy.

Hold on, he told himself. *Hold on.*

Hash playfully dangled the snake by the neck and smiled. "Don't you wish you had a pecker this big?"

"Cunt and cock world. Cunt and cock world," the parrot chimed from its perch.

"Very perceptive, Ibo. Ver-ee perceptive. Wouldn't you say so, Houston?"

The younger man nodded. The rhythm of his heart had become irregular. The room seemed much colder.

"You tried out that new woman—you know, Holly's niece?" Hash asked. "Oh, I'm sure you've tried. I forget myself. You are the resident stud at Orchid Springs, but back a few years I would have given you some competition. Now, if you'll excuse me, Danny Boy needs his goo—my name for his appetite renewer—egg and milk and bananas and anything else soft and swallowable."

For the next five minutes, Hash filled a grease gun with the milky white mixture and coaxed it into the snake's mouth, baby talking to the reptile as if it were a human infant.

"See that grin on his face? Means he's full. Yeah, he'll be eating pinkies any day now."

Then he held the snake's head so that he could examine it nose to nose.

"His eyes look clearer. Yeah, definitely clearer. Should have seen them a few weeks ago, I mean, hell, I thought Danny Boy was going blind. His eyes looked awful—you ever see that old Val Lewton movie, *I Walked With A Zombie?* Danny Boy had glazed over eyes just like the big, tall, black zombie in that movie—shit, that zombie gave me nightmares when I was a kid."

Feeding over, he gently returned the snake to the ceramic pot.

Ibo whistled, clucked, whistled again, and then sang out in an Irish tenor's voice, "Oh, Danny Boy, oh Danny Boy, I love you so-o-o."

Hash applauded. "Ah, that was sweet, Ibo. Wasn't that sweet?"

Houston shifted, but said nothing.

"I almost forgot," Hash exclaimed, reaching into his shirt pocket. "I have something you could be interested in." He tossed a small container the size of a tea bag onto the table; it was filled with a grayish-white powder.

Houston flinched. By the time his eyes focused upon the bag and he managed to grab for it, Hash, quick as lightning, cupped a hand over it.

"Nightmares," he whispered. "Weren't we talking about nightmares? Yeah. Yeah, I believe we were. Old

51

Val Lewton movies—ever see *The Leopard Man?* How about *The Cat People?* Scary shit."

"Give it to me, Hash. Come on . . . please . . . give it to me."

Leaning back, smiling smugly, sadistically, Hash held the bag firmly beyond Houston's reach. "First, tell me about *your* nightmares. Hey, it's only fair. I told you about mine."

"You know," Houston murmured, ". . . you know I only have one . . . the same one."

"And that's the one that interests me—the one about the creature. Now, what was it your old man called it?"

Houston closed his eyes; his upper body trembled.

Hash waited patiently.

Finally the younger man opened his eyes and stared directly into Hash's.

"Blood Wings," he whispered.

"Ah, yes. Blood Wings. And you have nightmares about this creature because . . . because you claim you saw it kill your old man years ago. Lots of nightmares. This so-called creature. This Blood Wings interests me. You wanna know why?"

Houston nodded vaguely, frightened not to go along with the game.

"Because of Mr. Bones. Oh, that's not his real name, of course. He doesn't want his real name to be revealed. You ought to see his place on Key Biscayne. Jesus, a gorgeous home. We're friends—no, not exactly friends. Mr. Bones is my patron. I dig up old bones for him, and I believe he would love to hear about Blood Wings—if such a creature exists."

"It exists," Houston murmured.

"I doubt it. I seriously doubt it. But a strange thing happened to me a month or so back. I was dredging at Pelican Pond, working the shit outta Bella, when something . . . when I smelled something so godawful the hairs on my arms stiffened. I was scared. Never been so scared. Ole Blood Wings give off a stink like that?"

Houston paused. He appeared to wander into the realm of memory. Then, returning, he nodded.

Propping his elbows on the table, Hash fingered the bag of powder. "You'd do anything for this, wouldn't you? Maybe someday help me catch that creature—what do you say?" He set the bag near Houston's folded hands and added, "You disgust me."

Hesitating, Houston watched to see whether the other man would snatch the bag away again. Suddenly the air in the room hummed; Ibo swooped down and in one motion released the bills and claimed the bag of powder, teasingly retiring with it to the protective surroundings of the shark teeth.

"Sorry sumbitch. Sorry sumbitch."

Houston stood up and slammed his fist upon the table. "God damn it, Hash, give it to me! I brought the fuckin' money!"

"Hey, talk to my accountant," Hash replied, chuckling, and yet his dark eyes never lost the glint sparked there by anger and repulsion. "Maybe if you said, 'please.'"

The younger man stumbled toward the perch.

"Okay, bird."

"Ibo . . . you have to do him the courtesy of using his name."

"Ibo . . . give me the bag. Give me the bag . . . please."

Fascinated, Hash watched. "If you get down on your knees and begged—"

"I don't have to put up with this!" Houston shouted.

"Oh, but you do . . . I believe you do."

The younger man stood, clenching and unclenching his fists. After a few moments, he lowered himself to his knees.

As he roared away from the cabin, Houston Parker heard nothing except mocking cries and laughter, and he could not determine which sounds emanated from the man and which came from the parrot.

Chapter Four

1

"Come in, dear. I'm sorry if you had to wait long. I can barely hear knocking on my door these days, and it takes me forever it seems to go from room to room. So many times it's someone wanting to sell something—health plans mostly. Nice young men come selling them, and I always listen politely, you know; but I tell them: 'I have no money. I have no money.' Mr. Bradshaw should keep solicitors out of Orchid Springs, doncha think, dear?"

"Yes, Granny Roth, and I'm real sorry to bother you. But you see, Wade hasn't come home yet, and I was thinking he probably was over here with Gillie." Anita stepped into the woman's dark little trailer and saw or heard no sign of the boys.

"Oh, no, dear. You saw me not an hour ago on the watch for him. I saw you, but you were so distracted. Gillie's not home, either."

"If you happen to see Wade, would you please tell him to make tracks home immediately? It's our rule that he's supposed to be home before sunset. The boys were together this afternoon, I know, because they came into Holly's while I was there."

"Sit down, dear. Please." The old woman gestured toward a threadbare easy chair covered by bath towels to hide worn spots.

"Granny Roth, I ought to get back. I left Timmy eating his supper in the kitchen, and sometimes when I leave him alone there, he plays with the microwave. He puts those little G.I. Joe figures in it—only the bad guys, he claims."

She laughed nervously; but the sudden spectre of her husband skulking outside her trailer projected into her thoughts, and she added, "It's not safe."

"Isn't it the truth," replied the old woman. "The awfulest things happen to children in the home these days. Why, just yesterday I read about a boy in West Palm who shoved his younger sister into the clothes dryer and turned it on, and she suffocated. She did. Several other children were lined up ready to ride in the dryer—the boy was charging them fifty cents apiece. Home alone is not safe for a child—no, not all. For old folks, neither."

Over and through Granny Roth's comments, a blackness was seeping into Anita's thoughts. The old woman noticed how quiet she had become.

"Dear, I'm sure Wade will show up. I have to warn you, though. Gillie's not a perfect influence by no means, and, oh, I've tried to control him some. Not much success. He goes his own way—summer's coming—I expect I won't see that much of him. Don't worry out of hand, dear."

"I'm afraid of my husband," said Anita. The sentence slipped from her mouth before she could stop it. She regretted it instantly.

"Oh . . . my dear. Not a week ago I read about a husband who brutally murdered his ex-wife after tearing off all her clothes and spray painting her whole body black. Can you imagine that? Times are not safe for a wife. Now, you take my husband, Vandy, though, he was a prince of a man. Never once laid a—"

"I don't want to talk about this, Granny Roth. I'm sorry I mentioned it, and I wouldn't have except that earlier I thought I . . . the kids . . . I'm afraid he'll kidnap them. He could be out there . . . I'm afraid he's out there, and I was worried about Wade not being home."

She stood up, and one of the towels clung to her. She brushed it away as if it were an unwanted hand touching her. "If you see him, send him home please."

"Of course, dear. Of course, I will. And don't you. . . ."

But Anita had clambered through the door before the old woman could finish her remark.

2

Anita was relieved to be out of Granny Roth's trailer, out into the south Florida evening; the muggy air bothered her less than the traplike atmosphere she had just escaped.

Stop acting like this, she scolded herself, and wondered why on earth she had alluded to Dean in the presence of Granny Roth, and why on earth her knees continued to rattle against each other and her heart continued to race full throttle.

On the way back to her trailer, Anita began to calm down; she considered detouring to Holly's trailer, then realized that her aunt would be busying herself at either the bar or the store.

There was no one to talk to.

She was worried about Wade, but the panic clutching at her throat had another cause: She felt alone. Terribly alone.

She took a detour, but not one leading to Holly's trailer. Unsteady legs transported her up concrete steps. She knocked timidly, stealing a glimpse at her shadowy reflection. She regretted not wearing lipstick and not combing her hair.

She waited, telling herself she was foolish, hearing an inner rabble that would not allow her to concentrate, and then when she had grown certain that he was not at home, Houston Parker switched on the overhead entrance light and swung open the door.

"Hi," she exclaimed, "I've lost something—my son. My son, Wade."

Shirtless, clad only in white runner's shorts, he stared at her.

"Anita," she muttered. "Anita Martin. We met at Holly's one morning and talked about your helicopter."

The feeling of foolishness mushroomed before he let her off the hook.

"Right . . . yeah, of course. Hello, again. Sorry for not recognizing you in the shadows. Come in."

Smiling the smile she remembered so well, he stepped aside. She managed not to allow her glance to linger too long on his bare chest and tanned, muscular arms.

To her surprise, the inside of his trailer displayed a neatness she wouldn't have expected from a young bachelor.

"Thank you. I'm checking around the trailer park to see if anyone's seen my Wade. He and that boy Gillie— Gillie Roth—apparently went out in a boat this afternoon. Did you by any chance see them?"

The first hit of Rapture had stolen his powers of concentration; Anita Martin's face had been surreal to him, but recognition kicked in, followed by the good feeling jolt of the drug. Most of all, the wings had disappeared, dissolved into some black night of his memory he could never illuminate. But the Rapture

58

reversed all of that—no sea of wings, no burning stench—leaving only a dreamy self-assurance that the world could not possibly be a better place.

Except for the addition of a beautiful woman.

Suddenly the world was complete.

He played back her question, then said, "As a matter of fact, I did. I saw them on one of my runs about mid-afternoon. They were in a skiff drifting down the slough just like Huck Finn and Tom Sawyer."

He smiled, and she nervously returned it.

"You make it sound innocent enough. But had they gone so far that it would take this long to come home?"

"Well, when I was a kid around these parts, I would boat the slough and raid gator nests in the saw grass. Gillie—I know him pretty good—he's probably teaching your son the fine art of lifting eggs."

"Is that dangerous?"

"Not really. Keep one eye open for mama gator. Gillie's an old pro at it; he's a wild kid, but he's learned enough about gators to avoid getting attacked by one."

His smile caught her, holding her for an awkward moment of attraction.

And you can cross him off your list.

The sudden intrusion of Holly's voice into her thoughts caused her to shake her head and laugh softly.

"What? What is it?" he prodded.

"Oh, it's . . . nothing, really. Just something Holly said to me this afternoon."

"Uh-oh. Holly. Mama Holly." He sat down on the arm of his couch and chuckled to himself as he ran his fingers through his hair. "Ten to one that *something* had me in it."

"Maybe."

"She said I was bad medicine. Stay clear. No doubt offered you my resume of delinquent activities."

"She's my aunt, and so I have to consider her advice,"

Anita countered. "She seems to care about you a great deal."

"But not enough to encourage a relationship between us; in fact, I'd wager she *dis*couraged it. Am I right?"

She smiled. "Sometimes advice like that can backfire. Can make a person want to go against it."

Eyes meeting, they gently broke down barriers.

Houston stood and stepped closer to her. "Glad to hear you say that. Holly—she gets her kicks from minding everybody else's business. There's more to my story than what she told you."

Anita half shrugged; the empty feeling of being alone had fled. "I would like to hear the rest of that story someday."

"And me yours."

"Oh, mine's nothing to hear—a bad soap opera, a country western lyric—love gone wrong. It's a story as common and everyday as the morning newspaper."

She hesitated, but the part of her that wanted his companionship and more was being shouted down inwardly by another part.

"My youngest son will be missing me. I have to go. Wade's probably home, and he'll have a doozy of an explanation for being late. His Huck Finn and Tom Sawyer days may be over."

"Don't be too hard on him; a boy has to explore. Wouldn't hurt to warn him not to go too far into the swamp . . . it can be . . . it's easy to get lost unless you've had a lot of experience in there."

"Thanks—if I'm not too angry, I'll mention it to him."

She smiled a good-bye, and he could read the reluctance in it. As she turned to the door, he caught her arm, firmly but gently.

"Come back when you've put your boys to bed."

She felt her throat flush, and she quickly pulled away from him. "No, I . . . I can't. I mean, I really shouldn't.

It's just that it's too. . . ."

"Hey, I'm sorry. My fault. It's too soon, right? I'm pushing too hard."

She smiled weakly and slipped out the door, wanting him to ask her to change her mind—wanting, as well, never to have to be faced with loving or trusting any man again.

3

The white, sticky, gooey substance had virtually glued the door to the microwave shut.

"I ought to give you a hard, hard spanking. If your daddy was still around, he would. Believe me, he would."

Timmy sat at the kitchen table tying and untying his fingers apprehensively.

"What on earth did you have in mind to do?" she demanded.

"Roast marshmallows. Six or seven or ten of 'em."

"Look at your marshmallows now! *Look* at this mess!"

"I put paper towel under 'em. You always tell Wade to put paper towel under the food, and I did."

"When I finish cleaning this up, I want you to go to your room, young man. No TV. No Nintendo. No Super Mario Brothers."

"Aw, Mom, *Fraggle Rock*'s on tonight. Could I trade and go to my room tomorrow night?"

"No. You're being punished. I've told you, and I've told you— do *not*, do *not* try to operate the microwave by yourself. Now do you understand that?"

"Yes. Mom . . . Wade's not home. He doesn't get to watch TV neither."

"I'll decide his punishment. Scat on to bed."

"Don't I get a hug?"

"No. No hugs for mess-makers and people who don't mind."

She watched as he trudged from the kitchen. She felt a painful tug, considered calling him back, but decided against it. Nevertheless, she embraced him in her thoughts and told him she loved him and apologized for not being a better mother.

But Timmy dissolved from that imaginary embrace, and in his place appeared Houston Parker, his strong, young arms holding her close to his body. Then, even that image dissolved as well, and she scrubbed hard at her fingers to remove the sticky marshmallow residue.

4

Everything looked vaguely familiar.

Having tied down the skiff, he walked up through the saw grass and across the road; a handful of cars stood bathed under the lights of Holly's store and the bar. The boy turned once to look back at the slough, but a giant, white screen blocked his view.

His only memory of the entire day was that he had eaten leftover popcorn for breakfast. He was tired, his legs rubbery; his whole body felt as if it were asleep. Disorientation came like gusts of wind; he could not recognize his trailer—not at first. He wandered from shadow to light and back into shadow before finding the number eight near the door of one trailer.

Wintergreen.

For some reason an image of wintergreen-flavored gum entered his thoughts—he could taste it. And it meant something, but the meaning eluded him.

When he entered the trailer, he could see that his mother was on the phone; she appeared distraught. Then, noticing him, she pressed one hand to her chest and rolled her eyes as if in relief. But there was also anger in her face, especially around the corners of her mouth. She suddenly put the receiver against her shoulder and pointed at the kitchen table.

"You sit right there!"

Wade obeyed, puzzled by her simmering fury.

"Yes, Mr. Bradshaw, I understand what you're saying. Wade just now walked in the door, and I promise you I'll talk to him and he will be punished. . . . No, I agree, stealing a boat is serious."

Wade listened as she continued her conversation.

Punished? Stealing a boat?

A fresh gust of disorientation hit him, then a calm. He went to the cupboard and got a box of frosted flakes and began munching on them mechanically.

He couldn't taste them. He sat down at the table again—and his mouth seemed to fill with the biting flavor of wintergreen.

"Yes, Mr. Bradshaw . . . I will keep a closer watch on him. No, Gillie is not over here. Yes . . . no, I don't want anything to jeopardize our living here. We like Orchid Springs. Yes. I'm sorry . . . yes. Yes, I will. Goodbye."

She hung up and closed her eyes tightly.

"What's the problem, Mom?"

For the next several minutes, Wade regretted the offhandedness of his question. His mother carried on loudly, tearfully, about a hundred things, though the central theme appeared to be the stealing of a boat. She ended the outburst by demanding, "What have you got to say for yourself?"

Nothing she had said made sense to him.

So he shrugged.

"Did you and Gillie steal Mr. Bradshaw's boat? He says you did. He says if you continue that kind of behavior, we'll be asked to leave Orchid Springs. What will we do then? Where will we go?"

Emotionally she was tightroping tears.

Wade swallowed hard. "I never stole a boat, Mom."

"Don't lie to me, Wade Thomas Martin! Timmy saw you! Mr. Bradshaw's daughter saw you! Houston Parker saw you! And another thing—I'm aware that you and Gillie took candy from Holly's without paying for it— don't think I don't know."

A smaller version of the giant, white screen fell between them.

"I didn't. I swear. I don't . . . remember anything about today," he mumbled.

"Did Gillie put you up to it?"

"Gillie? I haven't seen Gillie."

His mom lowered her face into her hands. "Go on to bed," she whispered.

"I don't remember anything, Mom. I'm tellin' the truth. I ate some popcorn for breakfast. That's all I remember."

"Go on!" she shouted. "Leave that cereal box here."

The boy pushed away from the table distractedly. He wasn't really hungry—only deeply confused. He wandered through the narrow hall leading to the bedroom he shared with his brother and switched on the light.

Not asleep, Timmy rolled over in his bed. "Mom's really yellin'. What's she gonna do to you?"

Wade stared at his brother. "Nuthin'. I didn't do nuthin'. I don't know what she's talkin' 'bout. I didn't steal no boat."

Timmy's mouth dropped open. "Goll-dang, you tole Mom a big lie. Goll-dang, you tole a big lie."

"I did not." He jumped on the bed and twisted Timmy's arm until he shrieked in pain.

"I'm gonna holler for Mom."

"Go ahead. I don't care."

With stiff, methodical movements, Wade crossed the

room and sat on the edge of his bed. Behind him, Dan Marino launched a touchdown pass from a colorful poster. But the boy stared at the opposite wall, at the white blankness just above Timmy's bed.

"Stop lookin' at me," said Timmy, then turned his face to the wall.

Wade watched as the wall transformed into a white screen, a depthless canvas that seemed to invite him to enter. It tugged. It pulled. It coaxed. It spoke his name.

He stood and walked toward it.

In the whiteness was memory—in the whiteness a lost day resided, all of its details intact. A shiver danced across Wade's shoulders. "What's in there?" he whispered.

Timmy wrestled over and, at the sight of Wade, threw up his hands protectively. "You better hadn't beat on me, Wade. I mean it. I'll yell like heck for Mom to come."

But then he could see that Wade wasn't attacking him; no, he was staring fixedly, trancelike, at the wall.

"You better not slug me . . . what are you gonna do? What are you lookin' at? Wade? Wade, stop actin' freaky."

Wade's forehead beaded sweat; it ran down, only to be detoured by his eyebrows, then found rivulets down his cheeks. His mouth opened, and strings of saliva threaded out from the corners. Mucous inched out of his nostrils and down over his lips.

"Oh, gross!" Timmy exclaimed, as he pitched back in fear.

A silent scream twisted Wade's mouth grotesquely.

Timmy ran, shuffling past the zombielike presence of his brother.

"Mom! Mom! Wade's freaked! Come see! Come see!"

Anita had shaken her son and shouted into his face for thirty seconds or more before he blinked his eyes and broke out of his trance, emerging like a newborn chick stumbling from its shell.

"Timmy, run and get mama a cold washrag."

Frightened, she rocked on her knees and clutched at Wade's body, hugging him tentatively as if not being certain what to do.

"Wade? Wade, honey, what is it? Snap out of this."

The boy blinked rapidly and began to breathe more normally.

"Here's the cold rag, mom. Has Wade gone nutso? Are we gonna have to send him to the crazy house? Are we?"

"No. No, Timmy."

She wiped Wade's cheeks and nose and mouth.

"Is he gonna throw up?"

"No. No . . . Wade, honey . . . what . . . is your stomach upset? Please say something."

Timmy slid onto his bed, tossing out a remark from a safe distance. "Mom, I bet I know what's wrong with him. He's got a poller-guy in him—just like in that movie—and this awful worm thing's gonna come crawlin' outta his mouth."

"Timmy, hush! Hush that kind of talk."

She continued wiping Wade's face.

"He doesn't seem to have a fever," she murmured, mostly to herself. "Wade, do we need to take you to a doctor?"

"No, mom," Timmy piped in. "We got to get an ole Indian exerciser to exercise the poller-guy out of him."

"Go! Go back into the front room, Timmy. Now. You're not helping."

The small boy embraced his pillow as a companion and reluctantly obeyed.

A few seconds later, Wade looked into his mother's eyes and said, "Why are you wiping my face?"

"You scared me. You were in some kind of . . . does something hurt on you? Did you have a bad dream?"

"No, mom. Nuthin's wrong with me. 'Cept I'm kinda tired."

"Are you hungry? Maybe you were trying to sleep on an empty stomach. . . . What have you had to eat today?"

"I . . . don't remember."

"Stop saying that, Wade. Stop saying you don't remember what happened today, or I *will* take you to a doctor."

Wade concentrated, staring past his mother at the wall. "I got up this morning . . . and I ate popcorn . . . and I think I had some wintergreen gum."

"Wade, if this is all a big act . . . is Gillie going to say he doesn't remember anything either? Don't you see that that's not a very good cover story. Too many people saw you boys take that boat."

"Gillie . . . I haven't seen Gillie, mom."

She could feel the corners of her mouth tighten in frustration and anger. "I'm very disappointed that you would lie to your mother. You and Timmy are all I have. . . . We have to be honest with one another. We have to trust one another."

"But mom. . . ."

"I want you to go to bed. We can talk about this some more tomorrow."

6

In the dark room, minutes later, Wade half listened to Timmy's incessant chatter about horror movies and whatever other nonsense occupied his thoughts. Eventually Timmy ceased, and Wade could hear the boy's eager, deep breathing—the sleep of the innocent.

But Wade could not sleep. He thought about the feel of his mother's anger, about her insistence that he had stolen Mr. Bradshaw's boat. Why was she accusing him of that? He tried to close his eyes and relax; but when he opened them and gazed into the shadows of the room, he saw something, or thought he saw something—the vague suggestion of huge wings, blacker than the shadows, on the edge of spreading and beginning to fly.

His stomach gurgled.

And the fear seemed to stream up from his toes to his scalp.

The wings settled and folded into the shadows. He watched for them to return. How long he watched and waited he could not be certain. The fear relented very little; so he climbed out of bed and, careful not to awaken Timmy, began rifling through the top drawer of his dresser—his mother called it "the disaster drawer." He did not bother to turn on the light, for he knew he would recognize the object he sought just by its outline.

Thirty seconds of effort netted the prize: a tiny, metal cross—a token he had received back in Missouri one summer for attending Bible School. One of the teachers had told the class that the cross would protect them. At that time, Wade had scoffed at such a notion.

Cross in hand, he returned to his bed and carefully placed it under his pillow. He rested his head on the pillow; exhaustion stepped forward, and soon he had joined his brother in the realm of sleep.

7

"Wade? Wade, honey, wake up."

Through the veil of sleep, he heard his mother's voice.

She was gently shaking his shoulder.

"Wake up, honey. Granny Roth is here, and she's very upset because Gillie hasn't come home."

"Gillie?" he muttered, twisting over, attempting to piece out his mother's face in the darkness.

"Honey, where do you think he could be? When you came back in the boat, where did Gillie go?"

"Mom . . . I wasn't in no boat. I told you that . . . and I haven't seen Gillie."

"Wade, stop it. Now Granny Roth is beside herself with worry. She's about to call the police; she has no idea where Gillie is. No more game playing, Wade . . . this is serious."

"I'm tellin' the truth, mom. Why won't you believe me?"

Exasperated, Anita said, "Has he run away? Has he run away and you've promised not to rat on him?"

"Gillie? Run away?"

"Wade, no one's blaming you if he did. But Granny Roth should be told. The poor woman is so worried I'm afraid she's going to collapse right out there in our front room."

"Mom, I don't know where Gillie is. Maybe . . . maybe he could've runned away. I don't know nuthin' 'bout where he is."

His mother hesitated. He could hear her sigh anxiously.

"What am I going to tell that poor woman?"

"He'll come back . . . probably," said Wade. "Maybe he did run away . . . maybe he runned off to Miami."

He listened to a few ticks of silence. Then his mother rubbed his cheek, got up, and left the room.

The dream unfolded sometime later.

It was lyrical: A sun-splashed day; he and Gillie were

69

floating in a boat down the slough. Swamp birds framed the scene, their distinctive cries like Muzak. Wade lay in the bottom of the boat, squinting up at the sun, letting its rays warm his body. The change in the weather evolved slowly, yet inexorably. A dark nimbus surrounded the sun, then partially blotted it.

Gillie shouted, "Look at this!"

Wade scrambled to his feet, standing unsteadily next to his friend. A tremendous storm was gathering over the mangrove swamp, generating black pockets of clouds like some allegorical image of a storm god, its cheeks filled with wind.

But the storm was not the focus of Wade's attention; he could see something else approaching rapidly. It was a man. A man running on the surface of the slough.

"God, do you see that?" he exclaimed.

He directed Gillie's attention to the miraculous approach of the man, and yet Gillie claimed he saw nothing except the storm.

"He's coming, Gillie—don't you see him?"

"It's a bad storm," said Gillie.

At that point, the texture of the dream shifted, taking on an intense clarity. Wade noticed that the man was covered by an animal skin or fur, solid black, and that a pair of large wings grew out from his shoulders.

Then one more realization struck him: The man was Wade's father.

The angry snarl on the man's face—Wade knew it well.

"He's coming, Gillie—don't you see? Don't you see?"

Brightly colored balls of panic exploded behind Wade's eyes. As his father drew to within twenty yards of the boat, the boy jumped and was surprised to find that the surface of the slough did not support him. He plunged beneath it, then frog-kicked up for air.

His father spread silken black wings and appeared to

direct his predatory intent at Gillie, who continued not to see the dark figure.

"Run, Gillie!" Wade cried out. "Run, Gill-e-e-e!"

The giant, white screen, like a curtain closing, rustled between Wade and the boat, blocking off his view of the scene.

Silence claimed the end of the dream; Wade woke, sweaty, throat raw.

He slid his hand beneath the pillow and gripped the tiny, metal cross tightly.

8

It was soon evident that Wade's dream had exacted a price.

An hour later, threads of the vivid experience clung to Wade as if they formed a spider web he had walked through. He sat up in bed. He could not sleep. Old fears of his father had been rekindled, flaming up, threatening to consume. Yet, he sensed a conflicting feeling as well: He missed his father, or rather, he missed the father who once swept him out of school one late spring day and carted him off to a Cardinals game, buying him a big, red and white pennant sporting a redbird at bat. That day they guzzled cold drinks and downed hot dogs, and his father boasted that nowhere in America did beer taste better than in St. Louis, Missouri.

They applauded Ozzie Smith at shortstop and the ninth inning rally that fell one run shy to the Mets, but it hardly mattered. They were together, he and his father, with no competition for attention from Timmy. Could that father have been the same one who snarled and raged and hit, all the while spreading a net of blackness and dread over his family?

And there was Gillie.

Another source of his sleeplessness.

Why would Gillie run away from home and not tell him? Weren't they good friends? Disappointment surged through him. This was not like Gillie. Not like Gillie at all.

Wade listened to Timmy's ragged snoring and thought about his mother's accusation. How could she claim that he and Gillie had stolen Mr. Bradshaw's boat? Probably something Sara Beth cooked up, he reasoned. Hippo, hippo, hippo.

What is Gillie up to?

Then he knew, or thought he knew: Camping out. Of course. That had to be it. Gillie was camping out in the swamp—probably somewhere in the refuge. Often he had bragged about staying over there all night, under the stars, snuggled up in a sleeping bag.

In the darkness, Wade smiled.

And his heartbeat accelerated.

Having wiggled into his clothes, he sneaked to the window, hesitating once to glance at the sleeping form of Timmy. There were certain things a boy learned how to do: One was slipping out his bedroom window preternaturally, noiselessly, even when it involved removing the window screen as well as crawling through and leaping to the ground, avoiding bodily injury.

A half moon sliced through the shadows, parting them as if they formed a dark sea. Smiling, feeling free, Wade bounced on the balls of his feet and tracked through the maze of mobile homes and then past Holly's store and out onto the bridge leading into the refuge.

There were no nightwatchmen, no security personnel; in fact, only once a day did a police car from Homestead or Florida City venture into Orchid Springs. Crime hadn't impacted the area.

On the shell road winding through the refuge, he jogged, eyes scanning the mangroves lining the water for

72

any sign of a low campfire winking through the darkness. *Won't ole Gillie be surprised,* he thought to himself. *Maybe I'll sneak up on him and scare him.*

The notion delighted him, buoying him as he scurried along. A southerly breeze tasted of salt and cooled the muggy air left over from the day. Night birds offered their lonely notes from a distance; some took flight as he passed.

Tiring, he slowed to a walk. No points of fire punctuated the mangroves.

How far in here had Gillie gone?

Growing discouraged, he continued, but at an ever slower pace; up ahead he heard something—a man's voice. Singing? In the partial moonlight, he could make out the tall frame of an observation tower and, below it, Hash's cabin.

"Who the hell are you?" the singer boomed at the boy.

Wade stopped. Thirty yards away a man was urinating near the cabin.

"It's me . . . Wade . . . Wade Martin."

He wished he hadn't given his name.

"The new boy, huh? Well, come on over here. It's not polite to stare. Ain't you never seen a man bleeding his lizard? Too much rum—that'll do it. Say boy, you know that rum turns your piss green? It surely do."

The image of a pirate sprang into Wades mind: *Hash is modern day pirate. But is he dangerous?*

"Whatchoo doin' in the refuge, boy? Not supposed to be here. It's closed, you know."

"I know. My friend, Gillie . . . I'm lookin' for him. I think he's campin' out somewhere, and I'm gonna find him."

"Not likely he is," said the man. "I'd uh seen him. Say, boy, you want to see a big damn snake have breakfast?"

"Well . . . sure."

"Come on in. Your mama know where you are?"

"No."

"I didn't think so. No damn matter—come on in."

Wade followed the man into the dimly lit cabin. Where furniture should have been, there were shadows, scattered boxes—some containing bones—and nets, ropes, hooks and digging utensils, fishing gear and several stuffed, baby alligators.

It was the kind of cabin any boy would love.

Over in one corner there stood a rollaway bed with no sheet and a dingy-colored pillow. A tiny kitchen occupied another corner.

"Pissant! Pissant!"

Wade jumped back reflexively from the doorway at the sound of the harsh voice.

"Quiet, Ibo. Don't scare off our visitor."

"Oh, it's your parrot," said Wade. "He talks real good."

From Ibo's perch came the inevitable echo matching Wade's voice. "Oh, it's your parrot. He talks real good. Talks real good."

"Dang, it sounds just like me." Wade walked over under the shark jaws. "Hi, Ibo, how you been?"

The parrot squawked, then gargled low as if clearing his voice. "Pissant sumbitch! Pissant sumbitch!"

Wade laughed. "You teach him all them dirty words?"

Hash, busying himself with what appeared to be a small wire cage, said, "I'm guilty as sin. Not all my fault, though. Ibo exercises no judgment in which words he repeats and which he chooses not to. I've tried reading Shakespeare to him, but . . . here, I'll show you."

He set the cage aside and whistled at the parrot to get his attention.

"Ibo—listen: 'To be or not to be, that is the question.' Give us a little *Hamlet, por favor.*"

The bird cocked its head and shifted on its perch.

Hash coaxed it.

"Come on you contrary bastard, a little *Hamlet*."

"Ibo pretty, Ibo pretty," the parrot exclaimed. Then, imitating Hash's voice: "'To be or not to be,' sumbitch, contrary bastard. Give us a little *Hamlet*."

Wade giggled. "He can't talk without cussin', can he?"

The bird intruded before Hash could say anything more. "Ibo a stud. Ibo a stud. Sumbitch."

That brought another round of giggles, and Hash said, "Aw, quiet up. You're no stud—I've seen your pecker and it's pitiful."

"Why did you name him Ibo—that a parrot name?"

"Voodoo, boy. In the voodoo tradition, Ibo is like a god of the word. Course this one's full of shit."

"Deep shit! Deep shit!" the bird echoed.

"See what I mean?"

"I think he's a neat bird," said Wade as he wandered over to investigate what Hash was doing with the small cage.

"Don't pump up his ego no more; he fills up like a balloon if you make over him. Impossible to live in the same cabin with him sometimes."

Suddenly the bird began whistling, and the whistling turned to lyrics: "Suicide is painless, and it brings on many changes."

"Hell in a handcart . . . wait a second, Ibo . . . I'll get the goddamn tape."

"What's he doin'? What's he want?"

Hash rifled through a cardboard box brimming with video tapes.

"It's not what *he* wants. It's what *I* want—some fuckin' sanity. If I don't put in this tape of *M*A*S*H*, he'll whistle and sing the theme song all the damn day long—like a marathon—non-stop."

"Really?"

Hash gestured for him to watch. Below Ibo's perch was a portable TV, similar to those in airports, mounted on a swivel base. A cheap VCR rested on top of it. Hash shoved the tape in, and in a matter of seconds the parrot lapsed into silence, his undivided attention devoted to the movie.

"There," said Hash. "Korea and Hawkeye and Trapper—no more whistling and singing."

Ibo appeared content.

Hash turned to Wade. "I believe I promised you the spectacle of a big damn snake eating his breakfast, right?"

"Yeah."

"Okay, see what these are?"

Wade peered down into the cage. "Umm . . . baby mice?"

"I call 'em pinkies—cuz they're pink like titties. You know about titties yet, boy?"

"My friend Gillie has some *Playboy* magazines. That's 'bout all we know. Gillie told a girl at school he'd give her two dollars if we could see hers, but she said she wanted ten bucks."

"Smart girl. No matter—you got plenty of time for that kind of thing."

Hash lifted a pair of finger-length mice from the cage and dropped them onto the floor as if they were cookie batter being dumped onto a cookie sheet.

"These are like sausage links for Danny Boy."

Wade stepped back as Hash brought out the boa constrictor. "Don't he want the mice to be dead?"

"No. He likes to feel 'em wiggle down his gullet. Here, you wanna touch him? This is Danny Boy—real name is Danbhalah—the name of the serpent god in voodoo."

Hesitantly, Wade tapped his fingertips on the snake's skin. "Will he bite?"

"Naw . . . least he isn't poisonous. Thing is, he's too weak to do much harm these days. Won't eat worth a damn."

76

"Do you give him medicine?"

"Oh, yeah. I think maybe he's just depressed. Wants to be back in the jungle—hell, I don't know. He don't have much of a sex life around here, neither."

He winked at Wade, and then placed the snake on the floor, creating a tangle that resembled a loose fire hose.

"Look alive, Danny Boy," said Hash. "I fixed you some pinkies just the way you like 'em."

Wade giggled again. "He don't act very excited," said the boy.

"Sure don't. Could be he's constipated."

The snake slowly uncoiled, and though it appeared that it smelled the mice, it made no move toward them.

"This ole raggedy floor—it give Danny splinters, and he won't hold still when you try to tweezer 'em out."

"Oh, hey, the mice are crawlin' right at him."

And they were. Blind gropings. They squeaked their tiny squeak, bumping into the snake's neck, brushing at it with their tiny paws, unable to locate a mother's nipple.

"Eat your breakfast, Danny Boy," Hash coaxed. "Come on . . . yum, yum."

"Maybe he don't want us to watch," said Wade.

"Naw, when he's good and hungry, he'll snap up pinkies one right after another. Don't make no difference if I'm around or nobody else."

They waited. Danny Boy tolerated the squeaking for as long as he could, then began to slither away.

"Damn it to Friday, Danny, you got me worried," said Hash.

"Is there a snake doctor in Miami?" Wade asked.

"Wouldn't surprise me, but I hate like hell to let some vet whose hand smells like dog and cat shit mess with my Danny."

He gathered up the snake and returned it to its ceramic pot.

Wade glanced around; he was much too enthralled by

his surroundings to want to say good-bye.

"Why do you got all these bones?" he asked.

From a flask of rum, Hash poured three fingers into a plastic cup and sat back. "Green stuff, little friend. Some of those bones bleed green stuff."

Puzzled, Wade said, "They do? Instead of blood?"

Hash laughed. "M-O-N-E-Y. Money. Green stuff. I sell 'em."

"Bones?"

"Some aren't ordinary bones—here, hand me that box on the second shelf."

Wade obeyed. The metal bookcase overflowed with boxes, and in turn, the boxes overflowed with bones and shells.

Hash dug around in the box, his eyes measuring and probing each bone and shell.

"Take this one, for example." He held out what appeared to be a rock the size of a baseball, except shaped into a rough rectangle.

Wade examined it. "What is it?"

"Tusk fragment from a mammoth."

"A mammoth what?"

Hash chuckled and sipped at his rum. "Prehistoric elephant—you've seen 'em."

"Is it worth a *lot* of money?"

"Naw—but if you find enough of 'em, it'll buy you all the rum you could ever want or need. And one of these days ole Hash is gonna maybe find something back in that swamp that makes him filthy rich. A big hit, boy. That's what ole Hash lives for."

"If you got a *lot* of money, what would you do with it?"

"Buy me a whole fuckin' island in the Caribbean," Hash replied without hesitation. "Buy me a rum distillery. Buy me the biggest damn yacht I could— maybe Donald Trump's yacht, you know. And I'd buy me some bea-u-u-tiful women, and all of 'em would have big

78

bea-u-u-tiful knockers, and I'd have 'em rub those knockers on my bea-u-u-tiful bald head about a dozen times a day. Turns you on, don't it?"

Wade giggled and rocked back and forth nervously on the balls of his feet. "Me and Gillie, we might could go huntin' for bones in the swamp. We're gonna go on lots of adventures, you know, this summer. School's out next week."

"You guys my competition, huh? Well, let me tell you something, little friend. That ole swamp can be a bad mother. You kids stay away from Pelican Pond, you hear me? Gillie knows what I'm talking about. It's my dredging spot—all mine—you understand? Got a dredger pump I call Bella set up there—don't you kids fuck around with it, or I'll hang you by your balls from that tower outside."

"No problem," said Wade. "We ain't really interested in bones anyway."

"The big hit's mine," Hash mumbled, his words suddenly slurring.

He closed his eyes, and his chin swung down against his chest. Wade studied the man as he dozed off. In the background, Ibo continued quietly to be absorbed in its movie. The boy then followed the faint pipings of the baby mice, located them, and slipped them back into their cage.

He took a final survey of the cabin and whispered, "Good night, Hash."

The man stirred, but said nothing.

Out on the shell road, Wade searched for Gillie another thirty minutes or so. The suggestion of dawn far to the east, spreading across the ocean, obliterated a few thousand stars. The moon was down.

Disappointed, Wade headed home.

Chapter Five

1

It was a complete sabertooth skeleton.

As Bella sucked at the watery mud at the bottom of the sinkhole, Hash could hardly believe his eyes.

"Mr. Bones! Mr. Bones!" he chattered gleefully, rubbing his hands together.

His mind instantly began to calculate the removal of the magnificent find, considering possible ways to keep it intact. How many thousands would Mr. Bones pay for this?

Stay calm, he told himself.

A plan unfolded: Inflate some inner tubes—tractor sized—lower himself into the sinkhole, dig the muck away from the skeleton, tie the tubes to the skeleton, and wait for the next rain. The water would float the whole shebang right up into his wallet.

He heard the wings before he saw them, before he saw his attacker. He flailed his arms, and the predator screamed, beating him with its wings. Hash woke thrashing and cussing, fear clawing at him, but relieved somewhat that his attacker wasn't huge.

He rolled out of bed, continuing to protect his face.

81

"Sumbitch! Sumbitch!"

Wings hovered, then gained height, and with a harsh squawk, the parrot flew up and landed on its perch.

"Goddamn you, Ibo, whaddaya think you're doin'! Christ almighty!"

Anger burning off the threads of sleep, Hash grabbed a large bone fragment and pitched it at the bird, missing wide.

"Sorry sumbitch! Sorry sumbitch!"

"I'll show you who's sorry. When I get through with you, you'll be nothin' but a pile of feathers."

The next object he could lay hands on was a bamboo pole; he swung it ninja-style and whooped out a battle cry.

"Feathers! Nothin' but feathers!"

But the parrot easily dodged the weapon, circled the room once, and escaped through the front door, which Hash had left open much of the night. He pursued the bird a few yards beyond the door, shouting, swinging the pole, disturbing all the creatures active at dawn.

His head pounding as if someone were driving a nail in it, he eventually retreated to the cabin, knowing that Ibo would return, and knowing, as well, that he would, in time, forgive the bird's attack: *M*A*S*H* had reeled to an end, and that always sent Ibo into a thirty second or longer frenzy.

Coffee. Hot, strong-as-sin, coffee. He needed it to recover. Rum. God blessed rum. Demon rum. No, to Hash, rum harbored no demonic tendencies. A better comparison existed, and Hash knew it well: Rum was like a particular type of woman a man could never possess— some mysterious *anima* figure who steps into his life and tortures him physically, igniting his sexual drive, and yet demonstrating to him that there would always be something about her he would never understand.

Freda Schreck.

Miss Freda.

The memory spoke to him in an elusive cadence; it seeded images, and those images sprang to life, neon pinks and greens and other ice-cream-parlor pastels. In his memory, he drove by the hotels along Ocean Drive, each freshly painted in the colors of the Deco District: yellow, aqua, peaches and cream. This was Miami's South Beach. Years ago—how many? They spent a weekend at the pale pink Astor.

In his kitchen, Hash held on to the memory as the coffee perked and he methodically beat a trio of eggs in a bowl and sloshed milk into it. Three slices of bacon sizzled in a skillet. He poured the eggs in with the bacon and stirred and stirred, his mind transported to that long ago weekend after Freda's husband had passed on and she was solely in charge of the refuge and he had become her foreman.

Some curious mixture of loneliness and desperation and suffering led her to ask him to take her away from Orchid Springs for a few days, though he had assured himself, or fantasized at least, that she wanted him, needed him physically and that perhaps she was a little bit in love with him.

Sloughing off her grief, she looked beautiful that weekend—tanned, breasts and legs much firmer than any other woman in her forties could reasonably hope for. During the days, they walked the beach and sunned and swam; evenings they went dancing—she loved to dance. And when the dancing ended, another closeness began in their hotel room, a lovemaking that surprised him because of her intensity.

He wanted to love her more tenderly, but she insisted, or her body did, on something more furious, climax after climax. It was as if she had determined to rid herself of all sexual desire for the rest of her life in one weekend of orgasmic purgation. Hash obliged her, still thinking,

83

hoping, there was a future for their relationship.

But at the end of the weekend, she told him two things: First, that her husband died having knowledge of a destructive force, a guardian spirit in the swamp—Hash did not believe her; second, she informed him that they would never be together again, that she could never truly love another man besides Maxwell Schreck—and again, he did not believe her.

The years testified to the truth of her second declaration—but the first?

Hash drank his strong coffee and leaned over the plate of steaming food.

He could not eat it.

2

It was Hash's day off.

No feeding the gators, the kangaroo, or any of the other creatures. No picking up litter after thoughtless tourists. No repainting of the bird-watchers' tower. No road mending or a hundred other small chores that needed doing at the refuge. Saturday was Hash's day off.

The purr of his low horsepower outboard sang a song of freedom and release to him; the hour was early, dawn spraying its pinks and golds from some cosmic fire hose. Sluggish and serene, the slough invited a similar mood, but Hash had business on his mind—specifically Pelican Pond and a date with Bella.

"Bella, Bella, she's no fella!"

From a perch Hash had fashioned at the prow, Ibo disturbed the quiet; bird and man had forged an uneasy truce, the mitigating factor being that Hash liked a little company on his sojourns into the swamp—it was not a place a man should enter alone.

"You're jealous, birdbrain. Bella's my lady. My love."

84

"My lady. My love," the parrot screeched.

"You can go straight to hell, Ibo. No movies down there—you wouldn't last five minutes."

Ibo rattled some reply, but Hash wasn't listening. As boat and man and parrot glided along, Hash breathed in the mangrove swamp, never ceasing to marvel how it touched some secret cell of his heart. How it made him feel alive. Something beyond himself, something transpersonal surrounded him. You had to believe it more strongly than you believed in politics or religion or perhaps even money.

Except for an occasional profane outburst from Ibo, they boated in silence for miles. Once or twice, Hash found his thoughts straying to the breathlessly marvelous weekend and the eager, willing body of Freda Schreck. And to her dead husband's secret.

"Pelican Pond up ahead," Hash exclaimed, having lapsed into a profound ennui regarding the past. It was time to face the present.

"Sumbitch! Sumbitch!"

Where the slough necked into the pond, Hash switched off the motor. An old silence greeted him. Even Ibo respected this environment.

"Let's go check on Bella—God I've been missing her."

But something, some subtle nuance of water and mangrove roots and the solitude, bound him hypnotically. He allowed the boat to drift freely in the lazy swirl.

Hash wrinkled his nose. "Jesus!"

Ibo ruffled his feathers. "Deep shit! Deep shit!"

Swallowing back his apprehension, Hash scanned the mangroves, his eyes steady and piercing, focused by an accelerating fear. The stench represented no new phenomenon. He had smelled it before. In fact, it was not as penetrating, not as cloying, as he had known it to be.

The boat meandered right, following the lead of the

current, slipping out of the pond into an ever-thickening, low-growing forest of mangroves.

Hash stood up. Something had caught his attention, though the stench had caused his eyes to water slightly. He secured the boat to a mangrove root and climbed gingerly into the thick and tangled branches.

Twenty yards beyond him, an object hung upon a vaulting branch. At that distance he could tell what it was, and the sight of it piqued his curiosity. The object's blue-green color was all too familiar.

Walking on the springy branches was like walking on a trampoline. Hash bounced and stumbled, watching for snakes, sniffing the air at moments to see whether the stench had increased.

The Miami Dolphins cap rested on a branch like an odd-sized piece of blue-green fruit. But as Hash reached for it, another object caught his attention.

"Know who's been here," he exclaimed. "I surely do."

He pulled Gillie Roth's spear loose from the clutches of the mangroves.

And smiled at the adventuresome nature of the boy.

"Told that kid to keep his ass away from Pelican Pond," he muttered.

Ibo winged over and balanced on a nearby branch.

"The young explorer left some of his equipment, Ibo. Look at this frog sticker."

Hash raised the spear as the parrot flitted to another branch some twenty feet away. Beneath the bird's feet, the mangrove leaves glistened.

"Christ almighty!"

Once, years ago, as a kid growing up in the Bronx not far from Yankee Stadium, Hash had toured the back alley scene of a gangland-style murder—three men emptied of their blood. The amount of blood splashed and splattered over the mangrove leaves and branches appeared to

86

match the quantity he had witnessed that day in the Bronx.

"Get away from there," he shouted at Ibo.

The bird reluctantly obeyed.

For the next several minutes, Hash steadied himself close to the gory spectacle of blood and shreaded skin and entrails. He battled nausea and desperately wished he had brought along a flask of nerve-deadener.

A dozen thoughts paraded through his mind, a collage not unlike the advance promotion of a carnival. Some thoughts dictated reason and caution: *This could be the remains of an animal. Or: Don't touch anything—there's a real possibility of foul play—tell the authorities.* Some thoughts appealed to selfish interests: *Don't report this or you'll have a flood of people surging through Pelican Pond. This is* your *spot. You have to protect your interests in it.*

Some thoughts wore grotesque masks: *Something unimaginably horrible has happened to Gillie Roth. And if you don't haul your ass out of here toot sweet, you might meet the same fate.*

He loaded the boy's spear and cap into the boat and headed back to the cabin.

And by afternoon had drunk himself into oblivion.

3

They appeared in the living room the way toadstools pop up on a freshly cut lawn after a summer rain. At the center of attention, Wade felt uncomfortable; for the better part of an hour, two deputies from the Dade County Sheriff's Department carefully asked the same question over and over again. His mother consoled a teary-eyed Granny Roth, and Mr. C.M. Bradshaw, a heavyset man in a coat and tie, injected his concerns.

"We have to consider, of course, that there's a simple explanation for everything. After all, the boy could have merely left his windbreaker and shirt in the boat—could have forgotten about them when something else took his fancy and poof—off he went."

Bradshaw punctuated his remark with a sharp clap.

Granny Roth jumped.

Officer Ford, a fatherly looking man, spoke softly to Wade.

"Son, understand again that we are not accusing you of anything. It's our job to investigate a missing person's report and, in this case, to follow up on the suggestion that your friend may have drowned. Do you still want to stick by your story that you don't remember the events of yesterday?"

"Yes, sir."

"Honey," said his mother, "are you positive Gillie never mentioned running away from home?"

"Yes, mom. Not to me."

Bradshaw turned to the other officer, a man named Butler.

"Gentlemen, I think it's only proper to mention that the *Miami Herald* plans to send a reporter and photographer to Orchid Springs in the next week or so—doing a feature story on our fine little community, and, of course, if word gets out that your people are dragging the slough for a suspected drowning victim—well, the *timing* is all wrong."

He chuckled nervously, gesturing, parading the histrionics of a born salesman and public relations man.

Granny Roth buried her face in Anita Martin's shoulder.

Wade felt sorry for the old woman—and disliked Bradshaw and wanted to be free of the incessant questions.

The second officer, Butler, assured Bradshaw that

there was no intention of creating negative publicity for the area, but that a dragging operation might be in order.

Bradshaw shrugged and twiddled his thumbs.

Officer Ford once again directed his comments toward Wade.

"Your brother, Timmy, and Mr. Bradshaw's daughter report that they saw you and your friend Gillie push off in Mr. Bradshaw's skiff following the current of the slough west into the swamp. Do you remember—?"

"No!" Wade shouted.

He stood, legs suddenly weak, skin flushing hot in a tight mask over his face.

"I was *not* in a boat! Why don't you believe me?"

The adults blurred in his vision; the room elongated until it seemed that he was looking through the wrong end of a telescope.

"I don't know where Gillie is!" he cried.

Then he ran out the front door and continued running in no particular direction, feeling much like an escaped convict, or, at least, what he imagined an escaped convict might feel.

Over the bridge into the refuge he pounded.

Would he be thrown into jail for shouting at an officer? He wondered.

"Gillie," he whispered breathlessly. "Where are you, Gillie?"

He looped his elbows onto the fence surrounding the white gator's pen.

Why is Gillie hiding?

The white gator basked motionless in the warm sun.

But a cold equation registered in Wade's thoughts: Something very strange apparently had occurred yesterday, something about which he had absolutely no recall.

It touched him like the hand of a ghost in a dream.

Saturday and Sunday passed. No sign of Gillie.

Wade stayed to himself, playing video games or wandering the shell road through the refuge. But he avoided Hash. He avoided Holly. He avoided Timmy and Sara Beth. He exchanged only a few words with his mother.

He dodged out of sight whenever he saw Granny Roth. Or a patrol car from the sheriff's department.

On Monday morning, the last day of school, his mother said, "Whenever you feel like talking about all of this again, Wade, come to me. I promise I'll listen."

He let her hug him.

"I'll listen, too," Timmy echoed.

Wade, however, had no desire to talk; he had nothing to say. Whenever he forced himself to recall the missing Friday, a giant, white screen would loom in his thoughts. He could not see through or around or above or below it. The day was lost just as anything might become lost—a sock, a pencil, or whatever.

At school, Wade discovered he could not share in his classmates' celebration of the rites of the last day. There could be none of that pulsing, joy-stick, off-the-wall excitement without Gillie. He came home that afternoon dispirited.

Before sunset he sprawled on the grassy bank of the slough, joining numerous elderly folk as well as Mr. Bradshaw, to watch a macabre operation: the dragging of the slough by raincoated members of the county rescue squad. In a trio of boats, they probed both sides of the slough, tossing a heavy grappling hook out, gaining a dull splash, pulling, hoping against hope that the prongs would not make contact with a human body—Gillie Roth's body.

At one point, Bradshaw left a knot of elderly residents

to hunker down next to Wade.

"You know, son, this business here," he said, gesturing out at the dragging operation, "creates the impression that Orchid Springs isn't safe for kids. When people hear about this, they could be reluctant—very reluctant—to consider buying into one of our fine condo units or setting up a mobile home in our park. It's a shame. So unnecessary, too, if . . . if you'd simply tell the authorities what happened. You're the only one who knows, son. The only one."

Wade pushed to his feet. He felt like slugging the man.

"You don't care nuthin' 'bout Gillie," he exclaimed. "All's you care 'bout is your stupid ole condos so's you can get richer and richer. Just leave me alone. Leave me alone."

He tromped away from the bank, disappointed with himself that he had allowed Bradshaw to get to him. He sought out the bridge leading into the refuge, a good vantage point for surveying the rescue squad. Once or twice, as he watched, one of the men would call out that his hook had locked onto something solid; other men would gather, and one of the two divers in glossy black wetsuits would venture into the murky slough and emerge with a tangle of mangrove roots, or, once, an abandoned automobile tire.

But each time the call rang out, Wade's heart stopped beating.

"Sara Beth says a gator probably already ate Gillie—you think one did, Wade?"

The boy turned to meet the searching eyes of his younger brother and the tentative approach of the pudgy girl.

"You guys go on. Get away from me."

"It's a free country," Sara Beth piped up.

"Not for hippos and little nerds. Go on, before I pound you."

They wouldn't leave, but stayed their distance nonetheless.

"Wade, who's gonna deliver Gillie's newspapers?" Timmy asked.

A good question, Wade admitted.

"I don't know. Gillie—he'll come back."

"My father says he probably ran away to Miami and's gonna get hisself in big, big trouble—maybe sellin' hisself to dirty men and bein' in nasty pictures and stuff."

"Oh, Sara Beth, you make me wanna puke. Gillie wouldn't do that."

"My father says Miami could corrupt a saint."

"What's 'corrupt'?" asked Timmy.

"Means you start doin' nasty things and never, ever be nice to anybody ever again," Sara Beth answered.

"Wade, do you get Gillie's spear?" Timmy continued his line of curiosity. "If a gator ate him, who gets Gillie's spear? If you don't want it, could me and Sara Beth have it? You got dibs on it?"

"Man, you two are unreal. Friggin' airheads. I'm gettin' outta here."

Wade stormed off.

But there was nowhere to go. Not really.

God, I miss Gillie.

He fished around in his pockets, located enough change for a can of Cherry Coke, and straggled into Holly's, closing the door on the echoing calls from the slough.

Chapter Six

1

"Definitely not the face of a boy who's outta school for a whole summer."

Wade shrugged as he plopped his can of soft drink on the counter. He didn't look up at Holly.

"You want something more?" she continued. "How about a pack of wintergreen gum?"

Puzzled, Wade could suddenly taste wintergreen.

"I don't like wintergreen, Aunt Holly."

"Oh, news to me. The other day seems like you went to a heap of trouble to get a pack of it."

"Huh?"

"Never mind." She smiled. "You been watching the men out on the slough. Gives me the willies, doesn't it you?"

"Willies?"

"A scary feeling."

"Yeah, sort of. 'Cept Gillie, he couldn't never drown in the slough. He's too good a swimmer. He just wouldn't never drown."

"I suppose then you're saying he ran away."

"Maybe so. But I don't understand why he . . ."

"Why he didn't tell you he was going—or where?"

Wade paid for his Cherry Coke and popped the top.

"Yeah. 'Cause, I mean, me and Gillie, we was gettin' to be pretty good friends, and so it seems like he would tell me—maybe ask me if I wanted to go along."

"Gillie's independent. I've known him for longer than you have. He's a hard one to predict; he may have gotten a wild hair and taken off. But my guess is that he didn't."

"It is? What happened to him, then?"

Holly had to pause to wait on an elderly woman who was attempting to buy a package of suppositories when she actually wanted to buy aspirin—at least that was what Holly discovered when she questioned the woman. Mistake corrected, the woman made her purchase and shuffled out.

"Mrs. Bordeaux doesn't see so well no more," Holly explained.

"Aunt Holly, what are you sayin' happened to Gillie?"

She took a deep breath, and her jowls quivered like jelly.

"I agree with you that he never drowned. Those men are wasting their time. And I don't really think he ran away neither."

She hesitated long enough for Wade to stop mid-sip on his drink.

"Not drowned *or* runned away?"

She nodded. "And that's what makes it all such a mystery," she said.

"They think *I* know something . . . mom and Mr. Bradshaw and Granny Roth and the cops . . . but I don't remember nuthin' 'bout Friday."

Holly tottered out from behind the counter, placed her ham hock arms on his shoulders and stared into his eyes, holding that stare for a dozen heartbeats, though to Wade it seemed longer.

"You really don't remember, do you?"

94

"No, ma'am . . . I've said it uh jillion times."

"You don't remember coming in here, trailing behind Gillie when your mom and I were standing at this counter talking—don't remember Gillie filching candy and a soft drink—don't remember when *you* took a pack of wintergreen gum?"

"Stealed stuff? Gillie and me? No. No way, Aunt Holly."

She studied his reaction. "You either don't remember or you're the best bluffer I've ever set eyes on. And you don't remember going off in that skiff?"

Wade started to pull away, but she held him, her strength surprising him.

"I don't remember nuthin'."

"Okay. Okay. I believe you. Your Aunt Holly believes you—but this is more than passing strange."

The boy relaxed some.

"The cops, you know—the sheriff's department— they want me to see a hypnotist 'cause they think I might uh had a bad shock and disremembered what happened to Gillie."

"What do *you* think?"

"I . . . I got uh bad, bad feelin'. But everything's all white, you know . . . just a big ole white wall ever time I think 'bout last Friday."

Holly was about to say something further when a robust-looking man, tanned, shirt sweat-soaked, slammed into the store carrying a stack of newspapers.

"Where the Sam Hill is Gillie these days, Holly? I got folks all over Orchid Springs down on my ass about not havin' a mornin' *Herald*. Now, I gave that boy a chance, and he's blowin' it; and *I'm* the one catchin' the flack, and *I* don't like it—no, not one damn bit."

Holly chuckled. "Come in and cool off, Jack," she said. "Wade, this here's Jack, our *Miami Herald* man—the state's worst complainer—complains if it rains, complains if it doesn't rain. Just loves to complain."

The man shook Wade's hand firmly—a little like shaking hands with a piece of steel, Wade thought to himself.

"You seen Gillie?" Jack asked the boy.

"No. Huh-uh. I sure haven't."

"What am I supposed to tell our customers? I give Gillie the morning route for all of Orchid Springs, and look at this. Dumps on me. Kids today are no damn good. When I was a boy—"

"Oh, Jack, spare us, please. We don't want to hear about when you were a boy delivering papers to all of Miami. Your problem is that you need a better carrier— need one like Wade here."

The boy's face flushed.

Jack put his papers down on the counter and, hands on hips, gave Wade a good once over.

"I got my doubts, Holly. He's real green, I'd wager. Boy, you ever deliver papers?"

"No . . . but, I mean, I've helped Gillie. I know his whole route . . . know where ever paper spozed to go and all that."

Squinting, rubbing his chin, Jack winked at Holly.

"So you've helped Gillie. . . . Well, you know, a good carrier's got to get his ass outta bed early—I'm talkin' five o'clock—when it's still dark and you'd lot rather be sleepin'. I dump my load of papers right here at Holly's at fifteen minutes after five, rain or shine."

"I can get up . . . I can do that."

"Then you got to roll each paper and rubber band it, and you got to keep good books . . . and another thing— every lost paper comes out of *your* pay. You hear me?"

"Sure, I know that. Gillie told me that."

"Shootfire, Holly, seein' as how I'm in such a bind, I'll give him a try."

Wade beamed. "Aw, right. That'd be great."

96

"Whoa. Who-a-a," Holly exclaimed. "Hadn't you better ask your mother. She ought to have something to say in this."

"Yeah, I'll go ask her, but she'll say yes—I bet she will."

"One more thing," said Jack. "Now, the second Gillie comes back, I may have to decide again who keeps the route. Could be you could go halves on it."

"Sure. No problem. I'll share it with Gillie. That'd be okay with me."

"Let's shake on it," said Jack. "And if your mom agrees to it, you can start right away."

Again, the steel grasp.

Wade, feeling better than he had in a long, long time, rambled out of the store to find his mother.

2

"It's a big responsibility, Wade. Do you think you can handle it?"

"Mom. I'm eleven. Almost twelve. Dad had lots of jobs when he was a kid. He told me all 'bout 'em. Say I can have the route, mom. Please."

They were standing on the bridge; Anita had come to round up Timmy for supper and had lingered to watch the dragging operation. When Wade mentioned his dad, she felt something dark and cold stir in her stomach. But she could think of no good reason to deny her son's request—a job might help him to grow up faster. With no father in the home, he would need to, she reasoned.

"All right. Go tell the man you have my permission."

Wade clenched his fists and punched the air in celebration. "Thanks, mom," he cried as he skittered away.

Timmy, who had been listening to the exchange,

hugged her leg for attention.

"Mom, could I have a paper route, too? Please, mom."

"Oh-h-h, Timmy . . . when you're Wade's age—about three more years—then maybe you could have one. But paper routes are for bigger boys. Three more years."

She held three fingers out, and he matched them, staring disconsolately at them as if they represented an eternity.

"Aw, dang," he muttered.

She smiled and squeezed him close and thought about Wade and how soon he would be a teenager—troubled years ahead. She wondered whether she would be able to corral him. Was Holly right? Would the boys increasingly need a father figure around?

"Hey, there. You two let anybody else stand on the bridge? Or do you have exclusive rights to it?"

She turned to find Houston Parker's dynamic smile.

Timmy thrust three fingers at the man and said, "In three more years, I get a paper route."

"Well, hey, sounds super," Houston exclaimed, sweeping the boy up into his arms.

Anita drank in the scene, warmth stirring in her throat. Timmy was giggling happily.

Stop it, she warned herself.

"Tourist traffic been slow today?"

Their eyes met and held.

"Double slow. I've only gone up twice in the chopper. But it'll pick up. I can't compete with this sideshow anyway." He gestured toward the dragging operation.

"It's such a scary thing, a horrible thing. I can't push the thought out of my mind of what it would be like if one of my . . . my boys were missing."

Houston gazed at the road leading out of Orchid Springs.

"Gillie's probably hitching it somewhere. He's a free spirit; like as not, he'll show up some morning telling

98

tales of what he did in Miami or up the coast at Lauderdale or West Palm."

"I hope so," she murmured. "Granny Roth is devastated, and my Wade—I'm worried about him. He's either covering up for Gillie or else something . . . oh, I'm not sure what I'm thinking. I thought Orchid Springs would be such a nice, safe place."

"It's all in your perspective. When you see this area from the vantage point I have every day, well, you see its beauty. Not to say it doesn't have an element of danger. It does, but—hey." He jostled Timmy. "You want to ride in my chopper and take a look from wa-a-a-y up in the sky?"

Timmy chortled a yes.

Houston took Anita's hand. "How about it?"

"I really should get home and fix the boys some supper before I go to work—shouldn't be late my first week on the job."

"Hey, we'll only be gone a few minutes. You'll love it. Come on."

When she saw the anticipatory glee in Timmy's eyes, she couldn't say no. Or perhaps it was something in Houston's smile, a smile that exiled all of Holly's warnings about him.

"All right. This won't be dangerous, will it?"

Houston's smile widened; he winked at her. "Every good thing has some risks."

He guided them onto the copter pad and secured them in the shotgun seat next to him, buckling Timmy onto Anita's lap.

"Wait'll I tell Wade 'bout this, mom. He'll freak."

Giddy herself, Anita kissed Timmy's forehead and whispered, "Not scared are you?"

He shook his head eagerly, yet his eyes said, *Yeah, maybe a little.*

Anita turned her attention to Houston, to the rugged outline of his tanned face as he donned reflector sunglasses and a headset. Her thoughts registered a series of questions:

What are you doing in my life, Houston Parker?

Are you anything more than a man I'm physically attracted to?

Has Holly been fair in her judgment of you?

What do you think of me?

Am I only something, somebody, for the moment?

Am I going to fall in love with you? And you with me?

Are you another Dean?

At that instant, Houston smiled and gave Timmy the thumbs up, and the boy giggled and returned the gesture. The copter thrummed. Anita looked through the bubble of glass to her right, squeezed Timmy, and watched as the Maxwell Schreck Refuge fell away and they lifted into the late afternoon Florida sky.

A breathtaking scene opened beneath her. The greens of the swamp area battled to control her eye, and the world of Orchid Springs—the dottings of mobile homes and condos—appeared safe and serene, a pleasant microcosm surrounded by water and lush vegetation.

Over the hum and ruffling roar of the aircraft, she said to Timmy, "See Aunt Holly's down there? And our trailer?"

The boy strained to see, then nodded and pointed.

Houston's voice suddenly filled the cockpit. "Say so long to civilization."

They banked right; Timmy cackled; Anita's stomach tilt-a-whirled, and her smile searched out Houston's. It felt good, felt exciting and stimulating and yet reassuring as well. She trusted the man at the controls.

Half a world of sky and half a world of swamp seemed to yank the copter violently, and they balanced there, rushing along, insignificant in the midst of so much beauty and wildness.

When they reached cruising speed and altitude,

Houston asked, "How you liking this?"

His passengers smiled and nodded their approval.

"Hey," he said, "look two o'clock to your right." He pointed, and Anita followed the angle of his gesture. On a pine-clad hummock, she could see them, a pair of white-tailed deer, a buck and doe running breakneck speed, tails flicking. Anita showed Timmy, and he squealed his delight.

Such beautiful creatures, she thought to herself. Wild and free.

The magnificence of what spread below her was dazzling; it transported her out of herself to where the future and the present seemed to coalesce with the past, and the resultant sensation buoyed her.

Verdant mounds of pond cypress raised toward them like extinct volcanoes, some of the craters filled with water, and one of the larger, denser hummocks touched her imagination as a giant teardrop surrounded by brackish-green sloughs. Where mangroves had clogged streams, small creeks had formed, striking the eye as hairline fissures in the massed vegetation.

Houston's voice brought Anita out of her reverie momentarily.

"The mangroves are the best place to be during a hurricane—nothing can uproot them. They're solid. They belong."

His final words echoed in her thoughts.

But do I? Or my boys? Here in this strange and beautiful piece of the world?

It was a labyrinth of meandering water courses unimpeded by man, perhaps even hostile to man. Against the beauty of it all, Anita also experienced the darker feeling of being lost. Here was an alien realm on the edge of the civilized confines of Orchid Springs. *What's down there?*

She was comforted by the sudden realization that she

would never be forced to find out. Houston banked the copter, the world tilted, and they headed safely home.

3

"You oughtta been along 'cause we went way, way up and way, way out over the swamp, didn't we, mom? And Houston turned real, real far over, and I 'bout throwed up on mom; and he let me talk into his mike, and I'm gonna get a pair uh sunglasses just 'zactly like his."

Breathless, Timmy waited for Wade's reaction, certain that he had thoroughly impressed his older brother.

"Big friggin' deal."

"Wade, none of that language," said his mother.

"Friggin's not the baddest word. It's like heck or shoot. Don't even have God or Lord or Jesus 'long with it," Wade explained.

"It's 'bout like turd," said Timmy, "or poop, isn't it, Wade?"

Anita frowned. "All right, boys. I don't want to hear any more trashy mouth talk. Eat your supper because I have to go to work soon. Marcie will be here any minute."

"Aw, mom," said Wade, "Sara Beth's big sister is a bigger hippo than Sara Beth. Why do we need a sitter at all? I'm old enough to watch after Timmy. I mean, geez, this is embarrassing, havin' uh sitter when you're eleven years old and have your own paper route."

"Yeah," Timmy added, "but you didn't get to ride in Houston's chopper and I did, and he's my buddy—yeah, he told me he was. He said, 'Timmy, you're my buddy,' and I am and you're not."

"So, big smelly deal—Houston Parker's a dopehead, and ever'body knows that; and if you want a dopehead for a buddy that's your tough luck—I can't stand the dude. Hope his copter crashes sometime when he's all

102

doped up."

And with that, Wade took a final bite of macaroni and cheese and stormed back to his room. His mother called out something of a reprimand, but the words died a quiet death in the hallway.

Seeing the hurt in Timmy's eyes, Anita sat down beside him and brushed the hair off his forehead.

"Don't pay no mind to Wade, honey. He's pretty upset these days what with his best friend missing. He's having a real hard time, and so he says things he really doesn't mean. You understand?"

"No," said Timmy softly.

She smiled and hugged him. "Maybe, just maybe, Wade's kinda jealous of you, too—getting to go up in the helicopter—but, you see, he doesn't want to admit it."

"Mom, what's a dopehead?"

Taking a deep breath, she surveyed his innocent face and an expression there that demanded an honest response.

"Well, I think it's someone who uses drugs, you know . . . certain chemicals—sort of like medicine, but not medicine that a doctor would want you to take, or that momma would want you to take. It's more like bad medicine. Pills and powders."

"Why would somebody take bad medicine?"

"Because . . . because they get to feeling real, real lousy about themselves or their life, and the drugs make them feel better for a short time . . . but then they feel even worse later."

"Know what makes me feel better, mom? Nintendo. Chocolate donuts, too."

She laughed. "I'm glad, and I hope and pray you never ever use drugs."

For a few seconds, he burrowed into himself, and she could tell he was picking his way through some difficult thoughts.

"Should I quit bein' Houston's buddy? 'Cause he's a dopehead and takes bad medicine?"

"Oh-h-h . . . we don't know for certain what he does, Timmy. Whether he takes drugs or not. But if he does . . . well, maybe he does because he hasn't had many buddies, many friends in his life. Maybe what he needs is to have people care about him."

"You like him a whole bunch, mom?"

"My, oh, my . . . now you're prying into your old mom's personal life. Well . . . yes, I'd say I do like him a whole bunch."

"Me, too," the boy whispered uncertainly.

4

She liked her new job, though balancing glasses of beer on a tray was a skill that escaped her best efforts. She felt that she would do as well walking a circus tightrope. But she got along with Wick, the bartender, who bore a remarkable resemblance to Sam on the old TV western *Gunsmoke;* and the customers were friendly—most were elderly—and they tipped as generously as possible. Men noticed her; a few flirted clumsily. She could brush them off without antagonizing them into taking their business elsewhere.

By the second night on the job, she could track her way through the darkness of the bar like some animal intimately familiar with its burrow. She could not, however, shake the lingering dread she experienced every time a stranger entered, especially a dark-haired stranger—a shadowy doppelganger of Dean.

It was always a relief to discover that it was someone else.

Midweek, a routine had established itself: Lazy days of sunbathing, tending to domestic chores, including some time with the boys, then preparing for work, turning the boys over to Marcie, and adopting the role of barmaid.

Each evening Houston came late and stayed till closing time. She noticed that frequently the man called Hash would search him out. Intuitively she disliked Hash, always dubious as to why Houston would associate with him. Each evening the man who owned the world's sexiest smile—in her opinion, at least—walked her home and kissed her good night, and she would close the door on him and think about him far into the coming of day.

One evening the routine changed.

As Marcie left, Houston stepped inside and closed the door behind him.

"I want you, Anita," he said.

And the kiss was long and full. She led him to the plaid sofa, one leg of which threatened to collapse unannounced. And she whispered, "I need to check on the boys."

When she returned, he undressed her, a ritual replete with awkward moments; yet the passion was there and strong, and she touched him and kissed his throat and felt his muscular body against hers and forgot about everything but a need easily surrendered to.

The sofa held up under the first lovemaking, but not the second.

And the laughter felt so good to her that she might have convinced herself, then and there, that she would never feel alone again.

"We have so much to talk about," she whispered sometime during the night.

"There'll be time," he said. "Besides, talking never changes the things that mean the most to you."

She curled against him.

As dawn approached, she wondered how silence could turn a loving man into a stranger.

Wade clenched the tiny cross in his fist, hoping that having it in hand would make it more effective in warding off things lurching through the night, perhaps even bad dreams. He had awakened from one, a suffocating narrative in which he was poling down a slough he had never seen, a preternaturally silent body of water. He was alone.

Suddenly, breaking out around him was the thrumming of wings generated by hundreds of swamp birds; there were so many flocking together that they appeared to merge into some gigantic winged form. And he was lifted, screaming, battling the unseen attackers—or was it only one? The beating of their wings threatened to suck all of the air from his lungs and drive away any that he might breathe.

He thrashed and gasped and woke clawing at the air, sweating, then chilled, as he burrowed beneath the sheet. And that's when he reached for the cross. Momentarily, it did provide a sense of protection, some comfort which lasted until he began to doze off again and to catch the vague listings of sounds elsewhere in the trailer.

He fell asleep to the distant jingle of laughter.

A second dream unfolded: He was in the kitchen with Timmy and his mom; they had knotted themselves together there in fear. Beyond the walls of the trailer, they could hear the wail of a wind, but Wade knew it wasn't a wind, knew, instead, that the amassing of wings from the previous nightmare had returned. And they were striking the thin siding, clanging, thudding, searching for any possible point of entrance.

Over the cries and tears of Timmy, his mother was desperately trying to phone for help. Terrifyingly convinced that no help would respond, Wade shouted for her to get off the phone and for the three of them to barricade themselves at the other end of the trailer.

But it was too late.

Just like the tornado scene from *The Wizard of Oz*, the trailer began to rise, to spin, shaken loose from its foundation and anchor lines by the tremendous force of the attacking wings. The trailer was carried high above Orchid Springs; the door and the windows imploded. Wade looked up to see his mother and Timmy at the door, precariously close to dropping into an abyss or into the clutches of the attacking wings.

He screamed for them to get away from the door.

He woke, and the abruptness of the waking nearly catapulted him out of bed. His dark room testified that it had been a dream—only a dream. His hand ached, and suddenly he realized that he was squeezing the tiny cross with such force that it had broken through the skin of his palm.

Angry with himself for trusting it, he hurled the cross against the far wall; it tinkled faintly, and Wade felt alone. His mouth was dry. More fully awake, he got out of bed and trod to the kitchen. On the way, he stopped dead in his tracks and stared at the sofa, not at its broken leg, but rather at the bodies covered by a single white sheet and at the sleeping faces partially illuminated by the night-lite above the kitchen sink.

He recognized Houston Parker immediately. But the remainder of the scene defied all that he thought possible; in fact, he reasoned that he was mistaken—the other person *could not* be his mother. Could not.

Yet was.

He stood there, in the shadows of the living room, gritting his teeth, wanting—he wasn't certain why—to run at Houston and slam fists into him or hit him with a lamp or whatever other object he could find. He wanted to yell at his mother, wanted her to understand the spear thrust of hurt he was experiencing. Instead, he could

107

only stare.

They were naked under that sheet; he knew that. He knew, vaguely at least, what they had been doing. He felt dizzy; his cheeks flushed. He forgot about getting a glass of water. He went back to his room and concentrated upon the numbers of his digital clock radio. Less than an hour later, he heard Houston leave, heard his mother in the bathroom, then in her bedroom.

I hate him, he told himself. *I hate Houston Parker.*

Why?

Because Houston Parker did not belong in their lives—could not take the place of the man Wade still thought of as dad. Could not.

Another hour and it was time to go wait for Jack to toss the *Herald* out at Holly's.

6

Sitting with his back against Holly's front door, Wade took each copy of the newspaper, rolled it into a tight baton, and slipped a rubber band around it. In a dark projection, each paper became Houston Parker, and the boy was twisting the life out of the man, making him pay for entering their little family of three. But, at moments, it was hard to decide whether he ought to be mad at his mother instead of Houston.

How could she have done such a thing?

He thought about what Gillie might say if he found out. Confusion toyed menacingly with his emotions—hate, love, loneliness, hope and despair.

"God, I miss you, Gillie," he whispered aloud.

There was no one around to hear; Orchid Springs slept under a blanket of mist generated by the warm night air drawing upon the slough. From where he sat, he could hardly make out the bridge.

Gillie wouldn't be bothered by all this.

The thought hit him like a fist in the stomach.

Of course, he wouldn't. Gillie was bad-ass, street-smart. Didn't need anyone. Could take care of himself.

I got to be the same way.

Yet, that resolve failed to allay the ache that settled into his bones—or deeper—into his heart, into his soul.

"Come on back home, Gillie, damn you," he muttered, wanting to cry, but determined not to. He swung the heavy satchel of papers onto his shoulder and started on his route. A few yards from Holly's, he hesitated to watch a swamp bird, perhaps a heron or an egret, slice through the thick mist layering the slough; it swooped low, narrowly missing the bridge railing and the shadowy figure of someone standing there.

Wade felt hot needles prick his thighs.

He concentrated on the dark outline—not large enough for an adult.

"Gillie?"

The word slipped out so softly it was barely audible.

He ran several feet closer to the bridge and called out, "Gillie? Is that you?"

The figure did not move, but it appeared solid.

Satchel bouncing against his hip, Wade ran faster.

"Gillie, god darn, it's me—Wade."

He began to smile, to giggle almost deliriously.

"God darn it, Gillie, where the friggin' heck you been? Man, they drug the slough. Thought you was drowned dead. But I knew you'd come back."

He rattled onto the bridge planks. In the distance, a swamp bird cried a single, lonesome note.

The figure raised a hand as if in greeting, as if to say hello.

Wade clambered to within thirty feet of it.

"Jack gave me your . . ."

He slowed his steps.

109

". . . paper route," he whispered.

It was Gillie. For a moment.

He was there—then gone as quickly and completely as figures zapped on a video screen.

Very softly, Wade whispered, "Gillie?"

The word "ghost" seemed to hang in the misty air in front of him, hovering, stationary, like a phantom hummingbird—before flitting away.

Despite the morning's warmth, Wade felt cold.

He remained cold every step of his paper route.

7

As the morning wore on, Wade avoided nearly everyone: Timmy, Sara Beth, Holly, and especially, his mother. Still troubled by his encounter with Gillie's apparition, he stayed in his room, read his new baseball magazine, and surrendered to a profound sense of alienation.

He wished he could talk to his dad.

An idea flashed into his thoughts.

After lunch, his mom and Timmy left the trailer, his mom clad in her new hot-pink bikini and a towel. She looked good, but the thought that she was decked out that way to catch Houston's eye torched a fresh flame of anger in Wade.

I'll tell dad.

He lingered near the phone, trying to recall the name of the millwork on the outskirts of St. Louis where his dad was employed. Pulse hammering, he dialed for operator assistance—"What city please?"

"St. Louis. I want the number of a millwork, and its name begins with a 'G'."

The operator discovered one called Gateway Millwork.

"That's the one—it's where my dad works."

110

Excited, he scrambled around to find a pencil and, with trembling fingers, wrote down the number read off to him. He put the receiver on the hook to calm his nerves.

What would he say to him?

Come home, dad. Come be my dad, again.

He began to dial, his pulse throbbing in his forehead. He felt dizzy. He tried to imagine a tiny bead of white light spinning out from Orchid Springs, destination: St. Louis.

Number completed.

He took a deep breath.

"Gateway Millwork. May I help you?"

A pleasant voice—some secretary no doubt. He asked for his father, and the woman asked him to wait a moment. But it seemed more like an hour; the phone turned to lead. He had to hold it with two hands.

And he feared that his mom would return any second.

"Hello."

It was his dad's voice—no mistake about it.

"Huh-hello," Wade murmured.

"Hello—who is this?"

In that voice, the boy heard something he had forgotten: an echo of anger, the cocking of a hair-trigger temper poised to fire upon anyone who confronted it. The boy remembered a tapestry of dark scenes: his dad striking his mother, bringing a flow of blood to her nose; and Timmy attempting to protect his mom by swinging a whiffle bat and connecting with his dad's leg; and Timmy being tossed across the room, crashing onto the carpet like a bag of flour; screams, shouts and the hiding— hiding in a closet—or running, running to get away from a mysterious fury.

"Who the hell is this?"

In that voice the boy could imagine a hand raising or a fist clenching.

He slammed the receiver down before the imaginary blow more than a thousand miles away could strike him.

111

Visibly shaken, he ran to his room.

Hurt and fear stung at Wade like wasps. He wanted to cry, wanted to hit something. Or someone. He gathered up Timmy's tennis racket and a dead tennis ball and hustled out of the trailer.

"I hate you," he shouted as he ran.

And the *you* was many-headed: his dad, his mom, Houston, the world.

The Orchid Springs tennis courts provided an outlet for his anger; he spent the rest of the morning and most of the afternoon banging the ball against the tall, green backboard, hammering the sphere relentlessly until he neared exhaustion.

Some anger remained when he finished, so he took his brother's tennis racket and smashed it, the plastic rim dangling off to one side like a broken arm. The destructive act made him feel better. He then decided to seek out a companion. He had reached the door to Gillie's trailer before he remembered, *Gillie's gone.*

Fresh anger and frustration.

A memory of the ghost on the bridge.

Maybe I oughtta run away, too.

He wandered aimlessly through the warm, breezy late afternoon, finding himself eventually at Holly's door. Tending to several customers, his aunt did not see him slip in, did not see him hover near the candy racks—and he believed, or perhaps did not care, that she never saw him palm a Milky Way and scoot out the door.

At home, he taunted Timmy with the broken racket; predictably, Timmy tear-jerked a path straight to his mother, and at supper she opened up.

"Why would you be so deliberately destructive? What is wrong with you?"

"What's wrong with *you?*" he shot back. "Why would you let Houston Parker stay all night and sleep with you? He's a dopehead."

112

He ducked, but not in time to miss her hand raking across his shoulder.

"*That* is none of your business," she exclaimed. "You will *not* tell *me* how to live my life."

He dashed from the kitchen and, once again, found himself running.

Hungry.

Alone.

Feeling that the wings of the night could, without warning, swoop down and pluck him from reality as naturally as a hawk swoops down upon a field mouse.

Chapter Seven

1

"Wade has me at my wit's end, Holly. Breaking Timmy's tennis racket, talking back to me . . . I'm thinking about taking his paper route away just to show him he's not the boss."

Busy unboxing a colorful display of sunglasses, Holly shook her head. "Not a good idea, hon. The paper route's a great way for him to learn about making money, to learn that you have to work very hard to earn a living—don't mess with that, for heaven's sake."

"*What*, then? If Dean was—"

Again, Holly shook her head. "Bruises won't help, either."

"Wade's so angry all the time—it disrupts the whole household."

"Could be he has good reason to be angry."

Anita stared bewilderedly out the store window at the hazy morning.

"I jumped on him for breaking the racket, and I've had to get after him several times for not minding Marcie. I've told him that if he won't cooperate with a baby sitter, then I won't be able to work evenings, and we'll have to move to a shelter for the homeless."

Holly snickered. "Aw, come on, honey, the boy won't believe that. You make it sound like you're going to be featured on the six o'clock news—the boy's no dummy."

"How should I approach this?"

Anita followed Holly's stubby fingers as they fondled the display.

"There, how's that look? Would you pay ten bucks for a pair of those glasses?" The heavyset woman laughed heartily. "Got to put up some new displays today because Bradshaw has roped a reporter into coming all the way out here from Miami to do a feature on Orchid Springs. They may want a shot of the store and the bar. This apron too sexy? How's my hair?"

She playfully patted a suggestion of curls, and Anita was forced to giggle, aware suddenly of how expertly Holly was dodging the subject.

"Oh, Holly . . . I feel so stupid sometimes. Where are you supposed to learn how to be a parent?"

"*Phil Donahue Show,*" she quipped, and they both laughed. "Or you could watch that Geraldo fella and learn what to do if your lesbian lover is abducted by UFO aliens who are Elvis clones."

More laughter.

"You're not helping," Anita exclaimed through a broad smile.

Holly waited on two customers, then returned to her distressed niece.

"Give Wade some understanding. Give his anger some room."

"I don't follow you. Do I just *give in* to him? Is that what you're saying?"

"No, not at all. But put yourself in the boy's shoes: He's lost his dad, and he's apparently lost his best friend, and he's going to spend his summer in a strange setting— lots of adjustments there. Tell him you understand why

116

he's angry—tell him you're angry, too."

"I am?"

"Of course you are."

"No, Holly . . . confused maybe. But, thanks to you— thanks to the job at the bar—I'm feeling much better about myself."

"You do have a suspicious glow about you." Holly, who wore glasses, peeked knowingly over the lenses.

Caught off guard, Anita scrambled. "What is *that* supposed to mean?"

"Hmm . . . I wonder. Only one thing I know of brings on that kind of glow—a woman in love. And see there, you're blushing."

"Holly!"

The older woman sighed heavily. "I was afraid of this," she muttered. She raised a stubby finger authoritatively. "I warned you, honey. I warned you about Houston Parker."

"I'm not going to talk about Houston. Besides, there's nothing to talk about. We're friends. He walks me home after work, and he—" She glanced away. "Relationships are different today, Holly. No one commits unless—I know what I'm doing. I can take care of myself . . . and the point is, this has nothing to do with the problem I'm having controlling Wade."

"Are you sure of that?"

Why would you let Houston Parker stay all night and sleep with you? He's a dopehead.

Anita heard the pain in Wade's outburst.

Why didn't I hear it yesterday?

"I won't let a little boy decide who I can have a relationship with. I'm a grown woman."

Under her breath, Holly murmured, "Sort of."

"So you think he's jealous, is that it? Wade's jealous of Houston?"

Holly shook her head and allowed a smile born of a

117

wisdom that comes only with age and experience. "Jealousy? Oh, not necessarily. Could be the boy just has better judgment than you have."

"Oh, you're impossible, Holly," Anita exclaimed. "I came here for advice, and you're telling me my eleven-year-old son knows more about life than I do. You're impossible."

"No, hon. Tough, but not impossible."

"I'm leaving," said Anita.

"Don't rush off. Where you going?"

"Home to watch Oprah Winfrey," she replied, wishing she could muster some firebrand anger toward her aunt. But she couldn't because she feared the woman was right about everything she had said.

2

"I'm gonna call it 'Royal Orchid.' See, if you view it from above, the units form the outline of a crown. Say, you want to get a photo of this? Here you go, stand on this chair and point your camera down on the whole model. You have a wide-angle lens along?"

C.M. Bradshaw rubbed his hands together waiting for the reporter to show a little enthusiasm. The reporter stood and reluctantly climbed onto the chair. Below him Bradshaw had spread a large map of the Orchid Springs area replete with toy blocks to indicate a proposed expansion of the condo units, a high-priced wing for older and, presumably, well-heeled elderly folk.

The reporter went about his work indifferently, clicking a couple of shots, shaking his head as if he thought the project was a ridiculous idea.

"Say, what is it?" Bradshaw asked. "God alive, I've been giving you my best promo pitch on Orchid Springs for the past half hour, and I get the distinct impression—

118

and I've got to say that having been a salesman for over thirty years I can read people, read 'em like a damn book—you aren't a dog's leg interested or excited about my . . . my *vision*."

The reporter chuckled. "Vision? That what this is?"

"Listen to me, friend."

Bradshaw waited for the reporter to step down from the chair before thrusting a finger, a trembling finger, in the man's face.

"I've built Orchid Springs from scratch. From nothing. From right out of the God damn swamp. Now I've had some bad luck—the area hasn't attracted people the way I'd hoped—but I still have a vision, and no ink-smeared reporter's gonna poor mouth it. We straight on that?"

C.M. immediately regretted losing his temper. This was bad public relations. The reporter had the power to give Orchid Springs a real shot in the arm, provided the feature article he wrote had some zing to it, provided it painted a portrait of a place any retired person would want to come. Raising his voice to the reporter broke every rule in the PR manual.

The reporter smiled. "Can you handle a few words of advice?" he asked.

Loosening his tie, Bradshaw hesitated. His face had beamed a high flush; he took a handkerchief from his coat pocket and dabbed at his forehead and cheeks. In the reporter, he suddenly saw a different man, clearly one who had figured every angle, taken risks, witnessed con jobs, and experienced the way in which the world can rip a strand of barbed wire through your naked hands and leave you bloody, wallowing in self-pity.

"Yeah. Yeah, sure. Didn't mean to fly off the handle like that. It's just that I've sunk a bunch of years and a Brink's truck of money into this venture—and it's time I turned some big bucks on it because I'm fifty years old . . . and more and more these days I feel tired. You know what I mean?"

The reporter gestured for him to sit. "I've been in the newspaper business all my life—I know what tired is. I also know Florida, south Florida in particular. I've seen a couple hundred retirement areas mushroom out of swamps and bogs and sandy nothings. Saw some of them succeed—saw a hell of a lot go bust."

"So what's the bottom line? I got to come up with something bigger, better, newer, fresher? I don't have Donald Trump's money, you know. I got to build more slowly."

"I hear you," said the reporter. "But what you need isn't necessarily more money."

"Not money?"

"Not necessarily. Oh, course if you had fifteen or twenty million to pour into this immediately, hell, yes. But what you really need is a point of attraction."

"Point of attraction? We've got the Schreck Refuge right across the bridge from us. Folks come out to see it."

"Not that many," said the reporter. "I took a gander at it—not much there. An old kangaroo on its last legs. Pile of gators—but people can see gators everywhere in this part of the country. No, I'm talking about a special draw. I'd never heard of Orchid Springs before last week when that kid drowned out here."

"I wanted to hush that story," said Bradshaw. "Folks hear something like that, and they think it won't be safe for their children to grow up and play in the area. That there's no supervision. Sounds like a negative attraction to me."

"No argument there. But weird attractions are better than no attraction at all. Here's an example: You remember last year up the coast at that hole-in-the-road town called Heron Lake?"

Bradshaw thought a moment. "Oh, you talkin' about

where somebody's supposed to have seen a vision of the Virgin Mary? God alive, folks flocked up there like they's giving away money. I've never heard . . . wait . . . wait a second. I see where you're coming from."

"America's full of loonies these days, Mr. Bradshaw."

"I reckon you'd say a bass fishing rodeo wouldn't be strange enough—that right?"

"Probably wouldn't be."

"How about this? I could start a rumor that someone saw Elvis Presley over at Holly's store—that Elvis is alive and well and holed up in one of our condo units."

"Now you've got the picture," said the reporter. Both men laughed, and Bradshaw offered his visitor a cigar, not a cheap one, not an expensive one either.

"You need a few more photos, don't you? Then I'll treat you to some lunch over at our motel—not great food, but it's filling."

Outside, they strolled and talked; Bradshaw couldn't resist exercising the glib and oily art of sales and promotional rhetoric. The reporter managed not to hear a word he said.

3

When Wade saw them coming, he figured it involved the lingering mystery surrounding Gillie's disappearance. The man walking next to Bradshaw carried a camera; nothing about him suggested police. A private detective? Was Bradshaw still hot about the skiff stealing?

I didn't steal his skiff.

Why don't they leave me alone?

Suddenly it was too late to get up and run; the two men had angled off the shell road and were approaching where Wade had secured a spot on the bank of the slough.

"Good day for taking it easy, young man," said the camera toter.

Wade squinted up at him and mumbled in the affirmative.

"Hello, son," Bradshaw followed, hunkering down within a few yards of the boy. "This here gentlemen is Roy Johnson of the *Herald*. He's doing what's called a feature article on Orchid Springs. Says he'd like to get a photo of you. It'd show people that our little community is a good place for kids as well as for retired folk."

The reporter maneuvered closer to the slough so that he could frame Wade against the backdrop of some of the condo units.

"You don't mind if I take your picture, do you?"

"No," said Wade. "I guess not."

"You like Orchid Springs?"

Wade stole a glance at Bradshaw, who was nodding as if coaching the boy's response.

"I did till my best friend disappeared."

"Disappeared?"

Bradshaw grimaced, then interjected, "Yeah, you see . . . that was the Roth boy. At first, we thought he might have drowned, but since dragging the slough turned up snake eyes, we're thinking now that he ran away. The boy was troubled before he came to Orchid Springs—rough family situation, you know."

The reporter nodded soberly before turning his attention to Wade.

"Just sit there natural-like and be looking out over the water. Okay?"

"Like this?"

Wade leaned back lazily and gazed at the mangroves rimming the far side of the slough. The reporter clicked, repositioned, then clicked several times more.

"Good. That oughtta do it. You've just become immortalized."

122

Bradshaw smiled broadly and gently slapped the boy on the back. "Have a nice day, son. Enjoy your youth while you can."

Wade watched them amble toward Holly's. He felt restless and bored, and the gnawing in his stomach had a source other than emptiness—he was missing Gillie.

"Come back home," he whispered. "I'm friggin' mad at you for goin' away."

With that, he got to his feet and wandered aimlessly, a circuitous route leading eventually across the bridge to the Schreck Refuge, where he trod among a handful of tourists. He stopped at Ruthie's cage, then visited the white gator; his anger flared a moment at the copter pad as Houston Parker loaded a couple of tourists for a bird's-eye view of the swamplands.

He caught a glimpse of Miss Freda's aboriginal servant woman outside the white, sprawling cottage. The dark-skinned woman appeared to be as mysterious and intimidating as Gillie maintained she was.

Restlessness continuing to surge through him, Wade trailed along the shell road, one eye alert for Hash, for he believed that piratical old man and his foul-mouthed parrot understood his loneliness better than anyone else.

But Hash was not at his cabin. So Wade climbed the bird-watchers' tower and tried to read the future in the flight of a foursome of egrets. The southerly breeze touched his loneliness; the egrets sent an obscure message. Minutes later, he climbed down and hit the shell road, meandering, searching the tangle of mangrove roots for signs of corn snakes or any other interesting critter.

He tasted wintergreen.

Where does that come from?

In his memory, he vaguely connected the flavor with something out of reach, something forgotten, buried, repressed. But what?

Nearly a mile into the refuge, he slipped his sneakers off and waded into the shallow water from which the snarl of mangrove roots received their sustenance. Bent over, he scanned the murky bottom for the outline of turtles, or the flashing silver of small fish, or the camouflage of frogs. The mossy, vegetation-laden floor squished between his toes; it felt good.

He had groped along another fifty yards when something made him halt—a curious sensation that he was being watched. Turning slowly, glancing over his shoulder, he expected to see Hash. But there was no one. He straightened, stretched his back muscles, yawned, and looked to his left.

The gray-green collage of mangrove leaves and limbs reminded him of comic book features in which the reader is asked to find animals hidden in a mazelike drawing. Can you identify the ten woodland creatures in this picture?

Wade smiled.

And then he staggered back a step or two. And the smile faded.

He bit at his tongue to overcome a wash of numbness.

He used both fists to rub at his eyes.

His lips moved as if shaping some foreign language.

Nestled among the mangrove branches not fifteen feet from him, a grayish form, like an oversized fetus, curled upon itself. Sleeping? For a few seconds it was.

And then it opened its eyes.

Wade stumbled as he inched away from the sluggish-moving figure, and he sat down hard upon the shell road and cried out in pain.

The apparition of Gillie Roth thinned into a plume of smoke, rose from the labyrinth of branches, and dissipated into the late morning sky.

Wide-eyed, knees weak, face pale and cool, Wade negotiated the shell road in a daze. Tourists taking the scenic drive through the refuge waved at him, but most drove by him as if he were merely part of the landscape or one of the swamp creatures of no particular interest. Their cars raised white dust which he walked through, a daylight fog causing him to choke and cough.

Time after time, the gray, ghostly apparition of Gillie unfolded in his thoughts and played out its brief appearance to him. Virtually unaware of his surroundings, the boy slogged along. The minutes passed. He felt faint. His ears buzzed, blocking out, at first, the sound of a man's voice.

"Don't walk in the middle of the damn road."

Words filtered through the boy's mental as well as physical fog.

He stopped.

Hash, stationed in the doorway of his cabin, eyes concealed by sunglasses, gestured for him to come.

"You been out in the sun too long, kid. Come on in and cool your heels."

Wade obeyed, and gradually full consciousness returned. He entered the dark cabin, but the air inside was no cooler than outside.

"Pissant! Pissant!"

"Don't mind Ibo—he calls every kid pissant. Just bad manners on his part. Sit down, kid. Like a cold drink?"

Easing himself into a chair, Wade said, "Yeah, I would. Thanks."

"By mistake I bought a six-pack of this diet shit the other day. You like Diet Pepsi?"

"It don't matter to me."

Hash brought him a lukewarm can. "Look, I can pour a couple fingers of rum in that—won't taste as much like piss that way."

"Naw, it's okay."

Pushing his sunglasses high onto his head, the man, who continued to remind Wade of a pirate, twirled a chair around so that he could sit in it and prop his elbows on its back.

"You look zoned, kid."

Wade shrugged and glanced around. He brightened a bit as he remembered something.

"Did your big ole snake ever eat anything?"

"Danny Boy? Yeah, matter uh fact, that bastard of a worm did. One pinkie. Only one. 'Bout gagged on it, too. Tomorrow I'll try a pair of pinkies on him. He's in his pot sacked out or I'd let you say hello to him—sleeps late these days. Wish that loudmouth over there would." He pointed at Ibo.

The bird began to sing. ". . . troubles are all the sa-a-me. You wanna go where everybody kno-o-o-ws your name."

Wade laughed. "Hey, that's *Cheers*, ain't it? The song when *Cheers* comes on."

"Yeah, Ibo's a real couch parrot. Addicted to that tube. It's like a glass tit."

When the soft drink hit the back of the boy's throat, he began to feel better. Still haunted somewhat, but not as physically and emotionally at loose ends.

"You know anything 'bout ghosts?" he asked suddenly.

Hash chuckled hoarsely. "Ghosts? Hell, yes. Ever time I get sloshed I see ghosts of my former self—ghosts ever'where. Ghosts of when I was younger, stronger, more virile. Could handle half a dozen women a night, all the hard liquor you could pour in me, and kick ass whenever anybody wanted a fight. Yeah . . . yeah, I know all about ghosts."

"If you . . . you know, if you see a ghost that looks like

somebody—like a friend, or somebody—does that mean the person is for sure dead?"

"For sure dead?"

Hash took a lengthy swallow of his rum-laced drink and belched.

"You tellin' me you've seen a ghost? I mean, you're not shittin' me, are you?"

"No. I saw . . . I *think* I saw Gillie's ghost. You know . . . my friend Gillie Roth who's been missin'. I think I saw his ghost right back down the road."

He carefully described the incident, alive to any non-verbal reaction on Hash's part, but the sharklike demeanor of the man held firm.

"This ole swamp has some damn strange things in it. But probably what you saw was what's called one of them hallucinations. Things you think you see but aren't really there. Like . . . like mirages."

"You said *you* see ghosts. Donchoo believe I did?"

"Hey, my ghosts are different, kid. Mine aren't booga-booga ghosts."

On that note, Ibo, patiently biding his time, erupted.

"Booga-booga! Sumbitch! Booga-booga!"

Wade snickered. But he could tell that Hash had embraced more serious thoughts. Disregarding the parrot, the man said, "You ain't been down to Pelican Pond, have you, kid?"

"No."

"You know if Gillie's been there recently . . . I mean, you know for certain he's been there? He ever tell you that's where he was going?"

Wade shook his head. "Why you askin' me 'bout Pelican Pond?"

"No reason, kid. 'Cept I like to think I've staked a claim to it—don't like the idea of kids fuckin' around out there. Dangerous place."

"Why? Why is it dangerous?"

Hash's anger flared. "Because it is. Anywhere back that far in the swamp is dangerous, 'specially for kids or anybody who doesn't know shit about taking care of themselves."

"Gillie could take care of himself. And I can, too."

Laughing into his drink, Hash studied the boy. "You really are a pissant, kid. That ole swamp would swallow you the way Danny Boy gobbles up pinkies when he's feeling good. And don't you forget it. Maybe it swallowed Gillie. Hell, who knows. Fact of the matter is. . . ."

He paused, seemed on the verge of sharing some revelation, some dark secret with the boy, then decided not to.

"You think Gillie's dead, too, don't you?" Wade asked.

"Look, kid, I'm a man who survives because he abides by Hash's Law: Watch after your own ass and don't tell other people half of what you know."

"Could that be my law, too?"

"Shit, yes. I don't have a fuckin' copyright on it, or nothin'."

He smiled at Wade—the shark in the man's face receded some—everywhere, that is, except in the black, lustreless pools of his eyes.

At that instant, Wade's stomach growled. "Geez, I don't 'member eatin' all day."

"Tell you what," Hash followed. "I'll fry you a couple of the greasiest burgers you ever sank your teeth into if you'll be my partner on a job this afternoon."

"Sure. What kind of job?"

"You'll see. Give me ten minutes and I'll have those burgers for you."

Hash was right—about the ten minutes and about the state of the burgers. They were served up swimming in grease. Because Hash had no hamburger buns, they ate the grease-soaked meat slapped between pieces of white

128

bread—bread that quickly turned yellow and tore into greasy shreds. Hash opened a can of pork and beans which they shared, not bothering to dump them out onto a plate. Some stale corn chips and warm soft drinks— Hash's ice box wouldn't cool enough to produce ice— topped off the menu.

"This is good," said Wade.

"Lord love it, kid, your mama must be one damn lousy cook if you think this shit is good."

"Yeah, she's pretty bad. You can ask my little brother, Timmy. He'd say it, too."

5

"See why I gave you a machete?" said Hash.

"The slough's 'bout all the way stopped up," Wade murmured. "Man, I wish Gillie could see this. Bet it's a great place for corn snakes. We gonna hack a clearing through this?"

"You got it. Miserable damn job, too."

Hash had ferried them in his skiff to a fingering offshoot slough of the refuge, an ever-narrowing run of brackish water the color of strong coffee. At one point, mangrove roots had seized the slough in a deadly stranglehold, intertwining, choking, reducing the flow to a bare trickle of what it had been.

"Last two winters of dry weather helped cause this," Hash explained. "That and the fact that no gators nest here—gators, they're our best engineers."

"Engineers?"

"Damn good engineers. They can crawl along the bottom of the slough, nosing in the mud, you know, and they'll take a mind to tearing the mangrove roots with them sharp teeth of theirs—keeps this kind of thing from happening. Not healthy for the refuge to be clogged up

129

like this—sorta like being constipated, you know. You and me, we gonna be laxatives."

He winked at the boy, and they set to work. Skiff anchored, Hash showed Wade how to get down close to the roots and chop away at them with the machete. Knee deep in the sluggish water, Wade imitated Hash's motion, and soon the steady splash and crash of their machetes drowned out the cacophony of a nearby brown pelican rookery.

Pockets of oppressive humidity surrounded man and boy as they worked. Hash sang snatches of old Roy Orbison hits, and Wade found himself occasionally fantasizing that a protruding root was Houston Parker. After fifteen or twenty minutes of steady hacking, the boy rested long enough to wipe the stinging sweat from his eyes and trace the intermittent flights of swamp birds and the dog-paddle strokes of a turtle crossing the slough in search of a good spot to sun itself.

Hash paused to curse himself for not bringing beer.

"I could go to Holly's and buy you some if you give me money."

"Yeah, maybe later," he responded. "Hey, there you go . . . that lucky bastard caught himself lunch."

Wade twisted around to see what Hash was looking at. A hawk had taloned a large southern leopard frog and was, no doubt, transporting it to a nest where it would be devoured. The frog's legs kicked and twitched. Kicked and twitched.

A giant, white screen fell across the boy's view before it began to disintegrate, dissolving like tissue in the rain, revealing a much different scene from that of hawk and prey.

He could see Gillie.

And smell the stench. Stronger than dead fish, it burned the lining of his nostrils, generating a stream of mucous.

The air vibrated with the beat of wings.

Memory crystallized. From the protected reaches of his subconscious, Wade began to relive the forgotten, the repressed, experience.

"Gillie!" he screamed. "Watch out!"

His friend could not move; it appeared he was somehow tangled up in the mangrove branches. *He could not move.*

And the winged creature was upon him.

It opened its black, silken wings, and they seemed to spread forever. The only associations in Wade's chaotic thoughts were those of a bat, a giant vampire bat, as large as a man, and of an old movie poster of Bela Lugosi, black cape raised menacingly above an innocent young woman—the archetypal Count Dracula.

Yet, the sheer fear-inducing capacity of this creature transcended any image Wade could conjure: This creature was a terrifying combination of bat and man. The wings and clawed feet, the body, the imposing fangs, matched pictures he had seen of vampire bats. But the face had the dark suggestion of a man's—except that the predatory cast of it was more sinister, more evil than any other he had ever encountered.

"Gillie!" Wade screamed one final time.

His friend reached out, a halfhearted attempt to fend off the creature, and the massive wings shuddered, then slowly closed, rustling like a stage curtain.

Blackness folded over Gillie, but not before Wade saw the horror in his friend's eyes and heard a smothered cry.

The wings tightened; tendons pulsed.

Bones snapped. Gillie's.

Then the wings opened, slowly, deliberately.

Gillie Roth slumped down into the branches.

And Wade prayed that he was dead.

Positioning itself so that it could grasp the boy's body with one clawed foot, the creature lowered its head as if

131

carefully scrutinizing for signs of life. Then it cocked its head and opened its mouth, straining its jaws as immense fangs protruded.

And sank into Gillie's face.

Wade closed his eyes as tightly as possible. When he reopened them, he watched in horror as the creature used its fangs to tear at the boy's flesh, spurtings of dark red blood splashing against its glossy wings.

Gillie's face was gone.

The creature had shifted its devouring ways to the boy's chest and stomach; entrails were pulled taut like rubber bands, then snapped and torn and swallowed.

Wade screamed a primitive cry from deep within him.

The creature hesitated; its dark eyes appeared to look right through the boy. Disturbed by the intruding scream and the presence of Wade, it gathered the remains of Gillie Roth and, with a thunderous roll and thrum of its wings, lifted free of the mangrove branches, then skimmed low over the swamp, seeking out the far horizon.

Hawk and dangling frog returned to Wade's vision. He dropped his machete; vomit, sour and warm, emptied from him in a continuous gush, threatening to strangle him. He struggled to the skiff, gasping, choking on a sticky, liquid paste of hamburger and pork and beans.

"Jesus Christ, kid, what happened?"

Hash scrambled toward the skiff, splashing, slipping, nearly falling, but the boy, half out of his mind, could only respond by crying over and over. "God, it got him! God, it got him!"

6

It took as much energy as cutting through mangrove roots, but Hash eventually succeeded in transporting the terribly frightened, badly shaken boy to the cabin, where he encouraged him to lie down on an old army cot. Ibo, excited by the entrance of the babbling boy, launched into a frenzied tirade which forced Hash to slip the tape of the bird's favorite movie into the VCR.

On the cot, Wade tossed and turned, crying out, flailing at Hash, demanding that he do something about Gillie. The impact of Hash's slap jerked the boy's head to one side. And then Wade began to sob, and the man held him momentarily before taking him by the shoulders.

"You tell me exactly what the hell's going on!"

Afterthralls of tears rocked Wade's chest. Through glazed eyes he tried to focus on Hash, but reality kept shifting as if he were watching television and the channels switched on their own.

"You're scaring the piss outta me, kid. What's the matter with you? God damn it, tell me."

Gradually he did.

It took nearly an hour for Wade to narrate the experience, his story interrupted again and again by tears and the shock of it all.

"God, it got him!"

He threw himself into Hash's arms, but the man did not allow the embrace to last. A curious sheen masked Hash's face; he stared off to one side and muttered, "Blood Wings . . . Jesus . . . Blood Wings."

"Whuh-what's Blood Wings?" the boy stuttered.

He saw something most unusual in Hash's expression: Fear. But mingled with that fear was something mean and calculating—something dark and hidden.

"Never mind, kid. It's nothin'. Forget I ever said it."

"But we got to tell somebody about it. The sheriff. The police. They got to go get that thing and kill it. Somebody's got to kill it."

Hash grabbed the boy and shook him. Through clenched teeth, the man said, "Listen to me, kid, and listen good. We ain't tellin' nobody about what you

133

thought you saw. You hear me?"

"*Thought* I saw? Hash, I saw it. I saw it." Almost too weak to talk, Wade merely shook his head, exasperated that the man could even suggest doubt.

"No, you didn't. Cut and dried case here of hallucination. Now, don't try to tell me different. Look, you *thought* you saw Gillie's ghost this morning, then, out there in all that humidity, working up a swamp sweat, you had another hallucination. A bad one—I'll grant you that. But there ain't no such creature like you describe—there just ain't."

"But I remember the whole day . . . everything. Stealin' stuff at Holly's. Takin' the skiff. I remember everything. It got Gillie. Something got Gillie. I saw it." He felt so exhausted he wanted to lie back down on the cot and sleep.

"Bottom line is this, kid. I don't want nobody nosing around out at Pelican Pond. That's my territory. It's mine. I don't want the sheriff and every God damn curiosity seeker turning over every leaf out there and interfering with me and Bella."

"Pelican Pond," Wade whispered. "Hey, that's it. That's where it happened. I remember . . . but . . . how did you know Gillie got attacked there?"

"Damn it, kid. He never got attacked. Your mind's been playing nasty tricks on you."

The boy closed his eyes.

Maybe he's right.

The nightmarish vision. It couldn't possibly be true and yet, and yet. . . .

"You go on home, kid. But I'm warning you—if you tell the sheriff or the authorities about Blood Wings, they'll think you're looney as hell. They'll put you away. No damn way they'd believe your story."

Wade sighed. One side of his face burned from Hash's slap.

134

Confusion overwhelmed him, warring with exhaustion.

Hash helped him to the door.

"You go on home and forget about all this. In a few days, you'll realize it was all like a bad damn dream, and that's all. Here—here's five bucks for helping me. Go on. Get your ass home."

Chapter Eight

1

The five dollar bill shrank to a soggy wad in the boy's fist. He walked toward home, still a bit dizzy, still a bit disoriented, his legs seeming to have lost half their strength and flexibility.

What should I do?

Leaving Hash's cabin, he had vaguely reasoned that the man spoke true; the horrific flashback could be explained away as a daylight nightmare, much as was the apparition of Gillie among the mangrove branches. If he told anyone, if he recounted the flashback to the authorities, they most certainly wouldn't believe him. Worse yet, they might feel he needed to see a psychiatrist and possibly—"they'll think you're looney as hell"—to be put in some institution.

On the other hand, the vision had the unmistakable feel of reality. *God, it happened. I know it did.* The sour taste of vomit rose into the back of his mouth. An image flitted through his thoughts: Gillie's face was gone.

Wade stumbled and fell forward at the edge of the shell road. Above, swinging high and to the right, Houston Parker gave tourists an aerial view of Orchid Springs and

137

the refuge. But for an instant, the copter had sprouted silken black wings and was circling, hawklike, zeroing in on prey.

I gotta tell somebody.

He struggled to his feet, not bothering to brush the white dust from his shorts, and he began to run against the protest of his legs. At the bridge, he slowed to catch his breath. Timmy and Sara Beth called out to him, but he disregarded them, his thoughts pinballing.

Who can I tell?

"Wade, mom's lookin' for you. You're supposed to say where you're gonna be. You're in trouble, big as heck."

Timmy's voice trailed behind him as he started off again at a trot.

Holly. I'll tell Aunt Holly.

He beelined for her store, already mentally rehearsing his story. But on route he happened to see the reporter and Mr. Bradshaw entering Bradshaw's office, a small, pre-fab building beyond Holly's store. Instinctively, he altered his course.

When he burst through the door, Johnson and Bradshaw were sitting back talking, laughing, Bradshaw waving a cigar in his best imitation of a wheeler-dealer.

Wade changed the jovial atmosphere immediately.

"I got to tell you! I got to tell you what happened to Gillie!"

The two men swung to their feet, exchanging glances of puzzlement.

"Hey, hey, son. Hold on, now. Hold on," Bradshaw exclaimed.

They braced the boy into a chair, hunkered down near him and listened to a rambling account unlike any other they had ever heard. Bradshaw, face flushed, tried to calm Wade, assuring him that he imagined everything.

Johnson, however, began taking notes and asked the boy to recount everything from the beginning. "God

138

damn it! Why didn't I bring along that recorder?"

When Bradshaw saw the notepad, he grabbed Johnson's arm. "Are you crazy? Why are you writing this down?"

Johnson arched his eyebrows; his smile was knowing, the kind of smile a man flashes when he recognizes something that no one else appears to see.

"This is your ticket," he replied.

"What? Jesus Christ, no! You're not gonna print any of this, are you?"

"Do you want Orchid Springs on the map?"

Bradshaw's mouth fell open; he stared at Johnson, then at Wade.

"Aw, no, no-o-o," he murmured. "This is lunacy. You can't be serious."

He looked again at Johnson, who, in turn, patted Wade's knee.

"Never been more serious in my life."

Rubbing at his mouth, Bradshaw appeared to be deep in thought. On his knees, he clambered up to the boy. "Son . . . this is very important. *Ver-eee* important." He paused, blinked his eyes rapidly and took a breath. "Do you swear to God that you're telling us the truth?"

"Yes," said the boy defiantly.

"Wait. Wait just a minute." Bradshaw scrambled to his feet, and from his bottom desk drawer he retrieved a green-covered Gideon Bible. "Here—here, put your right hand on this and swear to me that you're telling the truth."

The boy obeyed, adding, "You got to call the sheriff, and somebody's got to kill that thing. Kill Blood Wings."

"Blood Wings?"

Interest piqued further, Johnson let the words parade through his thoughts. "What do you call it? Blood Wings? Is that the creature you saw?"

"Hash called it that. It's what he called it."

139

"Hash?"

Bradshaw broke in. "He's one of the workers at the Schreck Refuge. Been around this area for years."

Johnson was writing as rapidly as his fingers could move his pen.

"This is better than a vision of the Virgin Mary," he muttered. Then he concentrated on Wade. "Once more . . . I know this is hard for you . . . but could you walk through the entire experience one more time."

"I will . . . if you'll promise me you'll tell the sheriff and go get that thing that killed Gillie."

"Yes. Yes, of course, we will. But I want to get your story for the paper. Everybody's gonna want to read about this."

Bradshaw, renewing his battle with anxiety, said, "My gut feeling on this says it's a mistake . . . mistake to put this in the paper and let it get around. Public relations—Jesus Christ—I don't know."

"Trust me," said Johnson, flashing that knowing smile again.

His narrative interrupted once or twice by the threat of tears, Wade completed a retelling of the horror.

"I can't talk no more 'bout this. Please don't make me."

"Okay. Okay, fine," said Johnson. "I'm just gonna ask for one more thing."

He handed his notebook to Wade; it was opened to a blank page.

"Could you draw me a picture of this Blood Wings? Just a sketch. A rough sketch. Doesn't have to be very detailed or anything. I'd just like an idea of what it looked like beyond your verbal description of it."

Hesitantly Wade took the notebook and pen.

"It's like a big bat . . . only, its face is—"

"Could you draw it for me? Just a rough sketch."

The boy glanced at Bradshaw who, in turn, nodded encouragement.

"Go ahead, son."

Once he began, the sketch developed readily; he captured the creature, wings spread menacingly, and inked in everything but the head.

"It had these great big teeth, and, you know, the gums around the sharp teeth were real, real red . . . like blood. And its face."

He tried to translate the vision onto paper. The eyes, large ears . . . all the ordinary facial features of a man, yet pasted onto the horrific batlike creature, it darkly transcended anything resembling a man.

"This is the best I can do. It looked pretty much like this here."

Johnson took the notebook, studied the drawing several moments, and then handed it to Bradshaw.

"You've been a tremendous help, Wade. This might allow us to find what you saw attack your friend. You've done the right thing by telling us your story."

"I'd like to go home now," the boy murmured.

Bradshaw, scratching his chin thoughtfully, looked up from the drawing.

"Sure. Sure, son. Mr. Johnson's right . . . you've been a good citizen of Orchid Springs to come to us. You go on home. You've had a hard day, a tough day. We'll handle matters from here on."

Then he added, "One other question, son . . . who, who else have you told this story to?"

"Just to Hash."

"Yes. Right. Of course. He called the creature Blood Wings."

Johnson couldn't resist asking, "Has he seen this creature, too?"

"I don't know. I don't think so because he said it

wasn't real. It was some kind of hallucination or something like that."

The boy shrugged.

Bradshaw patted him on top of his head and guided him to the door. "Son, now, don't you be worrying about this. Orchid Springs is safe. Let's not create a situation, you know . . . let's not have folks panicking over nothing."

Wade turned to face him. "It's not *nuthin'*," he exclaimed, tears of frustration edging into the corners of his eyes. "I saw it. It was the most horrible, most awful thing—it tore off Gillie's face, and it carried him away, and somebody's got—"

"Hey, hey. I said we'd take care of it, son."

He smiled broadly and sent the boy on his way.

2

Absorbed in the drawing, Johnson lapsed into a silence that unnerved Bradshaw.

"My God, man, you don't believe any of this, do you?"

Johnson raised his eyes and gazed at the colorless wall beyond him. "Course not. Don't be idiotic."

Hearing those words, Bradshaw breathed a notch easier. "Good. Good, I was afraid you—but, you know, Jesus . . . that boy was upset, really upset. What in the hell *did* he see?"

"Maybe a big bird. A heron. Something like that. If you're up close to those things when they spread their wings, they look huge."

Dabbing at the sweat on his cheeks and forehead, Bradshaw said, "But how did a heron become a giant bat that—that did what he said it did to his friend? Lot of grisly detail there—my God, his story was giving me the shakes."

"Yeah, a terrific story . . . terrific. The whole country

142

will think so, too."

"I'm having trouble with this . . . a newspaper story . . . public relations. And the police, the authorities. How are they gonna react to all this?"

"Not hard to figure. Let's consider what we have in this situation."

He swung and leaned forward and used his hands as if he were counting off his fingers.

"First, we got us a kid, eleven years old, highly imaginative, probably watches a lot of TV, maybe a lot of horror movies or science fiction movies. Okay, second, his best friend has disappeared. Could be a runaway—there's a spate of them these days—or maybe the friend really did drown. Let's say he did. Let's say Wade *saw* him drown. The memory is so horrible to him that his mind creates something even worse—takes it out of the realm of possibility. Then, *voilá*, we get a totally fantastic account like this one."

Bradshaw appeared doubtful at first. He rubbed at his mouth as if it itched. "I don't know . . . this has thrown me for a loop."

"Blood Wings," Johnson whispered, seeming to admire the words.

"What are you seeing in this?"

Johnson smiled and tapped at the notebook. "I'm seeing that by next week at this time Blood Wings is gonna be a household name—Orchid Springs has its own Bigfoot, its own Loch Ness monster—and you, you lucky stiff, are in a position to reap the financial rewards."

"Financial rewards?"

Bradshaw warmed to the exchange.

"Talk to me. I'm listening, Mr. Johnson. I'm listening."

Anita Martin waited outside the examination room of the new county clinic serving rural Dade County. She was scared. During the night, Wade had awakened screaming, locked in a babbling, out-of-his-head flow of words focused loosely on Gillie Roth. For several hours she had tried unsuccessfully to calm him, opting finally to haul him to the clinic.

Timmy sat beside her, wrapped in a Walt Disney World sheet, Mickey Mouse wrinkled under his chin; he was falling asleep again, about to topple out of the chair. She lifted him into her arms and rocked him and kissed his head.

Dr. Corredera, a small, black-haired, dark-complexioned man, walked up to her and pulled a chair close. His smile was gentle and mildly reassuring.

"Mrs. Martin, we've given Wade a pretty thorough examination, and he and I have had a good, long talk. He's feeling better, though I'll write out a prescription for some pills I'd like for him to take during the next forty-eight hours."

"There isn't something seriously wrong with him, is there? I couldn't imagine . . . it scared me to death . . . the screaming, the wild talk. I thought he was having some kind of seizure—something, some kind of brain damage. . . . It's nothing like that, is it?"

He touched her arm. "No, no. I would rule out brain and neurological damage, and from the medical history you've provided, I would discount anything largely physiological as the source of the problem."

"Then what is it? His friend, Gillie . . . is he still having trouble accepting that his friend has disappeared? And the ravings . . . something about a creature?"

A frown ghosted across Corredera's face before he regained his professional composure.

"He has shared a most vivid, most unusual account, and certainly he appears to be quite serious that his friend was attacked and killed by some mysterious, winged creature. The obvious reading of it would be a trauma-induced hallucination—such things occur, though I must admit I've never encountered one so intense and detailed and told with so much conviction."

"Should I take him to a psychiatrist? Will he get over this? Will he keep having nightmares?"

"It's quite possible he will. The prescription essentially will help him sleep through the night. As far as a psychiatrist, I wouldn't hesitate to consult one if the extreme agitation continues. It might be necessary to siphon off some of the trauma and lingering shock. In fact, let me give you a couple of names; it could be beneficial for Wade to go through a preliminary session or two."

Accompanied by a nurse, Wade, looking tired, eyes puffy, face pale, joined them. Corredera clasped him on the shoulder.

"But I believe we're going to start feeling much better," he said, smiling at the boy.

"One other question," said Anita. "Wade insisted I call the sheriff, and the two deputies that talked to us before want him to show them where in the swamp he saw something happen to Gillie. Do you think he should? I'm afraid it would upset him all over again."

Glancing down at Wade, Corredera said, "How would *you* feel about that?"

"It'd be okay. I want to . . . I want to show 'em Pelican Pond. I want 'em to kill it . . . to kill that Blood Wings."

"I believe the surge of the initial trauma has probably passed," said Corredera. "But Wade, you must understand that doctors can't always predict the aftermath of very upsetting experiences, real or imagined. Let's hope that your nightmare doesn't return and you can plunge

145

into baseball and swimming and any summer activities you have planned."

Then he wrote out a prescription and jotted down names of two psychiatrists and handed the slips of paper to Anita, who took them, thanked the doctor, and herded her two boys out the door.

On the way home, Wade lay in the backseat, staring at nothingness.

That doctor doesn't really believe me.

The feeling, persistent as a physical ache, led him to wonder whether Johnson and Bradshaw believed him. Were they merely going along with him because he was a kid—just a kid making up a weird story?

Timmy thrust his head over the seat and studied his brother as if he were a stranger.

"Mom? Is Wade gonna freak out and stab a butcher knife in us?"

"Oh, Timmy, of course not. Wade had a very bad dream; he's worried about his friend Gillie. But he's going to be better. Dr. Corredera helped him."

Dissatisfied with her explanation, Timmy kept at it: "On *Saturday Nightmare* I saw this movie, and a little boy in it got a big ole butcher knife from the kitchen and stabbed his sister all up."

"Shut up, Timmy!" Wade exclaimed. "You're a super nerdy weenie!"

Anita called for a truce.

"We need to let your brother rest, Timmy. No more awful talk. Nothing like that is going to happen."

"Yeah, but, mom . . . do I gotta sleep in the same room with him?"

"Your bed would miss you, wouldn't it? If you didn't sleep in it, we'd hear it crying, 'Where's Timmy? I want Timmy to come sleep here.'"

"Would it really?" Timmy murmured.

"I don't care if he sleeps in the same room," said

Wade. "Let the weenie sleep in your room."

"Could I, mom? Just one night?"

"We'll see. We'll see."

Later that day Wade accompanied two sheriff's deputies down the slough toward Pelican Pond. He showed them the gator nest where he and Gillie had looked for eggs, and he tried to recall other details leading up to the tragic moment.

As the deputies guided their large, aluminum skiff to the edge of Pelican Pond, Wade involuntarily sucked in his breath.

"Is this the area?" one of the officers asked.

"Yes, sir. Gillie got out and went chasin' after a corn snake, but he didn't catch it. And he left his spear . . . he had this homemade spear and he forgot it, and when he went back to get it in the branches. . . ."

The officers maneuvered into the pond, all the while scanning the massively thick wall of low-growing mangrove trees.

"How would you ever find anything in there?" one muttered to the other.

Wade could feel frustration and agitation rising within him.

"You got to find it!" he exclaimed. "It killed Gillie and you got to find it and kill it!"

They reassured him as best they could in their "we're doing all we can" language. But he could tell that they harbored numerous doubts about his account.

"If there has been an attack, there should be bloodstains," said one, his tone carrying skepticism.

They conducted a brief search, climbing onto the jungle of branches, carefully picking their way into a labyrinth of vegetation.

They fired questions at the boy.

"Is this where you think you saw the creature?"

"Where did you last see your friend?"

147

"Where was the sun? What angle?"

"Describe your friend's spear for us?"

"In which direction did the creature head?"

Disorientation set in; Wade couldn't remember the exact location. His thoughts spun; directions turned a quarter turn.

"It's there. It's around there . . . where you are," he said, suddenly very uncertain of himself.

The officers tromped around in the mangroves for nearly an hour. They found nothing. Forty yards away Gillie's bloodstains were shading to brown on the glossy mangrove leaves.

4

For the next two days Wade could hardly stay awake. His mom and Timmy had to assist with the paper route. The prescription medicine kept him in a perpetual state of drowsiness, a fortunate situation in part because the microcosm of Orchid Springs was discovering the story of Blood Wings, and, in turn, curiosity mongers from throughout the country were about to discover Orchid Springs.

The evening of the day the story broke, Wade awakened from a nap—a common reaction to the pills— and wandered into the kitchen to find Marcie, Sara Beth, and Timmy chortling at the table over a newspaper spread. When they saw him, they immediately shushed.

"What are you guys readin'?" Wade asked sleepily.

"About the most famous boy in Orchid Springs," Marcie exclaimed, barely repressing a giggle. Sara Beth burst forth in a witchy cackle, and Timmy laughed until a lambleg of mucous slid from his nose.

Then Wade knew. He had seen the story that morning. The headline:

"I'm not famous or nuthin' like that," Wade protested.

"Of course you are," Marcie countered. "My father says you've done Orchid Springs a great service by making up this crazy story. Lots of people gonna come here, and maybe some of them will buy condos, and this'll put us on the map—that's what my father says."

"Yeah, it's a really weird story," Sara Beth followed, then turned and chased Timmy around the room flapping her arms and moaning, "Blood Wings is comin' to getcha. Comin' to getcha."

Wade watched in stunned disbelief.

He could feel anger walking through him like fire.

He grabbed Timmy's arm and swung him to a stop.

"Damn you all to hell!" he cried.

Silence reigned instantly.

Then Sara Beth buried a snicker beneath a cupped hand.

"Let go my arm," Timmy cried, yanking as hard as he could.

When Wade released him, the boy pinwheeled across the floor and crashed into the wall with a yelp.

"Wade!" Marcie exclaimed. "What do you think you're doing?"

"You can all go to hell and burn up!" he shouted. "I didn't make up no story. I saw that creature. I saw it, and I hope it comes around here and tears your face off and eats your guts. I hope it does."

He stormed away, scattered giggles trailing at his heels. He slammed the door to his room and locked it. And he stayed there all evening. A not so subtle imperative seized his thoughts: *Somebody's got to kill the creature.* It was easy to put aside the silly tauntings of Marcie, Sara Beth, and Timmy, and with some mental effort, he could look beyond the consistent manner in which adults discredited his story. But a more important fact remained: Somewhere in the vast mangrove swamp a creature slept in its lair, a creature unlike any he had ever seen, any he had ever imagined. Blood Wings.

The name caught in his mental filter; it breathed a life of its own. Blood Wings. Monolithic darkness. An ancient predatory intent. Something viciously opposed to mankind. And boykind. It had taken his best friend. Best friend. The words gained strength, building in his thoughts until they crystallized, set off in epic contrast. Best friend. Blood Wings.

Somebody's got to kill it.

But who?

Wade tried to sleep. No luck. Toward dawn, he slipped out his bedroom window; he battered himself with questions as he moved through the mobile home park, bracing himself against the cool, night air: Where did the creature come from: Would it attack Orchid Springs? Who could kill it?

The latter question cut a cold circle around his heart.

Who would be capable of such a feat?

Visions of the sheriff's deputies awkwardly climbing among the mangrove branches gave him little hope that the "authorities" were equipped to handle such a creature—robbers and drug dealers, but not a monster escaped from the darkest cell of the swamp.

The Army? The Marines? The Air Force?

The boy's thoughts toyed with images of military might directed at the winged thing. But would they be able to *find* it? To track down and kill Blood Wings, someone would have to know the swamp as well as they knew their face in the mirror. Someone would have to be tough and mean and somehow unafraid of the most horrible creature imaginable.

Wade raced over the bridge into the refuge; he raced through a torn curtain of mist and continued running as fast as his tired body would allow. Hash's cabin finally in view, he slowed. A muted light seeped out the front door. He could see the old pirate sitting at his small table, slumped over, a bottle near one hand.

Sneaking forward as quietly as possible, the boy reached the doorway and peered in. Ibo was watching TV and acknowledged his presence through a series of guttural sounds as if he were merely clearing his throat.

"People who creep up like that can get their throats cut."

Wade froze.

Hash raised his hand.

"I take it you didn't think I'd hear you," he continued. "Long as I'm not drunk enough to pass out, I can hear ever damn noise in this fuckin' swamp—ever one."

"I-I'm sorry," Wade muttered. "I thought, you know, you was alseep or somethin' and I was tryin' not to wake you up. I'm real sorry."

"Donchoo sleep at all, kid? Shitfire, only old men with nightmares for lovers are up this time uh night."

"Nightmares for lovers? What's that mean?"

"Means if I had a woman I could get myself fucked to sleep. As it is, hell . . . the cold hand of the night grabs hold uh me, tries its damndest to strangle me dead."

Wade's face appeared to register that he understood. "It's got hold of me, too."

"Well, hell, then, come on in and sit down. But I got to tell ya, I'm pissed off royally at you for talkin' to a damn newspaper reporter. You got any idea how many honyocks are gonna come out here, their heads up their asses, lookin' for ole Blood Wings?"

"I thought you didn't believe Blood Wings was real."

Hash rubbed at his bald head and attempted to pour some rum into a plastic cup, but found that the bottle

151

was empty.

"Shitfire."

He drained the final drops from the bottle and then peered into it as if it were a telescope.

"Dudn't matter if I do or don't—all manner of crazies gonna come outta the woodwork because of that story. Your doin's. Hope you're satisfied."

"I had to. I had to tell somebody else—somebody . . . somebody's got to kill the creature. Gillie was my friend. It's for Gillie—that's why I told."

"He's a boy that had trouble written all over him," Hash countered. "He'd uh gotten you in ever kind uh mess possible—you should feel lucky he ain't around to lead you slap fast into jail."

"He could take care of himself."

Hash chuckled softly. Then, leaning forward, those shark eyes throwing off sparks like a metal grinder, he said, "That so? Sounds to me like he couldn't take care of ole Blood Wings. Got his little smartass self killed. And so will you if you don't drop this whole fuckin' business. Stop spreadin' stories and talkin' to reporters. And stay the hell away from Pelican Pond."

"I can go where I want to," Wade challenged. "I can take care of myself."

"Smartass, ain'tcha? Just like Gillie. Whatchoo want comin' out here in the middle of the night anyway? Oughtta take my good alligator belt and whip your pink puppy ass till it yelps. Christ, I bet you give your mama gray hairs."

Wade took a deep breath.

Why am *I here?*

He hesitated several heartbeats. Ibo whistled low, but remained enraptured by the TV.

"I want you to track down Blood Wings and kill it. Those deputies . . . they don't know the swamp well enough, and you do. And maybe you could kill it because

152

I don't think nobody else can, 'cept maybe the Army or somebody with big ole heavy guns and stuff."

The boy paused, then added, "Would you do it? I'd help you. Would you kill Blood Wings?"

Hash rocked back and cupped his hands behind his head. He looked pleased.

"Wouldn't hurt to talk about it. Do me a favor first. Scattle over to my ice box—there's a liquor cabinet next to it—I'm done fresh out of rum. Bring me a bottle and we'll chew on this business, see if it's worth swallowing."

Spirits renewed, Wade sought out the rum. A full bottle in his hand, he had started back when the ice box thrummed and grumbled; his eyes grazed it, then locked onto something leaning against the wall beyond it.

An axe handle.

Nearly dropping the bottle, he stared at the handle; his mouth flooded with saliva.

"Can'tchoo find the damn bottle?"

He barely heard Hash. He stepped forward and saw the handle more clearly, saw the butcher knife lashed to one end of it, and crammed down between the ice box and the wall, tucked near the knife blade, was a baseball cap.

Gillie Roth's.

Fingers burning, Wade picked up the cap.

Behind him, heavy shuffling; a voice cleared itself.

"I asked you to fetch me rum—not stick your damn nose into things you got no business knowin' about."

Wade couldn't swallow all the saliva his mouth was secreting; he coughed, and a tear pricked at the corner of one eye, stinging like a thorn. He faced Hash. The cap trembled in the boy's hand.

"Why?" he stammered. "You found Gillie's cap and his spear . . . and you didn't. . . ."

"Didn't tell the cops? Shit, no. Look, there's no point in gettin' them involved. You want that creature killed? Then you got to do things my way."

Wade searched the man's face. "You lied to me. You told me what I saw wasn't real. Gillie's cap and his spear. You found 'em at Pelican Pond, didn't you?"

"So what if I did? God damn it, kid, I'm tryin' to tell you—you put crazies on the trail and you'll never get within miles of that creature."

Wade stood, silently swaying, wanting to be angry with Hash, wanting to slug him, and yet so confused he was willing to grasp at what seemed the best hope of vindicating Gillie's death.

"You believe it's out there . . . Blood Wings . . . it's real and it's out there."

Hash took the bottle of rum from him, opened it, and drank several long swallowfuls. He stared off to one side.

"I never used to, but, yeah, I do now. Blood Wings . . . it's out there somewhere."

The boy saw an involuntary shudder ripple across the man's shoulders.

Chapter Nine

1

"If you'll look straight at the camera, Mr. Bradshaw, the national broadcast will be coming to us live in about sixty seconds."

The black technician from a local Miami station steadied the skiff; Bradshaw, beaming proudly, tried to stand as still as possible in the anchored boat. For the "live" shot, the camera crew had selected a secluded spot along the slough, where the lush backdrop of mangrove trees framed the nervous man.

"Can you believe this?" said Bradshaw, dabbing at his cheeks and forehead, "I'm sweating like a—"

He caught himself in time; the black technician glared momentarily, then returned to business.

Bradshaw continued babbling.

"Never realized one TV spot took so many folks to put on, but, hey, you know, I'm getting used to all this media business. Yes, indeed . . . you see, Orchid Springs has been crawling this past week with reporters. And the Cable News Network, why, they've been doing daily updates. My telephone's hardly ever silent; fact is, yesterday the Bell folks installed one of those 800

155

numbers, you know, toll free, so's folks from all over the country, hell, all over the world, can call and ask about our creature. My oldest daughter, Marcie, I got her and a couple of other young women to work the phone. Exciting . . . damn, this is all exciting."

"Thirty seconds," said the technician, obviously disinterested in Bradshaw's utterings.

"The folks from the Geraldo Rivera show called—Donahue's probably next, you know, and of course, all those sleazy news magazines you buy at the grocery store—yeah, all of 'em goin' pig shit over Blood Wings—oh, hey, did my microphone pick up that? Damn, I'm sorry."

"No transmission yet," said the technician.

The main camera, anchored on shore, had a red light which winked twice. Bradshaw saw it and reflexively held up two bumper stickers.

"Can you get a good shot of these?"

The first one read: COME SEE BLOOD WINGS: YOU'LL GET CARRIED AWAY; the second one: BLOOD WINGS: NOT JUST ANOTHER BAT.

"Counting down from ten. Let's keep the boat steady. natural smile, Mr. Bradshaw."

Grinning a mouthful of teeth, Bradshaw heard a buzzing in the miniscule receiver behind his ear, then the pleasant, flowing broadcast news voice of a woman.

"Last week the tiny retirement settlement of Orchid Springs, Florida had its placid routine interrupted by reports of a giant, batlike creature in the nearby swamp. Orchid Springs is forty miles southwest of Miami and virtually borders the Everglades. With us live this morning is Mr. C.M. Bradshaw, a real estate developer and mayor of Orchid Springs. Good morning, Mr. Bradshaw."

"Good morning. Good morning, America. It's a beautiful day in Orchid Springs. Wish you were here."

156

The newswoman laughed.

"Tell me, has Orchid Springs changed much since the reports of the bizarre creature?"

"Yes, ma'am, it certainly has . . . and yet our settlement will never let all the attention upset its charm and easygoing pace. Orchid Springs is a delightful retirement area. We have several new condos and many more planned. But we'll monitor our growth closely. We wouldn't dare interfere with the natural splendor of the area."

"Mr. Bradshaw, just over your shoulder there is what appears to be part of a swamp. Could you describe the surroundings and tell us if the sighting of the creature occurred near there?"

Wheeling around so quickly that he almost lost his balance, Bradshaw gestured as the camera angled to a broad sweep across the tops of the mangroves.

"Yes, ma'am, the creature has been seen right close by, and all this, all these trees and this slough are connected to a great big ole mangrove swamp, thousands of years old—places in it no man has ever seen. Fact is—"

"Mr. Bradshaw, excuse me . . . Mr. Bradshaw, let me interrupt to ask you about the name Blood Wings— where does that come from and just what kind of creature do you believe is behind these reports?"

"I don't mind interruptions. Folks say I talk too much as it is. You ask about the name, well, we believe there's maybe an Indian source for it—maybe from the Seminole or some other tribe—and we've had state naturalists and other experts study the sketch we have of the creature; and to a man, they can't say for certain what it is—something remarkable—maybe prehistoric. Could have been living in the swamp for centuries as far as they know."

"Then you're saying that the experts truly believe Blood Wings exists?"

"Well, ma'am, of course some don't, but folks who know the swamp like the back of their hand think there's something out there."

"The boy who reported sighting the creature maintained that it attacked and carried off his friend. Can you substantiate that? And do you feel that the citizens of Orchid Springs are in danger?"

Bradshaw's face flushed. "No, no, no. No danger. No danger whatsoever. The first report contained, understandably, some exaggeration. But I can assure you that no evidence exists to suggest the creature is a killer or poses a real threat to Orchid Springs. On the contrary, we see Blood Wings in the category of a Loch Ness monster or something like that—a mysterious thing, but not something vicious. Everyone who comes around our jewel of a community is perfectly safe. There's an opportunity here maybe to view a natural wonder and to see our beautiful retirement properties."

At that moment, Bradshaw's receiver twisted free; he could not hear the woman thanking him and turning to other news. As a result, he held up the bumper stickers and said, "We want to invite everybody this coming weekend to something we're calling 'Blood Wings Days'— fun and free food and lots of memorabilia—and we'll be having an open house for our condo units, so head on south of Homestead on Highway 1 and—"

The black technician was delivering a throat-cutting gesture.

"End of spot. End of spot," he exclaimed.

"Oh, I got ya. Phew, man, that was exciting. How many million people you suppose saw this?"

Shaking his head, the technician began helping the camera crew to gather up their equipment.

"How did I look, Holly?"

"Sweaty. Nervous and sweaty."

"Was it that obvious? Damn. They made me stand in that skiff. I nearly fell on my ass. But you could see the bumper stickers, couldn't you?"

"Clear as day. And you sneaked in those plugs for your condos like a pro."

Bradshaw beamed. "Got to take advantage of this, Holly. Got to milk it. It's improved your business, hasn't it? Store and bar both, I assume."

"That it has." She gestured at the dozen or so morning customers and added, "I've got Wimp working day shift, and I've hired a new person for evenings."

"On the map," Bradshaw chirped. "Orchid Springs is on the map. Say, is that Coral Gables distributor gonna be able to deliver what we want on the buttons, stickers, and T-shirts?"

Holly raised a meaty palm. "Got the goodies hot off the press. Check these out. You can help me display them."

"O-o-o-h, this is fabulous," he exclaimed, unfolding a canary-yellow T-shirt replete with a huge and horrific bat creature, black as night, its fangs dripping blood. Beneath the creature, emblazoned in fiery red letters, were the words "Blood Wings: The REAL Batman."

"Quality airbrushing," said Holly. "There's one here somewhere that has Orchid Springs lettered on it and has a bat up in one corner."

"Fabulous stuff. Say, you don't think the creature looks too menacing, do you? I don't want to scare folks away. Blood Wings should be like that Loch Ness critter, you know."

As they set up a display of the colorful items, Holly chuckled. "Where did you come up with that nonsense about an Indian origin for the name? The Seminole never talk about big bats, do they?"

"Had to think fast. Who the hell knows where the name came from. Wade said it was something Hash made up."

"Drunk or sober?"

Bradshaw laughed. "Hard to say."

"The only thing I regret about all of this," said Holly, "is that Wade seems so serious. Anita has taken him to see a doctor, and the boy still insists he saw something attack Gillie—and, you know, years ago, when Houston was just a boy, he ranted and carried on about something attacking his dad."

"The man drowned is what I heard."

"The official cause of death was unknown—no body was ever recovered. My Roy used to take Houston back to the area where Gus Parker disappeared and . . . oh, no point in dredging up bad memories."

"Holly—hey, there's no creature—not like this one anyway." He pointed at the T-shirt. "Sure, the boy saw something, probably a big bird, and it probably scared him; but I think this whole story's designed to cover for his friend running away."

There was doubt in the woman's expression. "It has me baffled. It really does," she said.

"Hey, would I build up this carnival business if I knew there was some kind of dangerous creature that could threaten tourists as well as the citizens of Orchid Springs?"

"Claude Michael Bradshaw, I believe you would try to entice folks to Orchid Springs even if you knew that Jack the Ripper was living in one of your condos and the Boston Strangler in another."

Bradshaw winced. "No, no, Holly. You got me all wrong."

"Just be careful, or Geraldo will see right through you."

They laughed.

And a fresh handful of tourists trundled into the store.

3

"What's in it?" asked Houston, contorting his mouth as the liquid pinched the back of his tongue.

"Wick claims it's a jazzed-up Bloody Mary," said Anita, her admiring gaze moving slowly over the man's shadow-strewn face. "It was Holly's idea to call it a Blood Wings—good for tourism, she says."

I've fallen in love with this man.

And it was so, so easy.

"Has too much pepper or tabasco sauce in it. Holly should stick to her Headhunters—now that's a good drink."

"I'm not complaining these days," said Anita. "Business has been good. And I've gotten lots more tips."

She jingled her apron pocket and smiled her most seductive smile, only to notice that Houston seemed preoccupied.

"It's closing time," she followed. "I could use an escort home. You look tired. Need a backrub? I specialize in them."

He smiled weakly. "You hear those guys earlier in here shooting off their mouths about going into the swamp after the creature? They have no idea what they're up to. On my runs today, I saw three different boats deep in the mangroves, and I'd bet tonight's take that all three will get lost. I hope to God they don't start any fires—dry, dry summer so far—those hummocks could burn for weeks given the slightest spark."

"This creature uproar has upset you, hasn't it?"

"Yeah. Yeah, you could say that."

161

"Want to talk about it?"

"Not really." He took another drink of the Blood Wings and bit his tongue.

"You don't have to finish it." She laughed. "But I would like for you to talk to me about what's bothering you. I'm a good listener."

Her persistence earned a smile; and when Wick sounded last call and no one responded, she took Houston by the hand, and they wended their way from the bar out into the night and through the shadows to her trailer.

At the door Houston hesitated.

She touched his cheek reassuringly. "Would you rather go to your trailer? Does it make you uncomfortable that Wade saw us together here?"

He shook his head. "No. No, this is fine."

She unlocked the door. Marcie, doubling as phone operator for her father and babysitter for Anita's boys, had put Timmy and Wade to bed and gone home. The cramped living room seemed emptier than usual.

They sat on the couch—Houston had repaired it—and though Anita was feeling a rush of physical need for the man beside her, she recognized he was not in the mood.

"Sorry I'm not myself this evening," he murmured.

She rubbed his wrist and forearm. "I've been struggling some, too, what with Wade's problem. But I took him to a psychiatrist who assured me that he will get over this creature thing. The psychiatrist called it an 'extraordinary hallucination,' perhaps brought on by—"

"It wasn't," said Houston.

She frowned. Searching his expression, she said, "Wasn't?"

For a few seconds, he buried his face in his hands.

"Houston, what is it?" She reached for him. But he caught her hand and squeezed it to indicate he was ready to talk.

"Do you know how I got the name Houston?"

"No, but I'd like to."

"My dad . . . when my mom was carrying me, well, he had this—what he thought was going to be a great job opportunity. He specialized in helping companies locate potential oil fields, and this big operation headquartered in Houston, Texas, well, they offered him a lot of money to go there. He thought it would be fat city. I was born there."

He paused as if to piece together implications of the narrative he hadn't considered.

"The job went bust. Lots of hard times for my dad. Mom, too."

Houston looked away, but Anita could see tears welling in his eyes.

"I loved that man," he continued, choking slightly on the words. "God, I thought he was the whole world. I can't talk about him without—"

Anita pressed herself against his shoulder. "He must have been something special," she whispered.

"Yeah. Yeah, he was. To me, he was. Not by the world's standards, of course. Never made much money. Somehow we ended up in Orchid Springs. Mom hated this place. Dad loved it, and I loved it because he did. He scratched out a living doing various jobs. Nothing solid. He was happiest when he was out in that mangrove swamp. And he had one particular passion."

"What was it?"

Houston settled back and let her slide into his arms. "A white alligator."

"Like the one at the refuge?"

"Yeah . . . but he wanted to catch a big one, and so every chance he got, we'd load into a skiff and lose ourselves miles and miles into the swamp. There was something about a white gator . . . something . . . I don't know how to describe it."

"You mean, like something mystical?"

"Yeah. Mystical. It was like he was . . . incomplete without it . . . like his life would never have any real meaning unless he caught one of those gators—and they're pretty rare. I couldn't ever quite understand his feelings about them, but I tried to. He never caught one."

For several moments neither spoke. Anita sensed there was much that had been left unsaid.

"When I was telling you about Wade and what the psychiatrist explained, you said, 'It wasn't.' Does that have anything to do with your dad?"

He gently pulled away from her, leaned forward and clasped his hands together. "Anita, Wade saw something out there. It wasn't what the psychiatrist said. It's real."

"Real? The creature he sketched for the paper? You can't mean that!"

"I do."

"But there can't possibly be something like that—a giant bat, a man's face. And you believe this—this Blood Wings really attacked Gillie Roth and . . . ? You're not serious, are you?"

"Yes. Years ago, it killed my dad."

Anita was shaking her head; disbelief buffeted her like a strong wind.

"I saw it happen." And then he began the narrative of a warm summer morning. "I was about Wade's age . . ."

Midway through the account he stopped.

"I can't avoid reliving it . . . it hurts too much to. . . ."

"You don't need to finish. I understand."

"But can you? I mean, I feel that my life . . . so much of me died with him. I can't have a future, *we* can't have a future, until I resolve this. Every day is hell; I manage to survive but not without help, and it's bringing me down."

"I know about the drugs," she said.

164

"I guess you think I'm weak."

"No. I'm trying to understand."

"Funny thing is, I really feel sorry for Wade. No one believed me back then. People don't believe him now. All this bullshit publicity and hype . . . people think this is a big joke. For Wade it's not, I assure you."

"I wish you'd talk to him. Tell him . . . tell him about your dad. It could help him deal with what's happened."

"I feel bad vibes around him. Your son hates my guts, in case you haven't noticed."

"Maybe if you talked. . . ."

"Yeah. But for me, nothing will make a difference except going after Blood Wings. Nothing will be right in my life until I've gone after it . . . until it's dead."

Anita drew closer again, kissed his cheek and attempted to hold him.

He flashed a weak smile. "Just thinking about it scares me," he said, "scares the living hell out of me."

4

Hash's promise.

As Wade sleepwalked from one day to the next, largely staying away from the carnival atmosphere near Holly's store and bar, he thought of Hash.

"As soon as the crazies clear out of the area, I'll hunt down ole Blood Wings. You got Hash's word on it."

The boy had placed so much trust in the man—in his words. Neither the deputies nor the psychiatrist had been able to extract as much trust from him. Hash was different. He knew the swamp. He gave his word.

It was hard being patient, for the boy felt the presence of Gillie every day, a presence that seemed secretly to insist that Blood Wings be destroyed.

Around noon, Wade sought out the sun-drenched,

green-surfaced asphalt of the tennis courts. A breeze toyed with the ragged line of tarp at the top of one of the nets; the flapping was a lonely sound, a somewhat frightening sound. It reminded him of wings.

Huddled down against the backboard, Timmy and Sara Beth never saw him coming; he almost turned and left because he wanted to be alone. But he continued walking. When Timmy looked up, he jostled Sara Beth, who appeared to be reading a newspaper.

"It's Wade," the small boy exclaimed.

Sara Beth jammed the paper out of sight; the two of them were sitting, leaning against the backboard.

"Hey, I'm not a friggin' monster," said Wade. He sauntered up and plopped down beside them.

"Wade, Sara Beth says the creature's gonna come after you next because it got Gillie and you're Gillie's friend and so you're a goner."

The breathless words flew into Wade, provoking him to glare at the sweaty girl. "Sara Beth's an airhead and a hippo."

"Oh, you can call me names, but what I said's true. It says so right here."

She uncrumpled her newspaper—which turned out to be a sleazy tabloid—and pressed the headline story into his face.

BLOOD-THIRSTY CREATURE TERRORIZES SOUTH FLORIDA RETIREMENT AREA

And a related story—including a picture of Wade, declared,

"Boy Fears He's Next Victim of 'Blood Wings'"

"It's you," said Timmy, pointing a finger tentatively at the photo.

"I know it's me, nerdbrain. Let me see this."

He snatched the paper from the girl and began to read. He could hear the hot and heavy breathing of the other two and had to scoot a few feet away in order to concentrate upon the words.

"Don't be lookin' over my friggin' shoulder."

Then Sara Beth whispered to Timmy, "He's nervous because Blood Wings could swoop down and get him any second."

Timmy nodded, eyeballing the sky for the moment.

"Shut up, Sara Beth. Hippo, hippo nerd. I wanna read this."

But a few seconds into the story he exclaimed, "I never said that!"

Timmy and Sara Beth scrambled closer.

"Listen to what it says here: 'Wade Martin, who witnessed the creature attack his friend, fears his every waking hour. "Blood Wings talked into my mind and told me, 'You're next!'"'"

"Did he really?" asked Timmy.

"Course not—this is plain ole bullshit. They're making this up. Everybody's tryin' to make me sound like I'm nutso or something."

"Are you pretty scared?" asked Sara Beth.

"No, but I'm friggin' tired of people twistin' what I've said and tellin' me I didn't see what I saw and sellin' bumper stickers and T-shirts with that creature on 'em."

"Mom said I might could have a Blood Wings T-shirt," Timmy muttered.

"No, you can't!"

"Why not? You're not the boss uh me. Mom is."

"I'm gonna go eat lunch. You two are seriously afflicted with nerdness."

"I bet I know who would believe you."

Sara Beth's comment caused him to hesitate.

"So do I—Hash believes me, and he promised me he'd kill that creature."

"Miss Freda would believe you, too."

Wade hated to admit it, but it suddenly occurred to him that she could be right. Besides Hash, who could appreciate the wonders and mysteries of the swamp? Miss Freda. Yes. But what boy could be brave enough to seek her out? Hadn't Gillie warned of her strangeness?

"She's an old crazy woman," said Wade, as if that would close the matter.

"Are you scared of her?" Sara Beth teased.

"Course I'm not. Shut your fat mouth. I'm going home. So long, nerds. The sun's baked your brains."

He left, though he could hear a few trailing catcalls from Sara Beth, echoed, in turn, by Timmy.

"Dumb little farts," Wade whispered to himself; but dark images of the woman reverently and affectionately called Miss Freda flooded his thoughts.

What does she know about Blood Wings?

He realized, thankfully, that there was no need to find out. Hash was on his side. Hash knew enough. Hash had given his word.

Once home, Wade's mother fixed him a tuna sandwich and a glass of milk. She sat down at the kitchen table with him and looked warmly into his eyes.

"You feeling any better these days?"

He shrugged. "I guess, maybe . . . yeah, some better."

"No bad dreams."

He shook his head.

She paused to sip at some iced tea. She seemed to want to talk; she and Wade had patched up things between them—the rift over Houston—in fact, Wade appreciated the way in which she had kept reporters and curiosity seekers away from him.

"Lot of excitement in Orchid Springs these days. Houston says his business is booming like it never has before."

She paused again before continuing with caution.

"You know . . . Houston tells me he believes you . . . about the creature. He'd like to talk to you about it, and I wish you would, because I think it would help you."

"Not talking to him," said Wade. "Not never."

"You're not being fair. Houston and I . . . we care about each other, and he cares about you and Timmy."

The boy grew sullen.

She decided not to press the issue. "You don't have to talk to Houston. Not if you really don't want to. But there's someone else who would like to see you."

"Another reporter kind of person?"

"No. No, Mrs. Schreck called about an hour ago. She's invited you over at tea time for a visit."

Wade slowly put down his sandwich. "Miss Freda wants *me* to come to her house?" His voice had a lining of surprise and fear.

"I told her you probably would. I can call her back . . . or, if you want me to, I suppose I could go with you."

He didn't answer at first.

But he could not imagine himself entering that white house on the edge of the swamp.

5

At five minutes to four, Wade crossed the walkway to that house. He stepped onto the porch and took a deep breath, still undecided as to whether he would go through with the adventure. His heart beat so loudly he was convinced someone would hear it.

I wish Gillie could be here.

He reasoned that Gillie would not be afraid to enter the abode of the strange woman; he could almost hear his friend chiding him: "You got no guts."

"I do so," said Wade.

But why had he come? he asked himself. To prove he had courage? No. No, there was something more—some intuitive shove which had propelled him down that walkway and up to that screen door, dressed in his only Sunday outfit, shoes freshly polished, hair combed for the first time since school ended.

He pressed the doorbell.

Gillie would have been proud.

He waited, staring through the screen into a deeply shadowed foyer, and he continued staring until he realized, with a sudden heart-jumping start, that a pair of eyes had locked onto his.

And then the door swung open.

Wade felt a hard fist slam against his bladder, but the horrid spectre of pissing in his pants kept him from falling prey to one of a boy's most embarrassing scenarios.

The dark-skinned, black-haired woman nodded for him to enter. She had scars on her arms, and he found himself straining not to look at her but rather to tiptoe into the shadows.

"Mary, is that our young sport?"

The voice sounded pleasant enough, touched by an unfamiliar accent—British?—the boy knew it must be Miss Freda. *Sport?* Gillie had called him that, and he had disliked it; but at that moment he would have given nearly anything to hear Gillie's voice.

Mary made some perfunctory sound, more a grunt than an actual word, then pointed him to go to his left. His hands sweated. The bare-planked wooden floor creaked in protest to each step. He passed into a cool, slightly less dark room; an overhead fan soughed, and green plants of a dozen varieties crowded near him. Where the room opened into another and somewhat larger room, a curious object stood beneath a white, latticed archway.

Wade stopped in his tracks.

"Geez, oh damn," he murmured very softly.

The bottom half of a carved tree trunk sentried the

170

archway; from the core of that trunk, an old man's face was struggling to emerge. Bearded, eyes closed, the stunningly realistic face appeared on the verge of waking at any instant. The boy hurried on past it, lest those eyes open, provoking a scream.

In the next room, a jungle of green plants greeted him, and behind a silk screen painted garishly with depictions of kangaroos and turtles sat Miss Freda. She was seated on a high-backed, white wicker chair. To Wade, it looked like a throne.

"This must be young Master Wade. Do come in and be seated."

"Hello," he said.

"Oh, but first, please acknowledge Reginald—or he'll be quite miffed." She pointed a bony finger into a far corner.

Wade turned, then brightened.

"Hey, it's a kangaroo, a stuffed kangaroo."

"Ruthie's mate," said the woman. "You're acquainted with our Ruthie, I trust."

"Yes, ma'am." He walked over and petted the kangaroo's nose. "He looks pretty real—just like he could start hopping around."

"Goodness, I hope he won't, though it would warm my heart to see the life in him again."

This maybe's not gonna be so bad, Wade thought as he sat down, and almost immediately Mary brought a silver tea service and placed it on a small table between them.

Miss Freda smiled across at him, and his first impression of her kaleidoscoped into place: She seemed a contradictory mixture of goddess and grandmother. She had brilliantly white hair and a tanned face, skin like fine leather, black eyes, and a mouth that could turn cruel, he guessed, but chose not to for the moment. She wore a leather suit, bone white, and white thongs, and around her neck she wore a necklace of bone and rock and jewels

171

and beads. She looked relaxed, regal; her demeanor only hinted at a potential to be threatening.

Gillie was dead wrong.

Miss Freda raised her eyebrows. "Are you a ringer?" she asked.

Wade frowned. He recognized that the accent was definitely British.

"You're certainly not a jillaroo," she continued. "You see, in Australia, a ringer is a cowboy; a jillaroo is a cowgirl. Are you rough 'n tough?"

"Yes, ma'am, I guess so."

"Good. You'll need to be."

Wade felt an ice-cold rock drop into the pit of his stomach, but when the woman followed with a smile, he felt better.

"Quite a bloomin' good show at Holly's these days—a regular traveling wingding," she said, pouring him a cup of tea. "There's cream and sugar to your liking. And here are biscuits—quite good ones actually."

Please God, don't let me spill this, thought the boy, his fingers having transformed into dead fish. But he managed his cup of tea satisfactorily—even thought it tasted good—and munched on one of the hard biscuits, and when Miss Freda asked him to tell her about his family, he lost some of his jitters and launched into an overview of his mom and Timmy, alluding once to his dad—and to his dad's threat.

Miss Freda gave him a sympathetic ear; she did not ask about Blood Wings. Wasn't she interested?

Tea completed, the woman jingled a tiny bell, and Mary slipped from the shadows and removed the ornate tray.

"Now," said the woman, "shall we play at some games. All young sports enjoy games, am I correct?"

Wade shrugged and nodded at the same time.

"Mary, the carroms, please." She smiled her enigmatic

172

smile at the boy. "Have you ever played carroms?"

"No, ma'am. Are we really gonna play games?" He felt a wave of delight and surprise.

"Yes, unless you'd prefer not to. Myself, I've always loved games. It's the little girl in me. Mary does not share my affinity; she would prefer to paint in her leisure time."

So they played.

The boy and the mysterious woman.

But the boy was surprised to find that Miss Freda easily bested him at carroms—a game in which plastic rings were thumped into pockets rather like pool. Thumping the "shooter" ring hurt his finger, yet he didn't let on, for the woman shot tirelessly and accurately, never showing signs that her finger caused her any pain whatsoever.

Wade felt embarrassed.

"Geez, you're real good at this."

"Just takes practice," she said. "You do well for a beginner."

They played half a dozen games, the harsh clicking of ring against ring the only sound other than an occasional piece of advice from Miss Freda—"Here's a bank shot" or "Don't overlook this combination"—and sometimes the advice led to his successfully making a shot.

"Enough of carroms," she eventually exclaimed. "What say to a round or two of darts?"

"Sure. Yeah," said Wade, figuring he would fare much better away from the carrom board. "I know how to play darts. I'm pretty good at it."

And so was Miss Freda. Very good, in fact.

"In pubs throughout Australia, this is a popular sport," she explained as Mary removed a wall hanging to reveal a dart board.

The boy watched in awe as Miss Freda flicked dart after dart into the pie-shaped twenty-point slot or into the

173

twenty-five-point inner ring.

"It's all in the wrist," she told him, and after being thoroughly trounced several rounds, he started to get the hang of her method.

Geez, this has been fun.

The child in Miss Freda giggled and applauded and cheered. And Wade wondered how she had ever gotten a reputation as a people hater and much-to-be-feared woman.

"Now, then," Miss Freda announced after a score of rounds, "shall we retire to the artifact room?"

Having no idea what she was referring to, Wade nodded.

She led him into a long, rectangular room lined on all four sides with cedar paneling, and each wall was nearly obliterated by paintings and photographs and curious objects. There was even a slab of rock attached to one wall, and on the rock there appeared a perfect outline in white dust of two handprints.

"My treasures," she said.

And in her voice the boy heard the little girl in her retreat.

His eyes grazed over the paintings, which pulled him into them through their magnetism: colorful portraits of kangaroos, wallabies and emus.

"Mary painted these. Aren't they stunning?"

"Yeah, super neat."

"And these are artifacts from the aborigines, the most sacred, most beautiful people on earth."

For the next several minutes she offered him an informative lecture on bark masks, stone axes, bull-roarers, food bowls, knives, boomerangs, and a battle club known as a *nulla-nulla.*

"Wow! What is this one?"

"A *wirrie.*"

He was admiring a sharply pointed stick in a glass case;

a purple stain covered most of the object from the tip down.

"It's a particular kind of stick," Miss Freda explained, "that is left in a dead body to absorb poison. You are looking at an especially potent *wirrie*—a most dangerous and deadly object."

Ice crystals of fear suddenly coated the boy's throat.

He had heard more than enough about the *wirrie* and moved on to a handsome collage of black and white photos.

"There's you," he exclaimed, seeing one in which a younger Miss Freda was standing among a group of black-skinned men, many of whom had painted white circles and dots and other designs on their mostly naked bodies.

"Members of the Gagadju tribe. And this most handsome fellow in the photo is Maxwell Schreck, my late husband—one of the greatest anthropologists the world has ever known—and an expert on Australian aboriginals. Unfortunately, the scholarly realm failed to appreciate his brilliant, though unorthodox, theories."

The man in the photo, dark mustache neatly trimed, possessed a lean, athletic body and intelligent, piercing eyes.

"Did he ever get scared of these people?" Wade asked timidly.

"Oh, dear me, no. Maxwell learned from the aboriginals that overcoming fear is the most important capacity a human being can acquire. To be whole and dauntless in the face of fear, men must have women, and women must have men—one is incomplete without the other. This is the lesson of the frogs."

Wade giggled nervously. "Lesson of the frogs?"

"Yes, of course. I'm quite certain you've noticed that when you walk near the slough, frogs will jump into the water far ahead of your advance, as if they were frightened of you. Do you know why they are so skittish?"

"'Cause, maybe, they don't wanna be stepped on."

"Perhaps. The aboriginals tell a story that explains it another way. Would you like to hear it?"

"Sure."

"The story begins when upon a day all the male frogs grew dissatisfied with their wives and other female frogs, and so they went off to live by themselves. Not one of them felt he needed a female as a companion. So it happened that one night they were preparing their dinner on the campfire when of a sudden they heard a voice calling from the darkness, requesting food. The frogs were not a little apprehensive and asked for the source of the voice to identify itself."

"Did it?" Wade interjected, his interest piqued.

"No, it would not. It insisted on being fed, explaining that later it would, indeed, reveal itself. The frogs complied, giving it some fish to eat. The voice then announced that it was tired and wanted to sleep nearby. Again, the frogs agreed to the request. But that night one of the frogs could not sleep because he could hear the unnerving snoring of the mysterious entity; promptly the frog got up and began to cry. 'Who are you? I must see who you are.' To this, the voice replied, 'You shall see me coming across the plain on the morrow.' And at the dawn, the frog could hear the voice moving away, but saw nothing."

Wade smiled as the mystery thickened.

Miss Freda continued.

"The next day the frog perched outside the campsite awaiting the appearance of the voice. But all he could see was a willy-willy—a whirlwind—spinning across the plain and finally circling the camp. From within the willy-willy issued forth the voice saying, 'Here I am again,' but the frog demanded to see the voice with his own two eyes, to which the voice replied, 'You shall see me on the morrow night.' By the by, all the frogs had moved to a riverbank, and there the bravest of them—the one who had challenged the voice—sat upon a log, watching for the voice; and certain it did come, this time as a quite massive willy-willy, a hurricane which blew destructively along the riverbank. From a terrific blast of wind, a voice began, 'I am—' but even the bravest frog had grown so frightened that it jumped into the river, unable to face its fear."

Wade grinned. "And that's why frogs always jump in the water—yeah, a neat story," he said.

"Yes, and aboriginals teach that the fear experienced by the frogs came as a result of living alone. On occasion, my Maxwell would remind me of this legend to underscore his love and need for me."

The boy could sense the atmosphere in the room shift as the curious woman told of Maxwell Schreck's rejection by the scholarly establishment, of his humiliation and despair and bitterness, and of their move to Florida and the creation of the refuge.

"He loved this area and wanted to protect it—and he did—and despite the fact that this magnificent man no longer graces the earth, his legacy lives on—and so does the guardian of the swamp."

The tenor of Wade's visit darkened. He wanted to leave, but was afraid to say anything.

"Come with me into Mary's gallery," said Miss Freda.

The next room contained some of the strangest portraits Wade had ever seen. He noticed that in a far corner the dark, aboriginal Mary was seated before a canvas, but he could not see what she was painting.

"Maxwell's grand theory," said Miss Freda, "was that all of the horrific creatures present at the creation of the world, the so-called mythical beasts of the Dreamtime, were alive—yes, animated in a psychical dimension we as humans can experience only when those creatures wish

177

us to. His fellow scholars ridiculed him for such a theory. But Maxwell was correct. Here you see some of those beasts—Mary has captured them. See, the Myndie Snake, and there, the Devil-Dog, and there, the Whowie."

Wade was confused and speechless, feeling much like the frog of aboriginal legend ready to flee the mysterious voice.

Miss Freda looked into his eyes. "Aren't you curious as to why I asked you to my house?"

"Yes, ma'am," he murmured.

"I want you to sit down and tell me about the creature you saw out in the swamp. Tell me everything you can remember."

And so he did.

She listened, nodding from time to time, but at no point did she seem repulsed by the account or moved to sympathy toward the demise of Gillie.

When he had completed his story—a much-practiced narrative—she thanked him and said, "This creature—the one being called Blood Wings—is actually a Dreamtime beast known as a Garkain, a vindictive guardian of the mangrove swamps of Australia's northern shore. Half bat, half man, it lives alone. It smothers its victims before consuming them, and its victims, as you have discovered, continue to exist as restless, haunting spirits. And the Garkain emits a most, most disagreeable odor."

"Mr. Schreck brought one here from Australia?" asked the boy, trying desperately to understand.

"Brought two, in fact. Oh, not as cargo—not shipped to Orchid Springs as you would a kangaroo. The Garkain were transported in a most bizarre fashion, but that is of little concern at the moment. It would appear that the dry weather of the past several years has driven it closer to human settlement. There is extreme danger. Fires make the Garkain angry and vengeful."

"Hash promised me he would kill it," Wade suddenly exclaimed.

The boy did not like her smile.

"Mr. Hashler is a goomie, a down-and-out-drunk, whom I keep around merely because . . . because once I needed him and he did not turn away from me. But he poses no threat to the Garkain. There's only one way to destroy the creature, and no one except me and Mary possesses that knowledge."

"Why won't you go out and kill it before it kills somebody else? It killed Gillie, my best friend. Do you want it to live and keep on killin'?"

"It has killed in the past as well. Just ask Houston Parker."

"Houston?"

She motioned for him to follow her. "Shall we see what Mary is painting?"

He held back; she grasped his arm, and her strength surprised him. She ushered him around so that he looked squarely at the canvas.

The portrait seemed to leap out at him.

He clenched his fists. More than anything else he wanted to run.

"Is this the very image of Blood Wings?" she asked him.

The dark artist had rendered the creature in amazing detail; Wade could even smell some of its accompanying stench. His eyes watered; his nose ran.

"I have no compassion for mankind," said Miss Freda. "The world would be a more beautiful place if we could return to the Dreamtime."

She paused to allow a wisp of a smile to crease her lips.

"You may as well keep my secret to yourself," she said, "for I would never share it with the idiots who parade as journalists."

Boy and woman stared at each other.

He felt her hatred; it fell upon him like a heavy net.

"Now, good day, young sport," she exclaimed, brightening some. "Mary will see you to the door."

6

The weekend arrived in a whirlwind of activity. C.M. Bradshaw had orchestrated a promotion and celebration all in one: "Blood Wings Days." Tourists flocked to Holly's, where she sold memorabilia by the bushel. There were free soft drinks and hot dogs for anyone who toured the model condominium units; Bradshaw even hired someone to dress up in a bat-winged cape with "BW" in red letters across a shiny black, skindiver's suit. At the refuge, Houston Parker was taking as many loads of tourists as his copter would bear up under.

The whole scene depressed Wade.

He had to steal away.

At home he fixed himself a sandwich and a glass of Kool-Aid. His mom and Timmy were, no doubt, lost in the sea of balloons and buttons and music piped over a loudspeaker.

He finished only half the sandwich; it's hard for a boy to eat when there's a lot on his mind. In this case, his visit to Miss Freda's. He couldn't figure her out. The first part of his visit had been so much fun—carroms, darts, tea and biscuits—but something about her changed in the artifact room. A coldness, a bitterness, had set in. She appeared, more than anything else, to want revenge for the discrediting of her husband.

Hardest of all to figure: She seemed to want Blood Wings to continue killing.

It was more than a boy could wrangle with and not get dizzy and mentally lose his balance. And when he had asked his mom to explain the woman's erratic behavior, she had said, "Older people, especially when they're lonely, often become eccentric—they act strange, but mean no harm."

The words failed to satisfy him.

I'll go see Hash.

The old pirate would offer him some words of wisdom, he reasoned.

So he set out for the refuge, carefully skirting as much of the loud and garish celebration as possible. With the shell road beneath his feet and mangroves flanking him, he felt safely out of the reach of the frivolities. *They don't understand,* he told himself. They were treating Blood Wings like some cartoon character.

They might be real sorry someday.

Hash was not in his cabin; neither was Ibo. Disappointed, poised to leave, Wade heard someone exclaim, "Son-of-a-whore-bitch-dog!"

The boy smiled.

The gravel in that voice could belong to one man only. Wade found Hash loading supplies into a skiff from a small, dilapidated dock behind the cabin.

"Son-of-a-whore-bitch-dog!" echoed Ibo, in a perfect imitation of his master. The bird occupied its customary perch at the prow of the skiff.

"Hi, Ibo, how you been?"

"How you been? Pissant. Sumbitch," said the bird.

Hash was sucking two of his fingers. "Raked these mothers over a loose metal strip on the skiff. Sliced the shit out of 'em."

"You need a Band-Aid?"

"Oh, hell, no. I won't bleed long. I run outta blood in a snap and then start bleedin' rum."

Wade smiled weakly.

Hash cocked an eye his way. "Why ain't you at the doin's? I 'spect Holly's runnin' her fat ass off sellin' trinkets and all kinda shit, ain't she? You not interested in all that?"

"No."

"What the hell you been up to? I ain't seen you for a spell."

"I've been to visit Miss Freda."

Hash appeared to freeze in mid-motion. "You say, Miss Freda?"

"Yeah, she invited me for tea, and we played games and talked, but. . . ."

"But what?"

"She's pretty hard to figure."

"You got that right. Here, boy, I believe I'd like to hear what you two talked about."

He stopped his loading operation and fished a couple of deck chairs from the cabin, and they sat on the dock—Hash drinking rum; Wade sipped a soft drink—and watched the clouds shift and once or twice followed the line of Houston's copter passing over.

Wade told him everything that had happened and every one of the woman's remarks he could remember.

Leaning back, guzzling the rum, Hash chuckled. "A *goomie*, eh? Ole bitch. Well, she can think whatever of me the hell she pleases."

"Do you believe what she told me? Do you think she's crazy?"

"Yes on both counts. But she's flat out wrong about one thing." He paused to draw a response from the boy.

"What's that?"

"I can handle Blood Wings. If I set my mind to it—and stay away from the shit in this cup—I can do it."

Wade began to feel better than he had in days.

"I told her you could. I told her you could kill Blood Wings. But she said only she and that woman named Mary knew how Blood Wings could be killed."

"More 'n one way to skin uh cat is what I always say.

That right, Ibo, you ole bastard?"

"Skin uh cat you ole bastard," Ibo squawked, and Wade and Hash laughed.

"So does this mean you're goin' out this afternoon to kill it?" the boy asked eagerly, gesturing at the skiff.

"Got to track it down first, you know. Got to study its habits some. A fella can't head out there with his ass on fire and 'spect to bag a creature like Blood Wings, no sir."

"You goin' past Pelican Pond?"

"I'd say so. Silly ass weekend hunters have probably caused that creature to move deep into the mangroves. Should be some new hummocks what with this stretch of dry weather. When the fuck's it gonna rain again? This swamp is aching for a fire the way I been aching for a woman."

"Hey, wait," said Wade. "You're not takin' *this*, are you?" The boy pointed at a satchel from which protruded the necks of three bottles of Bicardi rum.

"Just something to steady my nerves. That ole swamp can come down hard on a man. Can steal his courage in the blink of an eye. Don't worry none about it."

"Okay," said the boy reluctantly.

Hash scanned the early afternoon sky. "Time to shove off. You ready, Ibo?"

"Sumbitch," rattled the parrot.

"Hash . . . could I go with you? Please. I could help you track Blood Wings. I could. I really could."

"Who-a-a-a, no. No, this is too damn dangerous goin' where I'm goin'. Sorry, kid. No can do."

His hopes deflated, Wade muttered, "Someday. You got to promise me someday I can go along."

"Sure, kid. Someday. I promise."

The boy helped him push away from the shore and gave him a good-bye salute.

Soon, Hash and Ibo were a dissolving speck on the great waterway of the swamp.

Chapter Ten

1

"Hello?"

Anita repeated herself several times and was about to hang up. There had been numerous crank calls lately from curiosity seekers and borderline personalities who, somehow, had gotten her number.

"Still got that sexy voice. Jesus."

She felt the sensation of hot water gushing through her.

"Dean?"

"Hey, you remember me. Helluva good sign."

"What do you want?" she snapped, noticing a catch in the rhythm of her question.

She heard a heavy, angry sigh.

"To make your life as miserable as possible, you sorry bitch."

She wanted to hang up, but there was something so venomously mesmerizing about Dean's voice—there always had been.

"You've accomplished that. You can't hurt me anymore."

"Don't be so damn certain."

"I have to go to work. I can't talk."

"Not asking you to talk. What you better do is listen."

There was an audible roar of hatred in his tone. She glanced into the living room where she could see Timmy watching television. Wade was back in his room.

They're safe, she reminded herself.

"Saw Wade's picture in a newspaper. Sounds like you've let that boy get some out of hand, telling wild damn stories. Well, it doesn't matter. That story made it a helluva lot easier to find you. Orchid Springs, Florida. Has a nice ring to it."

"Don't come here," she exclaimed.

And part of her wanted to add, "please;" part of her was willing to beg.

"Shut up! Shut your goddamn mouth!"

I don't have to listen to this.

I'm free of him . . . free of him.

"Soon as I scrape up some extra cash, I'll have to pay you and the boys a visit. But, the thing is, you'll never know exactly when. My surprise . . . my surprise."

The dial tone hissed like a poisonous snake ready to strike.

"Please don't come," she whispered as she placed the phone in its cradle.

2

"Why are you telling me all of this? It's between you and him. I don't think I should get involved."

They were at the bar; Anita was on her break, and she was reeling from the sting of Houston's response. She had told him the story of her marriage and profiled the menacing character of her former husband and his phone call.

"I'm not asking you to be a marriage counselor. I'm

asking you to help me protect the boys. Dean has threatened to come here, and I just know he'll try to take the boys, and I. . . ."

She fought the tears. Beyond her fear of Dean, there was the knife of disappointment wielded by Houston.

He looked away. Through gritted teeth, he said, "I can't handle this now. I can't make promises."

"I suppose you're going to claim it's the creature—the ghosts of the past are keeping you from being a man."

She knew she had hit below the belt, but she didn't care. There was too much of her own hurt and fear to deal with. It was a moment she had to seize.

"Can't you see what you've done?" she said. "You're using the death of your father as an excuse not to get on with your life, to wallow in self-pity. You blame everything on that creature you think is out in the swamp somewhere, but the only living thing that's at fault is *you*."

He turned once to look at her, but said nothing, though she desperately wanted him to defend himself. She hated his whipped dog expression, and she hated herself for continuing.

"Only one thing means anything to you—those little bags of gray powder you buy from Hash—I know about them. I kept denying to myself that you had a problem with it, but I was wrong. And I kept hoping we could have a solid relationship—not like I've had—but I was wrong there, too."

Visibly shaken, she tried to go back to work.

Houston left the bar.

The breezy, yet cloudless evening, replete with a star-filled sky, gave him no solace. Anita was right about everything. In the front pocket of his jeans he had just enough rapture for a partial hit. It would not kill the pain, only wound it.

Hash had not returned to his cabin.

And Houston wondered how to make it through the night.

3

"You better put away mom's Instamatic, or she'll give you a spankin' and not let you play Nintendo for a month."

"She dudn't know I have it," said Timmy, cradling the small camera to his chest.

Wade was watching an Atlanta Braves game on cable; they were losing, but he didn't mind. He was feeling good, anticipating the return of Hash from his scouting trip to locate Blood Wings.

"Just be careful so you don't break it."

"Guess what me and Sara Beth are gonna do," Timmy exclaimed.

"Don't talk so loud. Mom's takin' a nap."

More softly, Timmy said, "Betcha can't guess."

"I don't care what you and hippo are gonna do."

"You will when you hear it 'cause it's neat, and Sara Beth said her daddy said if somebody got a picture of Blood Wings, they'd get a lot of money for it. So we are."

"Pretty dumb idea. You'd never ever get close enough to Blood Wings, so just forget ever takin' a picture of it."

"Nun-uh. We can. Me and Sara Beth."

"Don't hang around Sara Beth no more. She gives you really stupid ideas."

Timmy chattered on in his annoying, little brother tone, eventually leading Wade to abandon the Braves and head for the front door.

"Where you goin'?"

"Somewhere."

"Can I go, too?"

"No. Definitely not. Tell Mom I'll be home for supper."

He heard a dwindling wail of protest as he left. There was no time for brotherly kindness. Wade had more important things on his mind: Hash, Blood Wings, and getting even for Gillie.

Yesterday's festive mood at Holly's had dampened considerably, a fact reflected in the near normal state of Sunday tourist traffic. As the boy crossed over the bridge to the refuge, he glanced at Miss Freda's cottage, experiencing anew a mix of emotions and sensations and impressions.

She's wrong about Hash.

A southerly breeze kicked up some white dust; he noticed that the water level around the knobby roots of the mangroves had dropped—south Florida needed rain. Everyone feared fires, even though old-timers in the area claimed that occasionally the swamp needed fires to serve as a catalyst for replenishing itself.

When he reached Hash's cabin, Wade almost turned around and beat it home. Houston Parker's Harley was parked by the front door.

What's he doin' here?

The cabin itself seemed to breathe its own silence.

No sign of Hash or Ibo. Danny Boy was curled, motionless, in his huge ceramic pot. But out on the back dock, Houston stood scanning the vanishing point of the mangrove-lined waterway. He wheeled around at Wade's approach.

"Hey, there," he said. "You looking for Hash, too? Got any idea where he is?"

The boy said nothing.

"Not speaking to me, huh? Neither is your mom. Must run in the family."

A stubborn silence held sway; both watched for the

swamp to surrender up Hash. Tiring finally, Houston hunkered down on the dock and, without looking at the boy, said, "I know what you're going through."

Wade felt a tingle in his hands, but continued his unwillingness to talk.

"No one really believes you," said Houston. "Maybe Hash does, but I'd say most others don't: Bradshaw, Holly, the cops, most of the tourists and reporters . . . and even your mom."

The tingle generated a fire.

But Wade held his tongue.

"I believe you," said Houston. "I thought you'd like to know that. Your mom . . . no, never mind. This is between you and me. Care if I tell you a story of what happened to me when I was about your age?"

The boy considered leaving; his dislike for the man, however, suddenly took a backseat to curiosity.

At once, Houston's story became an informative narrative and a spell of sorts; Wade wanted to break through the spell, but couldn't. He listened to the full account, and it opened the floodgates of memory: the attack on Gillie in all its cinematic horror.

"Blood Wings killed my dad, but no one believed me except Maxwell Schreck. He knew. So you can hate me if you want to, Wade; we have more in common than you realize."

Their eyes met.

Houston added, "That creature has ruined my life . . . or, I suppose I've *let* it ruin my life. I let the thought of revenge cut a dark hole in me. I've lived an empty life since then, trying to fill it with drugs and with relationships I end up destroying."

He started to walk past the boy, then stopped beside him.

"I've made this promise to myself that somehow, some

way, I'm going out into that swamp and kill Blood Wings—then maybe I'll be able to get on with my life. You just might be the only person around who really understands what I'm saying."

He left.

And the boy did understand mostly, and yet the spike that had been driven between him and Houston remained there, loosened somewhat, but still too firm to allow them to be friends.

4

The boy waited on the dock until suppertime approached, his thoughts tangled with reactions to Houston's story and the man's determination to hunt down the creature.

Hash never arrived.

Could be hot on the trail, Wade decided, and so he ambled toward home. Most of the tourists had gone; the boy waved at Holly through the glass doors of her store and then angled past the bar and out around the Orchid Springs Motel where a curious scene slowed his steps: A long-haired, frail, bespectacled girl, was grunting as she wielded a tire tool to remove a rear tire from a new-looking, quite fancy van.

Wade drew to within several yards of her.

In no longer than a minute or so, the girl wrestled the tire free, slapped on the spare, and lowered the van.

"Geez," said Wade, "I never saw a girl change a flat tire."

The girl stood, hands on hips, and swiped at a long strand of unruly hair that had draped across her nose. There was grease or dirt smeared on one cheek, shaping the letter "S." She wore a checkered blouse and blue

191

jeans and pixie-like boots.

"Well, first of all, I'm a woman and not a girl; and second, I do as many things for myself as possible. My name's Lark Garrison. What's yours?"

"Wade . . . Wade Martin."

She paused to clean a drop of perspiration from her glasses. When she put them back on she said, "I know you." She put a finger to her lips and appeared deep in thought. "Sure," she exclaimed. "Oh, this is my lucky day."

Excited, she ducked through the side doors of the van and returned with a folded newspaper which she perused a moment before saying, "And I thought the flat tire meant bad luck for certain—Wade, you're just the person I'm wanting to chat with."

The boy heard his stomach gurgle.

"My mom told me not to talk to any more reporters."

"But I'm not a reporter."

"What are you? You want to talk to me about the creature, don't you?"

"Yes, as a matter of fact, I do."

"Must mean you're some kind of reporter."

"Wade, have you ever heard the word, crypto-zoology?"

"No."

"Well, it means the study of mysterious animals. I'm a cryptozoologist."

The boy smiled. "Sure is a big, funny word."

"I drove clear down here from Chicago just to talk to you about the creature you saw. I've been all over the world searching for strange creatures. I've even written a book about them."

"You mean you chase after monsters?"

"Yes, I do. What do you think about that?"

"Women aren't supposed to chase after monsters."

"Oh-h-h, I *see*. And why not?"

192

"Because."

"Because?"

"Because they're not strong enough and could get hurt."

"I haven't yet, and I've searched for Bigfoot in the Northwest, for the Loch Ness monster in Scotland, and I've just returned from the Karatau Mountains of Kazakhstan in Russia where I examined a very strange fossil of a pterosaur."

"My friend Hash, he hunts for fossils, you know, bones, and he sells them. He's out looking for Blood Wings and he's—" Wade stopped, instantly regretting what he had said.

"This guy, Hash . . . do you think he can find the creature?"

"Sure. He knows more about the swamp than anybody. He promised me he'd hunt down Blood Wings and kill it."

"Why does he want to kill it?"

Completely nonplussed, Wade cocked his head to one side. "Huh? That's a dumb question."

"I don't think so. Listen, if you're not going to be late for dinner, come on into my van and let's talk."

The boy hesitated. "Well, okay."

The interior of the van was plush, housing comfortable swivel chairs ringing a small table. There was a fold-out bed and even a desk top jutting out next to it. Books, papers, flashlights and lanterns, hiking gear, a rack of clothes and camera equipment—lots of camera equipment—occupied the remaining space.

"Geez, this is super neat. You could *live* inside here."

"For the most part I do. But this week I'm trading my narrow, hard bed for a queen-sized mattress if the motel has one."

They sat around the table, and she offered him a cold drink from her cooler. The idea of someone traveling all over the country in a van appealed to the boy.

"You must make a bundle of money chasing monsters. Maybe someday I'll chase monsters and make money."

"I'm afraid there isn't much money in it. I've gotten some royalties from my book—see, here's a copy of it."

She retrieved a copy from a nearby stack of books and handed it to him. It was a glossy paperback titled, *Do they Exist?*; sub-titled, "A Search For Creatures Science Rejects."

"Yeah, it says, 'By Lark Garrison.' That's your name."

She turned the book around for him.

"Geez, it *is* you. 'Cept you're not wearing your glasses in the picture."

"As I was saying, there really isn't much money in cryptozoology. People do what I do because they're totally fascinated by it. You have to be dedicated to it. Or maybe obsessed with it would be a more accurate description."

"How'd you buy this van if you don't make much money?"

She grinned. "You're pretty sharp, aren't you? My father bought her for me—I think of the van as a she. My father's a banker in Chicago, so you see I'm a poor little rich girl; but I'm not really spoiled. I don't care for money, and I certainly don't want to become a banker. My parents don't understand; they don't like my being on the road by myself—and they cringed at the idea I might be driving a clunker—so the result is this. She's a great set of wheels. I love her."

Wade surveyed the interior more closely, then asked, "Where do you keep your guns?"

"Guns?"

"Yeah, you know, to shoot the monsters if you see 'em. Or do you use a spear or a big knife or poison?"

"I don't try to kill them or even to capture them. This is my only weapon." She picked up an expensive-looking

35mm camera, telephoto lens extending a foot or so from the camera body.

Shaking his head, Wade couldn't believe what he was hearing.

"You're not goin' out after Blood Wings with just a camera, are you?"

"I intend to, yes. You see, a cryptozoologist doesn't want to kill any of these fabulous creatures. We want to verify their existence to the doubting minds of scientists. Quality photographs are reasonably good evidence."

Wade became thoughtful. "Not me," he muttered. "Blood Wings has gotta be killed because it killed my friend Gillie. If Hash doesn't kill it, then . . . I will."

"Who else besides you and Hash have seen the creature?"

"Hash maybe hasn't, but he knows about it, I think. And Houston Parker. He's seen it. And maybe Miss Freda—she runs the refuge across the street. Her husband . . . hmm, maybe I better not say no more."

Lark busied herself jotting notes on a pad.

She glanced up and smiled as the boy finished his soft drink.

"I still can't believe my good luck, bumping into you this way. Could be it means I'll finally verify something truly, truly wondrous. Look, your mom probably has your dinner on the table, so you better scoot. But, tomorrow or sometime in the next few days, I want to go over the details of what you saw in the swamp. Would you mind sharing that with me?"

"Well, I guess maybe it'd be okay."

"One other favor: Is there any chance you could introduce me to your friend Hash?"

The boy shrugged, but a playful light glinted in his eyes. "He's got a parrot that cusses."

"He does? Must be an interesting man."

"He is when he hasn't been drinkin' a lot of rum."

Lark arched her eyebrows, and Wade added, "Yeah, I could take you to his cabin."

"Great. Thanks."

They got out of the van and the boy started to leave.

"You believe me, don't you," he asked hesitating.

"About the creature? Well . . . yes. Yes, I do."

Wade smiled. He waved good-bye and sprinted home.

Chapter Eleven

1

Hash cooked the big mangrove snapper over the open fire, savoring its fishy aroma and taste while remaining conscious of the distant laughter and the other campfire a hundred yards to the north. Flitting down from his perch, Ibo pecked without enthusiasm at a container of bird seed.

"Stupid bastards," said the man, his eyes narrowing toward the red-orange aura and twinkle of flame. "What makes some men so damn stupid, Ibo?"

"Damn stupid. Midges. Midges. Midges."

The bird ruffled his feathers, and Hash laughed.

"Get your ass closer to the fire and those midges won't bother you."

Nights in the mangrove swamp spawned furious hordes of mosquitoes and sand flies, the latter called midges by locals. Tiny, yet inordinately vicious insects, midges amounted to a pair of wings with jaws.

Earlier in the day, Hash had seen the three men flying low in their air boat, drinking, one or two brandishing revolvers—one wielding something that resembled a pitchfork. They had been somewhat typical of the motley crews drawn to the swamp in search of Blood Wings, or, more likely, in search of a weekend away from their wives and kids, a chance to raise hell, get roaring drunk, and engender a wild memory or two.

Hash knew the pine hummock where they had camped, for he had scouted it that morning and had made an amazing discovery: The far end of the hummock showed signs of being a nesting area—the lair, perhaps, of Blood Wings. And so he had poled here to sit and wait and watch and to catch a fish for his late night meal.

"Assholes got no idea what they're close to."

He estimated their campfire to be no more than fifty yards from the nesting area; their laughter and night cries, no doubt, had kept Blood Wings at bay. But for how much longer?

"If that creature takes a mind to return, he'll make supper out of 'em."

Hash realized that his words represented a curious admission. After years and years in the swamp, many of them spent denying the existence of Blood Wings, he felt—no, he *knew*—something was, indeed, out there.

"Mr. Bones—is this the big hit?" he whispered into the fire, musing on his wealthy Key Biscayne patron.

A shiver of excitement passed through his old body. He had come deeper into the swamp than ever before, and the possible reality of the creature, the hushed silence broken only by the drunken hunters and the drone of night insects, made him feel alone and vulnerable. Not feelings he was accustomed to.

Soon it was after midnight; Ibo dozed; the fire burned low.

Hash found himself thinking about Miss Freda and how the years had sweetened the memory of that one weekend, but memory usually had a bitter side to balance the sweet, and the emptiness of having no wife, no

198

woman companion in his twilight years, struck him full force.

He thought of the Bronx. The old stomping grounds. Saturday afternoons at Yankee Stadium in the late '50s and early '60s cheering for the Bronx Bombers: Mantle and Maris and Berra, Kubek and Richardson.

"God, what a team," he murmured.

And his metal salvage operation earned him a tidy sum. There were women in those days, as many as he had wanted. A few good friends. The lure of Florida had changed all of that. The lure of the "big hit."

He had come to the Sunshine State as a fortune hunter.

The fortune had eluded him.

"Hash, you miserable ole fucker—your day's comin', friend," he whispered to himself.

An image of Wade flickered through his thoughts. Vaguely, his promise to the boy came winnowing back. It meant little to him.

"He'll learn that a man only does things for himself. Ain't that right, Ibo?"

He tossed a firebrand at the bird, missing wide. Ibo shuffled his feet, swallowed a squawk, and slipped his beak under a wing.

Then Hash heard it.

The rioters on the hummock were leaving. A clamor of voices. The thrum of their boat. A spotlight. They were exiting in a fierce hurry.

Hash was instantly glad to be seeing them on their way, but their mad rush . . . ? He felt the skin on the back of his neck crawl. In less than a minute, they had gathered up and were speeding through the night water toward Orchid Springs.

"What the hell?"

Hash doused his fire.

199

"Come on, Ibo. Best go take a look."

The wind gusted, an uncharacteristic after-midnight breeze; strong, southerly, salty, it whipped at the man's legs. He set about lighting his gas lantern; next, he checked his .286 Mossberg and took a swig of straight rum. One, maybe two fingers of it.

He was scared.

"Jesus Christ, Hash . . . you sorry pussy," he chided himself.

Then he pushed off. He guided the skiff to his left, angling away from the end of the hummock where the hunters had been camped.

He poled slowly and as quietly as possible, not wanting to start the small outboard; it appeared that something had spooked the former occupants of the hummock, and he was not eager to announce his arrival to whatever that something might be. He continued his poling, the wind at his back, until he reached the first vaultings of mangrove roots. There, the trees grew to twice the height of those near Pelican pond, but not high enough to blot the sight of the hungry spread of flames.

"Those sons-uh-bitches. Campfire's caught the whole damn hummock on fire."

"Sumbitch! Sumbitch!" Ibo shrieked.

Hash suddenly stopped poling.

The skiff drifted.

The wind calmed even as the fire spread.

"Jesus," he whispered. "You smell that, Ibo?"

The bird ruffled his feathers once and fled, frightened by something neither he nor the man could see. Hash knew the parrot wouldn't fly far—just far enough to stay out of harm's way.

The man's eyes burned and began to water; from his nose, mucous began to flow steadily.

"Get this mother out of here," he snuffled.

But at that moment the night seemed to explode. Flames leaped into the upper branches of the dry mangroves, crackling, dropping burning leaves into the water where they hissed, and the hissing matched the immediate thrumming of wings. Hash turned. The stench thickened. He squinted into the semicircle of light spread by the lantern. And he heard an angry cry, half man, half beast.

The cry, together with the vibration of the night air, caused him to lose his balance and fall to his knees in the bottom of the skiff. He twisted around onto his back and saw the thing coming, swooping down from the stars it seemed, fangs protruding, eyes burning with hatred.

The creature dived, gearing itself for the kill.

Hash fumbled for his rifle, but could not lift it in time. The flapping of wings nearly smothered him with a gust of hot, stinking air; the man screamed at the top of his lungs when the creature narrowly missed him. Then, as it wheeled out beyond the skiff and prepared for a return pass, he seized his only chance to save himself.

Into the dark water he tumbled, praying to any God that would listen to spare him from the nightmare of wings.

2

"This morning's *Herald* claims it's a hoax," said Holly. "Has an admission from two teenagers that one of them dressed up in a mask and cape and went out into the swamp. All a big hoax. You believe that?"

Eyes dancing, the heavyset woman turned to Lark for a reponse. Biting his tongue, Wade listened carefully; he had brought the young woman by the store to introduce her. His mom and Timmy were there, too, and the boy felt a special pride in knowing someone who had actually written a book and had traveled far and wide on the trail of strange creatures.

"Naturally one always expects at least a strong possibility of a hoax," Lark began, "but in this case, I tend to believe my new friend here. Something out of the ordinary is in that swamp."

Wade felt a spreading warmth in his chest when he heard Lark refer to him as her "new friend." He glanced at his mom, who appeared interested in what Lark had to say.

"But what could it be?" she asked. "Wade described it as a huge bat—could a bat reach the size of a man?"

"Well, certainly no bat that we're aware of; however, the world has so many wild and nearly inaccessible regions in which some hitherto unknown species might live. We can't rule out the possibility, as extraordinary as it seems, that prehistoric creatures could exist in those areas—or in the seas. The coelacanth is a prime example; scientists had presumed that it had been extinct for seventy million years until one was caught in 1938. And we could one day discover that the Loch Ness monster is an elasmosaur, a type of plesiosaur which has somehow survived into modern times."

"But Orchid Springs isn't the Amazon jungle or someplace like that," Anita protested.

"It's a large area, though, and not completely explored. The press of development will eventually make it almost impossible for an unknown species to exist there undetected. Wade has given me a lot of good information, but I need to talk to people who know the swamp thoroughly."

"Are you really going out there?" Anita asked.

"I'm goin', mom," said Timmy. "Me and Sara Beth."

"Got to get the OK from mom first, cowboy."

Lark smiled and winked at Timmy before returning her attention to Anita.

"Yes, I am. Soon as I know my way around, or can hire a guide to get me where I need to be."

"Aren't you going to be just a little scared."

"More than a little, yes. But this is what gets my blood pumping. I love it."

"Hash can help you, I bet," said Wade.

Holly rolled her eyes. "Lots of luck. That man's about as dependable as a three-legged sled dog."

"What about Houston Parker? Wade says he knows something about the creature."

There was an uncomfortable silence.

Wade studied his mom, who after hesitating a moment, said, "I wouldn't count on him, either."

Holly nodded in agreement.

Lark smiled nervously.

Wade stepped in. "Miss Freda can tell you a lot," he said.

"If she has a mind to," Holly added. "Problem is, Freda Schreck is a hard nut to crack—changes moods like a chameleon changes colors on plaid wallpaper. I would be careful putting too much stock in what she had to say. She's been a bitter woman ever since she lost her husband."

"So many behind the scenes stories in Orchid Springs," Lark exclaimed, "that you need to be a detective to ferret things out. Lots of intriguing people. Your mayor seems real nice—Mr. Bradshaw. I met him at the motel restaurant last night."

Holly chuckled. "C.M.'s a bag of wind, but basically harmless. Blood Wings has been a dream come true for him. He's so excited these days he's about to split his britches."

Good-natured laughter filled the store, though for

Wade, anything related to the matter of Blood Wings could never quite be a source of humor.

"We better go," he said, suddenly claiming Lark's arm.

"Wade's offered to show me around the refuge," she said. "It was nice meeting all of you. I'm sure I'll be seeing you again."

Good-byes said, they walked over the bridge into the refuge and spent a few minutes gawking at the gators and at Ruthie and the other animals. Lark lingered a bit longer at the pen of the white gator; but Wade's impatience got the better of him, and he pulled at her hand.

"Come on. We gotta hear what Hash found out. Come on."

At a fast clip, they followed the shell road to Hash's cabin. Along the way, Lark pointed to a cloud of smoke on the western horizon.

"Could that be a swamp fire?" she asked.

"Yeah, it sure could." And something about the sight of that distant smoke tapped at a raw nerve in him. "Geez, we better hurry."

"Why? What is it?"

Wade did not answer. It was a warm, breezy day, and he was beginning to sweat along his hairline; but he couldn't be certain whether the heat or a sudden case of nerves was its source.

"Here's the cabin," he exclaimed as he hustled down to the front door, Lark in tow.

Once inside, they squinted into its shadows.

"Doesn't look like your friend's home."

Before Wade could say anything, Hash's voice thundered from the corner.

"Get this mother out of here! Sumbitch! Get this mother out of here! Sumbitch!"

Wade wheeled around. "Oh, it's just Ibo, Hash's parrot."

"He is rather profane, isn't he?" Lark giggled.

"Maybe Hash's out back."

He was.

At the dock, Wade and Lark stared down at Hash's skiff, where the man sprawled on his back, motionless.

There was fear in the boy's tone as he exclaimed, "Geez, oh, geez, is he dead?"

"Could be just asleep."

They edged up to the skiff, and Wade tied it down because it was adrift; its prow had reached shallow enough water not to allow the slough to coax it back into the swamp.

Lark took a few steps into the water and then reached for Hash's wrist. As she held it, feeling for a pulse, the boy crossed his fingers.

Don't be dead. Please don't be dead.

"He's got a pulse, but it's pretty weak. And his clothes are soaked." She leaned closer to his face. "Whew!" She wrinkled her nose. "I see the problem. He's wasted. Dead-to-the-world drunk."

The corners of Wade's mouth turned down in disappointment. "Damn him," he muttered.

"I suppose the only thing to do is let him sleep it off," said Lark.

"No. No, I gotta know what he found out. We gotta wake him up."

Lark arched her eyebrows doubtfully. "Well . . . okay." She glanced around. "Hand me that bucket."

She filled it from the slough. Hesitating a moment, she studied the derelict man, his surrender to unconsciousness, and his almost peaceful countenance.

"Forgive me, Mr. Hash. This is going to be a rude awakening." She looked at Wade. "Hope this doesn't kill him."

The man bullroared when the bucketful of water inundated him; he gasped and grunted and swore and spewed and jerked and twisted and coughed and spit.

"Good work," said the boy. "You didn't kill him."

Lark kept her distance. "Yes, but will *he* kill *us*?"

It was a struggle, but eventually they succeeded in getting Hash out of the skiff and into the cabin. Lark brewed coffee. Hash groaned and demanded they leave, and Ibo shrieked and whistled and generally raised a commotion until Wade turned on the television for him.

One cup of strong coffee allowed Hash to hold his eyes open. Wade introduced Lark to him, and after two more cups of coffee, the old man appeared reasonably alert and cogent. He took some dry clothes into the bathroom and changed.

"What did you find?" Wade demanded when he returned. "Did you see Blood Wings?"

Hash winced in pain. Pressing fingertips to one temple, he said, "Listen, do me a big favor—whisper. My head feels like holy hell."

Wade and Lark settled in around the small table across from the man and tried to be patient.

"Yeah . . . yeah, I saw him. Jesus, I did."

For the next ten minutes or so, he offered them a summary of his tracking experience, concluding with an account of the burning hummock and the attack of Blood Wings.

"I stayed under the skiff long as I could. When I finally surfaced, it was gone. Jesus, I'll never forget when that thing . . . oh, Jesus."

His body quaked, and he asked Wade to bring him a blanket.

"I'm interested in more detail," said Lark. "Approximate wingspan. Texture of the body covering—hair or fur? The face—everything you can recall."

"Little lady, trust me, you don't never wanna know about this creature—and you sure as hell don't want to get close to it."

"I came fifteen hundred miles to do just that."

"She's a crytozoo person," said the boy.

Lark grinned. "A cryptozoologist. Or, as Wade puts it, I chase monsters."

"No offense, ma'am, but a little thing like you would get scared out of her mind if you ever set eyes on Blood Wings."

"Don't count on it. I was camped in the mountains of Northern California one summer night when I heard a Bigfoot scream, and I felt the ground shake beneath me as the creature walked up to my tent. I heard it breathing, and it's a sound I'll never forget. But I don't scare easily."

"Have you ever seen a creature swoopin' dead upon you, wingspan twenty feet or better, six to eight inch fangs set to tear your heart out, and eyes . . . Jesus, eyes straight from hell?"

"You won't spook me," she maintained.

Wade inwardly applauded her courage. "Tell her, Hash. Tell her more about the creature. And tell her how you promised me you'd kill it."

"I've said all I'm gonna say about the creature. The fire stirred it up, so there's no tellin' what it'll do now."

"Fire makes it mad. Miss Freda told me that," said Wade. "So you gotta kill it before it attacks somebody else."

"Why does it need to be killed?" Lark interjected. "If no one were to disturb it—by burning it out of its home and shooting at it—it could live deep in the swamp as a wild and magnificently free creature."

"No," said Wade, "it's gotta be killed. It killed my friend. Tell me you'll kill it, Hash."

Still groggy, head pounding, the man tried to focus his

eyes on the boy. "I can't kill it," he said. "It's as simple as that."

Dumbfounded, Wade stared into his face until the man looked away.

"Can't do it? But you got to, Hash. Who else will if you don't?"

"Nothin' more to say, kid. I'm not goin' back in there . . . Jesus, I'm not. That creature . . . no way in hell I'm goin' back in there."

Anger balled in the boy's fists.

"You mean you're a coward, right? You're a friggin' coward."

He wanted to pound his small fists into the man; he looked helplessly at Lark, who let her gaze drop to the floor as if she were suddenly embarrassed to be overhearing a private argument.

"Maybe I am a coward," said Hash. "I don't give a good goddamn what you call me, or what you think of me. I'm not no fuckin' hero—never have been, never will be."

The hurt cut the boy like a razor.

"I'm takin' Gillie's stuff—it don't belong to you. Don't belong to a coward and a drunk. You're just a lousy drunk."

He ran to the edge of the ice box and retrieved Gillie's spear and hat. Hash made no move to stop him, and when the boy marched angrily out the door, Lark followed.

3

"You have been pursuing it, have you not?"

Hash, sober, dressed uncharacteristically in a sports shirt and slacks, knew exactly what Freda Schreck was referring to.

"A pretty sad attempt, yes."

208

She smiled. From the side porch of her cottage, they could see miles into the swamp; against the distant horizon they watched lazy spirals of smoke.

"Playing with matches on your hunt?"

"No. Some other crazy fools did that. A fair-sized hummock in flames. Should burn out in the next few days, but . . . we ain't heard the last of it."

"Whatever do you mean?"

"Blood Wings . . . the creature had a nesting area there."

"I see. Then you assume we may have an angry creature on our hands?"

"I'd say so. I came a whisker from being its first victim."

"Of course, I'm relieved that you escaped unharmed, and yet, I'm pleased. Maxwell would have been pleased. The guardian spirit he placed in the swamp is performing its assigned tasks, you might say."

Hash nodded.

He tried to imagine having made love to the woman who spoke those words, but the images failed to spring to life. The cool maliciousness of her tone almost made him shudder.

"You asked me to come because you had a message for me. What is it?"

"Oh, yes. Yes, of course. Forgive me. Your . . . your patron has sent word that he wishes to see you immediately. You may use my car."

"I appreciate that."

"I haven't forgotten that you helped me at a time of need."

"It might could be one of of these days all of Orchid Springs will be needing help."

To that, Miss Freda did not respond.

Only smiled.

Passing through the security gates at the Key Biscayne estate, Hash resolved to say no to whatever Mr. Bones would request, knowing intuitively that the man, doubtless, had one thing on his mind: the creature.

Twilight cast a breathtaking light upon the Andrea Palladio style villa rising before him at the apex of a circular drive. Four massive columns braced the centerpiece structure bordered by two impressive wings. Walking through the columns minutes later, Hash felt diminished by their size, just as he felt dwarfed by the hugeness of ego-will in the man whose vision created the place.

A servant met him at the door and asked him to wait in the grand foyer, the pink marble floor of which dazzled the eye. But as Hash awaited the appearance of Mr. Bones, his attention, as always when asked to the mansion on business, was drawn to a display of a looming skeleton, the skeleton of a massive, predatory creature sporting fangs as long as bayonets.

Hash found himself surrendering his fascination so completely to the beast that he did not hear the approach of his patron.

"His nickname is Smiley," cried a high-pitched voice, which sounded like glass breaking. It lifted above the irritating buzz and whir of an electric wheelchair.

"It's a Pleistocene sabercat—scientific name: *Smilodon*," the voice continued.

Hash rubbed at his smooth, bald head. "Nobody gave him any shit, I bet."

The small, withered man in the wheelchair laughed, a reedy giggle which echoed in the large foyer. "Mr. Hashler, welcome. I'm pleased that you responded so soon to my request."

Reaching out to shake his hand, Hash almost felt that a

formal bow would be more appropriate. The man's claw of a hand possessed surprising strength; but the remainder of his body was shriveled by childhood disease, so that only stumps of legs extended from the seat of the chair and a neck brace held the man's proud head in place. His white, scruffy hair contrasted with the flushed, heavily veined face.

"I needed a good excuse to get out of Orchid Springs."

"Yes. Yes, I can understand. I've been keeping up on the excitement surrounding your tiny community."

"I should have brought you a bumper sticker or a button," Hash joked, instantly relieved to see the man smile broadly, though the act of smiling grotesquely contorted one side of his mouth.

His name was Alfredo Comboni, a wealthy entrepreneur whose one passion in life beyond acquiring money was acquiring Florida fossils of the Pleistocene, Pliocene, and Miocene epochs. He was known to spare no expense, no amount of effort and pressure, to add to his collection.

"Come along into the east wing, Mr. Hashler. Myra has virtually taken over the west wing. She invites her biddies in twice a week, and their incessant cackling drives me as far away as possible."

Hash followed the man into a luxuriant sitting room, replete with a marble fireplace and a magnificent crystal chandelier. Dominating one corner of the room, and looking much out of place, a huge skeleton reared itself on its hind legs.

"Please be seated," said Comboni. Then, noticing where Hash's attention had been drawn, he smiled as if genuinely pleased.

"Oh, I see you've noticed Big E—the giant sloth *Eremotherium*, another Pleistocene creature. That one's over twenty feet in length, making it the largest land animal ever to live in Florida."

"Helluva big sucker. But slow, right?"

"Yes, a ponderous beast. Yet, I never cease to be amazed by their raw power and size. Can you imagine what Pleistocene Florida must have been like?"

"How long ago we talking about? A million? Two million years?"

"Not beyond 1.8 million."

Comboni paused to claw at his jacket for a cigarette. Hash made a move as if to help him, but the man gestured him away. He maneuvered his head and one hand to switch on a built-in lighter. Drawing deeply on the cigarette, he gazed at the stunning chandelier.

"I've been thinking quite a good deal lately about Orchid Springs—about years ago when we first met and you began digging fossils for me. I had several other good friends there. Now gone. Gus Parker and Roy Webster and, of course, Maxwell Schreck. I trust that Freda is well these days, isn't she?"

"Yes, I'd say so."

"Spectacular woman in her own way. A courageous act on her part to maintain the refuge after the death of Maxwell. And what about Holly Webster?"

"Runs the store that Roy started, and not long ago opened a bar. She's been busy as a bitch dog in heat what with all the Blood Wings excitement. Gave her business a shot in the arm."

"Blood Wings," Comboni murmured. "A most fascinating creature. Directly or indirectly, it was responsible for the deaths of Parker and Webster and even Schreck, I believe."

"Roy Webster's heart gave out," said Hash. "That's what I heard. And Schreck, who knows? He went into the swamp one day and didn't return."

"But the creature has returned?"

Fidgeting with his hands in his lap, Hash said, "Yeah, it's back. Definitely back. It killed that boy you probably read about in the paper and. . . ."

Comboni studied his visitor a moment. "And you've seen it, haven't you? You've seen Blood Wings."

Hash's eyes appeared to glaze.

His mouth slackened, and he stared at his palms.

"Yeah. Yeah, fact is, I have."

"Tell me about it, won't you?"

It was a slowly rendered, halting account; Comboni listened intently, at one point so enraptured by the narrative that he let his cigarette burn down to his knobby fingers.

Concluding his tale, Hash shuddered. "Makes me cold inside to think about it. That creature missed me by inches . . . I mean, Jesus, I'll guaran-damn-tee ya I was scared."

Comboni smiled softly. "Yes, I can see that."

For half a minute there was silence; Hash interlocked his fingers nervously; Comboni lit another cigarette.

"Mr. Hashler, I would assume that a man like yourself, a man intimate with the swamp and its inhabitants, would pride himself on mastering whatever he should happen to confront."

Hash looked at him. "What are you saying?"

Squinting through the smoke, Comboni said, "You went into the swamp to find the creature's lair. You found it. But you've left the job incomplete."

"Incomplete?"

"Next time you have to kill it. A man like yourself can't accept less."

Hash began to shake his head; his jaw tightened. "No. No, you're talking to the wrong man. I'll crank up Bella and dig for fossils. I'll sell you all the best pieces I can find. But . . . I ain't goin' after Blood Wings . . . not that creature. Not me. Not never."

Comboni blew a torch of smoke. "Have you seen my basement gallery, Mr. Hashler? Just recently finished.

213

Quite a grand spectacle—I'm quite proud of it. Wouldn't you like to see it?"

He nodded cautiously. "Yeah, I suppose so. That what you asked me here for?"

"Oh, no. No, I'll get to the matter of business in due time. Let's retire to the gallery."

From an adjoining room, they rode in an elevator which lowered them a few floors and opened into a high-ceilinged, glass-bound hallway that resembled a museum.

"I had this built to house my menagerie," Comboni explained. "The bone basement is what Myra calls it. Poor dear doesn't understand my compulsion to collect a complete skeleton of every marvelous creature ever to roam this fine state."

"Helluva place," Hash muttered.

There were dozens of glass displays housing large and entire skeletons.

"Allow me to give you a guided tour," said Comboni. "On the right here a pair from the genus *Canis*: *Canis lepophagus*, a Pliocene coyote, and *Canis dirus*, a Pleistocene wolf—quite a bit larger than any modern wolf."

The whir of Comboni's chair pitched higher as he shifted directions.

"Over here, my mastodons and mammoths—do you know the difference between them?"

Hash shrugged as he surveyed the huge skeletons mounted against a painted background scene of ancient Florida.

"This is a mastodon, genus *Mammut*. Note the vestigial lower tusks and strong upper tusks and the characteristic low skull. Mammoths, genus *Mammuthus*, are similar. But as you can see in this specimen, you have a high skull and no lower tusks. Beautiful beasts, aren't they?"

"Ever museum in the country would be pretty damn envious of your layout," said Hash, glancing up and down the long gallery. "You have about everything, I'd guess."

"No. No, not everything. Let me show you an empty display."

At the far end of the gallery they came upon the usual glass rectangle, the familiar modern scene of the mangrove swamp painted as a backdrop. Comboni pushed a button on the wheelchair, and the glass slid upward in a hum, disappearing into the ceiling. He reached for something at the edge of the display.

"Have you any idea what this is?"

Examining the object closely, Hash said, "The tooth and partial skull of a sabercat?"

Comboni seemed pleased that his companion was mistaken. "The fang is certainly large enough to belong to a sabercat, but the jaw fragment . . . it could only come from a primitive man."

"Where did you get this?" Hash whispered, feeling suddenly claustrophobic in the shadowy gallery.

"Years ago Maxwell Schreck was kind enough to present this to me. Returning a favor so to speak. You see, years ago there were two Blood Wings—but now only one." He paused to admire the rich color of the mangrove swamp.

"Before I die, Mr. Hashler, I have one rather inordinately strong desire: to see Blood Wings—a complete specimen, whole or skeletal—mounted here."

"I hope you get to do just that, but . . . like I said, I can't help you. I'm real sorry. I just can't do it."

Pushing a few buttons, Comboni busied himself with a pad and a pen. Slowly, almost painfully, it appeared, he wrote out something and tore a slip of paper from the pad and handed it to Hash.

It was a check:

Pay To the Order of Dominick Hashler . . . The Sum of One Million and 00/100 Dollars.

215

"You have my word that I will personally sign this the minute you produce Blood Wings for me."

Hash's fingers quaked.

His mouth seemed to be generating more saliva than he could swallow.

He coughed once and murmured something inaudible.

Comboni, satisfied by the man's reaction, added, "This is what you've been waiting for, Mr. Hashler. This is your big hit."

Chapter Twelve

1

Lark pointed down at the smoldering hummock and shouted over the rattle and roar of the copter. "That must be where he was attacked."

The sight of the blackened hummock, stray flames alive here and there, gave Houston a chill. Imagining the creature swooping full bore upon Hash's skiff caused his hand to tremble on the control stick.

"Fire's nearly out," he said, his voice garbled over the microphone.

Lark nodded.

Houston's dark glasses hid his occasional glances at her, not admiring glances exactly—not the kind he would use on a strikingly attractive woman like Anita Martin—and yet there was something interesting about Lark. Her courage. Her determination. She had paid him the regular tourist fee and then some to fly her deeper into the swamp.

She seemed no-nonsense. All business.

He liked that.

"I want to get close enough for pictures," she exclaimed, gesturing toward the smoking hummock.

"I'll circle once," he said.

But he did not want to. Despite the bright, cloudless afternoon, flying low over an area known to be the creature's territory trip-hammered his heart.

He banked the craft, and they began to descend.

"Can't we go any lower?" Lark asked.

She had braced herself against the right side bubble of glass, trying as best she could to steady her camera and the telephoto lens mounted upon it.

On the return swing to the starting point of the circle, Houston hovered momentarily, and Lark called out, "Thanks," and snapped off a dozen or more shots. As they pulled away from the hummock, she offered him a thumbs up and an expansive smile.

He sighed in relief and hoped she hadn't noticed how much his hand had trembled. On the way back, Lark busied herself sketching a very rough map of the area, noting layout, position, direction and mileage from Orchid Springs.

It was twilight by the time they landed.

"Buy you some dinner," she said, "unless you have other plans. I'd really like to hear anything you can tell me about Blood Wings."

"You're very serious, aren't you?"

She smiled. "Dinner?"

"I'll pass on that, but meet me at Holly's bar in an hour and you can buy me a drink. We can talk there."

"Holly's it is. Thanks again for the ride."

And she was gone.

Houston shook his head: *Curious woman.*

But his thoughts quickly returned to the creature and a vague sense of foreboding. Above all, he realized that the time had come for him to confront the creature or live constantly plagued by guilt and an inability to free himself from the ghosts of the past.

At his trailer, he showered and changed clothes and

wished desperately that he had a hit of rapture, but he had used up the last of it and was determined not to go to Hash for more. The idea of checking into a rehab center had crossed his mind.

I'll fight it on my own first, he told himself.

Traffic was not what it was a week ago; Holly's bar had only a sprinkling of customers. When Houston entered its comfortable darkness an hour or so later, he found Lark writing on a yellow legal pad, a tape recorder at her elbow.

"Hi," she said. "Thanks for coming."

"For a free drink—hey, my pleasure."

Anita waited on them. She was pleasant but cool. Houston planned to talk to her in an effort to patch up things between them. Seeing him there with Lark probably wouldn't help matters, but he assumed Anita didn't view the peculiar young woman as a threat.

Lark ordered a daiquiri; Houston a beer.

"Of course, it would have been more appropriate had we ordered a Blood Wings," she observed.

"No, I've tried one," said Houston. "They taste like a bad chili dog."

The laughter cut through the awkwardness.

They exchanged a round or two of small talk before Lark pressed to the point.

"It would be a big help to my research if you would be willing to share what you've seen of and know about the creature."

"I don't like to do this, but . . . I like your style. You seem to put your heart and soul into this. Very admirable. So . . . okay. Here goes."

Lark switched on the recorder.

Houston began.

Retelling the story was never easy, and when he

finished it, Lark carefully asked him to repeat certain parts of it, to clarify or elaborate upon specific details.

"There's something more," he said, watching her jot a few concluding notes.

"What's that?"

"I've really never mentioned this before. For several months after the incident, I would . . . I would see dad's ghost. At least, I thought I was seeing it. Sort of a gray film. Like fog or smoke. A definite shape, though. I guess I imagined it looked like my dad."

"Wade claims he saw something like a ghost, too. Of his friend, Gillie."

"I feel sorry for Wade. Except it seems that he has a few more receptive ears around than I had."

"He's experienced some real trauma, as I'm sure you did."

"Did? I still do. It's like . . . like it all happened yesterday."

"Why have you stayed around Orchid Springs? I would think you would want to get as far away from here as possible—away from the bad memories. What keeps you here?"

Houston asked for another beer, and Lark noticed the looks between him and Anita.

"Oh," she said, "I believe I see part of the reason."

"Or part of the problem. I've been fighting that creature in my mind for years; it won't allow me to live a normal life—to settle down and have some kind of future."

"It's none of my business, but . . . are you in love with Anita?"

"I think so. Hard for me to say because I'm filled with so much hatred for the creature—it represents everything in the world that's ever gone against me. Not much choice is there? I have to go after the creature."

"Looks that way."

"How about you? Why's this creature so important?"

"People who do what I do sometimes wait a lifetime to verify the existence of some creature science claims cannot exist. This is a tremendous opportunity for me. I can't let it pass by. What I want most is to get a good combination of still photos and live film footage—and that means I have to plan a trip into the swamp, preferably to the burned hummock."

"It would be dangerous."

"You're going, aren't you? I sense that you're resigned to it. And I have only one other question: Would you take me with you?"

Houston hitched back.

"Hey, no. Like I said, it'd be dangerous. And besides, I need to do this by myself. Just me and the creature. I don't mean for that to sound like some kind of stupid, macho talk. It's the way it has to be for me. I'm sorry."

"I understand. I have my fingers crossed that I can get my photos and the footage before it's destroyed—though I don't agree that it has to be."

The conversation waned momentarily before Lark picked it up.

"Aren't you curious about the origin of Blood Wings? No one knows what kind of creature it is. It would be a highly significant contribution if we could observe it and film it in its natural habitat; it fits into some wild niche of the biological scheme. Don't you want to know more about it?"

He hesitated, sipped at his beer. "It killed my dad. What else do I need to know?"

Lark lowered her head. "We have completely different motivations on this, don't we? You've been a huge help to me, Houston. Thanks, I wish you luck in dealing with what's haunting you. I plan to talk to Mrs. Schreck next, and then . . . if I have to go out alone and do what I came here to do, it won't be the first time."

Houston raised his beer glass. "To the both of us. We'll need all the luck we can possibly get."

2

"Can we talk?"

Anita had completed her shift and was helping Wick turn down glasses and wipe the counter. "Not much of a gentleman, are you?"

"What?"

"I noticed that you didn't bother to walk your date home."

"My date? You mean Lark?" He snickered.

Anita pushed past him. "If you intended to bring her here to make me jealous, you wasted your time."

"Look, first of all, it was not a *date*. She wanted to hear about Blood Wings. She's a fanatic when it comes to strange creatures. She's not interested in me beyond what she can learn about the creature. And I swear I'm not trying to score with her. Come on, Anita, you can't believe. . . ."

"I don't know what to believe. Too scared these days."

"Let's talk. Please?"

Reluctantly she nodded, and they left for her trailer. After checking on the boys, Anita returned to the living room.

"I want to apologize," she began. "Your social life is none of my business."

"Yes, it is. It is because I care about you. I explained about Lark, and I'm telling you the truth."

"All right. I believe you. I'm really very tired—if this is what you came to talk about, then fine, it's settled. Let's say good night."

"No. There's more. Just listen a minute. Look, I know you're worried about Dean coming back. I understand that, and I want you to know that I'll help you any way I can. If you need me, I'll be here for you. Anita . . ."

He reached for her hand. She hesitated, then allowed him to pull her gently down beside him on the couch.

". . . I love you. I'm trying to get myself off drugs . . . I'm trying to turn my life around, but please . . . you have to understand . . . that creature . . "

She touched his cheek.

"Do what you feel you have to do. Holly would say I'm out of my head crazy, but I'll wait for you. I'll wait until there's nothing standing between us."

3

A thunderstorm brewed in the night, bubbling, at last crashing down upon Orchid Springs and the mangrove swamp, bringing much-needed rain to the parched area. Rain beat against the roof of Houston's trailer, waking him from a restless sleep. Beyond his window, lightning sheeted and thunder rocked and rolled and the wind taunted the fragile bracings of the trailer.

Houston needed a fix. Needed one bad.

He went to his kitchen and popped the top on a light beer. It proved a poor substitute for what his system craved. Behind his eyes, colors pinwheeled and pulsed, some matching the jagged strokes of lightning, producing neon bolts of pink and green and yellow.

"God, I have to get myself through this."

He sprinkled sugar on the back of his tongue and washed it down with water. Calming himself at the kitchen sink, he thought of Anita.

I'll wait until there's nothing standing between us.

Only one thing stood between them: the creature.

Resolution came grudgingly. More than at nearly any other moment in his life, Houston Parker felt frightened.

223

"Dad," he whispered. "I need you."

He cried shamelessly. And when the draining, numbing sensation of having purged those emotions took over, he thought of the one object belonging to his dad that he had managed to keep.

In his closet, he found it in its leather case: a 12-gauge over-and-under Browning shotgun—a birthday present to his dad from Houston and his mother. It was a fancy firearm, sporting a hand-carved, wooden stock depicting duck hunters and a flock of ducks. Its barrel glinted silver.

Hefting the gun, Houston swung it in an arc, firing at imaginary prey or perhaps a clay pigeon, for his dad loved to take the weapon to the skeet shooting range and try his luck, and to teach his son how to handle it.

Self-consciously, Houston rubbed at his shoulder. It ached from memory, a good memory of attempting to be manly, and yet paying the price. The very first time he pulled the trigger on that handsome gun, he thought a cannon ball had ripped into muscle and bone. He had staggered backward, and his dad had grinned and slapped him on the back and said, "Good boy. Keep that shoulder hard against it. You can take it."

In the shadows of his living room, Houston whispered, "I can take it."

But spectres of doubt surrounded him. He sat in silence, losing track of time as the storm passed. Clouds having dispersed, the first light of morning pinked the sky out over the distant ocean.

He knew what he had to do.

He set about preparing methodically. The bare essentials found their way into a backpack. He loaded the shotgun and slipped a box of shells in with the other supplies.

Freda Schreck, doubtless, would disapprove of his taking the helicopter out so early, but his mission, he

224

reasoned, had overriding significance: He had to face the creature. Once and for all time. He had a good idea where he might encounter it. No more stalling. No more living life halfway from day to day just getting by.

The whop-whop-whop of the blades broke the silence of the refuge. He took a deep breath and lifted free of the pad and felt a shout of joy which seemed to build from the pit of his stomach and gain momentum as it approached his throat. His neck muscles tensed; his mouth contorted. And what issued forth as the glass bubble in which he hunched rose higher and higher was a primitive cry of release. An ecstasy of expression he had longed for.

He punched the copter west, rays of the sun spearing to either side of him, lighting his way. Below, the freshly washed swamp gathered drifting curtains of mist. The green of the mangroves and hummocks and saw grass dazzled the eye.

He felt good.

And continued to feel good until he sighted the blackened hummock miles from Orchid Springs. As he circled it, he thought of Lark and her interest in the creature and of Wade and Anita. but mostly, he thought of his dad.

Point of no return.

He gritted his teeth, scanned the hummock for a potential landing, and coaxed the thrumming machine down out of the sky.

4

Most of the hummock was sodden, and the rain intensified the odor of lingering smoke. He pitched a camp in some flattened saw grass, wishing he had brought hot coffee because conditions were too wet to build a fire. He had brought along a can of V-8 Juice, and as he settled

225

in, he sipped at it, shuddering slightly at its biting taste.

The stillness was total and complete.

He could see that the fire had burned about three-fourths of the hummock, leaving the far end unscathed. He knew that eventually he would have to explore that far end for signs of the creature, but he concentrated on the immediate moment. Sitting on the stump of a charred pine, he rubbed his fingertips over the stock of the shotgun. Touching it was like making contact with the spirit of his dad. And hearing the man's laughter. And his voice.

You can take it.

A thin haze to the east silk-screened the rising sun; the circle of morning fire rose, red-orange, huge and vibrant and breathtaking. It radiated an intensity that showered the swamp, cleansing it as if an act of cosmic ritual.

Houston felt alone. He could imagine himself present at the beginning of time. One man facing the unknown. He gripped the shotgun and stood, his legs protesting, his mouth dry, yet every nerve alive.

A breeze caressed his face, but it also stirred the charred and sodden grass and other vegetation. When the smoky air entered his lungs, he coughed, and the sound seemed to diminish him.

Where are all the birds? he asked himself.

Normally the mangrove swamp was alive with the frenzied activity of herons and brown pelicans and other wildfowl. This morning, nothing. Not even the croak of leopard frogs.

He glanced at the copter.

Smart money would have him climbing into that contraption and winging back to Orchid Springs.

Put the goddamn creature out of your mind and love Anita and hope she'll love you in return. You need each other.

He walked toward the copter, lowering the shotgun as

226

he did. The sun torched the bubble of glass, and in the reflection from the pilot's side he glimpsed his face.

And also the face of his dad.

"Oh, God . . . I can't go back."

The imagined reflection dissolved, leaving only his own. And it disgusted him. He raised the shotgun and kept walking toward the far end of the hummock.

A blaze of sun streaming over his shoulder, he saw his shadow, and the size of it, magnifying his stature, gave him a modicum of hope. He entered an area of unburned saw grass, some of it waist-high, and continued to a thick copse of mangroves, their leaves a brilliant green in the sunlight. The leaves quaked in the breeze, and as the direction of that slight wind changed, he stopped walking.

The first wave of the stench poured over him. His eyes began to water. His heart danced a dervish. He swallowed and tried unsuccessfully to stifle a cough as he scanned the outline of the mangroves, then the dense, intertwining of their branches.

It's near.

His finger nervously twitched against the trigger.

It's waiting for me.

He reasoned that the creature was perched just out of sight in the mangroves behind the first line of growth into which he was staring.

Waiting. Watching. Just like the way he got dad.

Houston lifted the barrel.

"Come on, goddamn you, I'm ready," he murmured.

But he was wrong.

He heard the low rustle of wings long before he determined their source and direction. A burst of screeching and frightened bird cries caused him prematurely to fire into a flock of brown pelicans fleeing the hummock beyond the mangroves.

The recoil of the shotgun staggered him.

227

His breathing tore at his lungs as if they were pieces of cloth.

Frantic, he wheeled around and looked into the looming ball of orange sun. He watched, mesmerized, as in the distance Blood Wings—and he knew with absolute certainty that it was the creature—dipped from above the rim of the sun, its massive size blotting out the light as it neared.

Holy God.

It was at least a hundred yards away when he initially sighted it, but it closed rapidly, maintaining an altitude of no more than six or eight feet—and its course was locked in on its prey.

Its wings pumped rhythmically, and as it reached within fifty or sixty yards, it began to glide, not swerving an inch off course.

Houston could not move. His arms lost all strength. He could not raise the gun to protect himself, and yet suddenly, for perhaps only a moment or two, he was not terrified. Instead, he experienced an ineffable sensation of awe.

The approaching creature was beautiful. Majestic.

Its glossy blackness, the stunning sweep of its wings, the indomitable position of its head . . . Houston could only marvel at the absolute wonder of it. And he was not freed from his helpless fascination until the final horrifying seconds when he could hear a high-pitched scream—a scream which hurt his ears—and he could see the creature's mouth opened wide, the upper fangs extended as the jaws strained.

And the eyes.

Unblinking, black holes of rage. And in their center, where they captured glints of light, they were dagger points.

A half second longer and Houston's fascination with those eyes would have cost him his life. He tore free and collapsed to his knees.

The creature dipped its talons like landing gears, then swung low, and Houston could feel the rush of air, could smell the hot stench. Shotgun in hand, he rolled onto his back and whooped a cry of celebration as Blood Wings swept out of its dive, climbing well above the mangroves.

"Missed me, you bastard! You missed me!"

But the right shoulder of his shirt had been sliced five or six inches as if by a razor, a precise cut suggesting the creature knew exactly how close it had come.

"Holy God, it *meant* to miss me," Houston whispered.

The chill from that realization penetrated to the bone.

He pushed to his knees and looked behind him; the copter was thirty yards away. If he stayed low. . . .

He turned, gained his balance, and started to duck walk while pressing himself as close to the grass as possible. But still wet from the night's rain, the grass caused him to slip. He landed hard on his elbows and dropped the shotgun.

"Shit! Damn it, man!"

Retrieving the shotgun, he crouched, eyes glued to the outline of mangroves beyond which Blood Wings disappeared. Tears, generated by the pungent odor, streamed down his cheeks. His nose burned and ran.

But he steadied himself, shotgun at his shoulder.

"Come on, you fucking monster! I'm ready to blow you away!"

For several seconds, he concentrated so intensely on the mangroves that his head began to pound, the pain pressing at his temples like a vise being tightened.

No sign of the creature.

He paused, caught his breath, and wiped at his nose with the back of his wrist.

"Gone. He's gone," he whispered.

The realization stung him. He had failed. He had journeyed into the swamp to kill Blood Wings and would return to Orchid Springs, conflict unresolved.

"Damn it! God damn it!" he shouted.

He looked up. He stood. He glanced to his right.

And heard the wind whooshing over powerful wings.

The creature had swung to the north and had drawn yet another bead on the man. This time Houston hunkered down, shotgun braced—*like shooting a big clay pigeon,* he told himself.

But as the winged fury plunged, the tip of the barrel would not hold steady; Houston's hands began to shake, tears and sweat clouded his eyes, and he started to cry in fear and anticipation.

Gun jerking out of control, he fired.

The pellets spread a pattern high and to the right of his attacker.

Once again, Houston crashed to his knees, but he kept the gun elevated as if to wield it as a club.

He screamed.

Blood Wings accelerated for the kill.

And Houston continued to hold the weapon, clutching it tightly as the creature slammed into the end of the barrel, causing it, in turn, to whip into the side of the man's head.

He saw strokes of lightning.

He felt hot fluids pour into his temples.

His ears filled with the roar of the ocean.

And then there was blackness.

5

It was the stench that made Houston come to.

His nostrils burned as if a match had been touched to them.

Slowly, ever so slowly, he opened his eyes and blinked at the high, blue sky above him. Propping himself shakily on one elbow, he raised his head. Pain bolted from temple to temple, nauseating him.

He surveyed his surroundings, at first unfamiliar with them.

"God love it. What in the hell . . . ?"

He sat up. The pain gradually slackened, though his nose continued to burn, his eyes to water. A numbness spread from his head to his shoulders. Behind him, a breeze lifted; the stench thickened.

"God," he whispered.

He groped on hands and knees for some sense of balance. He spun slowly around and shook his head to clear the fogging numbness. He glanced at his feet, and at the sight, anger mushroomed within him. The shotgun had been smashed, the handsome stock broken off from the barrel and trigger housing.

"Damn it," he muttered, as he tenderly picked up the carved stock.

"Oh, dad, I'm sorry."

Twenty yards beyond him wings rustled.

The creature stood watching, waiting, as if curious to see what terror could do to the man's face.

Something clicked in Houston's throat.

He assessed how far he was from the copter: Could he make a run for it? His eyes met those of Blood Wings. The face of the creature seemed almost human; but the eyes—something spoke there of total disregard.

He was the creature's prey.

Move your ass as cautiously as possible, he told himself. *It's your only chance.*

Hunkered down, he began to back away, judging as nearly as possible that he was on line with the copter. Blood Wings studied him, but made no effort to attack. Yet, when it spread its wings, the man's heart jumped into his throat.

The wings gently lifted. Then closed halfway to the

creature's body.

Keep going. Slowly. No false moves.

Suddenly the creature opened wide its mouth, fangs extended.

Dear God, this is it.

And then he realized that the creature was merely yawning.

Houston felt an involuntary shiver race across his shoulders. Tears and mucous flowed down his face. He knew that he had to move, move quickly before the creature decided the game was over. On hands and knees, he scrambled as fast as he could, slugging his way through the wet grass until he reached the copter and pulled open the pilot's door, bracing himself at every moment for the crush of fangs upon his shoulder.

Stumbling into the cockpit, groaning, gasping for air, he slammed the door and jerked around to find that Blood Wings remained precisely where he had been.

"You bastard!" he whispered. "You're playing with me."

His glance shifted to the control panel. For thirty seconds or more nothing seemed familiar. His mind went blank. He could not remember how to operate the machine. His body quaked violently.

Then, beyond the glass, movement caught his eye.

He winced in pain as if a giant hand had squeezed his heart.

Blood Wings approached.

Houston grabbed the control stick. And then slowly released it.

The creature flapped its wings eagerly and took flight as if its interest had been drawn elsewhere. Houston followed its ascent, struck again by its beauty. For the better part of five minutes, he sat in the pilot's seat which he knew so well. In that position, he had flown dozens and dozens of trips out over the swamp. But the terrifying experience with the creature had destroyed the intimacy between man and machine.

He did not understand what returned things to normalcy.

A burst of clarity. An epiphany of awareness.

He took a deep breath and punched the starter. Tears came to his eyes when the rotor turned and the blades thrummed, and the burned hummock sank beneath the landing rails.

Aloft, he circled the hummock once to get his bearings. He saw the broken shotgun and considered returning to retrieve it. Maybe it could be repaired, he told himself. His thumb tapped nervously on the control stick.

No. Not back down there again.

At the very thought of it, sweat beaded on his forehead.

Get out of here. Get the hell out of here.

He banked, gained altitude, and turned east.

It was a brilliantly clear morning, visibility unlimited. He reached for his sunglasses, and he basked in the warm, relaxing sensation of being, once again, in the glass womb hanging in the sky.

Below him, the labyrinth of the mangrove swamp invited his imagination to challenge its maze—from the safety of five hundred feet above. The beauty of the scene spreading before his eyes almost allowed him to shake the terror and to forget his failure.

He thought of Anita's touch and was on the verge of surrendering to a fantasy when he happened to glance into the right side, rearview mirror. He removed his sunglasses and squinted hard.

His stomach roiled, and his blood began to pump so fast that sudden sharp pains flared across his chest.

"No, this can't be," he murmured. "God, no."

Trailing the copter, fifty feet below and another twenty or thirty feet to the right, the creature flew effortlessly, its broad back and magnificent wings shimmering in the sunlight.

Steady, man. Don't panic.

Some kind of evasive action seemed the best and most obvious strategy. He wet his lips and fingered the control stick.

"Here goes."

The copter swung left and dipped, then angled sharply right. He was diving for the mangroves and found the water alley between two large islands of them. He leveled at approximately eighty feet and held it there as he searched the mirrors frantically for signs of the creature.

"God damn," he muttered. "Get off my ass."

Blood Wings glided not forty feet to his right.

Houston pulled back on the stick; the copter lifted. He lost sight of the creature, but when he leveled off again, it had circled around in front of him and was sweeping up toward him.

"Oh, Jesus!"

He banked right so sharply that he nearly lost control; the engine cut out once, and the copter lost fifty feet almost instantly. And the creature was there to his left, shadowing him, pressing closer, staying below the blades.

Houston desperately tried more evasive moves; nothing shook his attacker.

"One more. One more pass and I'll ram you, you bastard. So help me, God, I'll slice you in two with these blades."

It would mean losing control, crashing. Possible death.

But there appeared no alternative.

He steeled himself for the worst.

He lifted, wheeled left, glanced to both sides, and then below him.

And saw nothing but sky and water and mangroves.

Blood Wings had disappeared.

"I quit. That's what I said, and that's what I mean."
Freda Schreck gestured for Mary.

"Would you prepare some iced tea for Mr. Parker and me?"

After the housekeeper had left the room, Miss Freda leaned forward on the edge of her wicker throne and gently rested her chin upon her hand. The man seated across from her was agitated, alternately clenching his fists and running his fingers through his hair. His face was pale; sweat trickled from his hairline. The woman could tell that he had been deeply frightened, and the thought excited her.

"Now, Mr. Parker, when you arrived here you were quite incoherent. You nearly wrecked the helicopter in landing it, and you were most rude to Mary in demanding that you be allowed to see me. In the light of calm, please begin your explanation again, but temper it. There's no call for such frenzied ramblings."

"It's not safe out there," he exclaimed. "Not for tourists. Not for anyone. Can't you understand that? I'm quitting. I'm never going up again—God, I don't know how I got away—it kept after me—it kept coming. Like it was toying with me."

Miss Freda smiled benevolently.

Mary returned with the iced tea.

"Won't you have a glass?" Freda asked him. "Mary spikes it with just a leaf of crushed mint. It's most refreshing. Have a glass."

Glaring at her, he waved it off.

She straightened.

"Let me assume that you are speaking of Blood Wings, as the sacred Garkain is called locally. Please, start at the beginning and share the entire narrative."

He took a deep breath, but as he spoke, recounting the

whole of the experience, his eyes reflected moments of terror relived; his hands flung out nervously, and he shook his head constantly as if he challenged the truth of what he said.

"It will attack any aircraft—copter, low-flying plane, whatever—that enters the swamp. The copter tours are dangerous, and anyone air boating or taking a float trip back in there is taking his life in his own hands."

"And thus you are suggesting I cease the aerial tours and close the refuge to boating excursions as well?"

"Yes. You have to. If you won't, I'll go to the county sheriff, to Bradshaw, to anyone who'll listen."

"Don't threaten me, Mr. Parker. No one tells me how to operate this refuge. I won't be bullied."

Houston abruptly stood. "Fine. You do what you want. But do it without me. I won't be responsible. I've warned you—that creature has been disturbed—it's attacking, and I'm damn lucky I'm alive; and I think all of Orchid Springs had better be on the lookout."

"The Garkain," she responded, her voice cold and hollow, "is merely performing his assigned task—the task for which Maxwell brought him to the refuge—of guarding the mangrove swamp, protecting it from senseless individuals who have no respect for the wild state of nature. Occasionally, humanity has to pay a price for its insensitivity—I cannot stand in the way of nature."

Houston turned to leave, then hesitated. His voice quavered. "The blood will be on your hands—you're the monster."

Chapter Thirteen

1

Wade dreaded going to see Granny Roth, but his mom insisted.

"She wants you to have some of Gillie's clothes and toys—that kind of thing. I told her you would come over this afternoon."

"But mom . . . I mean, geez, do I have to?"

"She would be very disappointed if you didn't. It's not asking much of you."

And he began to wonder if, as an adult, he would be as successful at making his kids feel guilty. He decided to bite the bullet, and minutes later he was sitting in Granny Roth's front room, listening to the old woman's tear-laced words.

"I am going to leave Orchid Springs, though I dearly, dearly hate to. My health, oh, it's not good. The stress—the loss of Gillie—why, it's been too much. Too much entirely. So, doncha see, I am going to live with my younger sister, Clara, in Ft. Lauderdale. She has the most magnificent stand of redtips in her backyard. Oh, they reach as high as telephone poles. Just about that high. I won't be so lonely there, doncha see."

"Yes, ma'am," he murmured, his discomfort a balloon ready to burst.

"Gillie's gone. He ran away because, because, well, no boy wants to live with an old woman. No boy would. And so, doncha see, he ran away; and I see that he won't never come back, and I shouldn't ever have tried to take care of him."

The truth clawed at Wade's throat until he could not remain silent.

"He didn't run away. He didn't. The creature got him. Hash found his spear and his cap at Pelican Pond. The creature got him, don't you believe that?"

The hot sting of frustration filled his mouth. But Granny Roth seemed to block out his heartfelt exclamation.

"Would you like to go to his room and see if you would want to take any of his things? You were his friend, and so I thought before I boxed up all of it for Goodwill, I'd let you look at it first."

She smiled through tears, dabbing at her eyes with a ball of handkerchief.

Wade could not refuse her gesture.

She led him to the small room as if he had never visited it before.

"Doncha see, I left ever thing just like it was against his coming back so he'd see I never touched any of it. A girl comes in and vacuums; otherwise, it's just like it was. You look around—Gillie would want you to have anything that turns your head."

"Yes, ma'am," he whispered, for somehow it did not seem right to talk out loud in Gillie's room.

Granny Roth, choking on tears, waddled away.

A lonely, high-pitched whistle swept up through Wade's nose.

What'm I doin' here?

It felt all wrong. There might as well not have been any

furniture in the room—no bed, no dresser—and nothing on the walls—no Miami Dolphins posters or a pin-up of Madonna—because emptiness filled every inch.

For more than a minute, Wade simply stood and stared at the walls and at the dresser where Gillie's school picture leaned against a cedar box—Gillie's secret box. In the photo, the boy's blond hair shone like a halo; Wade envied it.

I can't take any of Gillie's stuff.

But he knew Granny Roth would be disappointed if he didn't, so he scrounged in the closet and found a half-inflated football and tucked it under his arm. He started to leave the room; but the picture caught his eye again, and he retrieved it and slipped it into his back pocket. The cedar box also issued its own siren call.

It seemed like trespassing on sacred ground.

Forbidden territory.

Before opening it, he wavered, hoping his friend would forgive him. There was only one object in the box: a small package of M & M's.

Lifted from Holly's. Wade smiled.

So he added that to the cache of football and photo.

At the door he turned as if anticipating a ghostly taunt.

"I ain't forgot 'bout you, Gillie. I promise you that creature'll get killed, and maybe I'll have to kill it. You'll see. I got the guts. You'll see."

He hesitated, then said, "I got to go home now and do something I've been wantin' to do. Well . . . bye, Gillie."

2

"Dang it, this friggin' stuff dudn't work right!"

Frustrated, one knee balanced on the lavatory, Wade frowned at the image in the mirror. His mom's hair lightener solution dribbled through his fingers. It smelled like Clorox and felt like liquid shortening.

And was successful on only half of his hair.

"Oh, geez, I look like a friggin' skunk!"

A broad band of blond inched up over the top of his head and into his bangs. Blond splotches gradually polkadotted other sections of his head.

"Got to put on more gunk," he muttered.

He mixed another round of the solution and began dabbing with the applicator as the directions indicated. Dark hairs surrendered to blond. Twenty minutes later, he surveyed a new Wade. And beamed.

"Just like Gillie's. All I need is a rat's tail," he told the mirror, and pledged to grow one.

The blond hair was his badge of commitment to the memory of his friend, and he was eager to show it to the world. His mom and Timmy were not around, so he made his way to Holly's, soaking in the warm Florida sunshine, hoping no one would notice that streaks of black peeked through the blond in spots.

Holly, however, noticed.

She screamed when she saw him.

"Dear Lord, boy, what on earth have you done?"

She held a fat hand to her bosom and fluttered her eyelids as if she were on the lip of fainting.

"Bleached my hair," he said. "Now it's just like Gillie's was."

Holly laughed and held her head, and two customers smiled benignly.

"Has your mother seen you?" the woman managed to ask, recovering somewhat from her laughter-induced tremors.

"Not yet. What's it matter? It's *my* hair."

He felt defiance rising within him and had, in fact, decided to leave, when Hash suddenly entered the store. The man strolled to the counter and asked for his favorite brand of small cigar.

He obviously did not recognize Wade.

Holly couldn't resist injecting a comment.

"You see what Wade here did? Halloween in June. He's a punk rocker or something strange like that."

When Hash finally focused on the boy, a lazy grin inched across his face. "Good Christ, kid, what silly ass idea got in your head to do that?"

"Hey, I like it this way," he shot back.

Hash shook his head. "Hard to tell who's weirder, kid—you or Houston."

"What's Houston done now?" asked Holly.

"Quit his job."

And Wade began to listen more closely.

Dropping some change in the man's hand, Holly said, "You making us drink sour milk? Why would he quit his job?"

Hash chuckled softly. "He came to my cabin and told me all about it. Seems he took the chopper out to that burned hummock and ran into company—just like I did. Ole Blood Wings let him know the swamp wasn't big enough for the both of 'em. The creature played with him like a damned cat battering a mouse before it crushes its back."

"Did it get him?" asked Wade, his voice filled with awe.

"Nope—just scared the livin' shit outta him, though. He claims the creature came after the chopper—I mean, Jesus, can you imagine that? When he got back to the refuge, he went straight to Miss Freda and told her what she could do with his job—he flat out wasn't goin' up in that chopper again—and he thinks all of Orchid Springs is in deep shit."

"So why would he come tell you?" Holly asked.

"'Cause we're friends," Hash exclaimed mockingly. "He knew I could help him out."

"Yeah," Holly sneered, "I have an idea that involved a

241

little purchase."

Hash shrugged.

Wade gritted his teeth. "Houston bought drugs from you, didn't he? He told my mom he was gonna stop—he's a liar."

"Hey, hey . . . he just needed something to calm his nerves. He'd had a bad scare. Hell, kid, don't be so damn hard on him."

"He's a liar, and you . . . you're a coward 'cause you won't go out and kill Blood Wings like you promised you would."

Turning to leave, Hash muttered over his shoulder. "Changed my mind. I'm goin' after Blood Wings. Tomorrow or the next day—that creature's mine."

As the man shuttled away, Wade glanced at Holly as if to see whether she believed him, but the woman busied herself at the cash register, having, apparently, no interest in Hash's declaration.

"Wait a minute," Wade called out to him, catching up to him just outside Holly's. "You really goin' after Blood Wings?"

Slipping on his sunglasses, Hash grinned confidently. "I am. But don't you go askin' me if you can come along, 'cause the answer's no."

"What made you change your mind 'bout goin'?"

"Well, let's just say it was a business opportunity."

"It's that guy in Miami, I bet," said Wade. "He's offering you a lot of money for the creature's bones, isn't he?"

"You're gettin' smart, kid. Maybe that blond hair gave your brain a kick in the ass."

"How much? How much will he give you?"

The man stopped walking and looked at Wade over the rims of the sunglasses; he grinned like a shark.

"It's the big hit, kid. The big hit."

Timmy and Sara Beth were playing Nintendo when Wade returned to the trailer, his thoughts geared to one desire: to get out into the swamp and be present when Hash killed Blood Wings.

I got to be there.

"Wow, look at Wade's hair!" Sara Beth squealed.

"Oh, man, who did that to you?" Timmy followed. "Can they do it to me, too?"

"Lay off, nerds. *I* did this to myself. And if anybody laughs, I'll waste 'em with this fist, got it?"

But Sara Beth could not restrain a giggle from leaking through the hand she had pressed over her mouth—she would have had an easier time holding water there.

"I mean it, Sara Beth."

Then he saw his mom's Instamatic by Timmy's knee.

"I told you not to mess with that. You break it and mom's gonna be seriously mad—madder than she's ever been, I promise you."

Timmy grabbed the camera as if fearing his brother would take it from him. "We need it."

Wade laughed derisively. "You still think you're gonna get a picture of Blood Wings?"

"Sure we are—ain't we, Sara Beth?"

"I guess so. Yeah, maybe."

"When? You guys would be too chicken. Puck-puck-puck."

"You'll see, Wade," Timmy exclaimed. "We're goin' this afternoon, and we'll bring back a picture. You'll see."

Wade shook his head, then noticed what his younger brother was wearing.

"Where did you get that? Did mom buy that for you?"

Timmy glanced down at the bright yellow "Blood Wings" T-shirt and pointed at Sara Beth, who became defensive.

"So what about it?" she said. "My daddy gave it to him."

"I hate those shirts. I oughtta make you take it off. That's what I oughtta do."

Sara Beth pushed to her feet. "Come on, Timmy. Let's get away from here. We're not wanted."

"Okay," he said, "but I'm takin' a sack of Oreos."

He switched off the Nintendo, and after wrestling the Oreos from a kitchen cabinet, he and the girl stalked out.

"So long, nerds," Wade called at their heels. "And I'm warnin' you, Timmy, you break mom's camera and she'll whip your friggin' little butt."

"I'll get a picture that'll make us rich. You'll see."

And then they really were gone, and Wade was relieved, but restless. He turned on the Nintendo and soon lost himself in Super Diamond Baseball.

Meanwhile, Timmy and Sara Beth broke into the cookies as they walked toward Holly's.

"You got any money?" he asked her.

"About seventy or eighty cents."

"Good—you can buy some Orange Crush."

"Why don't you ever have any money?"

"Because my mom says I lose it before I can spend it."

"My daddy says money burns a hole in my pocket," Sara Beth countered.

Timmy thought a moment. "Does it really?"

"Come on. Let's go in Holly's. It's too hot out here."

They trundled into the store and minutes later exited, each with a cold can of Orange Crush.

"Where's your daddy's boat?" Timmy asked as they sat on the grassy bank of the slough.

"It's around the bend, tied up where nobody can see it."

"Let's take it out and get a picture of Blood Wings."

"Are you crazy?"

Disappointment and puzzlement seized his expression.

"No, I'm not either crazy. You said you'd go with me. I got my mom's camera, and we got Oreos and a cold drink."

"Your mom wouldn't let you do it. She'd say you're too little."

"My mom's shoppin' in Miami. She won't never know we've been gone, and we'll be back by supper."

"Who's supposed to be watching you?"

He shrugged. "Wade, I guess. 'Sides, I don't never need nobody to watch me—I'm not no baby."

"Well . . . come on. I'll show you where the boat is."

They crossed the bridge into the refuge and walked the dusty shell road around the back loop, then plunged into some saw grass, continuing for another thirty or forty yards until the slough once again came into view. At a break in the tangle of mangrove trees, a small skiff was tied down.

Excited, Timmy said, "We gotta shake on the deal."

"What deal?" Sara Beth, sweating heavily, sat in the saw grass; she had finished her soda and was still thirsty.

"On the money we're gonna get for the picture of Blood Wings. We'll split it fifty-fifty, okay?"

"I guess so."

They shook hands, and Timmy clambered into the boat.

Fanning herself with her hands, Sara Beth grumbled, "It's too hot. Why don't we wait for a cooler day?"

"Naw, come on. I got the camera. If we don't go now, mom'll find out I have it and take it away from me and hide it."

"I'm still thirsty, aren't you?"

"Some."

"I got an idea," the girl announced. "Why don't I go home and fix us a thermos of lemonade, and when I get back we can talk about the boat."

Timmy frowned. "Okay, maybe. Don't be gone a

long time."

"I won't."

She scrambled to her feet.

"Bye," she cried.

"And don't make it real sour," Timmy called after her.

But that was the last he saw of her; when she reached home, her mother announced a spur of the moment trip to the Dadeland Mall. Sara Beth could not resist. She forgot all about Timmy.

So he sat in the boat and crunched Oreos and contemplated the rope connected from a ring at the prow to a mangrove root. And he experimented with the camera, snapping a shot of the saw grass across the slough. He pretended to see Blood Wings explode out of the mangroves, and he swung the camera into action, clicking nothing but blue sky.

He waited.

He ate his fill of cookies and decided to save the rest for the trip.

It was hot.

Although he knew he shouldn't do it, he gently placed his empty Orange Crush can in the slough; it floated for several feet before water flowed into the opening and it sank, producing a necklace of bubbles.

He contemplated the rope some more; his small fingers tugged at the knot.

He waited.

"Sara Beth, where are you?"

He worked at the knot. And to his surprise it eventually loosened. He stood up, then managed to lift the pushpole and angle it into the slough.

He thought of Wade.

"You'll see," he whispered.

He pushed hard. The sluggish current swung the skiff around.

Timmy smiled.

He poled into the main current and then sat down. He was on his way.

4

Wade stared at the twenty-foot cabin cruiser, its gleaming whiteness, the proud lines of its prow as a truck backed the boat down the ramp and into the slough. Having tired of Nintendo, he had gone to the tennis courts to channel his restlessness into pounding a ball against the backboard. The sight of the handsome boat being hauled into Orchid Springs drew him away.

As the boat gained its balance atop the water, and two men tied it down, Wade continued to admire it. A voice at his shoulder startled him.

"She sure is beautiful, isn't she?"

Wade turned and saw Lark. "Yeah, nobody 'round here has one like it. Whose could it be?"

"It's mine."

The boy's mouth gaped. "You kiddin'?" *That* boat?"

"Well, it's mine for several days, anyway. My father arranged with someone he knows in Miami to let me use it to go into the swamp. You're looking at my ticket to getting pictures of Blood Wings."

"Geez, it's some kind uh neat boat."

Suddenly Lark did a doubletake. "Wade! What have you done to your hair?"

"Oh," he muttered, "I bleached it."

"I can see you did, but whatever for?"

"Because of Gillie."

"Gillie? Your friend who . . . ?" She hesitated. "I think I understand."

"I'm glad somebody does."

Then Lark was called to one side to talk momentarily to the two men who had delivered the boat. Finished with them, she rejoined Wade.

"Let's climb aboard," she said.

"This thing's awesome," Wade exclaimed.

He scrambled to the wheel and sat in the captain's chair. "Who's gonna drive this for you?"

Hands on her hips, Lark shook her head. "Wade—why don't you think I can do anything? *I'm* the captain of this ship. And I'm so excited."

"When are you going into the swamp? Hash might be goin' tomorrow. And Houston quit his job 'cause Blood Wings attacked him."

"Wait, wait . . . run all this by me again."

So he did.

Lark bit at the corner of her lip apprehensively. "I had hoped to beat Hash out there, but I can't go before the day after tomorrow—I have some special film ordered, and it won't be in until tomorrow afternoon." She paused. "I'd like to talk to Houston, and I'd like to know what Freda Schreck told him."

"Hash said Houston was so scared it made him start takin' drugs again."

"Sorry to hear that. And I don't imagine he received a sympathetic ear from Miss Freda—she's very bitter. I had a chance to chat with her over tea."

"She's pretty strange, right?"

"Yes," said Lark.

And Wade added, "So's that black woman—you know, her helper."

"I got the feeling that Mary sees through Miss Freda's cynicisms, she recognizes that the woman's feeling about Blood Wings is extreme."

"Did Miss Freda show you the poison stick?"

"The *wirrie?* Yes. In fact, she claims it's the only way Blood Wings can be destroyed, but I assured her again and again that I wasn't interested in killing the creature—only in taking pictures of it and capturing it on film."

Wade had stopped listening.

Images of the *wirrie* flooded his thoughts.

So distracted was he that at first he did not hear her question.

"What?"

"I said: Do you want to give her a test run?"

"The boat?"

Lark nodded, smiling expansively.

"Well, yeah, sure."

"Do you know the way to Pelican Pond?" she asked.

The boy felt a sudden chill. "Yeah . . . I guess so."

"Help me throw off the ropes, and we'll be gone."

5

"Some places it gets pretty narrow," said Wade, concerned about the width of Lark's boat.

"I know, and that may limit where I can go in the swamp; but if I stay in the deeper runs, I'll be fine. This craft won't run aground easily." She was fiddling with her 35mm camera even as she kept one hand on the wheel. They were cruising slowly.

"How long are you gonna be gone?"

She shrugged. "Long as it takes. I spent six weeks camped out looking for Bigfoot."

"There really a Bigfoot? You know, a monkey-man tall as a basketball player?"

"I believe there is. I heard one, and there have been so many eyewitnesses that I find it difficult not to believe."

"Why hasn't somebody shot one and stuffed it?"

"A very good question—shows how elusive those creatures are. Of course, you could ask the same question about Blood Wings."

Wade nervously flexed his fingers. "I'd shoot it if I had a gun like Hash's."

"It doesn't appear to me that Hash is such a great hunter."

The boy frowned. "I thought he was my friend, but . . . my only real friend was Gillie."

"Hey, aren't *I* your friend?"

"Well, yeah, I guess maybe, sorta. But you don't want to kill Blood Wings, and I need a friend to kill it for me, or I'll have to do it myself."

"Okay, then, I suppose we can't be friends."

No one spoke for thirty seconds or more.

Saw grass passed to the left of them; mangroves to the right.

It was a hot, sticky afternoon. Lark's blouse clung to her; stray wisps of her hair began to fall onto her forehead, causing her to swipe at them. Wade felt the heat and humidity, too. They were approaching Pelican Pond, and he was struggling to think about anything except the stifling air and the inevitable memory of Gillie.

"You got a boyfriend?" he asked out of the blue.

She glanced at him, an impish smile stealing across her mouth. "Isn't that kind of a personal question?"

"Well, you asked me all about Gillie and the creature and what I saw. That was pretty personal."

She nodded. "Got me there." She sighed and stared straight ahead.

"Guys don't like women who do what I do," she began. "I mean, most of them don't. They want women with great figures and beautiful faces who like nice clothes and like to go out to restaurants and shows and parties and . . . I like doing what I do. The great naturalists who have been women have always sacrificed that part of their lives."

250

Wade studied her a moment. "I betchoo've had *one* boyfriend—at least one."

Her eyes twinkled from the reflection of memory. "Yes, one in particular. His name was Curry—Curry Thompkins, and I met him at Lake Champlain where I was on a photo hunt for Champ—that's the sea monster that lives in that huge lake. And, well, we spent most of one summer together. He was majoring in biology at the University of Vermont, and I thought we really hit it off super. I liked him a lot, an awful lot. I thought we had something special going. But when the summer ended, he went back to school, and we wrote to each other, and it still felt special. I wrote him a letter every day—was really hung up on him. Around Thanksgiving, I got a 'Dear Lark' letter. He had met this girl, some sorority fluff, and they had gotten engaged."

"Wow, that's a bummer," Wade muttered.

"You can say that again. A monster bummer."

The boy chuckled. "Monster bummer? Is that like a pun?"

"Sorta." And she laughed, too.

The boat eased into the area of Pelican Pond where not a half an hour earlier Timmy and the skiff had floated by, the small boy holding the Instamatic tightly, poised to photograph his quarry.

6

Forbidden territory.

It looked the same to Wade as it had that day weeks ago when he and Gillie had approached it.

"Right up there's Pelican Pond," he announced to Lark.

She shoved the boat out of gear, and as they drifted, she surveyed the scene.

"Incredible. So beautiful. It's like it could have been this way for millions of years."

Raising her camera, she clicked off numerous shots of the mangroves and the bottleneck leading into the pond itself.

"It's called Pelican Pond," said Wade, "but there really aren't many pelicans around. It's just a name."

Just a friggin' name, Gillie's voice echoed from memory.

The pink flush of Gillie's face ballooned to mind, and Wade wondered what his friend would think of his newly blond hair.

"This opening's going to be a tight fit," said Lark, bringing the boy out of his reflections.

The right side of the boat raked against the roots and branches of the reaching mangroves. Wade hustled to the rail and said, "It's okay. Maybe the side'll get a little scratched."

Clearing the bottleneck, the boat rode freely into the lazy swirl of the pond.

"Was it here?" asked Lark.

Her question caught him off guard.

She was looking at him queerly, half holding her breath.

"Here?"

And then he realized what she was asking.

"Oh, you mean. . . ."

"Where were you and Gillie right before it happened?"

Slewing gently against the outer edge of the mangroves, the boat held steady as the boy's eyes roamed the scene.

"Over there's Bella, Hash's dredger. See, over there. By the railroad ties—he digs up fossils with it."

Lark twisted around and snapped a couple of shots. "Is that where Gillie was attacked?"

252

"No."

"I'm sorry," said Lark. "I know it's a bad memory . . . I'm just interested in the layout . . . in the details."

"Gillie got out and climbed after a corn snake," Wade suddenly exclaimed. "Right in there." He pointed into the thickest tangle of the mangroves. "A big sucker. Six feet long."

"Did he catch it?"

"No, but you oughtta seen him go after it."

"What happened then?"

Wade scratched at the back of his head; he could still smell the lightener solution.

"There was a kinda funny noise."

"What did it sound like?"

"Like a couple thousand birds flying, and then like a whistle, only I never paid much attention to it because I saw Gillie had left his spear—the one I took from Hash. That was Gillie's."

"So the creature attacked him here in these mangroves?"

"More this way." He swept a hand to the right. "Could we start up the boat?"

Lark nodded and, excited by the boy's narrative, followed his directions as he guided her to inch the craft out of the pond into a narrow run.

"Stop here," he said.

He stood staring into the wall of mangroves and the slice of sky beyond them.

Lark began to take more pictures.

Tonelessly, Wade said, "I heard Gillie say, 'I found it,' and there was this awful smell. The worse smell I ever smelled. And then he called my name. He said my name two or three times, not real loud or nuthin'. But the way he said it scared me, scared me bad. I couldn't see him at first; so I moved the boat right to here, and I looked across there, and I saw him."

Wade's eyes met Lark's; his mouth quivered.

She hugged him against her breasts. After a few moments, he pulled away and said, "He started yellin' my name, and I heard that weird vibration again; but I couldn't tell exactly where it was comin' from. And a real bad stink. And then something happened to Gillie's voice—like, like when you put your hand over somebody's mouth and they try to scream. Like that. My nose and eyes burned, but I saw . . . I saw it. I saw Blood Wings. I saw what it did to Gillie."

He turned from the railing and sat down in the bottom of the boat and rested his forehead on his knees. Lark gently touched his hair and whispered, "I'm going to climb up there and take a look."

Five minutes later she returned; her face was pinched and drawn. With Wade's help, she backed into the pond, circled and squeezed through the bottleneck into the central slough.

She clasped him on the shoulder.

"Thanks," she said. "That must have been very difficult for you. I appreciate it."

The boy said nothing.

In his thoughts, a blackness rose and spread, a black curtain closing, then slowly opening upon an uncertain future.

Chapter 14

1

"What will he do? Does he have another job?"

Wade's mother tried to mask her concern as she set plates on the table.

"Pour some milk for you and Timmy," she added.

Still recovering from the trip to Pelican Pond, Wade shuffled to the refrigerator and pressed the container of milk to his chest. His mother was drilling him about Houston, a subject he did not care to discuss.

"Tell me again all that Hash said," she persisted.

This time his narrative became shorter, details sparser. He finished by saying, "He's back on drugs."

His mother did not speak at first. She was browning hamburger to be mixed in with a box of Hamburger Helper, and there was frozen corn in the microwave. She made the spatula dance through the frying meat; Wade could sense that she was very frustrated.

"Lark got a new boat," he offered, hoping she would change the subject from Houston. "It's super neat, and she took me for a ride in it. She's gonna take it into the swamp to get pictures of Blood Wings."

As she drained the excess grease into an empty can,

some of it splashed onto her wrist.

"Ouch! Damn it!"

She slammed the skillet down and hustled to the sink, where she wrapped a wet dishrag around the burn.

"Damn him! Why did I have to . . . I don't care what happens to him!"

She turned away from the boy, and he thought he heard her stifle a sob. Getting herself under control, she finished draining the grease and mixing the main dish.

"Call Timmy to supper," she said.

I hate Houston Parker.

I hate him for makin' mom sad.

Anger filtering all the way to the bottoms of his tennis shoes, Wade trudged into the hallway.

"Timmy! Supper! Come on!"

Back at the table, he watched his mother's stiff movements.

"How much corn do you want?" she asked as she started dipping it.

"'Bout two big spoons."

"Did Timmy answer you? Go back and make sure he washes his hands."

Wade groaned.

And found an empty bedroom.

"He's not in our room."

"That little scamp knows better than this. I have to go to work soon. He knows he's supposed to be home by now. Go outside and give him a call. Go on."

He did. And got no answer.

When he returned to the trailer, he said, "He's probably over at Sara Beth's. They been playin' together."

"Would you look at what I've done to my arm? It'll sting all evening."

She rubbed some Vaseline on it and went to the phone.

"Well, he's not over there," she said after a few

seconds of conversation with Mrs. Bradshaw. "Go out around where he usually plays. Check Holly's, too. And tell him I'm going to warm his bottom if he doesn't hurry home."

"Why do I have to get him? He knows how to get home."

"But I asked you to keep an eye on him while I went shopping—which you should have done instead of bleaching your hair. Haven't you seen him this afternoon?"

"No. Except when him and Sara Beth was here playin' Nintendo."

"Go look." She pointed at the door, repressing her apprehension.

Grudgingly, Wade made the rounds: the tennis courts, the bank along the slough, the kangaroo and gator pens, and Holly's.

"Dumb kid," he whispered to himself as he wended his way to the trailer, where he found his mother standing outside, the setting sun slanting across her face.

She looked worried.

"Did you see him?" The apprehension was building in her tone.

"Nope," he said.

"Oh, dear God," she suddenly exclaimed, pressing her fingers nervously to her mouth. "I was afraid of this . . . oh, dear God, it's happened."

She turned and practically crashed through the door, and the action sent a chill through the boy.

"Mom? Mom, whaddaya mean, 'it's happened'?"

But she was on the phone speaking rapidly, maintaining, from what Wade could overhear, that she believed her son had been kidnapped by his father. For several minutes she talked haltingly, describing Timmy and detailing her reasoning for assuming a possible crime.

Then she fired a question at Wade.

"What was Timmy wearing when you last saw him?"

He described the Blood Wings T-shirt, and she relayed the information to the person she was speaking to.

Her hand trembled as she hung up.

Her eyes teared. Wade went to her, and she hugged him.

"Mom, I don't think maybe dad took him," he murmured.

"Well, I do. He's threatened to. This happens these days. I'm going to call Holly and see if someone else can work for me this evening."

"Mom, Timmy's been talkin' 'bout goin' out in a boat with Sara Beth to take a picture of Blood Wings. Maybe that's where he is."

"Wade, I called the Bradshaw's—they haven't seen him—I just have a feeling I'm right about this. Oh, God . . . he's taken my baby."

"Mom, he coulda gone out to take a picture of the creature. He was carryin' 'round your Instamatic."

But his words fell on deaf ears; Anita Martin had convinced herself that her ex-husband had kidnapped Timmy—no other explanation would suffice. So it was that when Holly Webster showed up at the door to console his mother, Wade slipped out.

Mr. Bradshaw greeted him at the door of their condo, a rod and reel in hand.

"Hey there, Wade, what can I do you for?"

"Is Sara Beth home? I'm trying to find my little brother, and the last time I saw him he was with Sara Beth."

Bradshaw chuckled. "Maybe the boy's off fishing. A good evening for it—last quarter moon. White bass oughtta be biting. Roy Johnson and I are gonna hop down the slough a ways and test our luck. We put a lantern close to the water, and it draws 'em. Yeah, it does."

"No, Timmy dudn't know how to fish."

258

"When I was a wee lad," Bradshaw continued, "I would deliberately stay out after sunset just to aggravate my folks, you know. Then I'd wander home and make up some wild hair story to explain my lateness—kids do that kinda thing. Why, he's probably watching us right this second and snickering up his sleeve."

"Could I please talk to Sara Beth?"

"Oh, well, sure. Sure thing. Come on in."

Wade hesitated. "Could you please have her come to the door?" Bradshaw shrugged and smiled. "Suit yourself."

Wariness in her eyes, Sara Beth, moments later, waddled out to face the boy.

"Haven't you seen Timmy?" he asked.

"No, not for a long time."

"He's not nowhere 'round. You was the last one to see him."

The girl looked scared; she puckered her lips defensively. "I don't know where he is."

"Where did you see him last?"

She glanced away and blinked several times as if to jumpstart her mind into recalling. She was panting from the mental exertion.

"Well . . . you can't tell my father."

"Tell him what? Where's Timmy?"

"I said I didn't know where he is. I left him at the boat."

"The boat? Your dad's boat? The one he leaves tied up in the refuge?"

"Yeah."

"Geez, did you guys go out in that boat?"

"No way. I went home, and my mom and me went shopping."

"Where did Timmy go?"

She gestured that she had no idea.

"Friggin' bad. Okay, I'll go check the boat. That's

259

probably where he is . . . I hope."

"Wade . . . it's not my fault. He stealed your mom's camera, and I didn't tell him to . . . and I didn't want to get in the boat."

The boy gritted his teeth. "Oh, quit whinin', Sara Beth. Nobody's blamin' you."

He dashed away, a small flame of hope suddenly alive in his chest. By the time he reached the bridge to the refuge, darkness had a grip on the day, though the rising, partial moon provided some light, enough to keep him from returning home to get a flashlight.

Memory and intuition guided him to the spot along the shell road that angled off to the slough; he saw where the saw grass had been beaten down, a telltale sign that two kids had adventured through there.

"Timmy?" he called. "Timmy? Are you here?"

The saw grass and mangroves conspired to muffle his voice, and the modicum of hope he had collected began to evaporate.

"Timmy?"

He slogged his way through to a clearing; he could hear his heart pounding. A cold equation was forming in his thoughts: missing boat equals missing Timmy.

"Timmy!" he shouted.

But the night rhythm of the swamp took no special notice of his cry.

He fingered the tie-down rope, its empty ring, and forced himself to imagine where his brother might be.

"He's out there," he whispered. "Timmy's out there . . . out there with Blood Wings."

The horror of that realization sent him spinning, racing back to the shell road. He ran, not certain at first where to go or what to do. And behind him, the swamp held its darkness within.

"Are you postive he took the boat? It's possible, isn't it, that someone else could have taken it."

Lark's calm, reasoned tone dulled the edge of the boy's fears.

"I guess maybe so, but him and Sara Beth, they was there, and Sara Beth said Timmy got in the boat; so I bet he did, and I bet he untied it and, when it got out in the current, he's not strong enough to get it turned 'round."

A frown wrinkling her brow, Lark said, "Have you told your mom about finding the boat gone?"

Wade shook his head; the room started to blur. He was still trying to catch his breath from his mad dash out of the refuge. He had sought out Lark's motel room, interrupting her dinner of chips and soft drink. On her bed were scattered papers and books, a tape recorder, a camcorder, and a 35mm camera. She had been writing notes when he knocked on her door.

"She wouldn't listen. She thinks my dad kidnapped him, and she won't listen to anything else."

"Do you believe your dad would?"

The boy sighed heavily. The blur he had been experiencing resolved itself to clarity.

"I guess maybe he would."

"Has anyone seen him in the area? Has your mother seen him or talked to him?"

"On the phone she did—she said he called and told her sometime he might take us. She's called the sheriff."

"But they won't declare Timmy a missing person until he's been gone twenty-four hours," said Lark.

"Twenty-four hours—geez, he won't make it that long in the swamp. And Blood Wings . . . could we go out in the boat and look for him? Please. We gotta try."

"Oh, Wade, I couldn't navigate that boat in the swamp at night. Maybe Hash or Houston—"

"No, I don't want them. I don't trust 'em. I don't like 'em."

Lark rested her forehead onto one hand, surrendering as deeply into thought as she could. "I would be willing to take off at first light, but it wouldn't do anyone any good if I went out now. But if it still appears at dawn that he's gone into the swamp, then I promise you I'll go."

"And take me with you—right?"

"I don't know, Wade. Your mother has enough to worry about without adding something else."

"But you've got to let me. You've got to."

"Okay, I'll tell you what. You go on home and let your mother know what you discovered about Mr. Bradshaw's boat. It could be, of course, that Timmy's there at home already, or maybe they've verified the involvement of your dad. Regardless, you need to be with your mother. Don't do anything tonight to contribute to her troubles."

"I wish you had a gun," said the boy.

"I've told you before, Wade, I have no use for a gun or any other kind of weapon."

"But what if we have to kill Blood Wings?"

"Right at the moment, the problem is to locate Timmy. You go on home. I'll be ready to shove off at dawn. Holly has a CB outfit, so I can keep in contact with her, and the sheriff's department will help search, too, if we can convince them Timmy's out there."

"I'll be here," said the boy. "The second it gets light I'll be here."

Before she could object too strongly, he had scurried out the door, hope renewed.

3

When he reached home, he walked in on a gathering of his mom, Holly and, to his disappointment, Houston

Parker. And no Timmy. To the sober group he delivered his theory about the missing boat, but his mom rejected it.

"I called where your dad is staying and got no answer," she explained. "It has to mean he's come to Orchid Springs and taken Timmy, and there's no way to know where. . . ."

She broke down and began to cry; Holly and Houston pressed close to lend their emotional support. Neither said much. Frustrated, Wade went to his room and fumbled around in his closet until he located Gillie's makeshift spear.

"Gillie, Timmy's out there. Out there in the swamp. I have to get out there and kill Blood Wings before he attacks Timmy, 'cause Timmy dudn't have no weapon, no gun or even a spear; but I've got one and . . ."

Words and insight flashed into his thoughts like a vision from heaven, like some special effects lighting from a science fiction movie.

The wirrie . . . she claims it's the only way Blood Wings can be destroyed . . . .

"Friggin' right."

Wade knew instantly what he must do.

But the thought of doing it staggered him.

I've got to steal the wirrie.

"I can take care of myself," he whispered.

Then the cold, logical voice of some inner observer commanded his attention; Stealing the wirrie? Are you prepared to sneak over to Miss Freda's in the dark? How are you going to break into her house? Someone would hear you, and the worst part could be that she *doesn't* call the police. Instead, Miss Freda would devise her own form of punishment. Or she could direct Mary, the servant woman, to do something unspeakable. You would never be able to get away with it. Forget about the *wirrie*.

263

But he could not.

He switched off the bedroom light and plopped on his bed and tried to determine by the stream of light from the partial moon what time it was. Nearing midnight, he guessed.

Where's Timmy right this second?

The question stabbed him.

Wouldn't have a chance against Blood Wings.

In his darkest projections, he saw his little brother drifting beneath the moonlight, innocent, lost, no concept of the danger he was in. Unaware, he would glide into Blood Wing's territory. *Forbidden territory*. And that black curtain of wings, those vicious fangs, the overpowering stench—like a small rodent, the boy would be plucked from the boat and carried away and . . .

Timmy, God, hold on till we can save you.

He went to his door and listened. He could hear Holly suggesting that his mom get some sleep—nothing more to be done tonight. Some parting words from Houston as well, but Wade could not decipher them. A few minutes passed; the front door closed.

Wade scrambled onto his bed and pretended to be asleep.

Ever so gently Anita entered the room and crossed to the side of the bed. "Honey, don't you want to slip off your jeans to sleep? Come on. I'll help you."

"Mom," he murmured. "Don't worry 'bout Timmy. I'm gonna find him."

A lining of tears in her voice, she hugged him and said, "We have the authorities looking for your dad. They'll find him . . . him and Timmy. Your dad . . . I just don't believe he would do anything to harm Timmy. He's doing this to punish *me,* to get back at me for the hurt I caused him when we left Missouri. They'll find Timmy and bring him home, and then they won't let your dad ever, ever take him away from us again."

She said good night.

As before, Wade recognized that she would accept no other explanation; she had also apparently convinced Holly and Houston.

He closed his eyes and waited and continued to wage an inner war. Intuition told him he was right about Timmy and the boat; brutal necessity told him he must steal the *wirrie*.

After a half an hour, he could not bear to wait any longer. He rolled out of bed, pulled on his jeans, located a flashlight, and went to his window. The partial moon reminded him that quite possibly his little brother was out there somewhere in the swamp. Blood Wings had attacked Houston's copter—the creature had been provoked and would, no doubt, turn its fury upon anyone who trespassed into its territory.

Forbidden territory.

Wade squirmed through his window and sneaked through the darkness to the bridge, took a deep breath, and began a cautious approach to Miss Freda's. Crouched near her front porch, the full impact of what he was attempting slammed against his courage and determination.

A cold, sick, empty feeling gripped his insides.

He was on the edge of turning back, but at that moment he heard Gillie's voice ghosting from the past:

You know what your problem is, Wade, ole friend? You're a coward. Got no guts. I shoulda seen it before. You're 'fraid to go into forbidden territory.

"No, I'm not."

But it took him another several minutes of studying the darkened, silent house before he could free himself from his apprehension to test a few of the side windows. All were stuck too tightly to open without creating too much noise. He tiptoed along the porch, and as he passed the screen door, he tugged at it, assuming that it was latched.

It swung open.

Hot needles pricked his wrist.

Somebody forgot to lock it.

He couldn't believe his good luck. The screen cried a small protest as he squeezed through it. He paused to let his eyes adjust, and then he switched on the flashlight.

Suddenly he was immensely pleased with himself—almost giddy, in fact.

I'm doing it! part of him exclaimed.

He followed the pool of light into the artifact room. He felt confident as he swept the light over glass cases of stone hatchets, tools, and several boomerangs. But it was the *wirrie* that stopped him in his tracks; he stood before it nearly mesmerized, and in his thoughts he saw it lashed to the end of Gillie's makeshift spear, replacing the butcher knife.

Knowing he must hurry, he forced himself out of his reverie and reached for the handle to the glass case. He never heard the woman's approach.

"Why you want *wirrie?*"

Her broken English filled the shadows behind him; he spun around, and he could see only half of her face, the tangle of her black hair, and the gleam of one dark eye. His first impulse was to run, but she blocked his path to the door.

"You want to draw poison? You want to kill?"

"Please let me go," he stammered.

The flashlight jerked nervously in his hand; he felt as if he were standing in a frigid meat locker. He tried to say something more; instead, his chest heaved, he swallowed air, and then hiccupped, not able to control the involuntary reaction.

Mary stepped forward so that her face was bathed in

266

the reflection of yellowish spray from the flashlight. She appeared curious to hear the strange sound leaping out of of the boy.

"I paint Garkain," she said. "You want to kill Garkain?"

Though terrified of her possible reaction, he nodded. She glanced at the *wirrie*.

"Every boy learn not to fear," she said.

Wade judged that at any moment Miss Freda would awaken, or that the servant woman would awaken her, and then he would be at their mercy. They might go easy—they might tell his mom and recommend that the Martins leave Orchid Springs—or he might disappear. Everyone would assume that his dad had kidnapped him, or, as they had with Gillie, assume that he had run away. Or got himself lost in the swamp.

The woman opened the glass case and removed the *wirrie*.

The boy's heart froze. Cold chills fanned out in his chest.

"Please no," he whimpered through the nervous hiccupping.

Raising the tip to eye level, the woman seemed to be examining the sharp point as if sizing up its capacity to kill. "Garkain no longer sacred guardian of swamp."

She's going to jab that point into my heart.

He clenched his fist and tightened his grip on the flashlight, resolved that if she lunged at him, he would swing his pathetic weapon as hard as he could—he would fight.

"Men cause Garkain to hate. Garkain turn evil."

Pieces of her comments filtered through the boy's fear.

What is she saying? What is she going to do?

He calculated that possibly, just possibly, he could sprint past her and dodge the dangerous weapon.

"Garkain hate men. Must be killed."

Her eyes met the boy's. "You brave?"

Surprise caught his breath.

His response issued as a throaty whisper. "I can take care of myself."

But doubt siphoned off some of the energy from his confidence.

"Take *wirrie*. It has poison of Garkain. You kill him."

She handed the stick toward him. Hesitating, he eventually took it, holding it at arm's length as if it were about to explode. He searched her expression for some assurance that he could trust her, but before he could finish that search, another voice parted the shadows.

"Be careful, young sport. Maxwell Schreck killed the other Garkain with that *wirrie*. You, however, may discover that Mary's gesture is a fatal trap. You came here, a thief in the night. Let the day sentence you to an appropriate punishment."

His emotions feverishly alive, Wade bolted from the room and out the door and did not slow his pace until he reached his bedroom window. He caught his breath and flexed his fingers on the *wirrie*—and felt brave enough suddenly to battle all the world's darkness.

4

Deep in the swamp, a skiff runs aground on an isolated hummock, but the small boy curled up and asleep within the vessal does not stir. To his chest, he hugs a half-eaten sack of Oreo cookies. His throat is raw and sore from shouting for help into the indifference of the night; his eyes sting from crying.

Exhaustion had eventually taken its toll. Remaining vigilant as long as possible, he had finally relinquished his hold on his mother's Instamatic camera and slumped

268

down with the setting of the sun and the appearance of stars. For hours, he had listened to the orchestration of the swamp, occasionally breaking the silence to call out, occasionally fighting the rise of tears generated by fear and loneliness.

A mist gathers, its droplets causing the boy to shiver. Sleep chases away his terror.

5

Timmy Martin shifts once in the bottom of the skiff, but is oblivious to the silken rustle of wings as a looming blackness flies toward Orchid Springs.

6

Wick Thorndale loved a sky full of stars. He loved surrendering to their majesty, and although he knew only a sprinkling of constellations by name, he felt on intimate terms with those distant points of light. They were his only companions as he closed Holly's bar for the night.

He locked the rear door, checked it twice, and began to whistle. Sixty-four. That number was on his mind. Tomorrow it would be sixty-three. Sixty-three days until the end of August and the beginning of retirement. He had given Holly notice far in advance. This was to be his second retirement; the first came after thirty-five years at a small manufacturing operation in Jacksonville. He and his wife, Lurleen, had pulled up stakes and bought a trailer on the outskirts of Orchid Springs, their hearts and minds set on relaxation, fishing, a little travel, and no alarm clocks.

Reality raised its grim visage within a year, forcing the

269

man to seek employment to supplement the retirement checks—whose buying power appeared to dwindle every month.

"We paid it off, Lennie," he exclaimed as he walked along the road leading away from the bar and trailer park. "Bradshaw gave me the final payment receipt last week. This time, Lennie, this time we'll retire for good."

And, oh, didn't those stars look great.

He thought about his wife. He had always called her Lennie, a name she had acquired as a girl. He had fallen in love with her when he was barely fourteen and she was twelve; they had married six years later, and though their marriage had been childless—two miscarriages convinced them to quit trying for a family—he could not imagine how they could ever have been any happier.

Lennie was the only woman he had loved.

Fifty years of love; fifty years beside him, battling disappointments, sharing good times, dreaming of taking it easy.

"Soon, Lennie, sweet lady, soon we'll have it."

Wick enjoyed talking aloud when there was no one around to hear. The darkened trailers and condo units assured him not a soul would be eavesdropping on his mutterings.

A quarter of a mile beyond the trailer park, he reached the comfortable yet modest green and white mobile home he shared with the woman he adored. A pang of loneliness lodged in his throat as he climbed the steps and unlocked the door. Lennie would not be there. She had taken a bus to Jacksonville to visit her ailing sister in the hospital; she would return tomorrow afternoon.

"So empty," he sighed, after switching on lights and catching the faintest whiff of lavender bath spray— Lennie's fragrance.

He was not sleepy.

On the kitchen table sprawled futher evidence of

Lennie's habitation: jumbled stacks of envelopes and three by five notecards and a roll of stamps, tools of the trade for a compulsive sweepstaker. She entered as many as her arthritic fingers could stand, printing addresses relentlessly, watching the mail each day the way farmers reverently watch the skies for coming weather changes.

The only item she had ever won was a tiny, six-inch screen TV which they kept in the kitchen, and whenever Wick would suggest that she consider going cold turkey on the seemingly addictive string of contests, she would point proudly at the miniature object and chortle, "Listen sonny, who won that Sony?"

Then she would laugh at her play on words, and he would have to join her laughter because he loved her and couldn't imagine life without her.

"Let's go sit by the water," he said to the empty kitchen.

The partial moon provided just enough light for him to pick up two lawn chairs beyond the front door and stroll the forty yards or so to the edge of the slough—only he and Lennie would pretend that it was Caribbean beach and the water was blue-green and magnificently clear. At the edge of the slough, under the after-midnight sky, Wick set up both chairs. A bit self-consciously, he began telling the imaginary presence of his wife about the day, informing her that the mail had consisted entirely of bills and advertising flyers.

"Lennie, Anita Martin had some horrible news this evening. It seems her ex-husband has kidnapped her youngest boy—Timmy. I know you remember him. The cutest dark eyes. She didn't come to work. She's asked the authorities to investigate—such an awful situation. It's troubled me all evening. I've tried instead to think about the end of summer, but I feel so sorry for Anita, don't you?"

Patches of mist floated a few feet above the slough.

271

He pulled the empty lawn chair closer to him. He imagined he could still smell the lavender bath spray.

"I miss you, Lennie."

He half chuckled.

"Isn't that something? You're gone only a couple of days . . . and I 'bout can't take it. You know, Lennie, it seems like a morbid thing to say, but I've always sorta wished that when it comes our time to go . . . that I'd go first. I'd be so god-awful lonely without you."

He touched the arm of the lawn chair and then looked up at the stars.

"See there, Lennie? There's Orion. See his belt?"

A wave of something foul smelling poured suddenly over his shoulder.

"Wind carrying the stink from the sewage plant a good ways tonight," he said.

The dive of the creature sounded like the wail of a hurricane striking land. Wick turned as the blackness swept within a few feet of him, toppling the unoccupied lawn chair. He did not cry out. He watched as the creature banked, momentarily blotting out the partial moon.

On weak legs, Wick got up and retrieved the lawn chair.

"Get yourself to the house, Lennie."

The creature rolled and pitched in the air.

Wick's eyes burned; the smell choked at this throat.

He folded the lawn chair and held it protectively in front of him as Blood Wings dived again.

"Dear God, it's true," the man whispered.

A silken wing roared an inch or so over his head. He fell backward, but a talon caught the chair; and though he struggled, the man's elbow was looped through one of the aluminum armrests. When the creature jerked at the chair, Wick's arm popped out of the shoulder socket.

He screamed at the excruciating pain.

Writhing in the saw grass, he knew by instinct there

was only one possible escape: He began crawling, rolling frantically toward the slough. But the creature lowered itself upon him from behind, this time fangs bared. The bottom pair of fangs buried into his back, just above the kidneys. Shirt and skin and the top layer of flesh tore away like newspaper.

Wick screamed again.

He dragged himself on one elbow to the edge of the slough.

And the intense flame of pain in his back and shoulder curiously snuffed itself out. He thought calmly: *I'm sorry, Lennie.*

He could hear and smell another attack coming, and so, with a final push, he thrust his upper body into the slough. He could not hold his breath under water; he sank to his belt, his legs extending into the saw grass. Bubbles pearled up from his mouth and nose, and then he was silent. His legs twitched once, and then his body gave off no signs of life.

Blood wings circled, swooped low and landed near the body.

Then, as if satisfied with its destruction, it flapped its massive wings and lifted into the night.

7

C.M. Bradshaw dipped a hand into the icy cooler and wrapped his fingers around a can of Miller. "You need another hit?"

"Yeah, why not—the fish aren't biting worth shit," said Roy Johnson. He reeled in his line to check his minnow.

"That look like a damn turtle been eating on it?" he asked Bradshaw, who, in turn, laughed.

"Wouldn't doubt it. Wouldn't doubt it. This slough's

lousy with 'em."

Johnson took the can of beer, and both men popped the tabs.

"A man's favorite music," said Bradshaw.

He had had two beers and only one nibble, the combination being enough to provoke him to set aside his rod and reel.

"So what's the deal on your theory that white bass are attracted to lantern light. We been here since midnight, and turtles seem to be the only thing we're attracting."

"Be patient. Be patient. All good things come in due time."

The lantern light bathed Johnson's frown. "Ah, to hell with it." His mangled minnow slipped off the hook. Disgusted, he tossed his rod and reel into the saw grass.

"Wish the hell I could remember where I tied my skiff," said Bradshaw. "If we could get our asses out there in the current, we'd get some strikes."

"Yeah, three strikes and you're out," Johnson muttered, then guzzled at his beer. "You're wrong about a man's favorite music," he added. "A man's favorite music is the soft, rose-petal moan of some long-legged, willing blonde as you're driving your spike into her and she's coming and she's wrapped those long legs around your back and she's squeezing your lungs out."

Bradshaw snickered. He set his beer down and dabbed at his cheeks and forehead. "Jesus, friend, you're giving me hot flashes. I don't hear that music much these days. Hey, you just may be right—love to hear that moan."

They had another beer. The night wore on. Once, Johnson thought he heard a distant scream, but Bradshaw assured him it was a night bird of some kind. Their fishing spot was a half a mile into the refuge, a full mile or more from the point along the slough where Wick Thorndale had set up his lawn chairs.

274

Eventually, Johnson broke the lull in their conversation.

"Once upon a time, I loved the sound of a typewriter." He laughed self-deprecatingly. "Yeah, the click of those keys, the zir-r-ring of the carriage returning. Thirty years ago, I was gonna be another Hemingway, you know. Hell, I even spent time down around Hemingway's place in Key West just soaking up the atmosphere as if somehow that would make me a better writer. I copied his style. Short sentences. Lean, clean, mean prose."

"What went wrong?"

Johnson thought a moment. "Didn't press the right keys, I suppose."

A smile spread across his face. Bradshaw, slow to respond to the pun, winced as Johnson punched at him playfully and missed. Both began to laugh, beer-laced spittle escaping from their lips into the lantern light.

"That's royal," Bradshaw exclaimed, after curtailing his laughter. "Oh, Jesus. Well, I'll tell ya, I could never write a damn complete sentence. Never liked books—unless they were adventures about men searching for gold or lost treasure."

Suddenly his lighthearted, drunken tone shifted to one more sober.

"It's the sound of money, Roy. Who'm I kiddin'? It's the only sound I've ever really cared about.

"Makes the world go around," said Johnson.

"Yeah . . . sure as hell does. I love the jingle of quarters in my pockets. I love the paper whisper of a roll of twenties when you let their edges spin against your thumb. I love that crisp little cut you hear when somebody tears out a check to give you."

"You hearing that sound on a regular basis lately—that right?"

"I am. I surely am," Bradshaw admitted. "I may be a

piss poor fisherman, Roy, but when it comes to making money, I got the touch."

He punctuated his comment by rubbing his forefinger against his thumb.

"You selling a mess of those new condos?"

"Damn straight—six in the last three weeks. Six."

He held up five fingers and both men giggled.

"A mess of 'em," Johnson echoed.

"Royal Orchid's blooming," Bradshaw slurred. "Hey, that's damn good—oughtta be my slogan: 'Royal Orchid's Blooming.' Whatdoya think?"

The beer buzz rang in Johnson's head like a faulty phone connection. He pressed a cold can of Miller against his forehead and lapsed into a serious tone.

"You know who's responsible for your success, don't you?"

Bradshaw belched a few times, sour beer gas filling his cheeks until they looked like pouches. "Was it you? My ole buddy . . . it's you, ain't it?"

"Nah, nah, nah, nah—no, sir-eee. It is not. No sir."

Bradshaw's face collapsed into a comical frown. "Not you? Then . . . me, ain't it?"

Johnson shook his head. He crawled past the lantern to settle at Bradshaw's side. He leaned conspiratorially close and waited for Bradshaw's face to come into focus.

"Blood Wings," he whispered, his breath skirling against Bradshaw's cheek.

"By damn . . . I believe you're right about that."

"Let's toast that ole bastard," Johnson suggested.

"Yeah . . . hell, yes . . . a toast."

On rubbery legs they stood. Johnson thrust his Miller high above his head.

"To Blood Wings—the meanest, baddest motherfucker in the whole swamp."

Bradshaw tried to stay on his feet and second the toast, but his world canted sharply; he stumbled, giggled, and slammed down hard on his butt. And Johnson's whooping laughter broadcast through the night air.

Above their camp, the creature glided as smoothly as a woman's delicate hand slipping into a black, velvet glove. It could have been the laughter, it could have been the glow of the lantern, or some combination of the two, but whatever, the creature swung out of its glide, its wingtips tilted, its body balanced in a magnificent state of readiness—and it began to slice through the air, an emissary from the all-destructive, dark soul of the universe.

Still laughing, still holding his can aloft, Johnson said, "To all the long-legged blondes I never poked. To all their pretty faces I never kissed. All their pretty faces . . ."

He staggered. And Bradshaw watched him, propped on one elbow.

"Pretty faces," he echoed.

The stench rolled ahead of the diving creature like fast-moving fog.

Johnson squinted into the stars and saw dozens of them wink out.

"Pretty," he murmured.

The night froze in a crouching hush.

But a feral scream broke the silence. Bradshaw felt the hot rush of air as something huge—as large as a small plane, he imagined—swept down and knocked Johnson off his feet.

Something huge. And alive.

Bradshaw's eyes watered; the blur of lantern light heightened his confusion; he could not tell what happened, could not determine whether the split-seconds had been real or imaginary.

"Roy?" he whispered, his voice nearly inaudible.

His companion had been flung to the edge of the slough. Bradshaw grabbed the lantern to investigate, and reality continued to slip through his consciousness.

"Roy?"

His companion issued the most unusual and chilling moaning and groaning sounds, crazed, as if somehow beyond pain and terror, and his body was twitching and jerking like some animal hit by a car. It bucked and spun out of control into the saw grass away from the slough.

"God, Roy . . . let me help you! Let me help you!"

Bradshaw was shouting at the top of his lungs. He chased after the horrific scene of a man flopping like a fish out of water.

"Roy! Jesus!"

He caught up with him in deep grass, pinning the man's legs down. He swung the lantern up so that he could see where Johnson had been injured.

"Roy, let me help—"

The lantern continued swinging back and forth gently.

Roy Johnson had no face.

Or very little of one.

Several layers of flesh had been peeled away. His right eye was gone; his left eye appeared twice as large as normal, forced from its socket. The upper lip had been torn off, exposing bloodied teeth and gums. Blood. Blood everywhere.

The pulpy mass that had been Johnson's face seethed.

Bradshaw reeled back and vomited, vomited until his throat burned and he feared he would choke.

Johnson lay quietly as if napping.

Somehow, he was still breathing.

Scrambling away, Bradshaw found that he could not stand up. On hands and knees, he heard the approach of Blood Wings. Smelled it, too. A whoosh of air, like that created by a bus roaring close, blanketed him as he reflexively pressed himself as flat as possible.

"Jesus. Oh, God," he muttered. "The light . . . the light's attracting it."

Terror was the catalyst allowing him to push to his

feet. With as much energy as he could muster, he slung the lantern out into the slough; it splashed; its glass did not break; its sealed construction held, and slowly it caught in the sluggish current moving inexorably toward the swamp.

The darkness closed around Bradshaw. He ran. Disoriented, he couldn't be sure whether the shell road lay dead ahead or not. His breath came in heaves and gasps. He was whimpering, tears flowing down his cheeks.

He glanced over his shoulder once, but saw only a collage of stars and blackness. When he turned to look straight ahead, he heard the thrum of wings and detected a shadowy mass within the darkness. He ran harder, pumping his arms and legs. But he could not outrun the angle of the creature's attack.

It crashed against his right side. Two of his ribs snapped instantly. He cartwheeled through the air and landed on his shoulder, breaking his collarbone and dislocating his shoulder. The fire of the pain and impact of the landing slammed the breath out of him. His chin struck the ground, causing him to bite his tongue nearly in half.

The creature's talons had hit him like a fist of thorns.

His side was bleeding profusely.

And blood filled his mouth.

Losing consciousness, his last sight was of the creature bending down, its fangs extended. He reached out feebly with his left hand to try to push it away. The fangs entered his chest just above the heart. For that split-second, the pain was intense; then he gave one final strangled gasp and was dead. Thirty yards away, Roy Johnson stopped breathing, having outlived his companion by a few moments.

Blood Wings repositioned itself over Bradshaw's body. In the cold rhythm of predator dominating prey, the creature began to tear at the fatty flesh on Bradshaw's chest and to drink his warm blood. It fed, showing no emotion, working methodically until, apparently satiated, it took flight.

8

Her name was Brandy.

Jack Staimer had the hots for her so bad he could barely concentrate on the road. His ancient Dodge station wagon knew the route from Homestead to Orchid Springs unerringly—a good thing because the tank top young Brandy was wearing could not handle the swell of her breasts, creating a cleavage that mesmerized ole Jack. It made his mouth water and his jeans bulge, too, though he hoped his new delivery person didn't notice. Or did he?

Brandy, her frizzled hair falling in ringlets down around her mouth, gave her full attention to a crudely drawn map Jack had handed her. The Dodge's map light aided her very little.

"So do I have this figured right?" she asked. "After the Florida City and Homestead drops, Orchid Springs is the last one of the morning?"

"You got it figured."

He winked at her.

She clutched a can of Diet Dr Pepper against the crotch of her shorts as she looked away from Jack and studied the map a second longer before surveying the scattering of buildings and trailers as they entered Orchid Springs.

"This it?"

Her top lip curled upward.

Jack thought it made her look sexy as hell.

Suddenly she yawned and stretched, forcing her breasts against the overmatched tank top, and Jack found himself swallowing hot sparks of lust and skirting the ditch.

"I guess you're not married, are you, Brandy?" he managed to observe.

"Oh, this. . . ." She fluttered her left hand. "I don't wear my wedding ring. It gave me hives. Red, itchy splotches. So I don't wear it. My ole man—his name's Kenny—broke his leg doing construction work—fell off a roof. You see, that's why I need this morning job, because who knows how long Kenny'll be laid up—couple months probably—and so he's gonna stay home and watch our Polly. She's our kid. Our daughter. Be two in July. Terrible two's coming."

"Jesus, a kid, too," Jack muttered.

Brandy rattled on about Kenny's leg and how he used a coat hanger to get to the itchy places under the cast and how he could sing to Polly and it would make her stop crying. But listening carefully, Jack heard nothing of a warning not to come on to her.

He wished she wouldn't talk so much.

It interfered with the sexual fantasy unreeling in his thoughts of kissing that soft, pouty mouth and cupping those spectacular breasts and filling the backseat of the Dodge with night moves and night sounds—the histrionics of illicit passion.

"This is Holly's," he announced, brakes squealing as the Dodge lunged to a stop.

Both of them bounced out of the station wagon, and Jack swung the stack of papers at the front door to the store; it thudded and skidded a few inches, and he grinned, pleased with himself.

"Who's the route boy?" Brandy asked.

"Kid by the name of Wade Martin. A good one. Pretty dependable. But like all of 'em, it don't hurt to kick 'em in the ass occasionally—if you know what I mean."

"I know men," said Brandy, and she smiled so that the tip of her tongue rested on her bottom row of teeth.

Ole Jack had to clear his throat.

"This is the end of the route. Now you get to relax. You wan' another can of soda?"

"Sure," she said, dumping the remainder of hers on the ground. "What's across the bridge there?"

"That? Oh, that's the Schreck Refuge—alligators, birds, the swamp." He paused. "Say, would you like to see it? Good place to do some serious relaxing."

In the neon night-light glare of Holly's he gave her his best come on look, and she cocked a smile and said, "Sure. You got a connection? Copped some speed? I have some black beauties in my purse."

Jack looked puzzled, and yet the young woman appeared eager to see the darkened refuge—*so what the hell,* he thought, and drove them a ways into it, stirring up the white dust on the shell road. Picking an isolated spot in the dogleg angle of slough and mangroves, he pulled over and shut off the engine.

"Let's make something happen, honey." he muttered, hoping he sounded irresistibly sexy.

"Just a sec," she flounced. "I gotta go pee."

She jumped out of the car and waged her finger at him. "Donchoo peek."

Jack felt deliciously weak, nearly all of his blood having rushed to his groin. He smiled wickedly.

"I can't pass this up," he whispered as she moved away from her door. He tore into the glove compartment for a flashlight. "Sorry, honey."

He sneaked around the front of the station wagon, gained his bearings, and fanned the light out to the saw grass bordering the road. He heard a muted scream of surprise, and there she was, her shorts and panties around her knees, half-squatting, her naked bottom shining, at least to Jack, magnificently.

But she wasn't screaming at Jack's intrusion.

The night suddenly roared.

Jack thought a train must somehow be approaching.

Not in the damn swamp, his mind registered dully.

In that same instant, the creature's talons jolted into the young woman, snapping her neck. She was knocked forward across the road, her face burrowing several inches into the shell dust. She lay there, silent, her head twisted at an impossible angle from the rest of her body.

Jack ran to her.

He couldn't believe what the light revealed.

He dropped the flashlight, and lapsing into a terrified gibberish, he sprinted for the Dodge.

Get the gun! Get the gun!

But as he reached the tailgate of the station wagon, the creature dove again. It crashed into the roof, showering sparks and skipping toward Jack's head. He screamed and managed to duck in time; stench choked at his nose and throat. Survival was his only concern. He clambered to the driver's side door, slid beneath the wheel and cranked the Dodge to life, and in his frenzied hurry to get away, he thundered forward, crushing Brandy's head under the tires.

He never realized what he had done. Never became aware of anything except the next dive of Blood Wings, which shattered the front windshield and caused him to veer off the road and settle the front tires into three feet of slough water.

Scrambling over the seats, Jack found his revolver.

The night gathered a deep and almost palpable silence.

Jack climbed out of the Dodge and surveyed the sky.

The revolver trembled in his hands; he was shivering uncontrollably. He leaned against one of the passenger doors and rested the back of his head against a window. And he prayed the creature would not return.

The swamp began to gently vibrate.

And Jack's prayer was not answered.

Even in the partial darkness, he could see the creature's approach. From a platform of stars in the east, it swung toward him like a trapeze artist, down, down, gracefully, winging so gracefully. Using both hands, Jack lifted the revolver and tried to steady his aim. He closed his eyes and gritted his teeth and discovered he could not pull the trigger.

The creature hit with the force of a steel wrecking ball. Jack's ribs curled around his spine.

His head jerked.

In his final moment of consciousness, he heard glass breaking—not a harsh or unpleasant sound, but rather like that of a wind chime singing out in its own unique voice.

9

"Good Christ, Ibo."

Hash awakened. He had heard something. And he could smell something—something very familiar.

A multiplying fear shook him to full consciousness. He grabbed his rifle and switched on a flashlight.

"I'll be right back," he told the bird.

"Sumbitch! Be right back! Sumbitch!" it squawked.

Slipping cautiously along the road, Hash came upon the young woman first.

"Christ Jesus, no . . . oh, Christ," he murmured.

The scene staggered him. He turned away. And then he saw the station wagon resting partly in the slough.

"What the fuck is anyone doin' out—?"

Jack Staimer's body appeared to be dancing the limbo.

There it was, knees bent, upper body and shoulders pitched back as if preparing to slide under the bar—but the head . . . and all that blood.

Hash stepped to within twenty feet of the scene. He was a hard man, not squeamish in the least, and yet in that score of seconds he felt a numbness of revulsion he had never experienced. He reached out to balance himself against the tailgate. Three steps more.

Jack Staimer's head had created a nearly perfect hole in the side window. The head and neck were inside the car, but jagged projections of glass were working to free head from body as the weight of the slumping body exerted pressure.

Clicking off his flashlight, Hash held on to the station wagon tightly; his knees threatened to buckle. He scanned the night sky. He knew, of course, what had happened. The lingering smell added further evidence.

Hash, ole buddy, now's the time.

Go get that creature.

The big hit.

But courage was leaking out of him as fast as air out of a punctured tire. The grasp of the rifle helped him regain some of that courage; gradually he edged away from the scene, checking the stars and partial moon every dozen heartbeats for the return of Blood Wings.

"It'll be back," he whispered to himself. "It enjoyed killing too much to stop just yet."

At the cabin, he collapsed in a chair and poured a shot of rum. His hands began to shake so violently, however, that he could not hold the plastic cup. The rum jostled onto his wrist.

"God damn it!" he groaned.

"Sumbitch! God damn it!" Ibo followed, capturing Hash's tone perfectly.

The man stared toward the shadow-strewn perch. "Ibo, ole friend, I just seen a nightmare."

The bird cooed and cleared his throat and shifted his feet nervously.

"But a million bucks... Mr. Bones... a million bucks. I had the check right in my hand. Made out to me—Dominick Hashler. Biggest goddamn hit I'll ever have a shot at. Got to take it, Ibo. You understand me?

Got to."

As the minutes passed, his hand steadied, though he drank little of the rum. He checked his watch: two A.M.

"Time for more shut-eye, Ibo. First light, we gone."

"Sumbitch! We gone!" the parrot squawked.

Hash rested his head on his lumpy pillow and closed his eyes. His body tingled. His stomach roiled. In his thoughts images of the mangled body of the young woman and the even more grotesque corpse of Jack Staimer pulsed like neon signs.

He should have contacted the sheriff's department. Yes, he realized that, of course. It would have been the proper thing to do. And the fine folks of Orchid Springs should be warned: A bloodthirsty creature was on the kill.

A million bucks.

Cold reason seeped into the images of blood and twisted bodies.

Big hit.

Over and over in his mind, he played a simple explanation: *If you tell the authorities about the bodies, there'll be a ton of people out here. The creature will head for the swamp, somewhere deep within it, and you'll never see it again, never have a chance at the million bucks. Wait until dawn. Start after it. It may linger in the area. Give yourself a chance at it. A chance for the big hit.*

"Big hit," he murmured.

A smile animated his lips.

A fantasy unfolded: He had bought a seaside cottage on the island of Mustique in the Caribbean. His neighbor was Lord such-and-such from Great Britain, who came to the island only twice a year. Hash had a mile stretch of beautiful beach to himself. His days spread before him like a feast on a banquet table. Mornings he would sleep late, luxuriating in his own laziness. An island house-keeper would bring him fresh citrus for breakfast—steak

286

and eggs if he called for something heavier. And champagne. Champagne every morning.

Late morning, before the sun grew too hot, he would stroll the beach for exercise, kicking at interesting pieces of driftwood, picking up fascinating shells or feeding sea birds which would come to know him. They would flock around him, begging for food. And he would be "Papa" Hash and wear a magnificent straw hat. For lunch, he would retire to a hammock strung between two palms; he would sip at some delicate, fruity drink laced with rum and nibble on fresh fish or perhaps cheese or nuts. He would nap, and the sea breeze would relax every muscle.

Late afternoon, he might stroll to the village, avoiding the tourists—even the wealthier ones—and he would visit his favorite watering hole where, naturally, he had credit as long as his arm. The proprietor and every bartender would know him by name and listen, enraptured by his tale of hunting down a mysterious creature and of selling its carcass to a rich patron whose identity would not be revealed even at the point of death.

Good drink. Good food. And as night rolled onto the beach, he would find good company—a variety of beautiful women to choose from—and they would return with him to his cottage, and a night of lovemaking would be punctuated by the appearance of a brief thunderstorm and the calming effect of rain upon the roof.

The fantasy ushered him into two hours of sleep.

The screaming and wild, frenzied fluttering of Ibo awakened him.

"Help! Sumbitch! Help me! Sumbitch!"

Out of bed and on his feet, Hash yelled at the bird to calm down, and when Ibo returned to his perch, still wired with fear, another sound broke upon the cabin. Hash found his rifle, braced it against his chest, and listened. It was the thrum of wings, the raspy, metallic sound of an old threshing machine.

287

Like a hawk circling its prey, the creature was circling the cabin.

Hash could smell its stench filtering down and eventually through the screen doors, causing his eyes to tear.

"Hear that, Ibo? The bastard's comin' right to us. Christ, this is gonna be easy."

But beneath the bravado, the man's heart raced; his hands shook.

Suddenly there was a crashing thump upon the roof.

Blood Wings had landed.

Hash's throat went dry.

Behind him, shifting restlessly on his perch, Ibo muttered, "Help! Sumbitch! Get me outta here! Sumbitch!"

"Quiet!" the man hissed. "Damn you, bird!"

Everywhere the creature stepped, the roof threatened to cave in. Loose dust puffed down, and when Hash switched on the dim kitchen light, the dust created a fog within the shadows.

He carefully checked the rifle to make certain it was loaded.

"All right, you ole bastard. I smell money. One helluva lot of money."

He raised the rifle, eyes glued to the ceiling, calculating that one clean shot from the high-powered weapon might do it. The creature shifted, seemingly feeling its way over the rotted shingles as if testing points of entry.

The stench thickened.

Hash snuffled. Tears streamed down his cheeks. Mucous flowed from his nostrils. He wiped it with the back of his hand.

"God damn. Stay in one fuckin' place."

Unexpectedly, the creature screamed, an angry, uncontrolled sound.

Hash fired.

The ceiling exploded. Sparks and dust and pieces of rotted plywood showered to the floor. He fired twice more, creating new holes, but the creature took flight, giving no indication that it had so much as been wounded.

At the front door, Hash scanned the night sky.

Blood Wings had disappeared.

To the east, first light was breaking.

"Damn it, Hash, you sorry fucker, get your ass after him," he urged himself.

It took only a matter of minutes to load the skiff with everything he needed. He called for Ibo, and the parrot flew to its perch on the prow.

"Blood and money, Ibo . . . I smell 'em. A million bucks."

"Million bucks! Sumbitch!" squawked the bird.

As the rays of dawn struck the derelict cabin, Hash and Ibo pushed off into the slough.

Chapter 15

1

It sounded like Gillie's voice.

Some wisecrack, some one-liner, taunting, goading him.

Same ole Gillie.

At the window?

Wade rolled out of bed and threw himself against the screen.

Nothing.

Disappointed, he yawned. And then remembered.

Timmy's out there.

Time to get ready or Lark would leave without him. He hated not saying anything to his mom, but there was no way, in light of Timmy's disappearance, that she would give her permission to go on the planned mission into the swamp.

The spear.

The *wirrie.*

He hadn't assembled the new weapon yet, and so he scrambled into his closet and found Gillie's spear. He removed the butcher knife and then glanced around to see where he had put the *wirrie.* For an instant, his heart plunged into a well of despair—had it only been a dream? Had he really gone to Miss Freda's to steal the *wirrie?*

But, yes, there it was, leaning innocently against his dresser.

He let his fingers curl around it.

He felt its magic, its power.

I can kill Blood Wings with this.

The surge of confidence thrilled him like roaring down that first hill on a roller coaster.

He heard another voice; not the ghostly voice of Gillie; but the curiously resigned murmurings of Miss Freda's dark servant, Mary.

"Men cause Garkain to hate. Garkain turn evil."

Something of sadness lodged in her words, a kind of grief the boy could not quite understand.

"Garkain hate man. Must be killed."

And he heard her ask if he were brave.

I've got to be. For Timmy. For Gillie.

And, again, her surprising request—almost a command: *"Take wirrie. It has poison of Garkain. You kill the creature."*

The memory of her words fired him. There was something of sacred duty about the task he had committed to. But he could not forget, as well, the intrusion of Miss Freda.

"You, however, may discover that Mary's gesture is a fatal trap."

In his fingers, the *wirrie* felt alive.

Would he and Lark fall into the trap Miss Freda spoke of?

What would the day bring?

It was time to find out.

Quickly, yet carefully, he secured the *wirrie* to the axe handle with tape and string and wire. Holding it up away from his body, it felt invincible—it was Excalibur and every other magical, fantastic weapon in literature and history.

Before he left his room, climbing through his window into the emerging dawn, he held the weapon firmly, closed his eyes, and whispered, "This is for you, Gillie. And you, too, Timmy—hold on. We're comin'."

2

On his way to the motel, Wade slipped past Holly's. The sight of the stack of *Herald*'s set a hook in him, but he reasoned that his dark journey was far more important than seeing to it that everyone got a morning paper. Jack Staimer would understand, he assured himself.

As he approached the motel, he saw that Lark was already loading her boat. He ran to help her.

"Good morning," she said. "How's your mom? Any word on Timmy?"

Wade shrugged. "Mom's still pretty upset, I guess. I sneaked out and didn't see her. Timmy, he's . . ." His gaze drifted out to the slough.

"I'm gambling that you're right. That he's out there," said Lark.

"He is." the boy murmured.

She noticed the spear he clutched at his side. "I wish you hadn't brought that."

"We have to have a weapon," he protested. "You don't got a gun—what if Blood Wings attacks us?"

"I can't kill a creature I've come to revere."

"Revere?"

"You don't understand, Wade . . . and maybe I wouldn't be able to explain it anyway. Blood Wings is the opportunity of a lifetime. I pray that nothing happens to Timmy, but don't expect me to condone the destruction of the creature. . . . I hope it lives to die of old age or natural causes, at least."

293

"It kills."

"Because it's been driven to."

"You don't want me to come, do you?"

"Wade . . . first of all, I feel it's wrong for you to go with me without your saying anything to your mom. But I can sympathize with your wanting to find Timmy—I won't say no. I could get myself in trouble. You know that, don't you?"

He smiled victoriously. "Yeah."

Lark shook her head as if mildly exasperated with herself. C'mon, then, daylight's burning."

They clambered aboard and Lark cranked the engine to life, and Wade's heart leaped at the throaty thug-thug-thug. The boat glided into the current, and as both of them looked back at the scattered habitations of Orchid Springs, they heard sirens approach.

"Wonder what that could be?" Lark said.

"It's comin' pretty close. Not a fire probably. I can't see smoke."

At the opposite end of the community, the driver of a delivery truck hauling bread happened to notice the partially submerged body of Wick Thorndale and had called the authorities.

"You don't suppose that it's something involving your mother?"

"Probably not," said Wade, hoping intensely that it wasn't.

They settled in on their journey, the sun rising in a bright shout behind them. After a few minutes, Lark glanced at the boy's spear.

"Isn't that Miss Freda's *wirrie?*"

Wade nodded.

"Did she give it to you?"

"Sorta."

There seemed no way, and perhaps no reason, to avoid sharing an account of his late-night adventure. So he did.

Lark listened carefully.

"I wish now that I had talked to Mary at some length. She must have special insights into the nature of the creature. Are you positive she wanted you to kill it?"

"Yeah. She said so. But maybe . . . well, Miss Freda called it a trap. Maybe it is. Maybe the servant woman thought the creature would get me. Maybe it's what she really wants."

The young woman scanned the sluggish flow of the slough, the vaulting saw grass and the mangroves which crowded to the water like thirsty beasts.

"Unraveling the mystery," she muttered. "This is the exciting part. Today, Wade . . . perhaps today we'll unravel some of that mystery."

3

The kitchen swam around her; the glare of the sun slanted through the window above the sink. She squinted as she nestled the phone to her ear; the long distance connection spit static at every other word.

"But just because he's at work doesn't mean he hasn't hidden my son somewhere. I know, but . . . so you're saying it wouldn't do me any good to press charges? . . . No, no one actually saw him take Timmy . . . I'm sure it's what happened. . . . Yes, yes he did threaten to. No . . . all right, yes, but . . . I appreciate that. Yes, good-bye."

Weak from lack of sleep and from the emotional drain of the past twelve to fifteen hours, she hung up. She cried softly, not out of fear or sadness, but rather out of sheer frustration. There was no indication that Dean had taken Timmy.

As if in a trance, she walked down the hallway to the boys' room, certain for a heart-stopping run of seconds that she would find Timmy curled up in his bed, his face covered with an innocent mask of sleep.

Instead, she found an empty room.

4

"Wick Thorndale's been murdered, they're saying."

Anita, her mental stability on the doubtful side, stared at Holly as if the woman had spoken in a foreign language.

"Wick?"

Hovering near her CB unit, Holly said, "I picked up some of the sheriff department's transmission earlier. Then, Harold Lawrence—he's Wick's busybody neighbor—I phoned him and sure enough, they found Wick's body at the edge of the slough—lot of blood."

"Holly, my God!"

The heavy woman shook her head gravely. "Have you heard anything from St. Louis?"

Anita took a deep breath and gave her the whole story, including her discovery that Wade was also missing.

"Odd part of that," Holly added, "is that he didn't deliver his newspapers."

New fears stabbed at Anita.

"Holly, what's going on? Dean . . . has he sent someone down here? Has someone taken both my boys?"

Moving past the counter, Holly wrapped her fleshy arms around the distraught woman. "No . . . no, listen to me, honey. I believe I have an explanation. 'Scuse me a second."

She waddled back around to her CB unit and issued a call for 'Seeker.' Lark's muffled voice soon responded.

"Is Wade with you?"

There was a long pause.

"Yes, he is."

296

Anita scrambled to Holly's side and gestured that she wanted to speak.

"Lark," Holly said, "Anita's here and she'd like a word with Wade."

"Wade? Wade, what on earth do you think you're doing?"

"Mom," he began cautiously, "We're going into the swamp . . . to find Timmy. I know he's out here. I'm gonna find him and bring him home."

"Wade, I want you to come back this instant. You went without my permission. Tell Lark to bring you back."

"No. I won't come. Even if Lark turns the boat around. I won't come. I'll jump out. I'm gonna find Timmy."

Reluctantly Anita stepped away from the CB.

Holly wished them luck, and before signing off, Lark asked her to please stay close to the CB.

"We may need help." she explained.

5

Crossing through Pelican Pond, Hash sensed, uncomfortably, that he had passed some point of no return. Nerves jangled, he fought the pull of a bottle of rum he had stashed in the prow, hidden under a tarp and deflated inner tubes. The latter had been brought to aid in lugging home the bounty—the carcass of Blood Wings. Inflated, with a netlike travois strung between them, the tubes could sustain considerable weight.

"Leave the booze alone." he chided himself. "Start lookin' for signs of the creature."

He poled on, the sun generating warmth all around him; it was to be a windless, sticky day, the humidity strangling the swamp in its oppressive grip. A quarter of a mile beyond Pelican Pond, he was greeted by a choice—a

297

wide run to his right, a more narrow and unfamiliar one to his left.

Calculating the possibilities each way, the man rubbed at his bald head. He did not wear a cap, opting to burn the bare skin to a bronze over the course of the summer.

"I'll be pissed, Ibo. Which way?"

"Which way? Which way?" the bird echoed before breaking into a whistle, snatches of the theme from *M*A*S*H* filling the air.

"If you ain't gonna help, keep your damn trap shut."

"I'll be pissed," the bird shrieked.

"We're takin' the run not taken," Hash suddenly exclaimed, poling hard, turning the skiff left.

He had followed the run nearly half a mile before the usual landscape of mangroves and saw grass thinned to a dotting of hummocks and stunted grass and the water carried a blanket of duckweed and water hyacinth.

"Wait a goddamn second," Hash muttered. "Ibo, we got some freshwater springs around somewhere."

He hunkered down in the boat and cupped a handful of water and drew it to his lips.

"Damn straight. Hardly a lick of salt."

But what did it mean? And why, he wondered, hadn't he explored this run before?

Around the next bend, one point of significance presented itself. The run gradually widened; hyacinth and duckweed threatened to choke the flow of water, and two hummocks flattened into sun-splashed banks. And there was something more.

Hash leaned against his pole.

A chill skirled down his spine.

"Jesus H. Christ, Ibo."

The scene appeared to panic the bird, for he left his perch and fluttered in a tight circle around his keeper's head, screaming, squawking, locked in a curious out-of-control frenzy.

Protecting himself, Hash batted at his attacker.

"What in the hell!"

But Ibo wouldn't stop. He continued his wild, frightened cries, spinning wider circles until he swung out so far that he wheeled north toward the more familiar stretch of the swamp.

"Fuckin' looney bird," Hash muttered.

He wiped his lips with the back of his hand as the parrot disapeared from view. Then he returned his attention to the immediate scene. He was surrounded by the liquid sounds of living things slipping into the water.

Gators. Two dozen or more had created a feeding hole and, quite likely, a summer nesting area. It was unusual to see so many gathered in one spot.

As Hash poled through them, a big bull nosed the prow.

"Get the damn hell back!" the man shouted, jabbing savagely at the gator. It slapped his jaws and rolled; the skiff rocked.

"You ole son-of-a-bitch."

He grabbed his rifle, waited for the gator to surface, and then fired the high-powered weapon point-blank into its body. The barklike ridges of outer hide tore away in a hole the size of a baseball; the gator thrashed and twisted, animating the water and vibrating the skiff.

"Nothin' gonna get in my way," the man bellowed.

The wounded gator sank.

As Hash continued poling through the area, other gators eventually glided closer, almost daring him to shoot. He imagined revenge in their unblinking eyes.

"Go to hell, all of you. You or nobody else gonna take my million bucks away."

Laughing, he speared at several with his pole, desiring to aggravate them until one or more snapped, provoking more laughter, laughter that wafted into the secret recesses of the swamp.

Timmy stepped from a marshy hummock back into the small boat that had carried him miles from Orchid Springs. His throat was sore, and he was hungry, having eaten the last of his Oreos hours ago. And he was thirsty. Very thirsty. He waded a few feet into the slough and cupped both of his tiny hands into the water. But when he sloshed some of it into his mouth, he spit it out immediately, the brackish, salty bitterness coating his tongue and stinging his throat.

"Whew, that's nasty bad," he exclaimed.

He turned to step onto the hummock; the sticky swamp peat held one shoe firmly. He yanked, freeing his foot with a loud smack, but the shoe, which he fished out of the muck, looked as if it had been bronzed in slime. He tossed it into the low grass.

And that's when Ibo surprised him by landing on the prow.

"Hey, a bird. Pretty bird. Hey, bird, I'm lost."

Ibo ruffled his feathers. "Pretty bird. Hey, bird, I'm lost," it gurgled.

"Hey, you can talk. Gosh dang neat."

"Gosh dang neat," Ibo cooed.

Delighted at the bird's ability to repeat words, Timmy said, "You sound just like me. But I'm lost. I'm really lost."

"Really lost. Pretty bird. Hey, bird, I'm lost. Sumbitch."

Timmy giggled.

"Can you show me the way back home?"

The bird waffled and emitted brief, high-pitched whistles as the boy climbed into the boat and began to pole.

"Here, wanna sit on my shoulder?"

But when he made a move to reach toward him, Ibo winged away.

"Come back," Timmy called after him. "Come back.

I'm lost."

Then he rubbed at his throat and tried to swallow. The talking had made it feel as if it had been rasped with needles.

The small boat joined the current once again.

Timmy sat down, determined he would cry no more; and yet, beads of sweat trickled from his forehead, burning at the corners of his eyes like tears.

7

Wade sipped his cold drink while he studied the shape of his spear and the reddish-purple stain on the *wirrie:* the creature's blood. Yes, the poison. Blood Wings would die from the poison of its own kind. Was that possible? Mary said it was so.

"Which way?" Lark suddenly asked.

Scrambling to join her at the helm, the boy scanned the scene unfolding before them. "Geez, I don't know."

Lark flattened a hand-drawn map on the control panel in front of her. "I sketched this when I returned from Houston's helicopter ride, but I've lost my bearings. Wouldn't the current be more likely to have taken Timmy to the right?"

"If we go the wrong way, we might could never find him," said Wade, the cold reality of their dilemma clutching at him.

Taking a deep breath, Lark said, "Cross your fingers— we're going right."

On the broad waterway, they floated for the better part of a mile as the sun beat down, climbing to its noonday vantage point. Much of the time they stayed under the cabin's canopy. Lark kept her 35mm camera handy.

"Where's your movie camera?" Wade asked.

"Didn't bring it. We were so rushed, I never had a chance to get the special film I wanted. If I'm lucky, I'll be able to capture the shots I need with this. But finding Timmy is the main thing at the moment."

"Yeah, I wonder where he is. He's not strong enough to pole against the current, so maybe he just kept floatin' and floatin'."

"If this is the right route, then we ought to catch up with him eventually."

"But if it's not—Timmy'll die out here, won't he?"

"Don't say that. Don't even think it."

"It's true. Even if the creature dudn't get him, he'll die of thirst or somethin' else."

"Hey, knock it off. We have to keep a positive outlook. We have to." She jostled at Wade's shoulder, and he nodded weakly.

Then she said, "Look in that blue totebag. Should be some Granola bars and apples. You're hungry, aren't you?"

"Yeah, I guess I sure am."

So they munched on their snack, both keeping a vigilant eye on the passing vegetation and on the sky. The boat hummed along at a slow, trolling speed; brown pelicans skimmed the surface, fishing. On a distant hummock, two deer bounded into the open, but appeared to be running more for the sheer thrill of their high-speed run than out of fear.

Wade watched the deer blend into a copse of small pines.

"Are the birds and animals scared of Blood Wings?"

"They have a healthy, natural respect for the creature . . . at least, I would imagine they do. But we have no firm idea of the creature's diet. More than likely, it's a meat-eater—small mammals, but deer, too, and possibly fowl."

And humans.

The words flashed into Wade's thoughts, catching him by surprise like a sudden bang or crash behind his back.

"What's wrong?" Lark asked.

"Well . . . it's just that I get to thinkin' sometimes maybe the creature's not real the way all other animals, you know, living things are real. Is Blood Wings supernatural?"

"I can't quite bring myself to believe in the supernatural, but there's a theory among some crypto-zoologists that strange phenomena—like Bigfoot, for example—may have supernatural powers. Perhaps even the power to become invisible. Perhaps most of the time they exist in another dimension, one we humans can never enter, or only rarely enter or become aware of."

Wade thought a moment. "You mean like Blood Wings could be watchin' us this second, but from a dimension where we can't see it? Then, when it wants to attack, it flies into our dimension?"

"Something like that, yes."

"Geez. It's weird, ain't it?"

Lark smiled. "But exciting. I— Hey, look, there's a parrot."

Wade turned to find Ibo perched on the rear railing.

"Ibo. It's Ibo, Hash's parrot. You remember Ibo, don't you?"

"Oh, of course—the bird that talks dirty."

"Ibo, why ain't you with Hash?"

The bird gargled a few words and whistled a few notes.

"Won't Hash be delighted to learn we're out here in the swamp, too," Lark joked.

Wade made his way to Ibo, holding out a piece of Granola bar.

"Gosh dang neat," Ibo cooed. "Really lost. Pretty bird. Hey, bird, I'm lost. I'm really lost."

To Wade, the world suddenly held nothing except the sound of his little brother's voice channeling through the parrot.

"Lark!" he shouted. "Pull the boat over! Pull it over!"

303

"What is it?"

"I'll show you. Pull the boat over."

She did, reluctantly, switching off the engine, visions of it not restarting poking into her thoughts. As the boat drifted into the shallow water next to a hummock, she joined Wade.

"Timmy's not far away—I'm sure of it now," he said.

"How? Did you see him?"

"No, but Ibo has."

Both of them looked at the bird as he two-stepped along the railing, cooing, muttering to himself.

Lark's face was a mask of puzzlement. "But how . . . how do you know that?"

"Because he talked, and it was Timmy's voice, and he said he was lost."

Lark studied the bird and then Wade, searching for something in the boy's expression that would explain the curious turn of events.

"Wade, are you positive?"

"Yeah, I really am. Here, listen."

He raised his hand solicitously to the bird.

"Okay, Ibo, say it again. Say what you said to me."

The bird cocked its head and whistled. "Okay, Ibo, say it again. Sumbitch," it exclaimed, matching Wade's voice flawlessly.

"No. No, Ibo. Timmy. Tell us what Timmy said. Say it to Lark."

"No. No, Ibo. No. No, Ibo. No. No, Ibo. Timmy. Sumbitch. Tell us what Timmy said. Say it to Lark."

Like a taunting child, the parrot repeated itself over and over again, fluttering, dancing along the rail as if being playfully chased.

"Dang it, Ibo. This ain't no friggin' game," Wade cried.

"Wait," said Lark, "I have an idea."

"What?"

304

She tugged him away from the railing. "If we shooed Ibo, if we drove him from the boat, do you think he would fly to wherever Timmy is?"

Wade's face brightened. "Yeah. Yeah, I bet he would. That's a great idea. Let's try it."

Both spooked at the bird, succeeding in making him fly, but he merely circled the boat a few times and attempted to land again.

"Shoo on outta here, Ibo. Get outta here. Go to Timmy. Show us where Timmy is."

"Hey he's going. I'll start the boat. Don't lose sight of him."

"I see him. Hurry!"

The boat purred to life, and they continued down the wide slough for another quarter of a mile before slowing.

"I can't see him no more. I lost him. Right over in there's the last I saw him."

Lark guided the boat into still another marshy hummock area. The humid air lowered itself oppressively upon them. Mosquitoes and other vicious flying insects swarmed in dark clouds.

"Use my binoculars," she said. "I'll spray some more insect repellent on us before we're eaten alive."

Wade took the binoculars and scanned the far reaches of the hummock, and as he was doing so, Ibo once again landed on the rear railing.

"He's back," Lark murmured.

"Gosh dang neat," said the bird.

Disappointed, the boy lowered the binoculars.

"Really lost. Pretty bird. Hey, bird, I'm lost. I'm really lost," Ibo continued.

Wade wheeled around. "Did you hear that? It's Timmy. Timmy's voice. It's 'zactly his voice."

"Could it possibly mean Timmy's real close by?" She took the binoculars and began to sight the full sweep of the hummock.

"Good goin', Ibo," said Wade. "Want some more Granola bar?"

The bird eagerly crunched at it as the boy turned his attention to Lark.

"See anything?"

"Oh, Wade, it's like looking for a needle in a haystack. This swamp is so huge, and if we keep moving west, we'll end up in the Everglades."

Leaning on the side rail, the boy stared at the hummock. "We can't give up. We can't. Timmy's somewhere out here. Maybe not far."

Gazing at the western horizon, Lark said, "We'll have another problem before the afternoon's over. Storm clouds building. Look at those thunderheads."

He did and knew she was right. But his concentration returned to the hummock where the movement of a leopard frog—and one more thing—caught his eye. He frowned.

"Hey, what are you doing?" Lark exclaimed, seeing him climb eagerly over the side of the boat.

"I see something," he called over his shoulder.

Sloshing through the muck, he suddenly stopped and reached down.

"Timmy!" he whooped. "It's one of Timmy's sneakers!" He held the slime-covered object up so that Lark could see it.

"Can you be certain?"

"Yeah. Yeah, I know it is. He's been here."

They both began to yell out his name at the top of their lungs, overjoyed that they had discovered evidence the little boy was probably near. But after several minutes of hearing their voices echo emptily over the expanse of swamp, Lark said, "We've forgotten about something, Wade. Where's the boat? Where's the boat Timmy came in?"

The boy felt his heart sink, a physical sensation of the

blood-pumping organ withering, its beating faint and irregular.

"Maybe," he murmured, swallowing a hard ball of spittle, "maybe it got him . . . maybe that thing got him right here."

"No. no, we can't let ourselves think that. The boat. I'd say he's still in the boat. And I've got another idea. Come back on board."

She helped him over the rail; he held the sneaker pinched between his thumb and forefinger.

"What's your idea?"

"We've got to radio Holly for help."

"For the sheriff?"

"No. No, the sheriff's department wouldn't know this area well enough."

"Hash knows it, but he's already out here somewhere."

"We need someone in a helicopter—someone who knows the swamp and can cover this whole area and see much more than we can see."

"Houston!"

"Right. I'm going to call Holly."

"Won't do you no good—he won't come. Houston's a coward and a dopehead. He won't come. He's scared of the creature."

Lark turned. "He might be our best chance—somebody has to ask him. We have to try. Timmy's in danger in a lot of different ways. He may not have much time left. We have to try."

Chapter 16

1

Through the static, Holly's voice sounded as if it had been drained of all energy.

". . . Jack Staimer and some young woman . . . been killed . . . horrible scene, they say. C.M. Bradshaw . . . his friend are missing . . . the creature?"

"Holly, I'm not receiving you well. Listen, please let me repeat what I said. We've found indications that Timmy's out here, but we can't cover the area. We need a helicopter. Can you talk to Houston Parker?"

". . . won't listen to me."

"He has to, Holly. Please try."

Static tumbled through the remainder of the exchange.

"I'm switching off," said Lark, more to herself than to Holly or Wade.

"Is she gonna try?" asked the boy.

"I think so. Keep your fingers crossed. Let's keep looking for Timmy, and you help me watch for a helicopter in case Houston makes it up."

It was like being inside one of those glass-domed paperweights—some winter scene, perhaps a horse-drawn sleigh—and as the snow filters down, a blizzard cranks up around you with the flick of someone's wrist.

Snowstorm.

Right there in the living room of his trailer.

He had taken one snowman, a homemade upper, and little time had passed before the hit scored and the delightful fall of snow began. It disgusted him that he had resorted to chemical help, but the last several days had pushed him beyond the point of toleration. The attack of the creature, the disappearance of Timmy—and then, curiosity had taken him into the refuge, to the grotesque scene of Jack Staimer and the young woman.

Every man had that line of toleration.

Beyond it he shut down. Called it quits. Retreated from the world.

Houston watched the snow fall in his mind for five minutes or so before he heard a voice ghosting through it and a pounding, an incessant pounding, and the voice growing louder.

"Houston! Please! Open the door!"

The snow released him. He was thirsty. Incredibly thirsty.

On the way to the door, reality crystallized like a sharp rap to the side of the head, and his next sensation was that of holding Anita in his arms, hearing her frightened, tear-choked voice, and then sitting down with her, unable to decipher her words at first.

Gradually individual words made sense. Sentences formed. He heard her repeat herself.

"Would you? If Timmy's out there . . . would you, please, for God's sake, do it? Please."

"I'm still not following you," he mumbled. "What

do you want me to do?"

"The helicopter. Take the helicopter up. Lark and Wade . . . they've seen where he's been. He's out there alone in a boat."

The implications of her explanation suddenly swept through him like a hot wind.

"Timmy's in the swamp? Good God, why would he go out there alone?"

She shook her head and began to sob. He held her tightly.

I can't do it. Can't do what she's asking. Can't go up and face that creature.

Images of Blood Wings gliding below the copter filled his mind.

"Please. There isn't much time."

How? How can I tell her? How can I make her understand there's no way I can face that creature?

"Please," she continued. "Will you go find my baby and bring him back?"

I can't.

He shaped the words mentally.

I can't. I'm sorry. I just can't do it.

He looked into her eyes and saw much more than a distraught mother, more than simply the woman he loved—he saw a future and a resolution to the past.

But even so, he found it difficult to believe his own words.

"I'd better get going," he said. "Don't worry. I'll bring home your Timmy."

3

Sweat plastered his shirt against his back. It ran in rivulets down his face, over his top lip. He tasted the bitterness of his own fluid, but nothing could shake his

311

concentration. He had maneuvered his skiff under the protective branches of some mangroves, where he squatted, rifle ready, for any sign of Blood Wings.

The familiar stench drifted through the humid air.

How close am I?

Hash blinked at a trickle of sweat.

"Christ," he muttered.

And a thought niggled its way into his concentration: *Have I come too far into the creature's territory?*

A humid mist clouded low on the surface of the wide slough. Darkness loomed in the west; the storm was pressing full bore across the Everglades into the mangrove swamp.

Hour. Maybe two before it hits, he calculated.

He waited, and as his concentration waned, he began to imagine dark shapes winging up from the line of mangroves across the slough.

"Goddamn pelicans."

The birds swept along, hurrying from the scene.

Hash swallowed.

He needed a drink.

Holding the rifle so firmly had made his arms ache; his throat was parched; his eyes flicked to the end of the boat where the bottle of rum had been hidden.

"No," he whispered. "Got to concentrate."

But the bottle sang its siren song.

"Oh, Jesus," he exclaimed.

With the tail of his shirt, he mopped the sweat from his face. He took a deep breath and momentarily set the rifle down and stared in the direction of the bottle.

Nervously he licked his lips.

"Jesus."

The temptation was too great.

As he gingerly made his way toward the bottle, he heard the scream; he looked up in time to see the creature swoop and glide no more than ten feet above the man-

312

groves on a line that would bring it very close to his skiff.

"There you are," Hash growled.

He turned for the rifle, but tripped and crashed to his knees.

"Goddamn it."

Blood Wings drew to within thirty yards; its cry pitched higher, intensifying, cleaving the air like a giant sword.

Fumbling at the weapon, Hash rolled onto his back. Waves of the now too familiar pungent odor inundated the boat, burning his eyes and nose; the temperature of the warm air seemed to rise twenty degrees as the creature passed.

Hash fired three shots, each missing wide.

"Damn it!" he roared, pressing to his knees and then to his feet as quickly as he could, but Blood Wings had winged beyond view.

Sorry ass fool—you missed a damn good chance.

He stood. He dropped the rifle to the floor of the boat.

On shaky legs, jaws clenched angrily, he sought out the bottle of rum. He grasped it by the neck and smashed it again and again against the side of the boat, unmindful of the glass slivers cutting into his hand.

4

A hundred feet above the narrow finger of slough, the creature circled. It smelled a living thing. To the west, thunder boomed; crooked sticks of lightning walked down from the roiling blackness of low-hanging clouds. The wind gusted; swamp birds scattered safely from the creature's path.

The small boy stood in his boat, camera aimed skyward.

He was not frightened, or not deeply so.

Wait till Wade and Sara Beth see the picture I'm gonna get.

The creature continued to circle, its senses picking up odors a mile away. It could smell the sweat in the small boy's hair. It could hear the purr of Lark's boat and the thrum of helicopter blades far in the distance. It could hear the small boy's breathing.

It circled indifferently.

Or perhaps it was merely working up an appetite.

5

Amidst the chaos of the sheriff's department's investigation, Houston had little trouble stealing onto the copter pad. Later, he wouldn't mind if Miss Freda had him arrested for trespassing.

As the blades spun to life, only one thing mattered: finding Timmy—before Blood Wings did.

Having set the takeoff controls, he readied himself to lift, and at that precise moment, his insides turned to jelly.

God, man, hold on to yourself.

You can do this.

You've got to do this.

Visions of the creature began to bombard him from all sides. Knowing they were hallucinations, he blinked them away, and yet, at first, they kept coming, diving, winging straight for him, a dozen creatures, fangs and talons prepared to kill.

Houston squeezed the control stick and shut his eyes tightly.

For an instant or two his mind filled with falling snow.

Anita, oh, God, I'm sorry. I can't do this.

Then, beyond his glass bubble, he heard the wail of

314

a siren.

Reflexively, he pulled back on the control stick.

Slowly, tentatively, the refuge sank beneath him; the storm-threatening sky rushed forward to challenge him. He banked and swung west.

He had never been so terrified in his entire life.

<h1 style="text-align:center">6</h1>

"I can't make out anything she's saying." Frustrated, Lark slammed the hand piece of the CB back on its hook.

"You think he'll come? You think Houston will come? I sure don't."

"Keep your fingers crossed that he will, Wade. But in the meantime, we have to continue looking ourselves."

"Maybe his boat drifted into one of them little side runs," the boy suggested as both scanned the waterway ahead.

"I hope not. There are so many of them—who could ever find him? Even from the air, the vegetation might hide a small boat from view."

"I wish, you know . . . wish I hadn't been bad to him. He wasn't such a nerdy brother. He was an okay kid."

Lark hugged at Wade's shoulder. "Hey, don't speak of Timmy in the past tense. When we find him and take him home, you can start being nicer to him."

"Yeah, I guess I could."

She smiled at him, but he caught something in her expression that plucked at his apprehension.

"You're pretty scared for Timmy, ain't you?" he asked.

She tried unsuccessfully to flash a convincing smile.

As if to answer for her, thunder hammered.

"It's the storm . . . if he doesn't have some kind of cover when it hits . . . yes, I'm afraid for him."

"He's sorta like your little brother, too, now, ain't he?"

She had to clear her throat and turn aside. She brushed at the corner of one eye. "Yes, it seems that way," she muttered. "Hey, why don't you take the binoculars and see what you can see from the back railing. Ibo's still perched there."

"Okay."

The wind had started to kick up, ushering in slightly cooler air to mix with the thick layer of humidity. As they slowly passed each side run, Wade directed the binoculars deep within it. But the outcome was always the same—no sign of Timmy or his boat.

Tiring of concentrating on the runs, he began to study the approaching clouds, the dark, pulsing membrane of the central bank.

"Timmy, where the friggin' heck are you?" he whispered.

Through the binoculars, the storm clouds transformed into an elemental monster loosed upon the innocent landscape; so Wade swung his view to the east, and there, perhaps two hundred yards away, locked in a lazy circle, was the creature.

"Lark!"

At the sound of his cry, she shut down the engine.

"Come here! Hurry! I see it! Here!"

He handed her the binoculars and pointed to the northeast.

"I don't see— Oh . . . oh, dear God . . . I . . . I see it."

She stood watching it, bound by a fascination that was total.

"It's . . . it's beautiful," she murmured.

"No," Wade exclaimed angrily. "It's not. It's a killer."

"It's circling something," Lark commented. "There's something below it . . . it's tracking something. . . ."

Then she quickly lowered the binoculars.

316

She and the boy stared into each other's eyes.

And knew each other's thoughts.

"Keep it in sight," Lark commanded.

She hustled to the wheel. In seconds, the boat was riding the curve of the central waterway, then a more narrow run back to the right.

"I still see it," said Wade, excitement filling his voice.

Maneuvering the boat another twenty yards before slowing it and letting it drift, Lark rejoined the boy. He handed her the binoculars.

"I can't see what it's circling. Maybe it's not Timmy."

Lark felt her breath catch. "The creature . . . it's magnificent . . . those wings . . . it's like an engraving of Lucifer I once saw—one by Gustav Doré . . . from Milton's *Paradise Lost.* I've got to get my camera . . . this is it. These will be the photos I've always wanted."

"Lark, what about Timmy?"

She hesitated. "I know . . . we'll find him. We will. But I'll never have this opportunity again."

When she returned to the railing, camera in hand, Wade had his spear ready, his eyes following every graceful, lilting move of the creature as it soared and continued to circle.

The boat drifted, sliding closer to some mangroves.

"I'm so nervous I can barely focus the lens," Lark chattered. "Oh, Wade, I've never seen anything like it. And it's not a myth. It's real."

She raised the camera and began clicking off shots.

Blood Wings cut mandalas in the ever-darkening skies one hundred to one hundred fifty feet above a nearby hummock, but Lark's boat remained hidden for another thirty feet or so; and then it cleared the tangle of mangroves, and the sprawling hummock spread before them to the left.

Suddenly the creature dipped a wing, initiating a loose spiral downward.

"It's coming after us!" Wade cried.

"No," said Lark. "Something below it."

The scene blurred at first, as if she were seeing it through an unfocused lens. Then a zoom to clarity.

"Oh, dear God, it's Timmy!"

"Where?"

But there was no need for her to say anything more, or even to point, because his gaze captured the movement of a hand. His little brother was standing in a boat, not forty yards away, waving up at the creature.

And Wade's senses momentarily numbed.

Lark's voice jolted him back to reality. "Timmy! Get down! Lie down flat in the boat!"

The small boy turned. The sight of Lark and Wade brought a smile instantly to his face. He began to wave more animatedly, and they could barely hear his strained words.

"I got a picture," he said.

"Get down!" Wade shouted.

The creature, as if excited by all the shouting, plunged lower, skimming to within fifteen feet of Timmy's head. The boy ducked.

"Dear God! Oh, God!" Lark screamed.

"Timmy, stay down!" Wade yelled with all the strength of his vocal cords.

But then the unthinkable occurred.

The small boy panicked.

Instead of scrunching himself protectively low in the bottom of the boat, he scrambled over the side, intent upon running to Lark and Wade.

"No!" Wade screamed.

Reflex took over. Spear in hand, the boy climbed onto the railing and jumped into the shallow water hugging the hummock. He never heard the splash or Lark's words behind him. Every ounce of his attention was directed at Timmy.

318

His brother looked once over his shoulder and saw the creature negotiating a turn that would bring its powerful body ever closer.

Wade motioned frantically for him to dive into the grass.

"Timmy! Watch out!"

Then Wade began to run toward him, though he could not move rapidly through the muck; his steps squished and issued loud smacking noises, and once he slipped to one knee and nearly lost his spear.

"Timmy!"

The small boy stopped running; his cry tore at Wade's heart.

"Help me! Help me, Wade!"

Huge wings slanted against the sinuous frame as the creature set its sights in a concentrated attack.

The air thickened with stench. Lightning and thunder edged to within a few miles.

"Get down, Timmy! Get *dow-w-w-n!*"

Timmy slumped forward onto the grass and began to scramble on his hands and knees.

In the boat, Lark screamed.

Blood Wings lowered its talons.

To Wade, the scene transformed into a reel of nature footage, a slow-motion shot of a predatory bird swooping down over a body of water, clutching a fish in its talons and lifting majestically, prey struggling futilely.

It was an intense moment of both horror and calm: Wade could only watch, believing he was witnessing the death of his little brother.

7

At the controls, Houston shivered violently. He had never experienced such an inner chill, and yet he was sweating profusely.

"Hopeless. This is hopeless, Anita," he murmured to himself.

The last flash of lightning outran the thunder by only three counts.

No way I can stay up much longer.

I ought to turn around while there's still time.

Sorry, Anita. Honest to God, I'm sorry. I tried.

He slowed to bank left and prepare to full throttle it home ahead of the storm when he chanced to see a box of white below. It looked familiar, familiar enough to cause him to back off his wide circle and swing the copter and descend.

"Lark's boat. Damn, what is she—?"

And then he saw it.

The creature, wings unfolding, their glossy blackness seeming to darken the entire hummock, spreading like a blanket of night over the small boy.

Timmy.

Houston never paused to think; fear channeled through him, a molten, liquid metal flaming, sending off sparks, making him feel preternaturally alive.

Sucking in a lungful of air, he pushed the copter into a forty-five-degree dive.

One stray thorn of introspection pricked at him: *God, what am I doing?*

But it dissolved into the roar, into the white noise of terror.

He saw the creature hook the boy in its talons.

"No, you bastard!" he shouted into the roaring sky.

The copter rattled and shook.

Houston gritted his teeth and held on.

Glossy wings formed a deadly black pool beneath him.

"Timmy."

The word came breathlessly, a whisper.

Wade saw his brother's hands wiggle like pink tentacles, and then the clatter-throb-clatter of the helicopter emerged from some miraculous opening in the sky. An act of magic, pure magic, appeared to be unfolding.

The creature had lifted Timmy four or five feet off the hummock when Houston's machine brushed near the broad expanse of wings and the massive head.

Helicopter and creature curled away from the boy as he was dropped and tumbled headlong into the grass and watery peat. And Wade found himself running to Timmy's side; Lark was suddenly matching him stride for stride.

They descended upon Timmy at nearly the same instant, clamoring at him, trying to determine the extent of his injuries, while remaining aware of the astonishing sight above them. The small boy, wild-eyed, face flushed, seemed unable to speak, but he did not cry at first—not until Lark and Wade embraced him and began carrying him as quickly as possible to the boat.

Angry red streaks and scratches covered Timmy's lower back and his buttocks; otherwise, no serious physical wounds were apparent.

"Look at that!" Wade called out as they reached the side of the boat.

Like World War I fighter pilots, Houston and the creature looped, cutting paths that would inevitably cross. The copter spun out its metallic clatter, and Blood Wings, proud ruler of the swamp, screamed its scream in an attempt to frighten away its combatant.

The battle lasted only heart-stopping seconds.

Houston rode out his loop, maintaining a level

altitude, as if inviting the creature to attack. And it accepted the challenge, climbing fifty feet or more above the copter; then, wings extended, plunging, it sliced directly in front of the fragile glass bubble in which Houston sat so precariously.

9

It was a sudden rage of blackness.

Then a tremendous jolt.

Houston held the control stick with both hands.

"Good God!" he exclaimed.

A blade clipped one of the enormous wings.

The spray of blood splashed against the bubble as if it had come from a water hose.

The horrible odor of the creature squeezed at Houston's lungs.

Blood Wings screamed and catapulted into a spiral of agony before it righted itself and averted crashing. Wounded, it flew off to the west.

But Houston knew the worst was not over; he felt the engine cut out. One blade had broken, and the entire craft began to roll. He pulled back, hoping to gain any altitude. For several seconds, it worked. The damaged copter rose thirty feet, sputtered, then lost all power.

It swung hard to the right and locked into a spin, tail first. The cockpit bubble, being heavier than the tail, looped once, and Houston released the control stick and saw a bloody rain falling in his mind.

Chapter 17

1

"He's crashing!" Wade yelled.

Lark, carrying Timmy in her arms, turned in time to see the tail of the copter plunge into the swamp like a spinning dart.

"Dear God, don't let it catch on fire," she stammered.

"He saved me," Timmy chattered, tears stinging his face, a face that had drained of all color.

The crash itself echoed like just another clap of thunder.

"We got to rescue him," Wade insisted, searching Lark's expression for agreement.

"Let's get Timmy in the boat first," said Lark, "and then see how close we can maneuver to where Houston went down."

"I got a picture," said Timmy, holding the Instamatic proudly so that Wade could see it.

"Not now, Timmy," said Wade.

"My back hurts . . . and, look, it's bleeding!" Timmy cried.

The small boy had touched his fingertips to the deep scratch on his lower back.

"I'll put something on it, and then we'll go after Houston," said Lark.

In the boat, they helped Timmy strip down to his underpants; Lark made good use of her first aid kit.

"The cuts and scratches aren't too bad. Main thing is not to let infection set in. I'm afraid of shock, too. Timmy, we want you to lie down and keep your feet up. Wade, there's a blanket in that compartment under the wheel."

With the boy's injuries tended to, Lark guided the boat along the hummock.

"Help me find a run that will take us to the crash site," she said to Wade.

"This next one will . . . maybe."

The helicopter had gone down approximately fifty yards from them in an area in which thick saw grass separated the hummock from a tangle of mangrove trees.

"It's too narrow," said Lark. "Wade, I don't think the boat will make it through the run."

"Can't we try it? Houston might be dying."

"I know. You're right. We have to try it. Crawl out in front of the windshield and guide me."

The boy obeyed.

And as the storm continued its relentless approach, he gestured right and then left and then right again. The boat labored in the shallow water; the run narrowed to ten feet wide. Saw grass thickened. The run narrowed to eight feet. Then five.

"It's right up here. I can see the cockpit . . . I can see Houston," Wade exclaimed.

But the cockpit, lodged in the clutches of mangrove branches, was upside down. Houston was slumped over. When Wade saw all the blood smeared across the front of the glass, his breath caught.

"He's all bloody, and he's not moving."

Lark slowed the boat almost to a stop. She determined

324

that they were still forty or fifty feet away.

"I'll push it as far as I can," she said.

Another twenty feet. The saw grass closed on every side of the boat.

"No farther. That's it," she called to Wade.

Through the knee-deep water they slogged, shoving aside the saw grass.

"See. Look at all the blood," said Wade. "You think he's dead?"

"Oh, God, I hope not. Here, maybe if I can boost you up, you can grab the landing feet and pull the door to the cockpit open."

"Okay. Hey, he moved . . . hey, he's alive."

Houston's eyelids fluttered. They could hear him groan.

Steadied on a mangrove branch, Wade held on to the landing feet and yanked at the door to the cockpit.

"It won't open. He's gonna have to open it from inside."

Several seconds passed before Houston was conscious enough to realize what they were trying to do. Pain lancing across his face, he succeeded in shouldering open the door.

One of the fuel tanks was leaking, but, fortunately, had not burst into flames, though the acrid smell filled the air.

"Help him slide out. Easy, easy," said Lark, "he may have broken something."

"I think his head's been hurt."

"I'm okay," Houston muttered, wincing as Wade and Lark reached for him. He was upside down, and one of his legs appeared to be trapped.

"Ankle and ribs," he whispered. "God, where's the creature?"

"It's gone," said Wade. "You chased it off."

"What about Timmy?"

"He's in the boat," said Lark. "Cut and scratched up and in shock some, but I think he'll be all right."

They struggled, all three straining, moving tentatively, until at last Houston emerged, slipping free as if the cockpit had just given birth to him. But it took another few minutes of painful maneuvering before they could get him into the boat.

"Let's make room for him in the cabin," said Lark. "His ankle's swollen. Looks like a sprain."

With their help, Houston lowered himself onto his back and watched as Lark began to wrap his ankle.

"Where'd you learn to be so handy with that first aid kit?"

"When you spend your time in the wilds, you force yourself to learn—a survival mentality, I guess you'd call it. Sometimes you surprise yourself with what you can do under pressure."

Timmy, awake, face gaining a healthier color, crawled to Houston's side.

"Thanks for saving me. That thing had me. It really did."

Houston smiled weakly. "Wade and Lark pulled you out of the way. You ought to thank them, too."

Thunder growled above the boat. The swamp lapsed into an eerie darkness broken intermittently by sheets of powerful lightning.

"It's going to open up any minute," said Lark as she studied a purplish bruise on Houston's forehead. "You got a nasty knock there. How about your ribs?"

"Feel like hell."

"Probably cracked a couple of them. Does it hurt to take a deep breath?"

He grimaced. "Yeah. I slammed into the control panel when I crashed."

Standing away from the scene, Wade found part of himself wanting to thank Houston for his heroics; part, however, held back, and he wasn't certain why. He glanced up at the churning darkness. A single, heavy drop of rain fell upon his shoulder.

The wind gusted, and to the west an angry, yellowish hue flooded the horizon. And there was something more. An all too familiar odor.

The boy's mouth sagged open.

Winging through the threatening pall, screaming its cry of vengeance, Blood Wings directed its wounded body toward the boat.

"It's back!" Wade suddenly called out.

As he hustled into the cabin with the others, the creature swooped low. Its talons raked across the top of the cabin, creating a senses-rending noise.

Timmy began to cry. Lark reached for him to hug and console him.

Houston trembled.

"Get this boat going!" he shouted.

Wade grasped his spear; his heart drummed in his throat.

The sprinkles of rain thickened. Thunder boomed, drowning out the sound of the boat as Lark coaxed the engine to life.

"Jesus, here it comes again," Houston exclaimed. "Why isn't the boat moving?"

At the wheel, Lark gave it full throttle in reverse. She rocked gears—forward and reverse, forward and reverse —and the engine labored and moaned.

"We're stuck! The hull's run aground!"

Lark's words were sandwiched between a rack of thunder and the screaming approach of the creature.

And then another sound.

The deafening crash of a downpour of water.

The dark membrane of cloud tore, and the rain was so intense that from the cabin they saw only the gray outline of the creature as it pulled out of its dive.

Timmy scuttled to Lark's comforting embrace. Houston struggled deeper into the protective covering of the cabin, and Wade cupped his hands over his ears.

The deluge continued for over an hour, during which time no one spoke, or only in whispers, Lark deflecting Timmy's fears.

Wade wrapped his fingers ever more tightly around the spear handle.

And Houston stared into the solid curtain of rain with the eyes of a man who had just received a death sentence.

2

Beer number five took the steadiness from his hands and the clarity from his vision. The rain waterfalled in front of him and the boat, though he had maneuvered far enough under a canopy of mangroves to keep the full force of the moisture away. He held the tarp over his head, a makeshift tent in which the wandering Ibo also sought shelter.

Although he had smashed the bottle of rum, Hash had brought a six-pack of beer in his cooler; the rain had stolen his appetite, but not his thirst.

"Toad strangler," he murmured. "Ibo, you ole butt-licker, the swamp's tryin' to drown us . . . and you know why?"

The bird gargled and cooed, ruffling the wet from his feathers.

"'Cause I'm a mean bastard. But I had to be. You know why? I'll tell you why soon as I drink this last beer."

Weaving even as he reached into the cooler, he gradually righted himself, drank deeply, belched, and then, disgusted, tossed the half-empty can out into the pouring rain.

"You ever know what a bastard my dad was? Son-of-a-bitch. The king of sons-a-bitches. You 'member what he did? You 'member, bird?"

Ibo picked indifferently at the feathers on his chest.

"He never liked me . . . never knew . . . why."

He paused to wipe threads of saliva from his mouth.

"Hated my guts, fact is. You 'member my ashtray? No, course you don't."

Beneath the tarp, he began to shiver. His teeth chattered.

"Goddamn, what are we doin' out here, bird?" he stammered, pulling the tarp farther over his head. The fog of intoxication and exhaustion and bitterness reclaimed him.

"Ashtray," he muttered. "You shoulda seen it. Mahogany. I made it outta real mahogany—not scrap shit. Made it in shop. Mister . . . mister—what the fuck was his name?—the teacher, he helped me. I worked on that ashtray for four solid weeks. Spent my own money on it. One dollar and twenty-seven whole cents. One whole dollar . . . and twenty-seven cents. Lot of money in those days."

Lightning flashed close.

Ibo squawked.

"Jesus," the man hissed. And then returned to his memory.

"I was twelve years old. I loved my dad. He was a big, strong sucker. I thought he was the biggest, toughest man in the world. He worked on construction crews—built skyscrapers—called himself a skywalker. Jesus, I thought he was God."

He paused to wipe at his mouth again.

"Wanted to make him something. So, you see he smoked cigars at home, and my mom—God, she was a blessed saint—she gave me this idea to make him an ashtray. So I did. I hollowed out this piece of mahogany and sanded it down and varnished it, and it shone like a nigger's toe. And I brought it home one day, and that night after supper, I went to the living room where he was smoking his cigar. I told him I'd made him somethin'. Handed him the ashtray. God, I was proud. Twelve fuckin' years old—you never feel like that again in your life, ya know."

The rain relented a notch.

A pocket of mist rose from the accumulated by-splash of the downpour, a surprisingly cold mist which chilled the man to his bones.

"He looked at it real close-like. Then he looked at me, and I was feelin' so damn good I thought I'd split my britches. He tol' me he had to test it, you see, to find out if it was any good. And he took it in those big ole hands of his and held it out in front of him . . . and it snapped in two. Jesus, I can still hear the sound of that wood splintering. I was twelve years old."

He stared through the rising mist.

"So when I make it . . . when the big hit comes—and it's gonna, I feel it—I'm gonna buy me an ashtray—maybe a solid gold one, ya know—and I'm goin' back to St. Luke's Cemetery in the Bronx, and I'm gonna stand on that man's grave and shake that ashtray in his face and say, 'Here, you mean bastard, test this!'"

He swallowed the memory, then murmured, "I was twelve years old."

Then louder: "All my ashtrays gonna be gold, Ibo. You hear that?"

He swung an arm at the bird, who, in turn, cried out, "Come here! Hurry! I see it! Here!"

It was Wade's voice. Hash recognized it.

"It's beautiful. It's beautiful. It's beautiful."

Lark's voice replaced Wade's.

Hash smiled drunkenly.

"They're out here, ain't they? And they've seen the creature, ain't they? I heard a chopper . . . could

330

be ole Houston has more balls than I figured. But that creature's mine . . . gold ashtrays . . . big hit . . . all mine."

3

The red and blue lights spun methodically, spreading their eerie glow through the steely sheen of the hard rain.

"Another patrol car," said Anita. "Half of the law enforcement officials in this county have been around here today. Seems that way, at least."

She leaned against Holly's counter and surveyed the rain and listened to Holly crunch at some pretzels and sip at a cold drink.

"Wish you would talk some to me, Holly. I need to hear your voice."

"Sorry, honey," said the heavyset woman, halting the approach of a pretzel to her mouth. "Can't get my mind off Wick and Jack Staimer. Now they say they've found C.M. and his friend Johnson . . . it's so blessed horrible, it just makes me feel like not talking."

"If you'd like to close up the store, go ahead. No use staying close to the CB because Lark can't seem to get through to us or we to her. And when it stops raining, one of the officers told me they'd consider flying a helicopter over the area, but they'd rather wait till morning."

She paused.

"But I told him that my two boys might not be able . . . to wait till morning. They need to be found tonight. And so do Lark and Houston."

She turned to Holly, who reached out and gently pulled the young woman's head down onto her shoulder.

"Holly, I sent him out there . . . and he's not coming back. Something happened to him . . . to all of them. They aren't coming back."

331

She began to sob.

Holly held her, knowing that the tears had to flow.

A siren echoed in the distance.

No customers entered the store.

The rain continued.

When Anita succeeded in getting her tears under control, she said, "I didn't believe Wade, and I'll never forgive myself for that. Twice I haven't believed him. He knew somehow that Timmy was out in the swamp, and I doubted it. And he knew . . . he tried to tell us there really was a monster . . . that something killed Gillie . . . but I thought he was making it all up."

"No one else believed him, either," said Holly.

"Houston did. And I forced him to go out there and—"

"Let's just hold steady, honey. Hold steady and tell ourselves we'll see them again . . . we'll see all four of them again."

4

Lark switched on the cabin lights and began to wrap tape around Houston's ribs. The rain having relented to a steady, less-gushing stream, she could turn her attention away from Timmy.

Hearing Houston groan as his injured ribs were tended to, Wade thought again about thanking the man who had boldly flown into the swamp and had engaged the creature before it could carry Timmy away.

But suddenly he felt a small hand tugging at him.

"Wade, it 'bout got me. It did. It grabbed me, and I was up in the air, and it was gonna take me off and eat me."

Wade studied his brother's face. "Lark said you're spozed to keep laying down 'cause you might be in shock."

"You mean like poking a fork in a 'lectric plug thing?"

"No. Different kind of shock. It's like 'bout bein'

332

killed, and your body gets so scared all your insides are messed up . . . like your heart and your brains."

"Do I go in shock?"

"Well, maybe. Lark said you might. How does your head feel?"

"Pretty okay. My bottom's real, real sore. She put on some stuff that stings real bad."

"To keep you from gettin' infected and dying of germs."

"Am I gonna die, Wade? From the creature puttin' its claws on me?" The little boy raised himself so that he could look beyond the railing of the boat. "Are we never, ever gonna get outta the swamp? We gonna be stuck till we die and they just find our skel'tons?"

Wade frowned. "Don't be a dummy. We ain't gonna die. Not probably. It'll stop raining."

In a tiny voice, Timmy whispered, "Will the creature come back?"

Heat flushed from Wade's throat to the pit of his stomach. Reflexively he gripped at his spear. "I think maybe it might. If it does, I got a poison stick that'll kill it."

"Can I touch the stick?"

"Yeah, but don't touch the point of it."

Small fingers stroked the spear handle, carefully avoiding the *wirrie* at the end of it. "Where you gonna stab it? In the face? In the stomach?"

Wade shrugged.

Images of thrusting the weapon into the creature blinked on and off in his thoughts. He felt suddenly very cold, but didn't want his little brother to see him shiver.

"You gotta stab things in the heart," he said, "so's then the poison don't got to go so far to kill it."

"Wade?"

"Yeah?"

"Well, what if it, you know, bites off your arm or your face before you can stab it?"

333

"You ask the nerdiest questions. If it bites off my arm or my face, I can't stab it. Somebody else'd have to. Stop askin' me questions. You're spozed to be restin' and not talkin'."

He glanced over at Lark and Houston, both of whom were quiet, choosing not to battle the hammer of the rain to have themselves heard. Houston was lying on his back, shadows slicing across his face, his shirt open, tape wound tightly around his chest. He appeared to be in some pain.

Lark was sitting with her back against the wall of the cabin, knees tucked up, a notepad resting there. She was writing notes; her camera snuggled next to her like a very small pet of some kind.

Attention straying from the two adults, Wade reached into his back pocket and retrieved a photo. He examined it and smiled. But Timmy had noticed.

"Who's that a picture of?"

"See for yourself." He held it out so that Timmy could see it.

"Hey, it's Gillie."

"Yeah . . . I sure miss him."

"Hey, you know what I'm gonna do?"

Wade sighed indifferently. "No, what are you gonna do?"

Reaching behind him, the small boy recovered the Instamatic camera and grinned. "I didn't break mom's camera."

"So?"

"I'm gonna take a picture of you."

"You got no brains, Timmy. You can't take a picture at night—not here. Not without a flashcube."

"No. I mean, tomorrow I'll take one of you killing the creature."

Wade chuckled nervously. "Man, you really are uh airhead. Man, you're a mess."

334

"I can do it. This afternoon I took one. The creature, it was flyin' around up there, and I took one of it. I clicked this little button. I did. You'll see."

"Lark took some. She's gonna put 'em in a book, I bet."

"Maybe she'll put mine in her book, too."

Wade shook his head. "I don't think so, Timmy."

The rain softened to a light patter.

After a few seconds of silence, Timmy asked, "Wade? If you don't kill the creature, who will?"

"I can kill it. Don't worry about it."

"But what if it kills you?"

"Just shut up, Timmy."

"Could *he* do it?" The boy cocked his head toward Houston.

"He's hurt himself too bad, probably," said Wade.

"There's nobody else except . . . me," said Timmy. "If it kills you . . . I'll do it. I'll kill the creature."

Wade laughed, and Timmy's face fell.

"You couldn't kill a frog."

"Yes, I could. I smacked one with a rock. Ask Sara Beth. I did."

"Timmy, you're a little baby wimp nerd, and you couldn't fight the creature or nuthin' else, so just shut your trap. If you wasn't such a friggin' dummy, we wouldn't all be out in the swamp gettin' people 'bout killed. You're a friggin' dummy."

"I'm not either," Timmy whispered, but even in the shadows, Wade could see his eyes tear.

The sight squeezed at his heart.

Timmy lowered his head so that his brother wouldn't see how badly his feelings had been hurt.

"Friggin' deal," Wade muttered. "All right. I'm sorry, Timmy, for callin' you names and stuff. I'm glad Ibo came around and . . . hey, where is Ibo?"

"Flewed away, maybe."

"Yeah, I bet he did . . . when Blood Wings attacked you. Might coulda gone back to Hash, or coulda gone all the way to Hash's cabin."

"I hope the creature didn't eat him," said Timmy.

"Ibo's probably okay."

Wade glanced again at Houston, who appeared to be resting quietly despite the rattle of the rain on the cabin roof. Then he looked to Lark, who had set aside her notebook and seemed to be locked into some kind of trance.

5

Whenever she felt threatened, whenever the great fabric of reality showed signs of coming unraveled, Lark would visit her Protector, her inner Magician for advice and words of wisdom.

Her Aunt Glennis, years ago, had introduced the ritual to her. One summer, they had been sitting around the family swimming pool when Aunt Glennis, considered a whacko by the more stable of her relatives, sensed that Lark, thirteen at the time, was totally miserable with herself.

"Sweetheart," the redheaded, pale-skinned Glennis intoned, "you need to go on a trip, a journey."

"I do?"

At the time, Lark had convinced herself that no boy would ever show interest in her and that she was, hands down, the clumsiest, most unattractive human being on the face of the earth.

"Yes, you. Because you're a hopelessly tangled mess of loose strings. I can see it. At your age, I was that way, too. Luckily I discovered a source of inner wisdom . . . a friend I could talk to whenever the world treated me like batter in a waffle iron."

Lark had giggled at the image.

"Do I have this friend?"

"Absolutely. Do you want to meet her?"

"Sure."

"Listen carefully. Put yourself into a complete state of relaxation—deep, slow breathing—feel each breath—in, out, in, out. Deep, slow, totally relaxed. Imagine that you find yourself at the mouth of a cave. Initially, it frightens you because it leads to a part of you with which you are unfamiliar. You enter the cave. It's very dark but curiously enough, you feel encouraged to go forward. You seem to be following a path, and the farther you walk along the path, the more you realize that you exude a light which helps you see. You continue along the path until you come to a fast-flowing stream. And there you discover a boat."

"Should I get into the boat?" young Lark had asked.

"If your intuition tells you to, yes. Yes, get into it. It will take you to a small, rock-covered island deep, very deep within the cave. On that island lives your Protector, your Magician. Go to her and ask whatever you want to ask. You will always find a source of help there."

Lark had taken that boat ride many, many times over the years, and so it was that as the steady rain assaulted the swamp, she sought the mouth of the familiar cave. Down the path. Into the boat. To the small, rocky island.

And there her Magician waited.

An ancient woman clad in a scarlet robe, her Magician had ivory skin and hair as white as snow and the texture of spun silk. Her eyes sparkled the irresistible blue-green of crystal clear seawater.

Lark stepped onto the island and felt the all-embracing peacefulness of the Magician's aura.

"I come for your help, inner Magician. We are in danger, and I cannot see my way through this. Tell me what I must do."

But, to Lark's surprise, the Magician said nothing.

"Please," she implored, "I need your advice."

Steadfast silence greeted her.

Confused, Lark watched as from within her robe the Magician removed an object surrounded by an intense, white light. She handed it toward Lark.

"No, I cannot take this. I cannot do what you suggest."

Heart beating wildly, Lark clambered out of her meditative state, profoundly troubled by her Magician's apparent solution to their dilemma.

Have I misinterpreted it?

I can't be certain what the object was.

She felt someone grasp her wrist. Startled, she tried to pull away.

"Do you hear that?"

It was Houston, his grip firm.

"Stopped raining," he said. "The boat. Feel what's happening?"

Suddenly she could.

The deluge had raised the water level of the narrow, shallow run.

"We're not stuck!" Lark exclaimed.

Wade and Timmy cheered.

"I'll start the boat."

Houston struggled to his feet. "Wade, you and Timmy give me a hand bailing out some of the water from the back of the boat. We're headin' home."

To Wade, the words sounded better than he could have imagined.

Forget about the creature, he told himself.

Home. We're going home.

Chapter 18

1

The gentle rocking and lifting free of the boat fired a celebration of words and laughter and happy slaps on the shoulder. Lark switched on the cabin spotlight, and its brilliance parted the night as she carefully backed out of the narrow run.

Hobbling to the rear of the boat, Houston guided her, calling directions to go left or right, faster or slower.

The swamp around them shimmered its wetness; mist rose in diaphanous curtains; frogs and night insects joined in an evening chorus which added to the weirdness of the scene.

But no one on the boat gave particular heed to anything except the thought of curling up in his or her own bed and forgetting the day's trauma. Wade figured that matters had probably turned out for the best: They had rescued Timmy—a fact that would bring joy to his mother—; Houston had survived the helicopter crash and, in Wade's eyes, had gained some heroic stature; and Lark had seen the creature and gotten some photos of it.

Sorry, Gillie.

I didn't kill the creature for you.

Maybe Hash would, the boy reasoned. Hash knew the swamp and had a gun, so it only made sense that he should be the one to do the deed. He understood killing.

"You've got it!" Houston exclaimed.

The boat swung free of the run and its forest of saw grass.

In the west, a fresh round of lightning and thunder paraded across the sky, promising more rain before the night ended.

Suddenly, the glub-glub of the boat choked off.

"What's wrong?" asked Houston.

Lark wandered uncertainly out from the cabin. "Which way? How do we get back to Orchid Springs?"

His face turned toward the cabin, Houston squinted into the glare of the spotlight. Lines of puzzlement were etched at the corners of his mouth. Hands on his hips, he glanced left and then right. The mist had thickened, blotting out any possibility of detecting a landmark or guidepoint.

"Just a minute . . . I'm not sure. Damn, it's hard to tell. Which way did you turn into that run?"

"Left, I think," said Lark.

"Okay. Okay, let's start back the way you came. I'll look for something I recognize." Making his way to the cabin, Houston winced in pain.

"You shouldn't be putting any weight on that ankle," said Lark.

"I'll be okay. My ribs hurt more than the ankle."

He joined Lark at the wheel, and she pivoted the spotlight so that it radiated over the prow.

Timmy's fingers tugged at Wade. "Are we lost?"

"A little, maybe."

"Can Houston save us? He saved me from the creature."

"Nobody's got uh save us, Timmy. We just have to find the right way home."

340

"You think mom misses us?"

Wade shrugged. "Yeah, I guess maybe she does. Last night she was pretty upset. She thought dad had kidnapped you."

"Really?"

"Yeah, and she called the sheriff and everything."

"Would dad really kidnap me?"

"I don't know. Maybe."

"Would you want him to kidnap you?"

"No."

"Why not?"

"Because."

"Wade?"

Growing impatient, Wade growled, "What now?"

"Well . . . why do they call it 'kidnap'? 'Kid' and 'nap'? A nap is what mom used to make me take every afternoon."

"It's a different word, dummy. Don't ask no more questions."

"I'm thirsty."

"Go up there by Lark and get you a drink. Don't be so helpless."

"That's just what mom says."

"Sometimes mom's right."

When his brother had shuffled off, Wade felt strangely relieved to be alone. He leaned against a side rail and let the cool mist brush across his cheeks. He looked up, but could see no stars. Lark had restarted the engine and they were moving at a cautious speed. The spotlight speared through the mist, suggesting a giant laser beam to Wade.

Wet mangrove leaves winked in the darkness, then seemed to shrink within themselves when caught in the bright light. The sour odor of rain-soaked clumps of peat bubbling up around hummocks touched the boy's nostrils. He had set aside the *wirrie,* and he had, in fact, marveled at how easy it was to push aside all thoughts of confronting the creature.

Lark and Houston appeared to have the boat under control. Tomorrow, he reasoned, this entire episode would begin to become only a memory, and the summer would spread before him like the vast, blue-gray expanse of the ocean. Things would get back to normal as long as Blood Wings remained deep in the swamp.

Relaxing another notch, Wade heard his stomach growl.

Hope Lark has something else to eat.

He wondered where she would go from Orchid Springs—off to find the abominable snowman or a sea serpent? Sounded like fun unless .... Suddenly the image of the creature bearing down upon Timmy seized his thoughts. No, what she did could be dangerous. Very dangerous.

And what about Houston?

He and mom gonna get married?

The panoply of questions dizzied Wade. Life was confusing.

Too friggin' confusing.

Except when you were hungry. Then life became bugshit simple.

Wade had turned away from the rail to hunt for food when he sensed it. Not the peculiar thrum of wings. Not the characteristic stench. But it was out there.

He wheeled around to search the night sky.

But he could see nothing.

Clouds blanketed the stars and moonlight.

Again, he sensed it. Watching. Circling with predatory intent.

The boy's body felt as if every vein were alive with squirming ants, animated by some unseen threat.

"Hey!" he shouted. "It's back! It's back!"

342

He ran toward the cabin and nearly knocked Timmy over.

"Dang it, Wade. Why doncha step on my face?"

"I mean it! It's back!"

Lark and Houston had shifted their attention away from the wheel to him.

"Where?" said Houston. "Which way is it coming?"

"I can't tell. I haven't seen it, but I know it's out there."

Lark grabbed for Timmy. "Everyone stay in the cabin."

They waited.

In the distance, faintly, they could hear its cry.

"It's looking for us," said Houston. "Give the boat more throttle."

Pulling away from Timmy, Lark followed his directions. And as the boat picked up speed, Wade began to breathe easier. Everyone huddled closer to the wheel.

"I'm going to try the CB again," said Houston.

He was balancing mostly on one leg, avoiding any extra weight on his swollen ankle.

"Try the emergency channel," said Lark.

He did. And his efforts produced only static.

"Nothing," Houston muttered.

"Maybe the creature broke the radio," Timmy whispered.

No one spoke.

Lark slowed for a bend in the slough.

And then she screamed.

2

"Get down!" Houston shouted.

For one moment frozen in time, Wade saw the

343

mesmerizing approach of the creature as it skimmed low over the slough and charged into the spray of the spotlight. Its blackness seemed to swallow the light.

Its muscular wings, the tip of one crusting blood, appeared to reach across the entire slough. And just before the boy ducked beneath the control panel, he saw the creature's talons splayed and ready for attack, and he saw the creature's face, its fangs.

And its eyes.

Both burning like a flame on the sharp point of his *wirrie*.

Eyes that could poison.

The collision of creature and boat slammed bodies together. The glass beyond the wheel shattered like a gunshot. The housing for the spotlight was ripped away; sparks skirled into the back of the boat. There were two nervous pops and the scraping of talons on the cabin roof.

And total darkness.

3

Hash had guided his skiff to within fifty yards of the spotlight.

"Christ, it's on 'em!" he exclaimed.

He could feel his blood quicken as all the lights on Lark's boat went out.

"Ibo, hang on to your balls, friend. Things could get ugly in a hurry."

His lantern cast its yellow-white glow in a muted circle at the prow. He poled firmly, methodically, his rifle at his feet; he hoped he could maneuver for a clear shot, though he knew that every yard away from the protective covering of the mangroves put him at high risk—an easy target for the creature.

344

"You see it, Ibo? You see that ole bastard?"

Hash scanned the darkness, but even when the approaching lightning flashed, he could see no sign of the creature.

He poled a few yards closer to Lark's boat; he could hear the occupants talking in frightened tones. He waited, choosing not to pull alongside and make his presence known.

"We best keep to ourselves," he told the parrot.

And with that he began poling away.

The night tightened around him like a fist.

"Don't like how quiet it is. No, not one damn bit I don't."

Ibo gurgled and preened. "No, not one damn bit I don't. Sumbitch. No, not one damn bit I don't," the bird echoed.

Hash chuckled nervously. "You're an asshole, Ibo. You know that? Oughtta shoot you and roast you on a spit."

He sat down and laid the pole aside and groped around in a canvas bag at his feet.

"Bologna sandwich. These fuckers'll make you sterile, Ibo. It's what I hear. Damn . . . wish I had another beer."

As he began munching on the sandwich, he kept one eye on the cloud-covered night sky. The rain front was gathering momentum from the west.

"You ready to get your ass wet again?"

But the comment had barely escaped his lips when Ibo took flight.

"Hey, where you—?"

He sat up, suddenly so alert he felt light-headed. He tossed the partially eaten sandwich into the slough.

"I smell it." His voice was barely audible.

Instinctively he reached for his rifle and stood, his knees creaking, threatening not to keep him erect.

"Come on you ole bastard. Bring your million dollar carcass right here to Papa Hash. I got a slug with your name on it."

There was no wind, no swamp sounds save the dripping of rainwater from the mangrove leaves.

"God damn," he murmured, realizing that he was squeezing his rifle so tightly that it was hurting his hands. He glanced down at the lantern.

Somewhere high above the boat, the creature circled.

And Hash knew something more.

"It's the light, ain't it? It's what drew you to the other boat. Now it's my little ole light's drawin' you to me."

A grin spreading across his lips, he lifted the lantern to eye level.

"Here it is! See it! I'm ready for you!"

His yelling echoed along the surface of the slough.

"Come on! A million bucks! All mine!"

He never saw the angle of the creature's attack, for it dived at him from straight above. He heard the shriek and felt the vibration of air, but the moment unfolded so rapidly that he had virtually no chance to respond. It was like having a bomb dropped upon him.

The lantern crashed to the floor of the skiff, snuffing itself out.

Hash swung an elbow up at the very last instant to protect himself.

And felt talons gash open his flesh from elbow to wrist.

He cried out as the creature's dive crushed him to his knees, and he toppled to one side banging his chin.

"God damn," he groaned.

Though knocked woozy, he gathered himself almost immediately and fired off three rounds from his knees.

"You bastard," he muttered.

He touched his forearm and felt the rapid oozing of blood; he gritted his teeth and began to shiver. He knew his shots had missed.

He slumped against his tarp and heard a rattle in his breathing. He closed his eyes tightly and fought to remain conscious.

Got to tend the wound.

Not gonna bleed to death.

With as much energy as he could muster, he tore off a strip of his shirt and began to wrap it around his forearm. Pulling a knot into place with his teeth, he sank down.

"One more chance . . . Jesus."

In his thoughts, an image of Mr. Bones tearing up the million dollar check materialized.

"Not yet. One more chance."

He opened his eyes as wide as possible, for he believed that if he let them close, they would never open again.

4

"It's Hash's rifle. I recognize it," said Houston.

"I heard the creature's scream. It must have attacked him. He could be hurt," said Lark, an urgency in her tone. "I feel like we should go check on him."

"No. No, we have no lights. You can't navigate this slough in the dark."

"Shouldn't we do something?"

"Yes . . . we'll wait. Nothing more we can do. Hash can take care of himself. He's tough, and he's been around this mangrove swamp for years—knows it as well as my dad did."

Wade had been following their exchange when he heard something in the distance. He listened as Houston's words ushered in a brief silence.

"Helicopters!" the boy exclaimed. "Hear them?"

Everyone scrambled out of the cabin.

To the north, a mile or more, a couple of searchlights crisscrossed, piercing the night. The helicopters were

347

moving slowly to the west and maintaining an altitude of less than one hundred feet.

"Is it the sheriff's department?" asked Lark.

"More than likely," said Houston.

"They're goin' the wrong way to find us," Timmy whimpered.

Lark put her hand on his shoulder. "They'll probably circle this way . . . we need to wave and make some noise. I have a flashlight somewhere . . . we can signal to them."

"Save yourself the trouble," said Houston. "They see how fast that next band of storm clouds is moving. They're turning back."

Wade felt the disappointment surge into his throat hot and sour.

A cool wind chilled the air. Nickel-sized drops of rain began to patter, and the four of them sought out the cabin once again.

"I'm cold," Timmy whispered to his brother.

They leaned against a wall, and Wade gently pulled him over so that they sat shoulder to shoulder.

The rain came, not as hard this time, but steady; the lightning and thunder were intense, eye-burning and ear-ringing.

"This definitely halts the sheriff's rescue mission," said Lark.

She and Houston had huddled in the darkness near the wheel.

"They'll be back first light most likely," said Houston.

"Timmy's cuts and scratches need more attention and medication than my first aid kit allows. What about you? You feeling any better?"

"Just stiff and sore. There'll be hell to pay when Miss Freda finds out about her helicopter."

"Such a curious woman. She seems to delight in the fact that the creature has killed and continues to viciously attack people."

"She's crazy. Simple as that."

"I wish that she had told me more about the creature."

They paused as if to listen for sounds penetrating the rain. Eventually Houston said, "What's out there? What do you think it is?"

"At first, I thought it was something genuinely prehistoric. A million years ago there were giant bats in this part of the world, but none the size of Blood Wings—and certainly none with such human facial features."

"God, it does have—like a man's face. I've seen it up close." He shivered involuntarily.

Lark, clearly interested in the subject, shifted to a more comfortable position in the darkness before continuing. "But Freda Shreck's account of the Dreamtime creatures—like the Garkain—the description fits what we've been seeing. It's a living myth. There's nothing quite like it in the natural realm."

"It makes me wonder, you know," said Houston, "*why* it exists. More than an ordinary predator."

Quietly, Lark spoke again, and her words carried Houston into memory. "I believe it exists because Nature understands the need for savageness. Such a creature makes every other living thing around more alive—stirs the blood, sharpens the instincts, reminds us that survival is the first law of the beating heart. We all need fierceness in our lives."

Whatever mechanism releases memory had been touched.

Houston fell silent.

The years dropped away like leaves, and he was a boy again—around the age of Wade—and he had accompanied his dad into the swamp. As usual, they were looking for a white gator.

A surprisingly cool dawn had encouraged them to strike a campsite and to start a small fire on one of the hummocks. His dad had used some of his coffee water to fix Houston a cup of hot chocolate.

Steaming cup warming his hands, the boy had asked, "Do you think we'll find one today? Do you think we'll find a white gator?"

His dad chuckled softly. "Maybe so. Maybe not. Will you be disappointed if we don't?"

"Yeah. Some, I mean. We got up awful early not to find something. Even a real small white gator would be better than finding nothing."

"But we have found something . . . or, maybe the way to say it is—we've been *given* something."

"Given?"

"Yes. A gift."

"Where is it?"

His dad set down his coffee cup and gestured widely, both arms extended, at the surrounding swamp.

Houston followed the movement of his dad's arms.

"Right here."

"What do you call our gift?"

"You can call it whatever name you choose. I like to call it wildness. We have been given the gift of wildness. And, you know, a great writer—I don't recall his name, but I read him in school—he once wrote that we humans need wildness. We need to see and feel our limits transgressed."

"Wildness," the boy whispered to himself.

At that moment, he had felt it.

Wildness.

The primitive, potentially savage scene of the swamp shaking itself awake—he saw it for the first time, and while he could not fully understand his dad's reverence for that wildness, he knew that it existed and that the white gator was part of it.

The memory faded.

The darkness of the swamp assumed a crouching hush,

the susurration of the rain the only sound.

The creature.

Houston recognized that it, too, was part of the wildness. Perhaps it was out there for a purpose—to penetrate the shell of security modern man had covered himself with—to make everyone with whom it came into contact feel more fully alive.

5

Ibo had judged it safe to return.

The groans and moans of his master piqued his curiosity, encouraging him to fly to the rim of the skiff. The rain had lessened to a drizzle.

Hash, his head throbbing, raised himself with his right arm, for it was the left arm that had been gashed and continued to seep blood. But the pain had relented; a tingling had spread to his shoulder, and yet he was cheered somewhat by the fact that he could still wield his rifle with his right arm.

"Come on back, you ole bastard."

He coughed hard. His tongue felt as if it had been attached with Velcro to the roof of his mouth. He could barely swallow, and he could not repress images of Blood Wings possibly returning to finish him off.

He fumbled for his lantern, but when he recovered it, he found that he couldn't relight it.

"God damn worthless thing," he growled, and tossed it angrily into the slough, and the night around him seemed, impossibly, to darken further.

He heard Ibo cooing and gargling low in his throat.

"That you, bird?"

Other sounds sirened toward him from beyond, and the surrounding mist appeared to whiten; the slough spawned filmy, ghostly images which glided atop the surface: the wispy figures of young women, naked, beautiful, nubile, seductive. They swept past him, generating a smile from his lips.

The drizzle beaded cold drops on his forehead and cheeks.

He longed for warmth and fantasized about pressing against the naked flesh of a real woman. He thought of earlier days. Of Freda Schreck.

But there on the slough another ghostly image rose: Alfredo Comboni in his wheelchair holding out the million dollar check, enticing Hash from his fantasy. Mr. Bones had hooks in him and would not release his hold.

"Jesus," Hash murmured. "Big hit."

His left arm was completely numb. He flexed his fingers, but could not tell whether they had moved.

The hallucination of Mr. Bones faded.

Sleep crowded near.

His eyelids grew heavy.

He listened to his breathing and placed a hand over his heart.

And he thought: *Don't give out on me, you ole fucker.*

His head lolled. He reached for his rifle, patting it reassuringly.

By degrees, he surrendered to sleep.

In the distance, a feral scream radiated into the night.

Hash stirred, but did not waken.

6

The crew of Lark's boat slept. They had scrooched within the cabin. The only screams they heard were in their dreams.

352

Hours after midnight, the rain ceased.

Houston rolled to one side; his ribs protested, sending an ice pick jab of pain into his nerve endings.

"Oh-h-h, God," he muttered.

Lark and Timmy were still asleep

Wade, flashlight in hand, was returning from the head.

"Be light in about an hour," Houston said to him.

Sitting down across from the man, Wade groped for his spear. In the spray of the flashlight, the poisoned tip of the *wirrie* appeared to gleam.

"That's quite a weapon you have there," Houston said, hoping to coax the boy from his silent treatment.

"I took it from Miss Freda's."

"You did? Guess that makes us two of a kind—I took her helicopter."

The boy started to switch off the light, but decided against it. The circumference of its spray partially illuminated Houston's face. Wade wanted to see his eyes. Wanted to know whether he could truly trust the man.

"The stick has poison on it."

"Could I take a look?"

His fingers flexing nervously on the handle, Wade hesitated.

"Okay. Be careful 'bout the point." He handed it to Houston, who examined it carefully.

"You think it would kill the creature?"

Wade shrugged. "Miss Freda told Lark it was maybe the only thing that could."

"That right?"

"Yeah, but I'd rather have a big gun, you know . . . a rifle or a pistol."

"I tried to shoot it with my dad's shotgun—a beautiful gun. The creature smashed it; I was lucky I got away from it alive, and I'm hoping our luck holds now."

"You think the creature's comin' back, doncha?"

"I do. And it is."

"I'll be ready for it," said the boy.

"Don't, Wade. You can't stand up to that creature with a sharp stick—poison or not. You just can't."

The boy's face flushed hot. "I can, too. I can take care of myself. Don't need your help or nobody else's."

"I'm not asking you for my sake—it's for your mom. I love her, Wade, and I told her I would bring Timmy back safe—and I mean to do the same for you, too."

"Nobody's gotta watch after me. I'm gonna kill the creature 'cause I promised Gillie I would. I'm not no coward."

"Doing the smart thing doesn't signal you're a coward. The smart thing for us is to stay out of the creature's way and get back to Orchid Springs."

Wade's throat prickled as Houston slid his shoulders along the wall and closed his eyes, intent upon some sleep before dawn arrived. Before the boy switched off the flashlight, he swung the beam out upon the slough where particles of mist danced. Behind where they had anchored, tall mangroves sent their strong limbs twelve to fifteen feet above the boat, forming an arbor of sorts, but to Wade it seemed more like being inside a natural cathedral. And he drew upon the strength it exuded.

I'm ready for you, Blood Wings.

He lay down, snuggling the spear close to him like a security blanket.

8

He was awakened, not by the muted light presaging dawn, but rather by a runny nose which he wiped on the back of his hand. He glanced around. Timmy and Lark were asleep in the small compartment just below the deck

354

of the cabin. Houston had slumped to the floor and was snoring as if in a deep sleep.

Wade rubbed his eyes.

The air was thick with moisture; pockets of mist yellowed with the advance of the eastern light. The boy wrinkled his nose.

And then tensed every muscle.

He recognized the odor.

He struggled to his feet and searched the overcast sky; he saw nothing, but he knew that the creature was near. He debated a few seconds whether to wake Houston.

No, I can fight the creature myself.

On stiff and aching legs, he stood. The overhanging mangrove branches dripped morning moisture whenever their leaves rustled. He followed the line of the archway they formed.

Suddenly his eyes stopped.

Sharp tails of mist continued to lift as if seeking out the mangrove branches as a place of refuge. Twenty yards beyond the rear of the boat, the mist had parted momentarily, and it created the sensation of being able to peek through a stage curtain before a performance offered first lines.

Reality seemed to turn inside out.

Upside down.

Walking cautiously to the back railing, Wade cocked his head, doubting what his eyes focused upon.

It was an odd-shaped block of darkness.

A giant black cocoon.

Wade took a deep breath and stared.

It was the creature.

And it was hanging, batlike, upside down, anchored by its talons to a mangrove branch. Its huge wings completely enfolded its body; its head hovered only a few feet above the slough.

Lark would say it's beautiful.

355

It seemed a peculiar thought to be dominating the boy's reaction.

He raised his spear, bracing it against his chest.

Then, as if on cue, the creature's silken wings began to unfold in a raspy whisper. The eyes remained closed; the face, from that distance, struck the boy as serene, almost peaceful. Its fangs were partially hidden.

Determined to be ready if and when it attacked, the boy climbed as quietly as possible onto the railing and balanced himself there.

"What is it, Wade?"

Houston's voice caught him by surprise; he teetered, then regained his balance. He returned his attention to the creature.

It had opened its eyes.

For Wade, reality turned another quarter turn. It blurred into images of imprecise but frightened movement. And voices—Houston calling to Lark and shouting for the boy to watch out; of smells—the stench of the creature and the sweaty panic of the boy's own terror; of touch—the brush of the creature's wing on his cheek as it roared past. And the helpless feeling of the spear dropping to the deck and of himself losing balance and falling, falling into the deeper-water side of the boat. He was aware of the explosion of the splash, and no more than a second or two later, a second splash as Houston plunged into the slough after him.

On board, Lark spoke frantically, reaching out from the boat to give Houston a hand, but then turned as the creature completed a circle and swept beneath the canopy of mangrove branches to see Timmy standing at the back railing bravely hoisting the spear and *wirrie*.

Wade heard her scream, heard Timmy's name cried out in absolute terror.

And he felt Houston's strong arms as reality crystallized.

Lark couldn't believe how tiny he looked.

Framed there at the rear of the boat with the mist rising beyond him, Timmy stood, ramrod straight, brandishing the spear, and he appeared to be shrinking like some Saturday morning cartoon character.

For Lark, the scene stirred a memory of being in New York City years ago with her parents, of being in the Warwick Hotel and peering down at the street ten floors below, of her mother holding her by the waist so she could see her father materialize as if the sidewalk had spawned him.

She had waved. And the stump of a man, her father, had returned the wave and had walked on, growing smaller with each step.

"He looks so tiny," Lark had murmured to her mother.

And she had feared that some monster lurking among the skyscrapers of Gotham City would step on her father and smash him into a pool of blood and flesh.

He looks so tiny.

The memory and the thought flashed and dissolved in a millisecond.

"Timmy!" she screamed.

But he stood his ground as the creature bore in upon him.

Panic seized her.

She fought through it and leaped for the small child, catching his ankles, tumbling him to one side as a second later the creature grazed the railing, generating heat and a nauseating odor.

The spear clattered to the floor.

Timmy struggled to find it, but Lark held him and carried him, slipping on the wet surface, falling to her knees, scrambling forward, arms and lungs aching, until she had shoved the boy into the safety of the cabin.

Knowing the creature would return, she wheeled around.

Houston had Wade under one arm and was straining to lift him free of the slough. She started to slide along that side of the boat to help him when an intense, white light caught her eye.

At first she assumed it was the rays of the sun knifing through the mist. Heart pounding like a kettle drum, she blinked. There was a blaze of scarlet and a glistening of spun silk, and the bright light began to dim, though she felt herself being drawn toward it.

She clambered forward and reached out.

The handle of the spear felt solid.

"Take his hand," Houston called to her as he tried to push Wade onto the railing.

But Lark saw the creature cutting through the sky, wings beating as if intent upon one final dive.

"Get back!" she cried to Houston.

On her knees, she raised the spear.

No, not this. Not this.

Seeing the approach of the creature, Houston yanked Wade from the railing and heard the thrum of wings, and it reminded him of power lines whistling and skirling in a high wind.

Lark held the spear, mesmerized by the sweep of the creature's blackness—its wings seemed to her a huge shroud threatening to cover and suffocate her.

Her entire body trembled, and she screamed as the creature pulled up, wings spreading to slow its flight, its talons extended. It slammed into the back railing, rocked forward, and then gained its balance. It perched there, not fifteen feet from her.

Tears flooded her eyes; mucous streamed from her nose.

The spear threatened to drop from her fingers.

Blood Wings stared down at her.

358

It was a magnificent creature, a paragon of power and savagery, an entity forged by Nature from great darkness and primitive fury.

"I can't," she whispered.

Then she heard Houston climbing at the side of the boat, splashing, reaching for the railing.

Its eyes never leaving hers, the creature opened its jaws; fangs extended from the blood-red gums, and it pressed forward for the kill.

Lark screamed again and began to scramble away. The wet floor brought her crashing to her elbows; on hands and knees she began to push herself forward.

Until the pain exploded in shooting trails of violet and orange lights.

The fangs of the creature locked onto one of her calves.

She felt herself being dragged toward the creature, felt it release its fangs and loop its talons around her ankles. And in those moments of unimaginable terror, she experienced, as well, a counterbalancing peace.

This is endgame.

Don't fight it.

Sliding along helplessly on her stomach, she nearly let go of the spear; she held on to it as someone might a lone, stray limb when dangling from a cliff. Eyes dimming, she forced herself to concentrate on the object and again, curiously, she saw a bright light emanate from it. She thought of her inner Magician.

Can't do this.

She rolled onto her back and felt herself being lifted.

All around her voices were colliding: screams, yells, panic-stricken shouts. Houston had climbed part way over the railing and was beating at the creature's wings with his fists.

Pressure from one of the talons relented.

The creature rocked its head back and issued a loud

shriek. From its fangs, Lark could see her lifeblood dripping, and the sight of it galvanized her into action.

She pushed herself to one knee, her hold on the spear firm.

Snarling, lashing its magnificent head to one side, the creature lunged at Houston, causing him to release his hold on the railing and splash back into the slough. And when the creature righted itself, Lark tore free of its grasp. She raised the spear and gritted her teeth.

And drove the point of the *wirrie* forward with all of her strength.

She saw it pierce the creature's throat; she felt it penetrate muscle and slice through a main artery, sending a shower of blood out into the slough.

Blood Wings roared, but the sound dissolved into a pathetic gurgle. It beat its wings, and in one gargantuan effort, it stumbled into flight, slanting off low over the slough, unable, at first, to gain altitude. Then it banked and wheeled. The *wirrie* remained lodged in its throat, but the creature fought the poison seeping into its system and swept upward a hundred feet or more.

Lark, Houston, and the boys watched its struggle in wordless awe.

Having achieved as much altitude as its condition would allow, the creature appeared to shudder. One wing crumpled. There was a final, agonized death scream, and it began to fall.

Like Lucifer, thought Lark.

Doré's illustrations for *Paradise Lost.* The fallen angel. There it was, tumbling into the fiery lake of Hell.

It crashed into shallow water.

Frightened birds cried out and burst into flight nearby.

No one spoke as the massive creature thrashed one wing, churning the water. It rolled over, then beat at the water a few seconds longer.

And then it was silent.

"Nothing. Their unit must be out," said Holly.

She and Anita had gathered at the store.

"Helicopters from the National Guard are going into the swamp," said Anita. "Sheriff's department is sending one, too." She was standing at the front door, arms folded against her breasts.

"There'll be a patrol boat heading out shortly," Holly added. "I overheard the sheriff mention that."

"Everything's so quiet. Orchid Springs is like a tomb," Anita murmured.

"All roads blocked off. But it won't be quiet long. The media will attack us this morning like sharks after fresh meat."

The pink light of dawn created a nimbus around Holly's head.

Anita turned around. "Thanks for bringing me through this so far, Holly."

"It's almost over, honey. The authorities will find them. In the meantime we'll just pray for the best. Keep good thoughts."

"Good thoughts," Anita whispered numbly.

11

Houston forced a smile as he bandaged Lark's calf.

"I'm returning the favor for you patching me up yesterday. Much pain?"

Lark shook her head.

Houston examined the bandage when he had finished.

"Course, you'll need a tetanus shot. The wound's not as deep as I thought . . . but you should see a doctor right away."

"Any of them around here make swamp calls?"

Houston chuckled; humor seemed so alien in the context of what had just occurred.

There was an awkward silence before Lark spoke softly.

"I never wanted to see it killed. I wanted it to live. To go deeper into the swamp and live its life away from people."

"You did what you had to do, Lark. You protected Timmy, and you protected yourself. Self-defense. The creature would have killed you."

Using his shoulder as a crutch, she pressed herself to her feet.

"The boys okay?"

Houston glanced at the rear of the boat where they were standing, gawking at the carcass of Blood Wings some thirty yards away.

"Yeah. This will give them a lifetime of memories . . . nightmares, anyway. Both of 'em are pretty tough. Maybe they'll be able to handle it better than I handled my memories of the creature."

12

"It's not really, really dead, is it?"

Timmy had pressed himself as far over the back railing as possible to see the carcass of the creature, so far that the angry, red scratch Lark had tended to on his back was visible.

Wade heard his brother's voice only as a very distant whisper. He felt as if he were in a dream, everything filtering through a yellowish lens, emerging like an impressionist painting—a world of flecks and dots, yet not wholly connected. At any moment, the boy thought that he would wake from the dream and the creature would rise from the slough and shake off its ties to death

362

and fly triumphantly away.

"Is it, Wade? Tell me. Is it really, really dead?"

Swatting the air as if he were swatting at an insect, Wade said, "What's it look like, dopey?"

"Like it's pretty dead."

Wade took a deep breath and let his eyes roam over the silken blackness of one wing that extended from the water at a forty-five-degree angle.

"It ain't movin'," he said. "The *wirrie*—that's what killed it. Just like Miss Freda said it would."

"Lark killed it," Timmy muttered. "She stabbed it right in the throat and killed it dead. I saw her do it. Did you, Wade? Did you?"

"Yeah."

"Wade?"

"Yeah, what?"

"Are you sad *you* didn't kill it?"

Wade felt the skin on his chest flush. "No. Not really. I thought maybe I could, but . . ."

"What would Gillie think?"

"Whaddaya mean?"

"Lark's a girl. Or a woman, I mean. And she killed it, and none uh us guys could. Would Gillie think we was wimps?"

Reaching into his back pocket, Wade pulled out Gillie's picture. It was sodden from his plunge into the slough, but the image of his friend remained intact.

"He'd think it's probably okay. Dudn't matter who did it. Only thing's important is—it's dead. Blood Wings won't be attackin' people no more."

Just behind him, Houston was assisting Lark to the rail. She limped noticeably, and she had her camera. Wade noticed how pale and drawn she looked, her eyes, red-rimmed, her every move tentative.

"What should we do with it?" Houston asked. He stared out at the carcass as if still not quite able to believe

363

that the creature was dead.

"Let's take it back and sell it," Timmy exclaimed, pounding a tiny fist eagerly into a tiny palm.

"Shut up, dopey," said Wade. "Nobody wants to hear what you think."

Lark smiled weakly and brushed her hand lovingly through Timmy's hair. Continuing to avoid Houston's question, she glanced at Wade.

"Your dark hair is coming back. Your days as a blond are numbered."

Her smile flickered; somehow it wasn't able to connect with her eyes.

Wade felt embarrassed and looked away.

Houston hoisted one leg over the railing, then gingerly swung his bad ankle onto the railing so that he could gain some balance.

"I'm going out to take a closer look," he said. "I'm really not sure what to do with it." His expression seemed to plead with Lark for her judgment on the matter.

Her eyes met his, but she could offer no more than a slight shrug.

"Could I go, too?" Wade heard himself ask.

"Don't see why not."

"And me. How 'bout me?" Timmy whined.

"Oh, no, Timmy . . . you stay here with me," said Lark.

"Why don't you go?" he countered.

"I can't let the swamp water get into my wound. Please stay here with me."

He reluctantly agreed, and immediately Houston and Wade entered the water. To Wade it seemed unusually cool, seeping up past his knees to his waist and a few inches above.

Houston clasped his hand and led him along so that neither of them lost his balance. When they were twenty feet or so from the creature, the extended wing twitched violently, slapping the surface, creating a loud smack.

Wade instinctively jerked back, but Houston held him. "No, wait," the man said. "It's okay. It's dead."

Turning to search for Lark and Timmy, Wade saw the young woman raise the camera, and he was inwardly cheered because he knew she would have another remarkable photo to add to her Blood Wings collection. The book she would write, no doubt, he reasoned, would create a sensation. She might even become famous.

But she lowered the camera; she had clicked off no shots.

What's wrong? Wade asked himself.

Houston had closed to within ten feet of the creature.

"God, Lark's right—the thing *is* beautiful," he exclaimed.

Wade stepped forward; the water became more shallow. The boy raised a hand to point at the creature's head.

And that's when the shot rang out.

Chapter 19

1

"It's mine!"

All eyes turned.

Hash, pushpole in one hand, rifle in the other, maneuvered his skiff next to Lark's anchored boat. His left forearm was heavily bandaged, and even from a distance Wade could see a wild, on-the-edge determination in his face.

"The creature's mine!"

The man fired glances from Houston to Lark and then back to Houston.

"It's my big hit! All mine!"

Wade noticed that Ibo was with him, the bird settled nervously on his perch.

"No need for the gun," Houston said.

Hash squinted into the slant of the sun's first rays of the day.

"Who got it? Who killed it? Was it you?" he demanded.

For several heartbeats, no one spoke. Then Timmy squirmed away from Lark to the side of the boat.

"Lark did. She stabbed it in the throat. She took

Wade's spear and stabbed it dead. I saw her."

Offering her a mock bow, Hash said, "Nice piece of work, miss. You saved me the trouble. . . . I would have gotten the bastard sooner or later—don't think I wouldn't have."

They watched as the man wrestled inner tubes from the floor of the skiff and tossed them into the slough; they were connected to a heavy rope and a metal clip.

"Sorry to do this, miss, but I'm gonna need this boat of yours."

"What? What do you mean?" Lark stammered, pulling Timmy away from the side.

"Just a damn minute, Hash—"

Houston's words broke off with the loud report of the rifle, its bullet whistling off over the mangroves like a low-flying jet.

"Don't nobody give me no shit on this," said Hash. "I got a bad cut on my arm, and it's hard for me to think straight; so don't get in my way."

He continued talking as he tossed the meager remainder of his supplies into Lark's boat.

"Ever last one of you's gonna help me, ya see? Houston, you and the boy'll give me a hand tying the inner tubes to the creature. They self-inflate, and I believe they got enough buoyancy to float that sucker. We'll tug it back to Orchid Springs, and I'll make a little phone call to a man who'll be tickled to death to have that carcass. This ole sorry man you're lookin' at's gonna be so fuckin' rich . . . my big hit. I deserve it."

Wade couldn't stop the words from tumbling off his lips.

"You don't deserve nuthin'," he cried, anger warming his cheeks. "You're just a coward and a drunk." Then he turned to Houston. "Why should he have the creature? If it belongs to anybody, it belongs to us. To Lark. Not to him."

368

"Wade, it's okay. You're right. But long as he has that gun on us, I'd suggest we do as he says. Lark, you too. Let him have the boat for the time being."

Hash smiled broadly.

"Talkin' sense, Houston. Good man. Now, don't get me wrong—I ain't gonna leave you out here. You can ride back. Just don't get in my way. I've come too far, got myself too close to some real money to allow anything to stop me. You got to understand that."

He propped the rifle in the skiff, then tied the rope to a towline loop on Lark's boat. And for the next half an hour he and Houston and Wade struggled with the bulky carcass of the creature, their eyes watering, noses running from its horrible smell.

"Give the whore's a rip," Hash eventually ordered.

A pneumatic hissing broke the serenity of the swamp as the bright orange inner tubes unfolded and shaped themselves into giant doughnuts.

"Hot damn!" Hash shouted.

The carcass of Blood Wings slowly lifted free of the slippery muck.

Hash's eyes gleamed.

"What do ya think that fuckin' monster weighs?" he shot at Houston.

The man thought a moment before saying, "The body's not as heavy as it looks—lot more wings than body. Still, it must weigh four hundred pounds."

"Makes it worth, oh, what . . . better'n two thousand bucks a pound to me."

"Miss Freda may have something to say about this creature," said Houston. "It was killed on her property. And what about the sheriff? He won't be exactly elated to hear you pulled a rifle on us."

"You let me worry about all that shit," said Hash.

Wade heard a desperation in his tone that hollowed the boy's chest. He sloshed his way to the boat where Lark helped him aboard. Moments later, Hash and Houston joined them. Hash directed Houston to bring up anchor and Lark to start the engine.

At the wheel, she said, "We don't know the way out."

"*I* do, miss," said Hash. "I got every angle covered. Just follow what I tell you."

2

"Will they throw him in jail for takin' our boat and shootin' his gun at us?" Timmy asked.

Hash had ordered the two boys to the rear of the boat along with Houston, where he could keep an eye on them.

The morning air was heating rapidly. In the distance, Wade believed he could hear the faint thrum of helicopters.

"I don't know. He's actin' real crazy. Don't do nuthin' to make him more upset," Wade replied.

Behind the boat, the carcass of Blood Wings, buoyed by the inner tubes, floated heavily, only wing tips visible on the surface of the slough.

Timmy had Lark's camera and was fiddling in little boy fashion with the f-stop ring.

"You better hadn't break Lark's camera. Better put it down," Wade said.

"She said I could hold it."

Wade glanced away from his brother to Houston. "What's he gonna do to us?"

"There's nothing to worry about . . . just don't do anything to get him riled up. Trying to bring that carcass in has done some strange things to his head, but he wouldn't hurt us—no point in forcing the issue, though."

The boy was disappointed despite realizing that Houston offered good judgment. Hash's bold takeover angered him; he wanted, somehow, to get back at the man, and he vowed he would commit violence if Hash did anything to Lark.

"Hey, Wade, watch. I'm gonna take a picture of the bird."

Timmy had the camera aimed at the railing upon which Ibo perched, preening his feathers.

"Don't be doin' that, dopey. She dudn't want a picture of that bird. You better just give me that camera."

But Timmy pulled away when Wade reached for it, and the matter was dropped when Lark made her way to the rear of the boat. She sat down by Houston; Wade saw worry lines around her eyes.

"Does he know where he's going?" she asked. "This isn't the route we came by."

Houston studied the swing to the left Hash had negotiated.

"It's a back run. No, it's not familiar to me, but you gotta remember—Hash knows this whole swamp pretty well."

The thrumming Wade had heard earlier suddenly grew louder. Two helicopters were visible to the north within perhaps a mile, bearing west, southwest. The boy and Lark and Houston caught sight of them at about the same time.

"That larger bird is from the National Guard," Houston explained. "Our rescuers finally made it."

It was a moment in which everything seemed upbeat, a moment that promised the long nightmare would soon end.

"I can't see any pictures of the creature!" Timmy announced.

Heads turned.

And Wade could not believe his eyes.

The gray-black spool of film slithered through Timmy's small hands like a snake.

"Nuthin' on the whole thing."

"Timmy!" Wade roared. "You stupid, stupid dope-head! You ruined Lark's pictures!"

Timmy shuddered. "No, I didn't. See . . . never was any on it. All blank."

He handed the film to Lark, whose lips were moving, but she wasn't speaking, wasn't, in fact, visibly reacting much at all. She appeared to be in total shock. She took the film and examined it as if somehow, miraculously, it hadn't been exposed.

Her fingers quivered.

"You stupid dopehead!" Wade shouted again, and this time he added a hard punch to Timmy's shoulder, sending him into an immediately wail.

"No. It's all right," said Lark weakly.

She dropped the film and reached for Timmy and began to console the sobbing child.

"I'm sorry, Lark," said Houston. Then, as if uncertain what more to say, he got up and went toward the cabin.

"You stupid dopehead! Sumbitch! You stupid dope-head!" Ibo shrieked a perfect imitation of Wade before the boy, frustrated, took a swing at the bird, missing, but causing him to flutter and sidestep.

Lark was rocking Timmy, telling him not to cry, when Wade scooted over next to her.

"You won't have any pictures of the creature for your book," he said.

She shook her head. "Not going to worry about it," she said. "Besides, the carcass is still intact. I can take plenty of pictures of it. No one can deny the physical evidence."

She was putting a good face on the matter, and Wade found himself wanting to hug her neck and to tell her how much he hoped all her wishes would come true.

Then he glanced at her feet and saw the spool of film coiled there in sad disarray.

The morning heated like a furnace, humidity pressing down upon the boat like a giant hand. Hash remained at the wheel, brandishing his rifle, squinting into the glare of the emerging day. Houston kept his distance from him, and Lark huddled with the boys. Wade read in her expression that her leg wound was giving her trouble; ugly red streaks branded her skin just above the bandage.

Hash guided the boat into less and less familiar territory, provoking Houston occasionally to question the route.

"I know damn well what I'm doin'. Donchoo try to tell me no different." Hash's voice was cold.

The air continued to boil up another degree or two, and exhaustion clawed at the occupants of the vessel as insects stormed at them. Wade could not remember ever being more miserable.

"They're back," Timmy murmured as the heat tightened its hold upon them.

Like Radar on *M*A*S*H*, Wade's little brother heard the helicopters before anyone else did. Wade looked immediately toward the cabin; Houston was scanning the sky, and Hash had shifted the boat into neutral so that he could also investigate the approaching racket.

"Sons-uh-bitches!" he raged, shaking his rifle barrel above his head. "Nobody's takin' my million bucks!"

And then as both copters winged to less than a hundred yards, the man shouldered the rifle and opened up—a half dozen rounds shattered the stifling calm of the swamp.

"You outta your mind?" Houston screamed.

He lunged toward Hash, but the man reacted instantly, swinging the butt of the rifle up in time to slam it into the side of Houston's head.

He crashed to his knees. Hash stood over him, then

fired a few more rounds at the helicopters as they banked, heading out of rifle range.

Wade ran to Houston's side. Lark hobbled to him as well; he was conscious, but barely. The boy helped Lark administer a cold rag to his head. Timmy crouched in wide-eyed fear by them.

Lark's eyes darted to Hash.

"He's insane," she murmured.

And Wade felt a clutch of dread.

Satisfied that the copters were gone, Hash stepped near to where Lark was hovering over to Houston.

"Next time somebody makes a move on me like that—there's a bullet for 'em. I damn well mean it. Don't get 'tween me and my big hit."

He returned to the wheel and kicked the throttle.

Wade hunkered at Lark's shoulder. "How bad is he hurt?"

But before she could answer, Houston pressed himself forward. He moaned once and took the washcloth and wiped his face.

"I'll live," he whispered. "If I don't do something else stupid. The rest of you okay?"

For several minutes, they talked softly, all except Timmy, who tugged at Lark as if she were his security blanket. They reasoned that Hash's action would bring a full force of support personnel. Stay calm, they reminded each other. And don't cross the man with the rifle.

4

Another quarter of a mile of swamp slipped past.

Wade, his chin propped on the back rail, watched the carcass of the creature bob and weave along the surface of the dark slough trailing thin ribbons of blood.

Images of what Hash might do next haunted him.

Everyone seemed balanced on a rim of fear, and even if more help managed to find them, there was no guarantee that in his crazed state Hash wouldn't turn the rifle on each of the other crew members. There was no way to anticipate, no way to ease the terror of the moment.

Hummocks sprouted on either side of the boat. Freshwater melded with salt. Duckweed formed greenish-yellow islands; the slough widened into an almost circular pond. Ibo shifted restlessly not a yard from Wade's chin. And despite the palpable air of tension, the boy smiled at the bird.

The boat suddenly slowed.

Wade heard Hash order Houston and Lark to take the wheel.

"Bastards better keep their distance," he heard the man exclaim, but he wasn't talking to Lark and Houston.

Then Wade saw movement at the edge of one of the hummocks.

With eager, businesslike quickness, the gators began to slide into the water, drawn by the prospect of an easy meal.

"Get the hell out uh my way!" Hash shouted.

And Wade felt himself being shoved roughly to one side.

"Oh, no you don't, you bastards!" Hash growled as he shouldered the rifle, and Wade peered over the railing in time to see two gators converge on the carcass. A shot clamored out. Wade held his ears; one of the gators twisted, blood pouring from its flank.

"Not my big hit! God damn you!"

Three more shots. Rifle smoke filled the boy's nostrils.

From an island of duckweed, several more gators advanced, the blood of their comrade seeming to stir them into a frenzy. And then Wade saw a gator fasten its jaws on one of the creature's wings.

"Bastards! God, stop it!"

Hash emptied the rifle, but the gators continued their onslaught. Desperate, the man swung himself over the railing, wielding his rifle like a club, and splashed toward the churning, blood-colored whirlpool, at the center of which was Blood Wings, a magnet attracting a dozen or more gators.

Wade heard a cry of anguish tear from Hash's throat.

Having stopped the boat, Houston rushed to the rail.

"Don't try it!" he yelled.

But Hash had set a direct course, swinging the rifle, cursing, shouting at the top of his lungs.

Hesitating a moment, Houston gripped the railing.

"Don't try it, Hash!" he called out again. Then Wade felt his heart hammer so hard that it seemed to beat against his ribs like an iron fist—Houston had lowered himself into the slough.

"Let him go!" Wade screamed.

Lark and Timmy raced to join the boy, but all they could do was stand there helplessly as the spectacle unfolded.

"Hash! Come back! Don't try it!"

Struggling through the waist-deep water, Houston reached wildly for the man, catching him by the elbow. Swinging the rifle around, Hash fought off Houston's attempt to stop him.

"God damn it, leave me alone!" he roared.

The gators snapped and tore at the carcass as if they hadn't eaten for days. A fury of terrifying sounds filled the morning air, and yet Hash continued his advance, jabbing the barrel of the rifle into the bloody, foamy swirl of water and beasts.

To Wade's relief, Houston turned back toward the boat.

Anticipating the final scene of horror, Lark pulled Timmy away from the railing; Wade started to look away as well, but found that he couldn't. As Houston climbed into the boat, Wade saw Hash submerge into the chaos of jaws and blood and roiling water and heard him call out one last time—something indecipherable.

A gator locked upon the man's arm and ripped it from his body.

Wade jerked away. He had seen enough.

The horrific noises continued to echo on all sides of the boat for several minutes. Then the boy felt Houston's hands on his shoulders. Together they surveyed the scene once more.

The gators, a dozen of them, had calmed; some were gliding away, one carrying a talon and shreds of flesh.

There was no other sign of Blood Wings.

The creature was gone.

And so was Hash.

Chapter 20

1

One week later.

"Are you sure this will make him better?"

Houston frowned as Wade coaxed another spoonful of milky-colored goo down the snake's throat.

"Hash said it does," the boy replied. "When Danny Boy's feelin' better, he'll eat 'pinkies."

Houston shook his head and smiled. He held the snake uncertainly as if he were looking for a handle on it somewhere. He glanced around the cabin.

"Miss Freda will probably want to bulldoze this ole shack to the ground now that she's closing the refuge."

"What'll happen to Danny Boy and Ibo?" Wade let his gaze wander momentarily to the parrot's perch, where the bird rested uncharacteristically silent.

"Lots of pet shops in Miami would take them—I'll check with some of them."

The boy nodded.

They finished feeding the boa and carefully returned it to its ceramic pot.

"Hash never got his big hit."

"No—he let his greed for money go to his head—he had completely lost touch with reality when he took over Lark's boat and shot at those copters—and going into the middle of those gators to save that carcass, well . . ."

"There won't be none of it left, will there? None of it left—not even bones, will there?"

"If you cut open a few gators . . . but no, no indication the creature was around except, of course, for the deaths it caused."

"Lark didn't even get a picture of it for her book—thanks to my dopey brother."

They continued talking as they walked from the stuffy cabin into the morning sun splashing across Hash's back dock.

"Timmy's a good kid," said Houston. Then his tone shifted. "Your mom tells me he's had some bad dreams this week . . . and that you have, too."

"Yeah . . . some. She took us to that shrink guy again. Dudn't help much."

"Could be it'll just take time. It did for me when my dad . . . It'll take time for all of Orchid Springs to get over it. But the media attention should die down in another week or so."

Wade stared out at the sluggish slough; he had been wanting to say something to Houston. Had been mustering the courage. And perhaps it was a stray thought of Gillie that finally prompted him—the thought that Gillie hadn't needed grown-ups, but that he, Wade, did.

"I guess I was wrong about you," he said.

Surprised, Houston looked out at the same spot on the slough where Wade's eyes had been drawn.

"How's that?"

"Thought you was a coward and a dopehead and . . . I didn't want you 'round my mom."

"Can't blame you for thinking that way. I just had to

380

grow up a lot and face some hard things about myself . . . and the past. But I'm ready for a good future."

"You gonna marry my mom?"

Houston smiled. "You cut through to the nitty-gritty, don't you? I like that. Well . . . yeah, I'd like to marry her . . . if she'd have me. What do you think about that?"

Wade's chest heaved.

He bit at the corner of his lip.

"Do I got to call you dad?"

Houston chuckled nervously. "I'd leave that up to you."

"Seems like I don't got a real dad. He never ever calls me or comes to see me. Mom's scared of him."

"You wouldn't ever be scared of me, would you?"

"Nah, you don't scare me none."

Houston laughed again. "Listen, I've been thinking maybe if your mom and I got married we'd leave Orchid Springs. Thought Orlando would be a good place to start fresh because it's a growing city. Lots of opportunities. You and Timmy might like it—Disney World and all."

Wade said nothing, but he forced a smile.

Then he turned and reached out his hand; and Houston, again surprised, extended his, and Wade shook it firmly.

"Thanks for savin' Timmy from the creature," he said.

For a moment, Houston was speechless. Something stirred in his throat—something warm and good.

2

"Never realized I had brought so much stuff," said Lark as she loaded another box of folders and books into her van.

Wade and Houston had returned from Hash's cabin,

and while Houston ducked into Holly's to see Anita and Timmy, Wade went to help Lark.

"Is your leg feelin' okay?"

"Better. Still sore. Ironically the bite mark could turn out to be one of the main pieces of physical evidence to show that Blood Wings existed."

"Where ya gonna go from here?"

"Back home first. To Chicago. To rest and think about things."

"But you'll write your book, won'tchoo?"

"Eventually. Though books and chasing strange creatures won't ever be quite as important to me again. Not after Orchid Springs."

"Why not?"

She hesitated.

From a canvas bag she lifted a small, white envelope. "Let's go sit by the slough a minute."

He followed her out into the bright, Florida sunshine. The slough's current inched by, and a breeze played with the saw grass.

When they had sat down, Lark said, "I have something to show you."

Out of the envelope she took a color photo; paper-clipped to the photo was a negative.

"You got one!" Wade exclaimed. "You got a picture of Blood Wings! But I thought Timmy ruined your film."

"He did. This was in the roll of film he shot with your mom's Instamatic. I went ahead and had it developed."

Wade shook his head in disbelief: There it was, a reasonably clear photo of the creature in flight—indisputable evidence of its existence.

"Wow! Timmy's picture's gonna be in a book. Wait'll that little nerd hears this."

But Lark was smiling as she shook her head. "No," she said. "I'm not going to use it."

"What?"

"In fact, here . . . I wanted you to be with me when I did this." She stepped toward the slough and dropped the print and negative onto the surface.

"Hey, are you crazy? Hey, that's a pretty good picture!"

She caught his arm before he could retrieve it. It swirled, and then the current embraced it.

"Photos are false images, Wade," she explained. "Blood Wings is much more than that. Much more than Hash's Miami patron thought or any of the curiosity seekers who've been descending upon Orchid Springs."

"I don't get you," said Wade.

"That creature—the one I'm going to write the book about—is a reflection of all the dark and destructive powers within each of us. We know it when we read about such a creature—we know that same power is hidden within us. We need for our imagination to work at connecting with the image. A photo would only interfere with that need."

The boy did not understand, but Lark appeared so firm as if she had secretly peered into the nature of something virtually unknowable and seen it, translucent and whole.

The print and negative floated on inexorably into the heart of the swamp. The sun occasionally glinted from them, winking a mysterious code.

Wade and Lark watched them until they disappeared from view.